Octavo

OCTAVO

MARTY NEUMEIER

HARKER

For Eileen

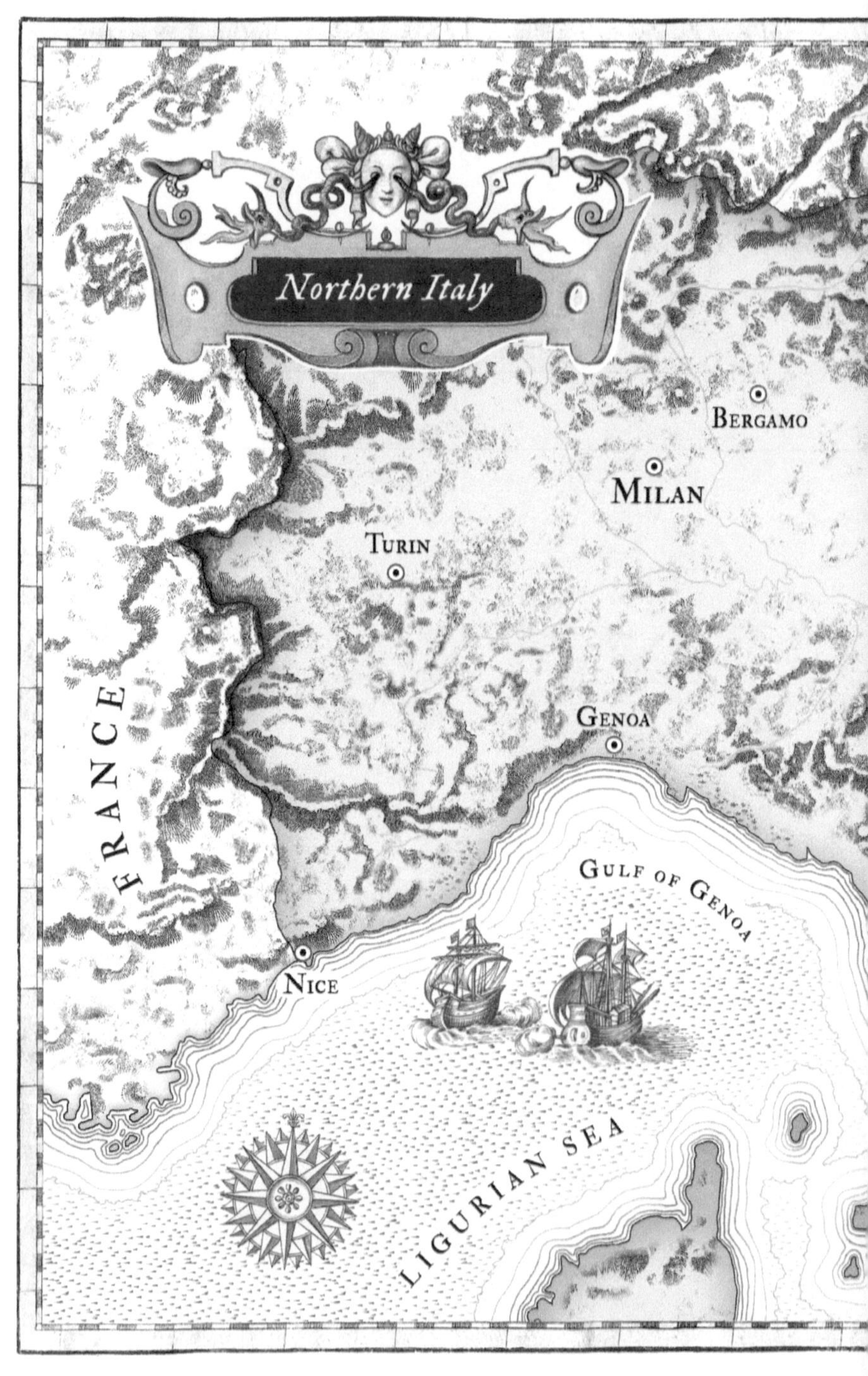

Northern Italy
BERGAMO
MILAN
TURIN
GENOA
FRANCE
GULF OF GENOA
NICE
LIGURIAN SEA

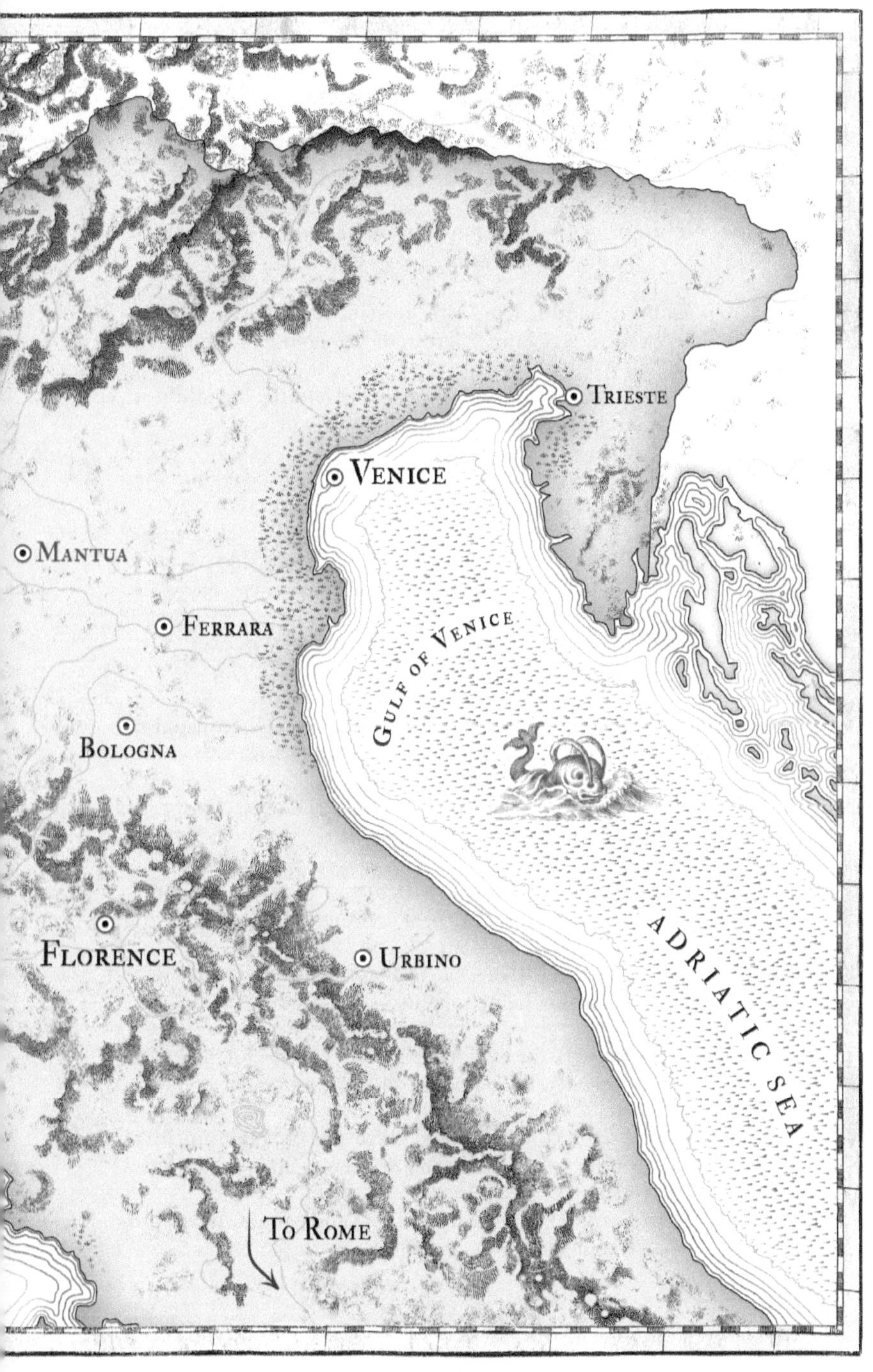

TRIESTE
VENICE
MANTUA
FERRARA
BOLOGNA
GULF OF VENICE
FLORENCE
URBINO
ADRIATIC SEA
TO ROME

GUIDE TO RENAISSANCE FIGURES

Leonardo da Vinci Artist and inventor, widely considered the leading polymath of the High Renaissance (1452–1519)

Francesco Melzi Leonardo's last pupil, painting assistant, and secretary at the end of his life (1491–1570)

Salaì Leonardo's long-time assistant and occasional lover, Gian Giacomo Caprotti da Oreno (1480–1524)

Zoroastro Leonardo's friend and collaborator, the metallurgist and alchemist Tommaso Masini (1462–1520)

Aldo Manuzio AKA Aldus Manutius, proprietor of the Aldine Press, Italy's most innovative publisher (1450–1515)

Pietro Bembo Poet and literary theorist who helped Aldo Manuzio popularize portable books in Italian (1470–1547)

Francesco Griffo Typographer who designed timeless typefaces including the first italics (1450–1518)

Lucrezia Borgia Duchess of Ferrara, wife of Alfonso d'Este, daughter of the pope, and Bembo's lover (1480–1519)

Isabella d'Este Marchioness of Mantua, wife of Francesco Gonzaga, and Lucrezia Borgia's sister-in-law (1474–1539)

Fra Luca Pacioli Franciscan, mathematician, and Leonardo's friend, known as the "father of accounting" (1447–1517)

Galeazzo Sanseverino Duke of Milan's son-in-law and member of the Academia Leonardi Vinci (1458–1525)

Dr. Marliani Physician at the former Milanese court and member of the Academia Leonardi Vinci (c. 1460–1520)

Donato Bramante Architect, painter, and planner of St. Peter's, member of the Academia Leonardi Vinci (1444–1514)

Bramantino Bartolomeo Suardi, architect and painter, Bramante's friend and former student (1456–1530)

After fact-checking the 16th-century manuscript, Harker editor Peter Chenoweth concluded that the translation and validating details provided by the two authenticators were sufficiently accurate to proceed with publication. We decided to let the entire text stand, including the remarkable commentary by the two women. The only addition is a postscript by the surviving partner.

—Katherine Cavel, President and Publisher

Part One: Discovery

Subject: BOOK QUERY
From: Scarlett <scarlett527@codelock.com>
To: Peter Chenoweth, Harker Publishing
Attachment: 8VO_1.m4a

Hello Mr. Chenoweth,
Please listen to the attached audio file.

My name is Scarlett. It's not my real name, and this isn't how I sound. I took the precaution of running this audio file through an app that disguises your voice. I'm using the name Scarlett—you know, from the movie *Lost in Translation*—because that's pretty much how I feel these days. But mostly because Artie and I can't reveal our identities. That would be an exercise in stupid.

Listen, Mr. Chenoweth, we have a book for you.

Really, *the* book.

It was written by someone else, someone a long time ago. Our only role—mine and Artie's—is to add supporting commentary from our analysis. You're free to treat the commentary however you like. Hand it off to an editor. Hire a ghost writer. Bury it five miles deep on the dark side of the moon—we don't care. All that matters is that the book gets published. Our part of the story is there for context and to prove that the manuscript is authentic.

We have zero doubt you'll want this book. There isn't a publisher in the world who wouldn't give his firstborn testicle to get his hands on it. You'll probably win Publisher of the Year—maybe Publisher of the *Century.* But you'll have to move fast. I realize speed is not a hallmark of your industry, but that's the deal. Artie and I will dictate chapters on the fly and send the audio files as email attachments, like I've done here. When we're finished, we'll vanish into the woodwork. Meanwhile, don't try to find us. Or ID us. It's not important, and you won't be able to do it.

As to the money, we're anonymous and want to stay that way. A contract is useless. Instead of sending checks for the usual half-now-half-on-approval, you'll pay our advances in crypto, one chapter at a time, using Lucra. We can't just walk into a Swiss bank and collect our money. We'd be scooped up in seconds.

One more thing. The most crucial thing. The text has to live in the public domain. Yes, we want the advances—expenses, escape money, yada yada—but we don't want the rights. Not for us, not for you, not for anybody. It's up to you to make your book better than the others. You're smart. You'll figure it out. And besides, you'll have a considerable head start.

I'll be honest with you, Mr. Chenoweth. If you publish this story, your life will change. Mine took a sharp turn toward the bizarre, and I don't see it ever getting back on track. Some decisions are irrevocable.

Before I go on, I need to know if you're interested. If I don't hear back in the time it takes to pee, we're moving on to another publisher.

EDITOR'S EMAIL

That has to be the most charming query I've ever gotten. So few authors would think of using the word *testicle* in a book pitch. And yet I'm tempted to say "no" in spite of your generous offer. I actually like my life. And why voice recordings? Can't you just write emails like a normal person?

8VO_2

SCARLETT: Charm isn't my strong suit, Mr. Chenoweth. I've been pushed around a lot in my life, and in this situation I need control. High-stakes negotiation rattles my amygdala.

The reason I don't send emails like a normal person is because, number one, I'm not a normal person. I struggle with dysgraphia. It's like dyslexia, except it messes with your writing. Had it since I was a kid. One of my workarounds is voice recording. It speeds things up and frees my hands for things like driving. Or research.

Number two, we're in a hurry. Artie could probably handle the correspondence herself, but she's got enough on her plate with all the translation work.

Mr. Chenoweth, we chose Harker not only for the quality of your books, but for you, personally. Please understand that we want to trust you. But also understand that if you betray that trust, even a little, the deal's off. If you talk to anyone outside your executive team and your legal counsel, the deal's off. If you play for time—which we don't have—the deal's off. If you give us any shit about the deal, the deal's off. I'm sorry to go all Bugsy Siegel on you, but that's how it is.

Can we try again?

EDITOR'S EMAIL

Scarlett, let's see if I understand. You have an item of value. You haven't said what it is. You can't tell me unless you can trust me. You can't trust me because you don't know anything about me. Would it help if I told you the story of a ten-year-old boy who shoveled snow from a neighbor's driveway for a dollar, then trudged two miles through icy drifts to pay his library fines? It wasn't me, but I could tell you about it.

C'mon, Scarlett, I'm a busy man. I can't help you if I don't know what you're selling.

8VO_3

SCARLETT: I'm a pushover for a sick sense of humor. But just so you know, I can also be suspicious, judgy, and vengeful.

Artie is nodding. *Bitch.*

Okay, start from the beginning. About a week ago we got hired for an assignment, a preliminary report on an old painting that turned up in Northern Italy. I'm a university graduate with a master's in biophysics. My side hustle is authenticating art pieces.

Artie's an art historian, just retired from another university. She's fluent in most of the romances—Latin, French, Italian, Spanish, plus English and her native tongue. She's a qualified authority on Renaissance art.

Artie, my little joke.

ARTIE [MUFFLED]: A very little joke, dear.

SCARLETT: See what I have to put up with?

We were working for a man we'll call Mr. Dickson. Dickson, because his father was an even bigger dick than he is. I probably shouldn't say that about a client, but facts are facts. He made his billions running a security software company. Gobbled up competitors with a predatory zeal usually reserved for, I don't know, turkey vultures. Thinks he can buy anything. Now he wants to buy the Renaissance.

ARTIE: That's a little much.

SCARLETT: Artie says I'm being harsh.

I knew Italy was a big deal when he asked us to download some heavy-duty encryption software. He's in the security business, but still. He'd just received a text from a European art advisor about a bunch of objects that turned up in a townhouse, a 15th-century workshop that an American couple had been converting into a residence. The workers pulled up the floorboards, and *voilà*. The advisor said the artifacts look like the real thing, and that one in particular—a panel—was, quote, intriguing. Dickson lost no time arranging travel for Artie and me.

We meet in the lobby of the hotel, an old pile of a place close to the site. Tall, narrow structure, leaning to the south like a sunflower past its prime, piazzetta out front. In the middle is a fountain that looks like it's under permanent repair, judging by the weeds and the rusted wire fencing.

We'd both worked for Dickson before, but this was the first time as a team. Naturally, it was hate at first sight. I'm all grungy and irritable after my long flight, and she looks like she stepped out of a department store window with the tags still on.

ARTIE: The grungy part is correct.

SCARLETT: Hilarious. Look at Miss Priss over there.

The townhouse is a short walk from the hotel, so the next morning we head over, rollaboards banging on the cobblestone streets. The owners are in St. Moritz on a ski vacation with their kids. Finance professionals. No interest in art or Italian history. The townhouse is their new vacation home, and they're already over budget on renovations. Hot for the free cash. I don't know about you, but people like that frost my tits.

We get to the address and find two doors, one for the house and one for the garage. Artie says medieval, judging from the limestone surrounds. An ancient wrought-iron fanlight sits over the narrow door. They left a lockbox on the latch so we can let ourselves in.

Looking back, it seems like a reckless thing to do, even for rich expat Americans. I'm not slamming expats. Or Americans. But considering the value of what was lying around in there, it was pretty dumb.

We put on our cotton gloves. You can't let the oils from your skin touch the surface of artifacts, or they'll cause deterioration. I take the key from the box and turn the lock. The door swings in and we're hit with the combined scent of fresh plaster, floor varnish, heating oil, and musty artifacts. That musty smell is the same all over the world. Intoxicating for us authenticators. The flesh on my arms goes all goosebumpy.

We can see that the owners hired an architect for this one. The walls are white. The floor is new bleached oak. The lighting is a combo of ceiling cans and Italian floor lamps. On a table to the right, organized into piles, are various notebooks, trays of graphite sticks, a canvas cloth with brushes and pens, a collection of wooden boxes, and several portfolios of sketches and drawings. A list of the objects is taped to the wall beside the table.

Leaning against the back are five oil paintings done on wood panels. The largest, the one on the right, is a full-length portrait of a Renaissance notable, beard descending in waves to the middle of his chest, white hair flowing over a brocaded rose tunic. His legs are covered in rich green wool, his feet in finely tooled brown leather. There's something about his face—a mixture of confidence and curiosity—that makes me think of the word *address*. This man, whoever he was, had it.

We move in closer. The painting is tempera grassa, a kind of egg tempera mixed with oil. The surface glows with a luminosity that photography can't capture. I haul over a Tolomeo standing lamp so we can get some light on it. The artist—whoever he was—applied successive layers of translucent oils to build depth, so when you move your head from side to side the image looks almost 3D, like you could dive right into it. The brushstrokes are so refined as to be nearly invisible. If you've ever seen the *Mona Lisa*, you'll know what I mean.

The *Mona*, of course, is darker, yellowed by years of oxidation. Smaller, too. The surface has thousands of craquelures—tiny breaks in the varnish. Makes it hard to appreciate da Vinci's trademark *sfumato* brushwork. The painting in front of us not only has decent *sfumato*, but also size, and what we in the trade call legibility. No craquelures or other defects, and the colors haven't been dulled by exposure to the elements.

This is the object we came to see.

We pull up a couple of chairs and get to work. The first thing we do is turn the piece around. The joined wood panel is in good condition. Five vertical planks and two horizontal planks, one at the head and one at the foot. On the lower half is an inscription in cursive, applied with a brush: *Il maestro di tutte le cose.* I look at Artie. She looks back at me, expressionless. The woman is exasperating.

The master of everything, she finally says, as if she can't believe my ignorance.

We turn the painting around to the front. She opens her laptop and starts reviewing museum sites. I'm not sure what you know about art historians, Mr. Chenoweth, but the way they work is—Artie, want to weigh in here?

This is Artie.

[SOUND OF FOOTSTEPS]

ARTIE: Good day, Mr. Chenoweth. First of all, I expect a painting by any artist to show similarities to other paintings by the same artist. I'll consider aspects such as composition, brushwork, color palette, handling of light and shadow, subject matter, materials, and overall skill. These may trigger a memory of past paintings, or perhaps suggest a time and place that could narrow the search. The *when* and the *where* are fairly easy. It's the *who* that can lead one on a merry chase.

To find the who, the attribution of the work, I'll sometimes use Morellian analysis, a technique that lets one identify individual artists by noting idiosyncratic patterns. Perhaps the brushstrokes are pitched at a distinctive angle. Perhaps the artist paints eyelids a certain way—or lace collars, or trees.

Once I form an hypothesis, I'll try to disprove it with comparative analysis. This can save time. But if I can't disprove it, I'll try to build a case for it. I'll see if I can match the painting to other paintings by the same artist. I'll spend a few hours on biographical research—diaries, account books, letters, and so on. I'll look for historical clues in inventories and estate records. Then I'll sit down in front of the work and imagine myself painting it, brushstroke by brushstroke, layer on layer.

SCARLETT: Here comes the woo-woo.

ARTIE: I can get a better sense of who the artist was by imagining the movements of his hand than I can from examining the finished painting. For me, every artist has a unique kinetic signature. This is what Scarlett calls my secret sauce.

SCARLETT: Woo-woo sauce. Drives me nuts. It's like she's in a trance. I twiddle my thumbs while she sits there for hours, peering through a magnifier and miming little brushstrokes in the air. She says all my fussing with paint particles makes her nervous. What makes me nervous are historians who fall ass over teakettle for anything beautiful.

ARTIE: I've always adored that expression.

SCARLETT: Mostly we try to stay out of each other's way. We're oil and water. Me, I need hard evidence. I get in close with the camera. I put small samples under the microscope. In some cases, I might send them out for carbon testing, which can date certain materials within 40 years in either direction. A good lab can work with a sample as small as 50 milligrams.

When I have a sense of the object's age, I'll analyze the painting to find out what materials the artist used. Different periods produced different fashions in substrates, paint composition, binding agents, surface primers, and so on. I'll compare these results with the materials found in other works by the same artist and assess the likelihood of a match.

Between the woo-woo—sorry, Artie, I mean your encyclopedic knowledge of art—

ARTIE: So kind of you.

SCARLETT: —not at all—and my technical chops, we expect to nail the artist, the period, and some idea of the object's worth within a day or two. We might even learn the identity of the subject, our gentleman in the rose tunic. I know this stuff's pretty geeky, Mr. Chenoweth. But we need you to appreciate the rigor we bring to our work.

When Artie lets me have a turn at the painting, I shave the thinnest splinter of wood from the back of the panel and place it under a microscope. Italian poplar. This is our first hard evidence that the painting comes from this area—Lombardy.

But when?

Lucky for us, no need for carbon dating. Plainly visible on the left edge of the bottom plank is a pattern of tree rings that includes—get this—the outer edge of the original tree. This lets me dendro-date the rings to find the year the wood was harvested. The chart for Lombardy shows the wood was cut in 1506, a year when there was very little rainfall. Given the time to dry and cure the wood, the painting was probably started around 1508, which would put it in the High Renaissance.

By the end of the second day, we've got it.

The painting, and probably the other works in the room, were done by one Francesco Melzi. The only reason Melzi is known to art historians is that he was the last pupil of Leonardo da Vinci. Needless to say, our hearts went pitapat.

Da Vinci's fucking assistant.

Then it hits us. Artie says it was like one of those movie effects, when the perspective shifts and your stomach does a double backflip.

ARTIE: The Vertigo Effect.

SCARLETT: Right, the Vertigo Effect. Because now we're thinking: What if the man in the rose doublet is Leonardo himself? The world has very few depictions of da Vinci, and the ones we do have are doubtful. This would be the first authenticated painting of the world's greatest Renaissance master. A full-length portrait revealing his proportions, his face, hands, dress, and maybe a few clues to the later part of his life.

No wonder Dickson has a hard-on.

EDITOR'S EMAIL

Alright, Scarlett, I get it. Leonardo's publishing gold. But I also know a little about art. How much can you really tell from a portrait?

8VO_4

SCARLETT: I hear what you're saying. But that's not all we found.

That night I can't sleep, so I get up in the dark and walk to the townhouse. The air's cold. The shutters on the houses are cinched down tight. There's no one on the streets but me. For most of our stay, the only souls we've seen are tourists, a few shopkeepers, and some elderly Italian women dressed in black, shawls over their heads. In my long black parka, I must have looked like one of them. Maybe someday I'll *be* one of them. *Gatto* lady. Between my black parka and Artie's dark complexion, we're nearly invisible around here.

I walk past the covered market, deserted and lifeless in the pre-dawn darkness. I cut across the main piazza and turn right beyond the arcade. I let myself into the townhouse and get to work, making notes on the remaining objects.

Two hours later, Artie shows up. She can't sleep either. She's been looking into the relationship between Melzi and Leonardo.

Artie, want to share?

[SOUND OF PAPER RUSTLING]

ARTIE: Francesco de Melzi. Born to a noble family in Lombardy. Raised in the Milanese court. Educated, well-mannered, trained in the arts. Leonardo meets him around 1507 at the Villa Melzi when he visits Francesco's father, Gerolamo, a military engineer.

Leonardo takes the boy under his wing, another dogsbody in a house full of pupils, assistants, and servants. Francesco soon becomes Leonardo's favorite, his amanuensis if you will, lending his elegant script and organizational abilities to the day-to-day chores of the studio. His start date tallies nicely with Scarlett's dating of the wood panel. He would have painted it one year after joining the studio.

SCARLETT: Mr. Chenoweth, you're probably wondering what any of this has to do with the manuscript.

Don't hit the stop button.

That afternoon, while Artie's preparing our report for Dickson, I'm rooting through the other sketches, studies, and drawings around the room. Buried in one of the piles is a small leather portfolio, all cracked and stiff with age. The tie-strings are so rotted they look like they could dissolve with a dirty look. They've recently been untied and then retied, probably by the owners of the townhouse.

I bring the object over to Artie. She puts on her gloves a finger at a time, taking care to straighten each one as she goes. *Come on*, I say, fuck's sake! At this point I'm ready to whack her with something paisley. She raises an eyebrow and waits for me to calm down. She takes a couple of tapestry needles from her toolbox, and teases the knots apart under a desktop magnifier. Several nerve-wracking minutes later, the strings come loose.

She tests the hinge of the portfolio. There's a quiet crunching as the leather stresses. Inside is a stack of paper about 30 millimeters deep. The top sheet is blank except for fox marks, those brown stains caused by iron salts and moisture, like the liver spots you see on the backs of old people's hands.

No offense, Artie.

ARTIE: None taken, dear.

SCARLETT: She pages through the sheets one by one. They're all blank until she gets about halfway through the stack.

Then, a letter.

It's filled from top to bottom with handwriting, all rusted with age. It starts with the salutation, *Al illustre signore Aldus Manutius.*

To the illustrious gentleman Aldus Manutius, I volunteer, waiting for Artie to correct me.

Mmm, she says. Italian, with his name in Latin. She closes the portfolio. On the cover is a small, discolored label with an inscription: *Per l'8vo.*

8vo, what's that? I ask.

Shorthand for *octavo*, she says, a book format from the Renaissance. If you fold a sheet of paper three times, you get eight leaves, or sixteen pages. You bind those sets of sixteen to make a book. Ever since the Renaissance, almost all books have been printed as octavos.

So. *Per l'8vo.* For the octavo?

She nods. She opens to the letter again and starts translating. After about twenty minutes, she looks up.

ARTIE: Mr. Chenoweth, may I read it to you?

To the illustrious gentleman Aldo Manuzio,

Pursuant to our discussion of 28 February 1509, I herewith enclose a complete record of the extraordinary events that took place in Venice, Ferrara, and Mantua in the year preceding. I authorize you to publish this text in one of your movable books, that a larger public may appreciate the astonishing talents of my master, and marvel at his skill to untangle the most diabolical of mysteries.

In the meantime, I shall continue to organize Leonardo's notes and drawings on the workings of Nature for a separate series of movable books. It is his wish that these be made ready in seven years' time.

I commend you for your courage in printing this truthful account of our grim adventures, and fervently hope it will go far to restore the good name of the Aldine Press. Yet I fear that some, especially the families of the Borgia and Este, will be displeased by its publication. I urge you to waste no time in protecting your household from the retaliation that may follow.

> *Your servant,*
> *Count Francesco Melzi*
> *Rome*
> *21 February 1515*

SCARLETT: How's that for a query letter? The fucking Borgias and Estes. Tell me *that* doesn't swizzle your stick.

EDITOR'S EMAIL

It's a lot to process. If Melzi's story is what it purports to be, I can imagine several audiences for it. Not just art, science, and history buffs, but everyone who enjoys a true-crime mystery. How about you? What are you seeing?

8VO_5

SCARLETT: Not to get too left-brained on you, but I count five items of interest in this one letter alone.

First, movable books. What the fuck is that? Is there such a thing as an *immovable* book?

Second, Melzi promises a peek at Leonardo's thinking process. We have 6,000 pages of his notes, but no written correspondence between the maestro and members of his circle—the philosophers, artists, mathematicians, engineers, doctors, and other intellectuals of his time. If he kept a personal diary, it hasn't survived. And the notebooks themselves tell us zilch about his private life, or how he felt about his family, friends, lovers, events of the day.

Third, it looks like historians will get new dirt on the Borgias and the Estes. Maybe less important than the Leonardo stuff, but still juicy.

Fourth, he gives us the target date for the publication of Leonardo's notebooks: February 1522. Something must have gone wrong, because the only notebooks we have are the handwritten originals. Maybe the manuscript will give us a clue.

And fifth—hello? Leonardo da Vinci, detective?

The only part of the letter Artie can't figure out is what looks like a date, probably added later, next to Aldo Manutio's name: *m. 6 feb 15*.

She carefully lifts the letter with a gloved hand. Beneath it are fifty or sixty pages of manuscript, written in a neat, tiny cursive. Melzi's grim adventures!

We check the list of discovered items on the wall next to the table. Oddly, the leather portfolio isn't on it. The owners must have decided that a decrepit portfolio with a stack of blank sheets was not worth itemizing. I suggest to Artie that we *borrow* the manuscript overnight. She studies my face, and says horns are sprouting from my forehead.

Remember, Artie?

ARTIE: I do believe you were born with those.

SCARLETT: Ignore her.

On our way out the door I grab a souvenir for good luck. It was in a box listed as miscellaneous tools. A strange silver stylus I couldn't identify. One end of the shaft forms a spiral, a kind of mushroom-shaped handle. The other end is tipped with a sharp red gemstone. I slip it into my bag. We close up the townhouse and return the key to the lockbox. Assignment complete.

ARTIE: Except for the part where you burn in Hell.

SCARLETT: One of the great benefits of atheism is that Hell is for other people.

ARTIE: I must remember to convert.

SCARLETT: Mr. Chenoweth, that night we hunker down in Artie's room. She starts translating the manuscript. The dim light from the frilly table lamp is just enough to illuminate Melzi's words as they dance across time to reappear on Artie's screen. The language Melzi used is a dialect of Milanese. She doesn't recognize some of the vocabulary, so she pulls up a scholarly dictionary to fill in the gaps.

The manuscript contains an account of a journey the two men took from Milan to Venice in the year 1508. Leonardo would have been 56, Francesco 15.

On the second page of the manuscript there's a reference to Melzi's portrait of Leonardo. He says he's just completed a painting of his master and set it aside to cure. That means if we can authenticate the manuscript, the case for the painting's a slam dunk. The painting, in turn, can vouch for the manuscript. A virtuous circle of proofs.

We send our report to Dickson by secure email, leaving out any mention of the portfolio. We know if Dickson gets his hands on the manuscript, it'll end up like the painting—locked away in his personal vault. It'll stay there until he dies, at which point some other rapacious billionaire will snap it up at auction. This—this *treasure*—belongs to the Italian people, to the world, not some jagweed collector.

What Artie and I do next shocks even us.

EDITOR'S EMAIL

What? You can't sell a stolen manuscript! Scarlett, what the hell are you thinking? It's one thing to publish a document without explicit permission from the owner. It's another to steal it first. Please say you're just messing with me.

8VO_6

SCARLETT: Mr. Chenoweth, this is where the trust comes in. What we're about to tell you could land us in big tub of hot water, if not prison. In which case, no book. And remember, I have your emails. You're a Known Associate. Do we understand each other?

Our plan is this: We'll sell the translation and the commentary, keep the advance, and deliver the original to a well-known Italian university, TBD. We'll assign the remaining royalties to a charity, also TBD.

Let's call that Phase Two of our plan.

When I say *our* plan, I mean my plan. As you've probably guessed, pulling off an international heist wasn't on Miss Priss's to-do list. But the fact is, I need her ace translation skills.

It took some persuading, believe me.

Look, I said, you've spent your whole life in classrooms and museums and libraries. You're childless, retired, widowed, and your only relatives live 4,000 miles away. Why settle for a tiny plink on the grand piano when you can play the final chord from *A Day in the Life*? Besides, if the manuscript wasn't on the list of contents, it really doesn't belong to anybody, does it?

She calls me a twisted Robin Hood. Rob from the rich, give to ourselves.

To my surprise, the next day she accepts. Right, Artie?

ARTIE: After first accepting Christopher Hitchens as my personal savior.

SCARLETT: So here's where we stand. We've got the manuscript. We think it's authentic, and we believe it's worth a fortune—far more than the value of the painting. Beyond that, we know it'll knock the book industry on its bony butt.

Mr. Chenoweth, Artie and I have gone underground. We've got new names and passports. We've got a complete digital arsenal. We've changed our looks and we're on the move. We're not worried about Dickson blowing the whistle. If he wants to hold onto the painting, he'll keep his lousy mouth shut.

We've trusted you, Mr. Chenoweth. Now you need to trust us. Talk to your team. Make an offer. If we like it, we'll share the first chapter of the manuscript. Remember, each chapter needs to be preceded by a fractional payment in Lucra. If you pull out at any time, we keep the payments.

It's our hope that, little by little, we'll start to feel like partners in what will surely become a global publishing sensation.

Mr. Chenoweth, I freely admit I'm not an honorable person. In fact, I'm quite literally a thief. But I do have compensating virtues. I almost always tell the truth. I'm a scientist with a degree in physics and a master's in biophysics. Suffice it to say, I have zero patience for self-delusion or magical thinking. To me, a thing exists or it doesn't. I mean, really, isn't this world magical enough without looking for fairies and conspiracies under every rock? I don't believe in all that shit.

Whatever you think of me and Artie, I can promise you one thing—we'll stick to the facts. The story we're going to tell is the truth, the whole truth, and nothing but the truth, so help me Dog.

I don't believe in God either, Mr. Chenoweth.

EDITOR'S EMAIL

I have to say, Scarlett, your ambition is breathtaking. But I need more information before I can approach my legal team. Can you tell me about Mr. Dickson? What's he like? How did you meet him? What claim does he have on the artifacts?

8VO_7

[SOUND OF CAR IN MOTION]

SCARLETT: Okay, I'll start with Artie. She met Dickson in London while giving a presentation on Renaissance art. So far, she's only worked with him at arm's length. Which is the safest distance IMHO. The man is a snake.

My own encounter happened a year ago at the university museum. I was there to authenticate a crate of antiquities, and he was there to lend some minor pieces to an exhibit. We struck up a conversation about scientific attribution. He seemed to know a lot about it, in that glib show-offy way collectors often have. Afterwards he hired me to authenticate some drawings, paintings, and sculptures from 15th- and 16th-century Italy.

Dickson keeps his treasures in a reinforced concrete vault in his fortress of a home, and shows his favorite pieces in a private gallery for the benefit of, I presume, easily impressed bimbos.

That ain't me, in case you're wondering. In my experience, it's men who are easily impressed. A toss of the auburn curls, a few strategic holes in the old jeans, the odd snippet of innuendo, and they're yours for the taking. I'm not the kind of girl who's perpetually ready to pair, like some over-eager Bluetooth device. But I *am* good with men. They only *think* they're good with me.

We get to talking in the museum, and he tells me about his interest in Transhumanism. The philosophy of extropy. Big deal in tech circles. I'm sure you've heard of *entropy*, the tendency for things to disintegrate and die over time. Extropy is the opposite—the life force that resists decay and brings order to the universe.

Dickson and his extropian friends think technology is fast-tracking us to a massive inflection point in human evolution. In twenty years or so, they believe, we'll leap the natural limits of our biology—i.e., live forever.

I mean, in a way, it's kind of hopeful. Who doesn't want to relieve suffering and extend your life?

Dickson says to me, you're a biophysicist. Imagine a world where if you needed an organ transplant, you'd just knock one out on a bioprinter. No more waiting for a donor. No more mismatches. No more autoimmune rejections.

Or, let's say you have a car accident with no chance of recovery. You could plug your brain into an AI array and live on as a fully conscious transhuman. Your life would continue, albeit in non-corporeal form.

Non-corporeal form. Blips on a computer screen. As if a transhuman is somehow better than a human.

What I imagine, I say, is a successful guy like you living forever at compound interest. Once you get going, you'll never want to stop. You'll pile advantage on advantage until you basically become God.

I give him my best pretend smile to show that we're fellow conspirators. Then I say, aren't you afraid of Transhumanist clout falling into the wrong hands? What if everybody started living forever? Where's the advantage in that?

He tilts his head innocently as if the thought had never occurred to him.

So I clarify. Wouldn't you be living—you know, forever—in the squalor of an overcrowded planet? The population would grow exponentially. The very technology that gave you immortality would bring everlasting misery to everyone, including you.

Here he lets the cat out of the bag.

Well, it's important that only the *right* people have that kind of power. Extended life should go to those who have earned it. It needs to be distributed on the basis of merit—as a privilege, not a right. I've worked hard for what I've achieved. I've built a business that keeps people safe from security risks. Don't you think I've earned the privilege of stewarding their lives, at least a little?

What I'm thinking is, his father set him up in business with profits from selling overpriced pharmaceuticals to the Cold War military. Those who've earned it, my ass. I'm so tired of the self-made-man schtick, followed by the pull-yourself-up-by-your-own-bootstraps crappola. It always comes from guys who can't deal with the fact that they've had gobs of help getting filthy rich. Jesus, we all depend on other people, from our parents to our friends to our teachers, even the government.

I mean, steward their lives? Really? Did these words just slip out before he could catch them? Or is this patriarchy on steroids? I can't tell if he's snapping the flag of white male privilege in my face, or if he really thinks the term doesn't apply. That, right there, would be the *essence* of white male privilege.

Dickson's father, on the other hand, really did earn it—or at least he yanked it off the tree with his own calloused hands. Hardscrabble striver who built the family fortune up from nothing. Lived large, took risks, and happily trashed the idealism of his workers.

He was also a notorious seducer of women. Especially the younger, more foolish types. In the Eighties—before my time—he was accused of the rape and murder of a 19-year-old girl. He used his connections to make it go away. Poof. He had a dealmaker's knack for teasing out the weaknesses of friends and enemies, which he used to great advantage. Out of the resulting largess, he was able to give Junior a leg up.

My dad was a dick, too, just not a rich one. How do you survive a dad who's an asshole? One of two ways. You either repudiate everything he stands for and create a life of your own, or you chase after approval that never comes and sell your soul in the process. I chose the former. He chose the latter.

Dickson waits for me to say something.

I give him my best Southern-belle eye flutter, and guess what? He offers to show me his vault. I open my greeny greens to their widest and say: My, my, sir, are you asking me to view your etchings? You do tempt a girl.

He gets my sarcasm and drops it. The last thing I would do is saunter into a vault with that man. Or with any man, for that matter.

I hope that answers your question, Mr. Chenoweth. As to your second question, as far as I know, Dickson has no legal claim to the artifacts in the townhouse. He's just another rich guy with a collection erection.

Scarlett, feel free to say what you *really* think—don't hold back. As you can imagine, your proposal raises more than a few legal and ethical questions. While we sort through these, can you send us a sample of the manuscript? I still can't promise we'll take the book, but I *can* promise confidentiality.

SCARLETT: I do appreciate your concerns. One of the reasons we chose you was your professional reputation. We're ready to share a translated sample, on the condition that, from now on, it's pay as you go. Sound okay?

ARTIE: Mr. Chenoweth, what I'm about to read to you is the first chapter of Melzi's account. Along the way we'll clarify one or two things that need some context. Five hundred years and change is a long time.

3 December 1512

The events I wish to relate, Dear Reader, might be taken as the ravings of a lunatic were it not for the details I have recorded in my notes. Even so, I myself have difficulty believing that such events did ever take place, so gruesome and fantastical they seem to me now. Yet I shall strive to serve the truth as I have served my master, with diligence and humility. My aim is not to shock or titillate. It is merely to shine a light on the prodigious creative powers of my master, Leonardo da Vinci.

On April 13, in the year of our Christian salvation 1508, the master and I set off on a journey from Milan to Venice. The winds were fierce and the roads muddy and rough from the rains. Leonardo had lent me his best mare, while he himself rode a young gelding in need of schooling. We ponied a dark brown jennet named Violetta to carry our bags.

Master Leonardo is an excellent horseman and quite strong despite his advanced age. Yet I worried for his safety lest we encounter a contingent of French soldiers or a band of brigands. On my person I kept two daggers, of which one was visible and the other hidden.

The object of our journey was an appointment with Aldo Manuzio to arrange the printing of my master's notebooks. Leonardo had met Aldo ten years earlier at his workshop in Venice. On seeing a printing press for the first time, my master had examined its workings with great interest. He surprised Aldo by proposing a mechanism for advancing the paper automatically, thereby saving unnecessary labor. Since then, Aldo and Leonardo have become good friends.

The matter of the notebooks had been preying on him for a number of months. He had just completed 30 folios while in Florence, where he had gone to settle his uncle's estate. Now he was eager to finish the rest of the work. He wrote to me saying, "Why in God's name have you not answered a single letter of mine? You just wait till I get there and by God I'll make you write so much you'll be sorry!"

I understood this to be a friendly gibe; I could tell he was annoyed by his own procrastination. With the master, there was always an urgent assignment or an unruly problem tugging at his boot like a stray dog. Given a choice, he would fain pursue a new idea than revisit an old one.

The further we rode, the more attuned he became to the landscape, feeling the spatial geometry of objects, weighing the quality of light. His attention flicked this way and that as he measured the world with the precise eye of a surveyor.

On our third day, after resting the horses, we continued our journey east through Brescia. Monte Maddalena was crowned with snow, and the air was clear and cold. Buckles shivered, reins jangled, and steam blew rhythmically from the nostrils of our horses as we trotted on a flat section of road. Leonardo passed the time by telling me about his first encounter with a printing press, or rather news of one.

"In 1466 I was apprenticed to Master Verrocchio," he said, a smile playing across his lips. "About the same age as you when you were first apprenticed to me," he added. "We had received a visit from Master Alberti. Though he was old in years, he was young in his passion for novelty. He had seen a mechanical printing press in Subiaco, and his thoughts had been racing ever since. He declared that printed books would soon revolutionize society.

"'Revolutionize!' The word echoed in my 14-year-old ears like a trumpet blast."

Leonardo's gelding shied violently to the left. He sat back calmly and applied pressure to the horse's left flank. Reassured, the gelding returned to his normal cadence.

"Alberti claimed that portable books would free the population from ignorance, and from the excessive power of the Church and the courts. Ideas would spread quickly. Reading would educate the world. His mind was on fire with the possibilities.

"Before he took his leave, I asked if he had any words for a young apprentice in need of advice. He guided me thus: 'Apply artistry to all your endeavors, but especially to three things: walking in the city, riding a horse, and speaking. This last,' he said, 'is the most important. To speak well you must read, read, and read.' Checco, you may think it strange for one who lacks a formal education, but that is what I have tried to do."

"I do not think it strange. For I have had a formal education, and all I did was read!"

"And yet you hold a brush well and write Latin like an angel."

"Omnium rerum principia parva sunt."

Leonardo's face went as blank as a sheet of paper. I remembered that Latin was a land he had not yet conquered. "The beginnings of all things are small," I said, ashamed for exposing one of his weaknesses, yet secretly proud that I knew something he did not.

"Ah. You must teach me Latin someday." He said, a teasing glint in his eye. "My projects leave me little time to learn as much as I would like."

Our journey to Venice had caused a halt to much of the work in the studio. However, I managed to complete a large portrait of Master Leonardo and set it aside to cure before we departed Milan. It was the first time he had approved of my sfumato. He was especially pleased to be depicted in his new embroidered tunic, cut from his favorite color silk, a dusty rose.

Leonardo himself was forced to suspend a number of his own projects, notably two Madonnas, one of which he had pledged to the King. Salaì had promised to manage the studio as if it were his own, which always worried Leonardo. He was eager to return as soon as possible.

SCARLETT: Did you catch the reference to the portrait of Leonardo? The *sfumato* brush strokes? The rose-colored silk? Artie also did some research on this Salaì character. Artie?

ARTIE: The pupil Salaì was born Gian Giacomo Caprotti da Oreno, the son of Pietro di Giovanni, a tenant in Leonardo's vineyard in Milan. Gian Giacomo entered Leonardo's household at the age of ten. His nickname was Salaì, a slang term for Little Devil. He had soft features, curly blond hair, and a classical Greek profile. He also had a tendency to steal anything that wasn't nailed down. Leonardo once described him as a thief, a liar, and a glutton.

Yet I daresay the boy's vices, far from disqualifying him, endeared him to Leonardo, who always forgave his faults. He bought the boy clothes for every occasion, insisting that he dress in the same elevated style as his master.

As Salaì grew older, he became Leonardo's lover. That's correct, Mr. Chenoweth. They were homosexuals at a time when one could be executed for it.

EDITOR'S EMAIL

I remember hearing speculation about Leonardo's sexuality. What do we know about these other characters, Alberti and Manuzio?

8VO_9

ARTIE: Hello, Mr. Chenoweth. Leon Battista Alberti was an architect, an artist, a poet, a linguist, a mathematician, a cryptographer, a priest, and a published author. Most historians view him as one of the premiere architects of his day—sumptuous churches, palaces, civic buildings. Whilst this is certainly true, it misses the larger point. He applied all these disciplines as if there were no boundaries between them. He was the very model of a Renaissance man, a fact that would not have been lost on Leonardo.

SCARLETT: It sounds like Alberti's athletic skills were dope. He rode horses like a circus performer. They said he could leap over a grown man. He was charming. Educated. Influential. Leonardo didn't want to be *like* Alberti. He wanted to *be* Alberti.

What impressed Leonardo most was Alberti's commitment to paying his achievements forward. He was constantly exploring new ideas with his buddies, and had a real jones for sharing these in print.

ARTIE: That brings us to Aldo, who used his Latin name in the trade.

SCARLETT: Aldus Manutius. The Aldine Press was a big deal in Venice. And Venice was a big deal in Europe. More books were printed in Venice than all of Italy, and Italy sold more books than all other countries combined.

Aldo had a couple of partners to help with the business, but his ace in the hole was a guy named Griffo, a punchcutter with an eye for a gorgeous typeface.

In those days you had to cut letters into the ends of metal rods, which you then used to punch out molds for the various sizes of type. Each size was a font. Most of the people who did this work were goldsmiths in a former life. You needed hand-eye coordination, and Griffo had it up the wazoo. His typefaces were so timeless that they're still around today.

ARTIE: By the way, Mr. Chenoweth, when Leonardo refers to Melzi as Checco, he's using a common nickname for Francesco. He had pet names for all his pupils. Back to the story...

[RUSTLING PAPER]

Master Leonardo had calculated the distance from Milan at 180 miles, a journey of one week with post horses, ten days with one's own horses. He arrived at this number using a clever device, invented in a single afternoon, that counted the turns of a cartwheel—so many turns per mile. He estimated that we were now about 25 miles from Venice.

After nine days of travel, happily without incident, we stabled our horses and mule in Mestre at the western edge of the lagoon. We spent a quiet night at the inn and woke to a brilliant sun reflecting off the mirrored surface of the water. A pair of boatmen ferried us to the Grand Canal and let us ashore near the Rialto Bridge. As one of the boatmen busied himself with the moorings, the other called for a porter. A man pulled a handbarrow to the edge of the quay and loaded our bags onto it.

We followed the porter past the debtors' prison at the foot of the bridge. Hands reached through the low iron grilles. Voices cried for money, or food, or intercession with the authorities. The porter shouted back, saying they would not be in prison if their hands had calluses.

The Rialto was a swirl of activity as men unloaded vegetables, spices, and large jugs of wine, stacking and unstacking their crates on the quay. Seagulls screeched and squawked over scraps on the fish market floor. The heavenly scents of cinnamon, pepper, and saffron mingled with the foul smells of rotting flesh from the nearby abattoir.

Leonardo objected to the wholesale slaughter of animals, and to foul smells in general. He held a perfumed handkerchief to his face as we walked through the Rialto piazza. Outside the church of San Giacomo, bankers and money changers sang out their prices. The giant clock above the church doors spoke more of Mammon than of God, but this has al-

ways been the way in Venice. The streets were filled not only with merchants, but with hooligans and scoundrels as well. There were simoniacal priests, relic peddlers, sellers of indulgences, and counterfeiters of papal bulls. There were alms seekers, fortune tellers, soothsayers, charlatans, and cardsharps. Fake paralytics lay at the doors of churches and knelt on the streets with their foreheads to the ground. We saw every type of person imaginable, scratching out a living in the overcrowded city.

One man sold ornamental birds in wooden cages piled high at the edge of the piazza. "Birds, birds. Every feather, every color," he crowed. Stacked on top were warblers, thrushes, and goldfinches, hopping from perch to perch. In the middle were magpies, blackbirds, and starlings. On the bottom were plovers, partridges, and turtle doves.

My master went up to the man, drawing his purse from his tunic. "What price for the birds?" he demanded.

"Which ones?" answered the man, gesturing first toward the finches and then toward the blackbirds.

"All of them."

The man tugged at the rim of his plumed hat as if to adjust his hearing. "All of them?"

Leonardo counted out fifteen soldi and placed the coins in the man's trembling hand. "Will this do?"

He grinned and nodded, unable to speak, so surprised was he at his good fortune.

One by one, Leonardo opened the doors of the cages. At first the birds did nothing. Then, as if responding to an unseen signal, they exploded from their wooden prisons in a thunderous clatter of wings beating against the air. They roared into the sky, their ascent so wild and joyous that the market sellers stopped their work to gaze upward.

"Master, why did you do that?" I said, full of amazement at this sudden impulse.

"Birds are not baubles to be kept in pretty boxes," he said. "They will die of broken hearts."

I could not but wonder if he was talking about himself instead of the birds. He relished his freedom above all else.

As we walked on, men wheeled carts full of stones and wet cement around us, and women carried baskets of soiled linens. Tinkers, masons, and basket-weavers loudly touted their wares. An albino swung out of an alley and nearly clipped Leonardo with the long roll of cloth he carried on his shoulder. I managed to block it with my forearm and gave the man a warning tap on the back of his hairless head. He spat and sped along without a backward glance.

We followed the porter onto the Ruga San Giovanni, where the flow of pedestrians thickened and echoed noisily under corbeled overhangs. The street soon widened into a river of herringbone brick, where a number of booksellers had set up shop. Men delivered barrels of ink and reams of paper, and boys, younger than I, dangled books from poles, shouting titles that had been newly translated into Italian from Latin.

At last, our inn came into view on the edge of a narrow canal off the main street. My master paid the porter, and we took our rooms. I lay down on a pallet against the wall. Within minutes I fell into a deep sleep and did not wake until the next day.

Aldo had agreed to meet Leonardo soon after sunrise the next morning, before the normal business of the day could interfere with their negotiations. At dawn, Leonardo was already dressed when he gently shook my shoulder.

"I hope your dream had long thick braids and fulsome breasts," he said with mock disapproval. I jumped up as if the Devil had grabbed me by the ears.

"I—I—I…"

"Ay-yi-yi is right!" he said. "It's almost time for lunch! Perhaps we should have taken the Rialto clock with us!"

I suddenly realized he was teasing. The sky was dark except for a pink band of light visible between the buildings. I too was pink, but not from the light. I quickly washed myself and set out the clothes I had brought for our meeting.

Leonardo had already gone out and come back by the time I finished dressing. He tossed me a warm biscuit. "Eat this for strength, lazybones, or you might mistake a printing press for a bed." I let go of my pants and caught the biscuit.

We left the hotel and walked diagonally across the Campo San Polo. Leonardo was attired in a silver embroidered doublet, his face glowing with the tantalizing hope of finally publishing his notebooks. He strode with his back straight and his head high, his white beard trailing to the side.

The campo was quiet that morning. But in the street ahead, a crowd had gathered outside a shop door. A group of men were whispering and gesturing in agitation, taking turns thrusting their heads through the doorway. As we drew closer I saw that the shop in question was the very one in which we were bound. The words on the sign said "The Aldine Press," carved under a symbol of a dolphin and anchor.

"What has happened, Master?"

"Come," urged Leonardo, grasping my wrist with surprising force.

I rushed in front of Leonardo and pushed several onlookers to the side so he could slip through the doorway unmolested. Then, dropping back, I followed him in. As our eyes adjusted to the dim light, we beheld a terrifying tableau.

EDITOR'S EMAIL

Wow. I have to say, Melzi's storytelling pulls you right into his world. His depiction of street life in Venice is truly vivid. As a publisher, I'm especially fascinated by the description of the kids selling books on poles.

What were all those people doing outside the print shop? Something terrible must have happened. A worker injury? Chemical fire?

8VO_10

ARTIE: Mr. Chenoweth, I hope you haven't just eaten breakfast. Here's the next part:

A man hung crucified on the back of a large printing press. His hands were impaled with steel spikes, struck deep into stout wooden uprights. Strewn across the floor were hundreds of pieces of metal type. Workers stood in small groups whispering amongst themselves. One made the sign of the cross.

Leonardo quickly closed the door behind us. A worker rushed over to lock it. Messer Manuzio walked towards us, his arms extended as if to apologize.

"Leonardo, I am afraid you have come on a very bad day. As you can see, there has been a tragedy. I arrived only minutes ago to find this poor soul hanging there."

I have seen my master in such situations before. Whereas most men become agitated and muddled when confronted with chaos, he grows calm and clear-headed. His visage becomes that of a bird of prey.

He turned to Aldo and said, "May I examine him?"

Aldo shrugged, grateful for the help of a friend.

Leonardo took an apron from a hook and slipped the ties over his head, checking first to make sure there was no ink that could stain his clothing. He instructed the pressmen to lower the man to the floor. "Be careful not to damage the body."

Two men held the victim in place while a third lifted his hands off the spikes. When they finished, they laid him gently on the floor, face up. The left side of his head was covered in blood. His skull had been crushed from the sides, causing his eyes to bulge forward in a hideous stare. His tongue was swollen and extended, falling outward onto his cheek. The sight of his face caused my stomach to rise to my throat.

Leonardo knelt beside the unfortunate man and loosened his tunic. The skin on his chest was black and blistered, his hands bloody and torn from the spikes. My master paused for a moment. Then he instructed the men to make an inclined pallet and place the body face down, head toward the lower end.

As they did this, he reached into his pocket for his eyeglasses and positioned them carefully on his nose. He stooped down to examine the pieces of metal that were scattered at our feet. Some of these he returned to the floor; others he placed in a pouch drawn from his doublet. He went back to the corpse and turned the man's head so the bloody side of his face was upward.

"Aldo, if you will, please bring me a wet cloth and a clean sheet of paper."

Aldo nodded to an assistant, who returned with the materials.

Leonardo took the wet cloth and carefully wiped the dried blood from the man's face. He waited for a moment, then placed the sheet of paper over his cheek. He pressed downward and rubbed his palm over the paper several times. The pressmen came closer, mesmerized by this curious procedure. Leonardo slowly peeled the paper from the man's cheek.

There on the sheet was a passage from a book, printed in the dead man's mortal ink. Leonardo passed the sheet to Aldo, who studied it, squinting.

"It is backwards—I cannot read it." He returned the paper to Leonardo.

My master, who was accustomed to mirror writing, read the words easily:

> "See how mutilated I am;
> Before me, another weeps as well,
> His face split from forehead to chin;
> And all the others you see here
> Were those who spread scandal
> And divided people up."

The workers looked at each other in puzzlement. Leonardo turned to Aldo, who took a deep breath. "It might be a passage from Virgil, or perhaps Dante. I can tell that the typeface was one Griffo had cut for my friend Bembo to use in his books."

"Is it possible to summon Messer Bembo?"

"I believe so. He is staying at the Palazzo Morosini on the Grand Canal while we print his poems." Aldo motioned to a shop boy, who quickly disappeared into the street. "But why? Surely the passage was chosen at random."

Leonardo looked surprised. "On the contrary, Aldo. It was the man who was random. The passage was purposeful. It is a message, and the man was simply the messenger."

Aldo was dumbfounded. "How can you know this?"

"You can see by his torn and soiled clothing that he was a man of little station. Therefore, his dead body had no other purpose but to serve as a substrate for this macabre message." Leonardo emptied the contents of his pouch on the table of the press. "I believe you will find that these characters match the characters in the passage."

Aldo picked up several of the metal pieces and noted traces of blood on their surfaces.

"Whoever did this took a chase from your workshop and pressed the poor man's head onto it." Leonardo pulled the lever arm and brought the platen down swiftly with a thud. "Like so."

Aldo shut his eyes tight at the image of a man's head being crushed in his own printing press, a device built to bring enlightenment, not death.

"After he nailed his hands to the uprights, he threw the chase to the floor, scattering the type." Leonardo bent down and picked up a broken wooden frame the size of a small window. "May I take this?"

Aldo agreed readily, then cast his eyes toward the mutilated victim. "Who would use such a horrible means to kill a man?"

Leonardo looked at Aldo as if he were a child. "My dear Aldo. Set aside such troubling thoughts. He was crushed by the press, yes, but he was already dead from the poison."

Aldo's jaw fell. This was too much.

Leonardo walked to the back of the press where the two spikes were still attached to the uprights. He reached up and twisted one of them until it came free. He turned it over in his hand. It was a steel punch, used to make typographic molds. "It must have taken a great deal of muscle to drive these punches into solid oak. Do you have any workers with that kind of strength?"

Aldo thought for a moment. "I do not think so. It must have taken the bicep of a giant."

At that moment the door of the workshop burst open and a wedge of light spread across the room. In flew the shop boy, followed by a man wearing the robes of a scholar.

"Pietro!"

Aldo rushed forward and clasped his friend's hands warmly. "I am sorry to call you here in such fraught conditions."

He quickly introduced Leonardo to Pietro Bembo. They exchanged courteous greetings, each aware of the other's reputation.

"I am acquainted with your father," said Leonardo. "A good man."

Bembo bowed slightly. He walked over to look at the body on the pallet. His face blanched.

Aldo said, "He seems to be a person of the street. I found him this morning, hanging from the uprights of the press with type punches driven through his hands. Leonardo believes it was part of a message."

"A message?"

Aldo handed Bembo the blood-inked sheet of paper. "These words were incised on his left cheek with a chase of type."

"It is printed in reverse."

"Come with me, dear Bembo," Leonardo said, leading him toward the window. "Turn the paper backwards and hold it to the light."

His lips moved silently as he peered at the passage. His face grew as white as the paper between his fingers. "It is from my translation of 'The Inferno.'"

Aldo raised his hands, palms up. "We were about to reprint it. The formes had been prepared and were stored on the shelf."

Leonardo had not taken his eyes from Bembo.

"What does it mean?" said Bembo.

"My very question," said Leonardo.

"The passage is Dante's warning to scandal mongers." He turned to Aldo. "What will you do?"

Aldo spread his arms in exasperation. "We shall notify the authorities, of course. Then the parish cemetery. After they remove the body, we shall clean up the shop. What else can we do?"

Leonardo cupped his hand under Aldo's elbow and turned him away from the group. "Tell me, Aldo, have you any acquaintances at the cemetery?"

"The gravedigger is one of our most devoted readers."

"Can you tell me his name?"

Leonardo and I left the workshop with the broken chase that once held the morbid passage from Dante. Yet as morbid as Dante's verses are, Dear Reader, the scene I would observe later that night would make the most stoic of souls wish for the inferno.

SCARLETT: If you're not hooked by now, Mr Chenoweth, ask your personal assistant to check your pulse. What we have here is a firsthand account of the world's greatest genius at the height of his powers, applying his unique talents to an undiscovered piece of history. It's bound to mess with the most cherished beliefs of da Vinci scholars. And—and—it was written by the only person with the knowledge, skill, and personal access to be credible. Melzi's account makes Vasari's *Lives of the Artists* look like a Marvel comic.

Keep in mind that we haven't had time to finish our fact-checking. We'll probably discover one or two errors before our first official delivery. But we do have corroboration for some of the items.

First, Melzi's description of Venice in 1508. They probably stayed overnight at the Locanda della Campana, a popular inn for visitors arriving from the west on horseback. The debtors' prison Melzi described is undoubtedly the Palazzo dei Camerlenghi at the foot of the Rialto Bridge. You can still see the iron grilles, low on the wall, where the prisoners would have reached out to people passing by. But the clincher for us was the books on poles. That's a quirky detail you won't find on Wikipedia. It strongly suggests a firsthand account.

Second, the way a murder was handled in Venice fits Melzi's description. Aldo would have called for the Signori di Notte, the Lords of the Night, who were charged with investigating prostitution, thefts, and other crimes. As to the victim's body, there were no hospitals or morgues in 1508 Venice. The corpse would have gone straight to the cemetery for burial, just as Aldo said.

Finally, there's the ability of a dead body to generate a bloody impression on a sheet of paper. This was a stretch for me. There wouldn't have been much bleeding by the time Leonardo arrived, but metal type could definitely dig into the flesh and release a lot of blood. If the murder happened recently enough, it was possible for the blood stored in his tissues to generate an image on a sheet of paper.

On this last point, you may be interested to know that blood sinks in the body after the heart stops pumping. Leonardo had the men place the victim on an incline to let the blood move down to his head and out through the broken skin. I'm speculating on this, but I know how scientists think.

Everything else checks out. The description of the marketplace, the herringbone streets, the corbeled buildings, the interior of the print shop. We have plenty of items on our punch list, but so far Melzi's account tallies with the known facts. There's no reason to think his description of the murder scene was any less accurate.

Now that you've had a sample, Mr. Chenoweth, it's time to bite. Or as my Aunt Mag would say, shit or get off the pot. Every minute we lose moves onto Dickson's side of the scoreboard.

Do we have a deal or not?

EDITOR'S EMAIL

Scarlett, I won't say this isn't a dangerous book for us. The legal risk of publishing a "borrowed" manuscript is certainly keeping us up at night.

Before we commit, I need to know we're aligned on our mission and that we're able to generate an abundance of trust. I'd like to have a word with each of you separately. Scarlett, would you like to go first? Find a quiet spot where you won't be overheard and let me know when you're ready. I need to ask you some personal questions—nothing that would give away your identity or location.

8VO_11

SCARLETT: Mr. Chenoweth, I have to tell you something. I can talk about technical stuff all day, but I'm not too keen on sharing personal details. Nobody wants to hear the sob stories of female scientists except for bored therapists pretending to give a shit. I hate them all. My life is my life. Are we clear?

EDITOR'S EMAIL

Got it. No personal details. But you must understand that publishing abook—*this* book—without ever meeting you, or knowing much about you, is nervous-making. My boss, Katherine, is feeding me some rope, but there's no telling how far she'll let it run before yanking me back. At this point I need to know a little more.

First, I'm curious about why you chose Harker to publish your book. Why not one of the other houses?

Second, I'd like to know more about your relationship with Artie. I sense you two don't always get along, which might become a problem in fraught circumstances like these.

Third, I wonder how dysgraphia might affect your output. If you have trouble writing things down, how do we know you're remembering everything correctly?

Finally, why are you doing this at all? It seems to me you had your life all figured out, and now you're ready to throw it away in an instant. I need to know how committed you are to this project.

I understand you have to hold some things back, Scarlett. I'm not asking for your life story. But since we can't have exclusive rights to the manuscript, we may need to include some or all of your commentary as a "product differentiator." That's marketing-speak for a competitive advantage, like putting a defensive moat around our book. Other houses might publish the same manuscript, but none will have the rights to the inside story, the story *about* the story. That needs to be ours alone.

Can you agree to be a little more forthcoming for the sake of a stronger book?

8VO_12

SCARLETT: Boy, you don't play around, do you? Right for the jugular. Okay, I promise to share more. Don't say I didn't warn you.

To answer your first question, we chose Harker because of *you.* More precisely, because of your success with books like *A Girl Named Aptly.* We also read that you canceled a book contract after you learned that the author had a history of sex abuse. You seemed to us like a mensch. It's amazing what you can find out online. I could tell you more about yourself, but I don't want to embarrass you.

As to my relationship with Artie, we only met a couple weeks ago. In some ways she drives me bananas. I think she's the fussiest, prissiest, most talented person who ever buttoned a cardigan. In my experience, most people aren't worth the carbon they're printed with. Artie's different. She's a net positive for the planet, a force for good in lavender pumps. I can't tell her that, or she'll be dressing me in Hermès scarves before I can dial 911. I want her to think I'm a train wreck, and to keep her distance

If you're wondering whether we can hold the band together, I won't make any promises. But I will say, when we're working, it's magic. I don't use the word lightly. I'm a scientist. Logic is more my thing. But it's like, I don't know, we're a pair of stick magnets. When we go head-to-head, we repel each other. But when we align our opposite poles, like when we're working together, we create a doubly powerful magnet.

Next question. Dysgraphia. Very annoying disability, but don't worry about it. Dysgraphia can actually improve your memory. Think about it—if you can't write things down, your best option is to memorize them. Sometimes I feel a little like Homer. He was able to remember incredibly long stories and reel them off word for word. *Sing to me of the man, O Muse, the man of twists and turns, driven time and again off course after plundering the hallowed heights of Troy.* I don't have perfect recall, but I remember a *lot*. It's one of my superpowers.

The tragedy of da Vinci's life, in my view, was that his notebooks never got published. His handmade originals just trickled out to random people when Melzi died. Leonardo's last pupil, the one he counted on to guard his legacy, blew his final assignment. It took something like two hundred years before the world got a good look at Leonardo's genius—too late to keep science and art together. Science headed for logic, and art headed for magic, never the twain shall meet.

You're right about me, Mr. Chenoweth. I did have my life all figured out. But if there's one thing that defines me, it's a burning desire for justice. Scarlett's Third Law: Every action demands an equal and opposite reaction. The scales must balance.

Imagine what it's like for a woman in science. People picture scientists as a race of kindly old men living the contemplative life on a philosophical plane removed from the corruption of ordinary mortals. Bullshit. They're a pack of feral, prize-snatching, grant-grubbing raptors. They'll destroy anyone who threatens their status. Women are the low-hanging fruit in this scenario. The only way for a woman to make it in science is to attach herself to a mentor. The mentor then wants to be paid in sexual favors or rank subservience for the rest of his life.

So along comes Mr. Dickson, a guy cut from the same cloth. He thinks he's an innovation genius and wants to own Leonardo just so he can bury him. I can't take it. I'm willing to sacrifice my own plans to balance the scales. I hope you can see this isn't some kind of zip-line thrill-ride for me. It's my destiny, Mr. Chenoweth.

EDITOR'S EMAIL

Call me Peter. I think we're going to be friends, despite my aversion to burning swords. I'll pass what you said on to Katherine, leaving out the more frightening parts. Can you let Artie know I'd like a word with her now?

8VO_13

ARTIE: I received your questions, Mr. Chenoweth. The red light is on, so I believe I'm recording. Audio files are not my usual means of communication. I'm making an effort to join the 19th century. The 21st seems like science fiction to me.

It's late here, and there's no one in sight. I'm walking along the street outside our hotel. The only movement I see is a tin streetlamp swinging like mad from a wire over the intersection, throwing yellow light all over the place. You can probably hear the wind rattling the rusty shade. I believe our conversation will be private.

I suppose you're wondering why I would sign on for a quixotic adventure with a woman less than half my age. It's a sensible question. I'm afraid I can't give you a sensible answer. I'm still trying to understand it myself.

But let me tell you what I see in Scarlett. She is young, yes. She is rude, certainly. She is irritating, willful, defensive, and headstrong. All those things. And yet she is completely brilliant. I've taught classes at university for three decades, and I have never seen a mind so utterly focused on getting to the heart of matters. She's a truth-seeking missile.

I don't fancy Mr. Dickson's chances if he tries to intimidate her.

Even though Scarlett can be caustic and antisocial, Mr. Chenoweth, I believe this is merely protective coloration. I've seen it before in some of my students. They simply need a little time to mature.

Allow me to offer an illustration of Scarlett's character. The night before last, we were walking back from a restaurant when my heel slipped into a crack between paving stones. My foot broke loose from my shoe and I pitched forward, landing on my hands and knees on the pavement. Scarlett rushed to pick me up, fussing and cooing as if I were a baby bird fallen from a nest. She helped me back to the room and spent thirty minutes carefully cleaning the abrasions on my knees and applying plasters.

Then she said, this doesn't mean I like you.

When her mask slipped that night, I saw who she really was. Hard as nails on the outside, sweet as cream on the inside. By the way, her given name is quite feminine. It doesn't fit her at all.

As Scarlett said, Mr. Chenoweth, we first met in the hotel near the townhouse in Lombardy. I knew she was Mr. Dickson's favorite authenticator and that I was hired mostly for window dressing. He needed the patina of European credentials in case he chose to resell whatever he ended up purchasing. I do love Italian art, so I took the assignment as a sort of busman's holiday.

I was unprepared for Scarlett's intensity. Whilst I confess to being swept up in her crusade, I believed our chances of success lay somewhere between zero and none. Scarlett says I have a no-can-do attitude. And yet she makes me wonder if I might not be one of those desert plants that grows slowly and predictably for a hundred years, only to explode with the most spectacular display of flowers imaginable.

I have an urge to find out.

In your email you mention the danger of being followed, and I second your concern. But Scarlett seems well-versed in the ways of spycraft. She found all sorts of clever tools and counter-surveillance devices online. One of her gadgets alerts one to all the GPS trackers, audio bugs, mobile phone bugs, or surveillance cameras that might be in one's immediate vicinity. Unlike myself, Scarlett is a digital native. Also unlike myself, she's confident in the superiority of her skills. Perhaps too confident, but that's youth for you.

I know you're worried about the risk of failure, Mr. Chenoweth. Given our tenuous partnership, the legal uncertainties surrounding our mission, and the enormous resources of our adversary, this is quite understandable. Success is far from assured. And yet I have an overwhelming feeling of rightness, of purpose, and dare I say it, destiny? The story of Melzi and Leonardo must be told. I hope you feel the same.

I promise to encourage Scarlett to share more of herself for the benefit of the book. I know she hasn't been very forthcoming. I can only imagine that her family history is less than rosy. Yet I'm inclined to let her work through her problems in her own way. My only goal—and it's a modest one—is to stop her from swearing so much. She's such an attractive young woman when she watches her tongue.

EDITOR'S EMAIL

Thanks to both of you for clarifying your commitment to the project. You'll be happy to know that Katherine is down from the ledge and the company is prepared to move forward. Offer attached.

8VO_14

ARTIE: Mr. Chenoweth...may I call you Peter as well? Scarlett and I accept. Please excuse any pauses in my reading. I have a distaste for grisly scenes.

After midnight we set out for the cemetery with a blanket concealing surgical tools and two dozen candles. As we walked, a slim moon led the way, darting ahead on the oily surface of the canal. Cats, both lissome and lame, slipped out from shadows, over bridges, and into narrow alleyways, looking for rodents and rotting pieces of fish.

We crept through a covered passageway, down a cobblestone cart path, farther and farther from the Rialto, each step taking us closer to the work that would surely become the subject of my nightmares.

Finally, we rounded a corner and beheld the church, a dark mass of bricks and tombstones—quite still, yet somehow alive. Glints of silver, reflections of the scant moon on scores of ex-votos, animated the exterior walls of the church. I ventured forward and ran my fingers over votives for broken legs, failing eyes, aching teeth, mangled hands, breasts, lungs, a uterus, a scrotum. Had the votives accomplished their purpose? Or do the victims now lay quiet in their graves, their prayers unanswered? The priests would say that all prayers are answered, but that God's will is un-fathomable.

I jumped as Leonardo touched my shoulder. He signaled me to wait in place with the tools.

At the far side of the churchyard was the bent form of a man, barely visible against the dark colorless trees. Leonardo approached him. Keeping their voices low, they exchanged a few words. Leonardo pressed several scu-di into the man's hand and started back towards me. Human dissection was allowed only for licensed practitioners, and even then, it was regarded by many as a branch of the black arts.

I followed my master into a one-room building behind the church. A single lamp illuminated the victim, who had been laid out on a raised marble slab with his clothes still on. Leonardo closed the door behind us.

"Now, Checco, light the candles!" he said loudly, rubbing his hands.

"Master," I said in a whisper, "are you not fearful of being discovered?"

"No one can hear us now, dear boy. Look at these walls! Not a window in sight, and the gravedigger is guarding the door. Our problem is not acoustics, young Checco, but time. We must finish our work by the hour the sun comes up, so the gravedigger can bury the body before the first mass."

I unrolled the blanket on the stone floor and lined up the tools, then moved a number of candles onto the slab around the body. As I did this, he lit them. I could not bear to look at the sight before me.

Leonardo began to hum. The tune was oddly cheerful given the morbidity of the occasion. His humming soon changed to whistling. The sound echoed off the walls in accompaniment to the dancing shadows thrown by the candles.

"Checco," he said, gesturing toward the corpse, "tell me what you see."

I took one look, then ran to the far corner of the room and immediately emptied the contents of my stomach.

"Now, now, Checco. You must not allow your emotions to reign at a time like this. The dead man is no longer a man, but an interesting collection of evidence."

I ventured forward, ran back, and vomited again.

"Ah, well, you will grow accustomed to it," he said, his hand stretched toward me with a scented handkerchief. He picked up his tune again, humming happily. I placed the linen fazzoletto over my nose so that it half-covered my eyes, allowing me to peek over the top as I found the courage. Fortunately, there was nothing left in my stomach.

EDITOR'S EMAIL

Grisly is an understatement. Artie, are you okay? Need to take a break?

8VO_15

ARTIE: Thank you for your concern, Peter. I merely needed a moment to recombobulate, as it were. Shall I push on?

The man's body had changed dramatically since the morning. It was now prodigiously swollen, black and blistered in some places, white and marbled in others. There was a greenish discoloration on his abdomen. I described what I saw.

"Well observed," he said. "What you notice is the deterioration of the body's tissues. The corpse has become bloated from the gas which has formed inside his cavities. The skin will continue to blister as the gas accumulates."

I shivered at the thought. More frightening than the bloated body was the man's crushed head, which looked like a prehistoric fish, half white, half crimson, the passage from Dante dark purple on his cheek. His eyes were open wider than human eyes should ever be, protruding wildly from their sockets. It was as if he had glimpsed the gates of Hell precisely at the moment of his death. I looked closer to see if an image of the murderer had been recorded on his pupils, as some say happens. But instead, his eyes were dull and blank.

"Superstition!" cried Leonardo without pausing to look. He had re-buttoned the man's clothing and was now searching through his pockets. He suddenly stopped. Repositioning his eyeglasses on his nose, he picked up something from the knee of the man's breeches. He held it to the candle-light: a thread. He reached for the notebook on his belt, and turning to the last page, neatly folded the thread inside.

"What is it?" I asked.

"We shall see."

He went over to his tools and picked up a scalpel. Without a moment's hesitation he proceeded to cut the man's face from the top of his forehead to the bottom of his chin.

I had believed there was nothing left in my stomach, but I was in error. He pushed me toward the corner with one hand and continued to work with the other.

When I returned, the skin on the man's face had been peeled back, and Leonardo was rearranging the broken bones of his skull. Thankfully, the victim's eyes had returned to their normal positions. Yet I had never seen such a sight, all the muscles and tendons exposed, with huge teeth that would frighten the Devil himself. I put Leonardo's handkerchief to my face and turned away so as not to embarrass myself further.

He wiped his hands on a cloth, then unfolded a blank sheet of paper *he had stored inside his notebook. He laid it on the table next to the man's face and began to sketch: first a head, then eyes, nose, mouth, and ears, all at actual size. Like magic, the dead man came to life, seemingly whole again.*

According to the drawing, the victim seemed to have fewer than 30 years, with dark hair, pale skin, sunken cheeks, and sharp features. He could have been Venetian, but he looked more like the foreigners I had seen coming from the east.

"Is he from Trieste?" I said.

"Farther, I think. The cut of his clothing."

"Then who is he?"

"My dear Checco, that is the wrong question. Not who, but why. Why would a man be plucked from streets, poisoned, then crucified in a print shop with a message impressed on his face? It defies logic."

I was already nauseated, and now I was vexed as well. To me this was another distraction designed to keep Leonardo from his more important work. "Tell me, Master, why do you bother yourself with this insoluble riddle?"

"Checco, I could no more ignore this riddle than I could ignore the question of how birds fly or why fishbones are found on the tops of mountains. What are philosophical questions but riddles? Every mystery is a twisted knot with a hidden order. Whenever I find a mystery, I am powerless to prevent my mind from trying to untangle it."

I nodded, although I secretly found this habit proposterous.

"More importantly," he said, "Aldo is the only one I trust to print my notebooks. The Lords of the Night do not have the patience to find the truth, and shall certainly close down his business as a substitute for seeking it. If we cannot untangle the knot ourselves, dear Checco, Aldo will suffer, and I shall be unable to publish my notebooks as I would like."

I had not considered this. "But where should we begin?"

"My brilliant Checco! This is the right question." He turned to face me and spread his hands. "While murder begins with a cause and ends with evidence, we must follow the opposite path. Namely, to begin with the

evidence, and by means of it, uncover the cause. A dead body is like a book. Nothing is hidden if you know how to read. But in this case, there is actual printing, not metaphorical printing, and it makes the book illegible."

I saw the irony. Perhaps I could untie the knot myself using Leonardo's methods. "Master, the passage on his face. It says,

'See how mutilated I am;
Before me, another weeps as well,
His face split from forehead to chin.'

"Master, who is speaking and who is weeping? The face of the one who is weeping is split from forehead to chin. How could anyone know that you would cut this man's face down the middle? Is it because the passage has put a spell on you? Perhaps the dead are trying to explain it to us. Could it be Dante, reaching out to us from the grave?"

"Checco, there is no such thing as necromancy. You must banish these superstitions from your mind. I suggest we start, not by engaging spirits, but by asking three questions of a more earthly nature."

I exhaled and nodded.

"The first is the cause of death. We can tell by the blistered skin that he was poisoned, perhaps by cantarella. That particular compound is odorless and colorless and dissolves easily in wine. We know he was poisoned before being crushed in the press because we found blistering and no signs of a struggle. There were no other bruises, cuts, or abrasions.

"The second question is the manner of death. Was it natural, accidental, suicidal, or homicidal? We can guess that he didn't climb onto the press and crucify himself. Therefore, he was most likely murdered.

"The last question—and perhaps the most intriguing—is the time of death. Aldo came upon him first thing in the morning, and we arrived at the shop shortly afterward. His skin was still warm. There is a chance that the person who crucified him believed he was still alive, which would mean there were two murderers, not one."

"It is magic!" I exclaimed.

"It is not magic. It is simple observation. Just as an artist learns to view the world as colors, lines, shapes, and perspective, and a musician tunes his ear to patterns that ordinary people cannot hear, so a natural philosopher trains his attention on details that for other people might pass unnoticed. Evidence cannot be wrong. It cannot become confused or forgetful. Every anomaly is a token that can lead to the truth. One simply has to have the eyes to see it."

Leonardo clapped his hands loudly. "And now, Checco, it is time to pack our tools and our candles, and let the gravedigger carry out his task. We have done a good night's work. Many things have become apparent."

"Apparent, Master?" I asked. "Now that we have two murderers?"

EDITOR'S EMAIL

You've got us on the edge of our seats. We sent the second payment to your Lucra account, but we haven't received the next chapter. Is everything alright?

8VO_16

[SOUND OF CAR IN MOTION]

SCARLETT: Keep your wife-beater on. We had to move out of our last hotel—people were getting curious.

On the bright side, the kid can really tell a story. I love the bit about scanning the dead man's eyes for an image of the murderer.

We've followed up on a number of the details and they all check out. He describes walking through a covered passageway, known as a *sotoportego*, on the way to the church. The passageway is no longer there, but we found a reference to it online. The church still exists. I suppose it's harder to move a graveyard.

I find it interesting that Leonardo's methods predate some of our modern techniques in criminology, like reconstructive sketches and a basic set of forensic questions. The cause, manner, and time of death are pretty much the same questions criminologists ask to-day. The only question missing is the *mechanism* of death, which he seemed to suggest was poisoned wine.

The effects of cantarella, or cantharidin, are pretty much what Leonardo described. Cantharidin is made from blister beetles, a group of insects from the family Meloidae. Today it's classified as a hazardous substance, but back then it was used as an aphrodisiac. Bad idea. In large enough doses, it mimics the effects of sexual arousal. And then you die.

Melzi's description of the greenish abdomen, the bloating, the marbling of the skin—that's all part of putrefaction, which takes place in the first twenty-four hours after death.

You might want to edit out these details so the kiddies can sleep at night. I have to admit I had a little trouble myself after doing the research. Artie, poor girl, may never be the same.

ARTIE: I think that's enough background, Scarlett.

Peter, Scarlett is driving, so I'll read chapter three while she minds the road. We have a lot to crack on with.

Late in the afternoon, the master and I rejoined Aldo and Bembo at the Aldine Press. The shop boys had cleared the type from the floor, and the pressmen were working furiously to complete Bembo's book of poetry. They knew the shop could be shuttered at any moment, and strove to get the last press sheets to the bindery by the evening.

I couldn't look at the press without seeing that poor man hanging from his hands on the uprights.

Leonardo produced the sketch of the victim's face from his notebook, smoothing it out on the workbench under the window. Neither Aldo, nor Bembo, nor the workers recognized him.

"Are you sure, gentlemen?"

They looked at each other and frowned. Bembo could not take his eyes off the drawing. "He looks almost alive. How did you make this, Leonardo?"

"That is unimportant, my dear Bembo."

Aldo signaled to Bembo with pursed lips and a sharp shake of his head. Bembo changed his question. "Who is he?"

"That also is unimportant. For now, the principal lines of inquiry are these: Who was the message intended for? Who was the instigator? And why would the perpetrator want to be identified? My dear Aldo, does anyone other than you have a key to the door?"

"Only my partners." His eyes widened. "You don't think one of them…"

"Not at all, not at all. So far, we can only draw a few rudimentary conclusions: This was a crime of warning, not passion; the victim and the perpetrator were extraneous to the motive; the perpetrator was a large man; and he worked alone."

The three of us stared at Leonardo in wonder.

Aldo blurted, "But, but—how can you know all this?"

"First, my dear Aldo, we know it was a crime of warning by the way in which the murder was carried out, and from the message impressed on the victim's face. Ordinary crimes are not staged as literary spectacles.

"Second, the victim was extraneous to the murderer's purpose, since he is unknown to you, despite being left in your place of business. The victim, therefore, was not the message—merely the substrate on which it was recorded.

"Third, that the perpetrator was also extraneous, or rather merely useful, can be inferred from the two facts that the door was locked and the perpetrator had a working knowledge of the press. If he were the instigator and not merely the perpetrator, he would have been more careful not to leave evidence of his identity."

Aldo began to sputter. Leonardo raised four fingers.

"Fourth, that he was a large man is clear from the depth to which the type punches had been driven. The force required to drive a nail into wood," Leonardo said, swinging his fist downwards, "increases in direct proportion to the surface area of its point. A type punch has a flat point, and therefore would require considerable strength to drive it into beams of such density.

"Finally, we can surmise that the perpetrator worked alone, since he had the necessary strength to carry the man's weight, a knowledge of mechanical presses, and a key to the shop. There was no reason to employ an accomplice."

Bembo tilted his head back, supporting his chin with the first two fingers of his right hand. His dark eyes sighted Leonardo down a long, thin nose, a crossbow ready to release its arrow. "I observe that your reputation as an artist is matched by your skill as a logician," he said curtly.

"My dear Bembo, you are too kind," said Leonardo, turning to me and arching an eyebrow. He then said to Aldo, "May I examine the other chases in the shop?" Aldo agreed. Leonardo began sorting through the formes one by one. He picked up a forme that had been locked tight for Bembo's translation of Plutarch. "Who prepared this?" he asked.

Bembo said, "The typographer Francesco Griffo. He had just designed a new typeface for the book."

"Griffo's work is remarkable," said Leonardo. "He is essential to the shop, is he not? Does he have a key?"

"He did have a key, but I am afraid he no longer works here," said Aldo. "We parted over business differences. I suppose he could have made another key before he left. He certainly had the skill to do it."

Leonardo considered this. "Is he strong?"

Aldo and Bembo looked at each other and then at Leonardo.

"A giant of a man," said Aldo.

Bembo nodded in agreement. "Strong as an ox. Strong enough to lift a man and nail him to a press. He might have been the instigator as well as the perpetrator. William of Occam tells us the most likely answer is often the most obvious one. Are we not making a tangle of a straight line? Perhaps the message was meant for Aldo."

"And what was the message trying to say?" asked Leonardo.

Bembo hesitated, then glanced at Aldo.

Aldo sighed. "Leonardo, I must tell you that our parting was not an amicable one. We said things we should not have said, and I am ashamed to admit that I let others know of my displeasure."

"Others in the trade?"

"Yes. Griffo had demanded—demanded!—to be recognized as a partner in the Aldine Press for his contributions. I categorically refused. So we parted, and to protect myself legally, I removed his name from the books he designed."

If Leonardo was disturbed by this, he did not show it. But I, as an apprentice with little say over my own work product, understood immediately the damage Aldus had inflicted on his subordinate. Griffo was not only refused status as a partner, but shorn of his position, his livelihood, and his standing in the trade. It would now be difficult to find other employment in the printing industry, except as an itinerant worker, a sort of gypsy. He was hardly in a position to start his own business. His reputation had been mutilated by scandal—scandal caused by Aldo— just as the passage from Dante had described.

Just then the door of the shop burst open and a large man filled the doorway.

EDITOR'S EMAIL

You're stopping there? So cruel! Aside from the brilliance of Leonardo's deductions, I found your explanation of early typography fascinating. These days we just license a digital font and don't think twice about it. Please send more ASAP.

8VO_17

[DISTANT HIGHWAY NOISE]

ARTIE: Sorry for the delay, Peter. We had to pull off the road for petrol. Scarlett's in the snack shop buying some crisps.

As you know, most people think of the printing press as the invention that launched publishing, but it was actually movable type which revolutionized books. The ability to create and reuse characters made all the difference. That was Griffo's speciality, the reason the Aldine Press were so highly respected.

In those days, letters and punctuation marks had to be individually cast in a mold, cleaned up, and sorted into cases where they could be used to assemble lines of type. The cases were shallow wooden trays—

[DOOR OPENING AND CLOSING]

—with small compartments, one for each character. There were two cases arranged on the typesetter's bench, an upper case and a lower case. The upper case held the capital letters, as you might suspect, whilst the lower case held what we now call lower-case letters.

SCARLETT: I love all this printing stuff. I just can't believe an art historian would know anything about it.

Here, have some.

ARTIE: Despite the ignorance of my young friend—

SCARLETT: Ouch.

ARTIE: —Renaissance typography was most assuredly an art form. The punchcutter's job was to create all the type needed to print a book, the success of which depended, to a large extent, on its formal elegance. This was no small task.

The process of making a character—a single letter or punctuation mark—required four distinct steps: cutting a steel punch with a raised letter at one end; driving the punch into a softer metal to make a matrix or debossed letter; placing the matrix into a mold; and finally pouring molten metal into the mold to make a piece of type. A good typographer could turn out a few thousand pieces a day from an existing matrix.

To build a book page, he would select the types from the two cases and assemble the text, line by line, in reverse. He'd lock the lines of type into a chase—a wooden frame to hold everything together—and mount it face-up on the bed of the press, ready to be inked by the pressmen. Most of this work could be done by ordinary typesetters after the metal types had been created.

What made Griffo so critical to the Aldine Press is that he designed original typefaces, not slavish copies. He was a punchcutter par excellence. Unfortunately, he wasn't much of a businessman.

SCARLETT: Remember how Aldo stripped Griffo's name from all his books? He also wrangled a ten-year privilege—a kind of patent— to get full ownership of Griffo's typefaces. Anyone hoping to catch up to Manuzio would have to make the same move: Exploit an artisan and fire him when he complained. Dickson's dad would have approved.

ARTIE: Yes, well, it's not an exaggeration to say the way we read books today was shaped by men like Griffo, toiling away in gritty print shops like the Aldine Press. Most of us hardly spare a thought for how the letters look on a page. We rarely consider the blood, sweat, toil, and tears—not to mention occasional backstabbing—that brought the printing industry into being. That's what I find so riveting about Melzi's account.

Shall I continue?

The man in the doorway looked as if he were sawn from a thick wooden panel and mounted there to block the light. From somewhere in his imposing silhouette came a stentorian voice: "I wish to speak to the proprietor of this establishment."

Aldo hurried over to introduce himself. The pressmen gathered up the last of the printed sheets and wheeled them into the back room.

"My name is Inspector Zanetti of the Lords of the Night," he boomed, as if he were speaking to a large crowd in the piazza. "I have a report that

says a murder took place in this shop yesterday morning."

For a moment my heart had stopped beating. I had thought it was Griffo, returned to take further revenge.

The inspector opened a notebook and began writing. "First of all, who are these people?" he said, gesturing toward each of us in turn. Aldo introduced Bembo, Leonardo, and myself, whereupon Zanetti sneezed—he seemed to be suffering from rose fever—and dutifully recorded our names and whereabouts at the time of the murder. "Now, can anyone tell me what happened?"

Aldo described how he found the body when he unlocked the shop, and how Leonardo discovered the passage from Dante on the victim's cheek.

"Yes, well, there have been irregularities," he said, narrowing his eyes. "I happen to know that the body has been tampered with. Can anyone tell me about the incident in the churchyard?"

We looked at each other with the mien of innocent babes. Bembo shook his head and said, "It is terrible, terrible, the perversions we find in the city today. A man cannot even die without being molested."

At that moment I was seized by the most inexplicable desire to insert myself into the conversation. Even as I spoke, I knew I might place my master and the others in jeopardy. I had the distinct sensation of leaping off a cliff into a dark abyss, but I could not stop myself.

SCARLETT: Just a sec. Coke Zero all over my jeans. Bad idea to drink and drive.

8VO_18

ARTIE: Sorry, Peter. We left off as Melzi was about to do something ill-advised.

"If I may suggest, Inspector, perhaps it would be instructive to look at the sketch my master made of the victim's face as he might have looked in life."

I was falling. My heart was pounding through my chest. Aldo and

Bembo caught their breath in unison, frozen by the fear that the Lords of the Night might discover Leonardo's unauthorized dissection and place him in a prison cell. The only one who showed little alarm was Leonardo himself. He unfolded the drawing and calmly placed it on the workbench below the window.

The inspector took one look and extended his arms, tilting his head to the side. "This—THIS," he said, altering his posture as if beholding a newborn child, "is the most beautiful thing I have seen in my life. It is exquisite! The face rises from the paper as if by magic. What manner of artist can capture the living spirit of a man with a mere stick of graphite? They have said you are a genius, Master Leonardo, but that was a malicious lie. You are an angel sent from the House of God!"

Leonardo responded with a faint smile and a bow. "You flatter my poor talents, Inspector."

"Is there any way you would consider parting with this sketch, for the sake of the investigation?"

"I am afraid I need it for my work, Inspector. Perhaps I can offer you a small drawing at another time."

"Ah. That would make me happy. He reached for his handkerchief and wiped his eyes. "So beautiful."

My legs were shaking. When I glanced at Leonardo he appeared as calm as ever. The inspector had softened his voice as if now speaking to friends. "Tell me, do any of you remember seeing this man before?"

We assured him we had not, and that his clothing suggested a man of the streets, perhaps a foreigner.

"He looks strangely feminine to me," said the inspector, tilting his head at the drawing. "He has the eyes of a female dog in estrus."

Bembo nodded. "Indeed, he has the eyes of a fallen woman seeking commerce with an incubus."

"No doubt a malefactor or an exile," said the inspector, sniffling. "Certainly not a Venetian. Still," he said, glancing at the printing press, "to crush the skull of a man like that. Such savagery."

Bembo replied, absently, "Quien quiere matar perro ravia le levanta."

I whispered to Leonardo, "He who would kill a dog must work himself into a rage."

Leonardo looked sharply at Bembo. "May I inquire as to the author of that quotation?"

Bembo hesitated. "I cannot remember."

"Perhaps it is from one of your poems," offered Aldo.

"Truly, I cannot remember." Then he adopted a more righteous tone with the inspector, summoning his status as a civic-minded scholar. "It is a shame that Venice cannot control the violence that is plaguing its people. I hope you can bring the perpetrator of this heinous crime to justice, Inspector Zanetti, and soon."

The inspector sneezed. He pulled out his handkerchief, which by now was sodden. "I am afraid the murder of foreigners is not our highest priority, Messer Bembo. There are so many these days, and the Council of Ten has more urgent matters to occupy its attention."

"Just so," said Leonardo, "the threats of war from the League of Cambrai. Therefore, Inspector, might the Aldine Press be free to continue its work, ensuring that Venice remains a powerful force in printing?"

"I fear that will be impossible."

"Inspector, as you are a learned man, I am sure you are aware that the Aldine Press is the leading printer of octavos?"

"Why, yes," he said, sounding not at all certain. "Of course I am."

"And that the octavo is the means by which Venice will spread its language and ideas to the rest of Europe?"

"I believe so, yes."

"Then you are also aware that, when every man can carry a book on his person, when every man can afford to read, Venice shall become the greatest city in the history of the world?" Leonardo seemed to be casting a spell on Zanetti.

He nodded, slowly, his gaze fixed somewhere in the future.

"In that case, you, Inspector Zanetti, by keeping the Aldine Press open, *will have played a historic role in the rise of that greatness."*

Aldo was on the verge of tears, suddenly overcome with pride. Bembo stifled a laugh, which came out as a cough.

A shadow slid across Zanetti's face. "I am sorry, Master Leonardo," he said, waking from his trance, "my instructions are to close this shop until the matter is cleared up. I am afraid it may take some time, given our current backlog. I have little power in this matter."

Aldo dropped his head in desolation. "How will I take care of my authors?" he moaned. "My readers? My workers?"

"There is nothing I can do, Messer Manuzio. In the eyes of the authorities, you are the one who found the body, and therefore you are a suspect. You must not leave Venice. A member of the Lords of the Night shall place a lock on your door this evening."

He made a quick note in his book, then turned to go as unexpectedly as he had come. Waving his notebook in the air as he walked out the door, he said loudly, "I hope you can grace me with a drawing, Master Leonardo." And he was gone.

"Jupiter's beard!" cried Bembo. "This city is the cesspool of Satan! How can anyone print books in such an atmosphere?"

He grasped Aldo's forearms and looked directly into his eyes. "Aldo, my friend, I must prepare for my journey back to Urbino. I know I can never repay you for your courage in completing my book in these circumstances. I regret that I cannot stay by your side, but I shall return." He embraced him and kissed him on the forehead. "May the Holy Spirit protect you." His red cape swirled as he disappeared through the door and into the night.

"Aldo," said Leonardo, pulling over two stools and bidding him sit. "It shall be my sworn and solemn duty to discover the instigator of this crime. You must continue your work—for Venice, for printing, and, selfishly, for my own humble writings on Nature. I would have no one else print my notebooks. Be of good cheer."

They sat mute for several minutes, Leonardo resting his old hands on those of his friend.

"I must tell you something," said Aldo. His face was mapped with worry. "Can you promise me your silence outside this room?"

"If it serves you, my friend."

Aldo seemed to be grappling with his conscience. "I do not believe I was the object of this warning."

Leonardo waited.

"A mutual friend confided to me that Bembo has had a long-time liaison with Lucrezia Borgia of Ferrara. Not merely a platonic one—a carnal one. They are lovers. I fear that her husband, Alfonso d'Este, may have known Bembo was here and staged this atrocity for his benefit."

"Who is the mutual friend?"

Aldo hesitated. Then, finally, he said the name. "Ercole Strozzi."

EDITOR'S EMAIL

Ercole Strozzi? Are we supposed to know him?

8VO_19

ARTIE: I believe Strozzi would have been familiar to members of Leonardo's circle. He was connected to the Este court through his father, Tito, who served as a magistrate under a succession of dukes in Ferrara.

Ercole was born a cripple and walked with a crutch, but he was talented and clever enough to attract female friends by making himself indispensible. He latched onto Lucrezia from the very start. He introduced her to the delights of Venice, making trips to the city to buy her the latest luxuries—velvets, brocades, taffetas, and silks of every color.

SCARLETT: He also introduced her to Pietro Bembo.

ARTIE: Bembo ticked all the boxes for Lucrezia. Elegant, tall, witty, cultured. An up-and-coming poet writing a book about love, in vernacular Italian no less. An intellectual *and* a radical.

SCARLETT: Lucrezia was total catnip for Bembo. If those two had any more chemistry they'd have to wear lab gear. In one of her letters, Lucrezia sent Bembo a medallion with the image of a flame on one side. She wanted his advice on a motto she could add to the other side, maybe a comment on their relationship, hint, hint. Bembo suggested a Latin phrase: Est animum.

ARTIE: It is the soul.

SCARLETT: As in, the fire of their love consumes the soul. Hot stuff. The medal is lost to history, but the story lives on.

ARTIE: Francesco Melzi's desire to help with Zanetti was touching, don't you agree? A teenage boy so solicitous of his master's welfare that he'd risk embarrassment, punishment, even physical harm to offer him whatever assistance his youthful skills could provide. He added this brief postscript to his chapter on meeting Zanetti:

Aldo closed the door behind us as we turned toward Campo San Polo and the inn. Leonardo grabbed the back of my hair and shook vigorously. "Checco, Checco, whatever got into you? 'If I may suggest, Inspector'? You are my apprentice, not my advocate!"

"Master, I apologize with all my heart for my hasty and ill-advised interference. I am the king of fools. Let the Devil devour my bowels! I deserve whatever punishment you deem fit—I will clean your brushes, groom your horses, change the chamber pots for a month—"

"Ah, well, that shall not be necessary, my dear boy," he said, relaxing his grip. "Your instincts are laudable. You attempted to change the tenor of the conversation, and you succeeded. It was cleverly played. That you failed to save Aldo's business is not your fault, as the decision had already been made. Of course, if you had gotten me thrown into a cell, I would

have insisted you join me so I could dump the chamber pot on your head!"

I tried to laugh but found I could not. We had come such a long way to print Leonardo's notebooks, and now we were further from it than ever.

Peter, I hope you can see why the Aldine Press was so important to Western culture. Their books were the first to be not only portable but easy to read. They were printed in everyday Italian instead of Latin or Greek. They had consistent punctuation, including the comma, the colon, the semicolon, the apostrophe, the accent mark, and the period. We take the humble period for granted, but it's only because Aldo Manuzio insisted on using it.

SCARLETT: Today we're all so impressed with Google's mission of organizing the world's information, but Aldo had a similar goal. He wanted to build a library so complete, according to his friend Erasmus, that there would be, quote, no boundaries but the world itself, unquote. The difference was one of technology, not ambition.

Of course, monks and scholars already had books, but these were giant, annotated bricks written in Latin. But now any reasonably educated person with a few scudi could carry around a lightweight *octavo*. Alberti was right when he predicted a revolution in printing. The octavo was as disruptive in the Renaissance as social media is in our own times. No wonder Leonardo wanted to harness it, shape it, make it his own. He wanted his ideas to spread, to go viral, in today's parlance.

ARTIE: A little background on how octavos were distributed. Naturally they were sold in bookshops, as Francesco Melzi noted in his description of Venice, but also in the cartolerias, those stationery stores—

SCARLETT: Artie, that's probably enough about the book trade. Tell Peter about the other thing we found, the time Leonardo went to prison.

ARTIE: Yes, well, Leonardo had once been incarcerated. As a young man he and three friends were arrested for sodomy and forced to spend the night in a cell. They were cleared of all charges, but it left an emotional scar. He realized that the official record of his youthful indiscretion could reassert itself at any moment, so he became careful around officials—notice that he didn't volunteer any information to Inspector Zanetti. And ever since his night in jail, he was circumspect about his sexuality.

SCARLETT: Who's being circumspect now? He was a fucking flamer! Sorry, Artie, I know I promised. But I mean, really, his obsession with clothes, the theatrics, the delicate manners? All those male pupils and not a single girlfriend? Come on, say it.

[PAUSE]

ARTIE: I wouldn't use *that* language, Scarlett, but I will say there's a certain…a certain, em, pattern. You can imagine the chill that might have rippled down his spine at the thought of being arrested for human dissection. Prison cells in the Renaissance were much like they are today—an unhealthy place for those of the homosexual persuasion.

SCARLETT: Not to mention ghouls.

ARTIE: Peter, I apologize for my colleague. She hasn't had the benefit of indoor plumbing and human parents. But then, it must have been comforting to curl up with the other wolves of a cold evening.

SCARLETT: I'm starting to like her.

ARTIE: If you promise to keep your lips sealed and your eyes on the road like a good girl, I'll continue reading to the nice Mr. Chenoweth. There are more surprises to come.

SCARLETT: I hate to be a killjoy, Artie, but our hotel is coming up on the left. We've got a big day tomorrow. Why don't we call it a night?

EDITOR'S EMAIL

Well, it couldn't have been easy for Leonardo. I can certainly imagine how his early brush with the law might have colored his behavior later in life.

I have to admit I've never actually heard the word *octavo* before. I feel like a furniture maker who's never heard of a dovetail joint, or a music producer who's never heard of the diatonic scale. Printing is so mechanized that we publishers have forgotten our own history.

How are you doing with the vetting?

8VO_20

SCARLETT: The vetting's going well. This morning we drove to a small printing museum, a *museo della stampa*. Don't try to look it up—there are dozens around here. We chose this one because it happens to be private, quiet, and out of the way.

We park the car outside on the street and walk up to a pair of steel gates set into a high stone wall. I press the buzzer. Nothing happens. After several more tries, an elderly woman appears in the courtyard and says something in Italian.

Closed, Artie translates. Come back after lunch.

So we sit in the car with our phones. I read about printing presses while Artie does research on Strozzi.

After a while I reach over and take a panini from the glove compartment and give half to Artie. No reason we can't eat and work at the same time, I say. We go back to reading, when suddenly she swallows hard and blurts out: The van!

I look up. What van?

The van that just pulled out from the curb!

The Ford Transit? What about it?

That same van was parked across from the townhouse when we locked up, she says. I remember the sign on the back: *Il tuo Salvatore, tuttofare. Tuttofare.* Handyman. It's a pun. His name is Salvatore, savior. He'll save you from, I don't know, your poxy plumbing.

There could be lots of handymen named Salvatore, I say. How do you know it's the same one?

I remember the cartoon on the side. It shows a comical handyman with six arms, each holding a different tool. A screwdriver, a squeegee, a plunger, a hammer, a weeder, and a crescent wrench.

You remember all that?

I have a facility with images. Art historian, remember? The cartoon is a reference to Shiva, the Hindu god of destruction. Shiva has four arms. The handyman has six. It stuck in my mind. It's cute.

To you it's cute. I can't think of anything worse than a six-armed man with hand tools. Maybe it's a franchise. There could be Salvatores all over Italy.

With a dent above the right rear taillight?

I consider this while we eat. A shiver crawls up my spine as I remember that the townhouse is a long way from the museum. What are the odds, I wonder?

Around two o'clock a docent opens the gate and waves us into the courtyard. He's sixtyish, balding, with a slight build. He speaks a little English. He seems thrilled to have visitors, and chatters a mile a minute as he leads us upstairs to the museum.

We enter a big room with high ceilings. Over in the corner is a Gutenberg press, like the one Aldo had in his shop. We make a beeline for it. I pull out my phone to take a few snaps. The docent wags his finger and says: *Niente foto, per favore!*

Artie reaches into her purse for a notebook and starts sketching instead.

I get out my measuring tape. The uprights are massive. It's clear that the press would easily accommodate a crucified man. I stand with my back to it, arms outstretched, resting lightly on the tray where the tools go. I thought the docent would shit a lawn chair.

Non lo tocchi! Non lo tocchi! he shouts.

I get off the press and say, *Scusi, scusi, mi dispiace, signore, scusi.* Artie thought I should learn to apologize in Italian.

ARTIE: I'm not the only one you rub up the wrong way, dear.

SCARLETT: Wrong-way rubbing was my ticket out of charm school.

When we finish with the Gutenberg, Peter, we start looking at the other items while Signor Nervoso hovers in the background. There are platen presses. Rotary presses. Linotype machines. Stitching machines. Machines for cutting bound books. Trays of wooden type. Glass case after glass case of hand tools.

One of these tools catches my eye. It's a stylus, like the one I swiped from the townhouse, only much plainer. No decorative spiral. Just a wooden handle in the shape of a mushroom cap. No gemstone either, but a metal point. I motion for the docent to come over.

Si, signorina, he says eagerly.

What's that? I say, pointing, my voice all innocent and girly.

That is a tool for the engraving, signorina. It is called, in Italian, *bulino.*

A graver, translates Artie.

He brings us over to another case with examples of copper plates. He says, the bulino he makes the groove in the copper, and the ink he goes in the groove.

I pull the purloined stylus from my hair, where I'm using it to secure a makeshift bun. My hair tumbles onto my shoulders and the man just about melts. The older they are, the harder they fall. He asks to see the graver up close. *Si, si,* he says, *un bulino.* He turns it over in his hands, studying the spiral handle. He holds the other end to the light. *Un rubino. Come l'ha ottenuto?*

Where did you get it? says Artie, translating.

I was tempted to say the Puces in Paris, but I can't lie, so I tell him I stole it.

He laughs. *Non ci credo. Lo venderebbe?*

He doesn't believe you. He wants to know if you'll sell it.

Quanto? I say.

He's not sure, says Artie, ten thousand at least. She gives me the old squint eye. I give her the sad-dog face. Ten thousand euros would buy a lot of Lambrusco and pizza. She doesn't budge.

Mi dispiace, I say.

At least we've confirmed that a printing press can bear the size and weight of a person, the main reason we came.

Artie tells the docent we have to go, but his *museo* is *molto, molto bello.* We can't thank him enough, she says.

He looks heartbroken.

We get back in the car. I check the glove box. The bug detector is blinking like crazy.

Artie, I say, give me your compact.

I jump out and crawl around the car on all fours, using the mirror to look under the car for GPS transmitters. Nothing. What do you want for 19 euros? I dial down the sensitivity level and toss the device back in the glove box.

We head over to our new hotel feeling like fools. The Great Van Scare. But it makes me more aware of the possibility of damage to the manuscript. I mean, we'd been transporting this thing in a Tupperware container. As soon as we check in, I walk down to a cartoleria to buy a secure metal box and a leather satchel.

EDITOR'S EMAIL

Well done, you two. It pays to be cautious. Still, aren't you worried that the docent might consider your behavior suspicious? What if he calls the police?

8VO_21

SCARLETT: To say what? A couple of strange women were asking questions about printing equipment? I can't see it.

ARTIE: Peter, here's the next chapter, in which Melzi describes a conversation with his master over a meal. I think you'll find it illuminating.

Leonardo and I dined in a dark corner of the inn. He had been turning over the day's events in his mind, and he asked if I might furnish my own interpretation of what had transpired. I set my goblet down and gathered the courage to offer my meager thoughts.

"It is clear that Griffo was the perpetrator," I said. "He must have made a key before leaving his employment. On the morning of the murder, he let himself in, carried the unfortunate man into the shop, crushed his head in the printing press, and nailed him to the uprights. He then scattered the type on the floor, let himself out, and locked the door behind him."

Leonardo nodded. "Just so. And why did he impress a passage from Dante onto his cheek?"

I thought for moment. "He wanted Aldo to know not only who had committed the crime, but why. Revenge is sweeter when the perpetrator makes himself known, and perhaps it becomes more righteous when it is justified."

"Was it justified?"

"Master, you must admit that Aldo treated Griffo unfairly in slandering his good name."

"Even so—"

The innkeeper suddenly appeared, refilling our goblets and lighting another candle.

Leonardo waited, and then lowered his voice. "Even so, Checco, how is it justified to sacrifice another human being to achieve one's personal revenge?"

I had to admit it. This was not a righteous act, and I was at a loss to justify it. Then I remembered what Aldo had said about Bembo and Lucrezia.

I said, "If Lucrezia's husband was the instigator, having already fatally poisoned him, perhaps Griffo felt absolved of the sin. After all, Master, the poor man was going to die anyway."

"And what about the sin of aiding Alfonso in his murderous scheme?"

There again, I was at a loss. It is one thing to send a warning to your wife's lover, but it is quite another to take the life of an innocent man. The whole enterprise was fraught. Griffo and Alfonso were complicit.

"And do we know Alfonso was the instigator?" said Leonardo. "We have only Aldo's conjecture."

"Master, you have said that murder begins with a cause and ends with evidence. And that to find the truth we must begin with the evidence and work in the other direction. We began with the victim, who led us to Griffo. Should we not look for Griffo and see if he leads us to Alfonso?"

"You have learnt well, Checco. But we are unlikely to find any trace of Francesco Griffo. To complete his revenge on Aldo, he had to sign his name to the crime. He will be many miles from here by now, and well hidden. No. We must use another means to discover who is next in the chain of evidence. Ah, here is the food."

We dined contentedly, myself on canal scallops and Leonardo on roasted vegetables. When we were finished, the innkeeper brought us figs and sweet wine. I was not used to so much drink. The room seemed to be bending of its own accord. I tried to counteract the distortion with sheer effort, that Leonardo would not think me weak. I made my voice as steady as I could. "Do you believe the man was poise, poised—poisoned—with wine in his blister beetles?"

"My dear Francesco, I believe you have been 'poised' by wine yourself! Did you know that potions made from blister beetles—cantarella—is a favorite of the Borgia family?"

My eyes refused to focus.

"Lucrezia is said to keep cantarella hidden in a ring with a secret compartment. I cannot vouch for that, but her brother Cesare was a well-known poisoner."

"What about Alfonso?" I said, trying in vain to make the room stop swaying.

Leonardo's hand paused halfway to his mouth. He placed the fig he was about to eat back on the plate. "Checco, we have been thinking about the wrong Este. The warning did not come from Alfonso, but Lucrezia! She is the one who poisoned the messenger. She is the one who hired Griffo to place him where Bembo could find him. Brilliant boy!"

"Am I, Master?"

"Yes, and soon we shall set out for Ferrara to prove it. Finish your wine. We must return to our rooms immediately and make a plan."

I drained my glass and hoped for the best.

EDITOR'S EMAIL

Francesco Griffo and Lucrezia Borgia, partners in crime? How did Leonardo come up with this theory? Next installment, please. The Lucra's in the mail.

8VO_22

SCARLETT: Artie's just wrapping up the next chapter. Meanwhile, I've got some background on the Borgias.

This Cesare dude was a bad guy. Brilliant, but bad. He was five years older than his sister Lucrezia, and they truly loved each other. Some say carnally. Hey—it was the Renaissance. The 1490s made the 1960s look like Sunday school.

In 1500, Cesare ordered assassins to strangle Lucrezia's second husband in front of her eyes. He once punished a libeler by having his tongue cut out, his right hand chopped off, and his tongue placed in his hand as a warning to other smartasses out there. Gives a whole new meaning to the phrase hold your tongue, doesn't it?

The Borgias didn't take kindly to having their reputation trashed. The usual response was violent revenge. Their father, Rodrigo, was a model Machiavellian. Cesare followed in his footsteps. In fact, Cesare was a poster boy for the actual Machiavelli, who quoted him constantly. Was Lucrezia simply channeling her brother?

I also did some research on our master typographer, Griffo. After he left Aldo's employ, he teamed up with another printer, Sonsino. Didn't last, though. He bounced around from shop to shop without much success. Most printers weren't willing to invest in original typefaces the way Aldo did. They'd rather use existing fonts and save their working capital, right? But since Griffo never got ownership of his designs, he couldn't offer his typefaces to other printers. He was known to have a bad temper in the best of circumstances, but he was getting more and more pissed off about his situation.

One day, years later, Griffo got into an argument with his son-in-law. He always thought his daughter deserved better. They'd been drinking. After dessert he cratered the kid's head with a steel rod, the same kind he used to make type punches.

Church records show that Griffo died shortly afterward. Maybe he went to the gallows, maybe not. Either way, we get a clear picture of a strong man with an even stronger temper, perfectly capable of crushing a man's head in a printing press or bashing the skull of a son-in-law.

ARTIE: The lead pipe in the library?

SCARLETT: The question is, how was Lucrezia acquainted with Griffo? We know she met Leonardo through her brother Cesare, who hired him as a military architect. In 1502, he and Niccolò Machiavelli tramped around Italy making maps for Cesare. Later they concocted all kinds of schemes together, like diverting the Arno to cut off Pisa's access to the sea. Crazy shit like that.

Fourteen months before Leonardo and Melzi went to Venice,

Cesare was killed in battle. Two years before that, Lucrezia's father Rodrigo, who was now pope, had died of malaria. Which left Lucrezia without any Borgia protectors. How would she react to being grilled by Inspector da Vinci and Lieutenant Melzi regarding a certain incident at a Venice print shop?

We're about to find out. Artie, hit it.

ARTIE: My pleasure, Miss Scarlett.

"Checco," said Leonardo in a boisterous voice, "take out your quill and compose a letter."

Every word was a hammer to my head. My brain felt hard and small in my skull, like a clapper rattling against the walls of a lead bell. I recalled little of the night before, except a vague notion that we might be going somewhere.

"To my dearest Lucrezia, esteemed Duchess of Ferrara," he said.

I reached bleary-eyed for a sheet of paper and a pot of ink "Anon, Master. Allow me a moment to ready myself." I dipped my quill and began writing. Leonardo waited before continuing.

"Too many years have passed since you have graced me with your charming presence. I hope you will grant a brief audience in the next few weeks, that I may offer you a small token of my esteem: a modest drawing I have done from memory."

He waited for me to catch up, which was difficult under the circumstances. The scraping of the quill against the surface of the paper was more deafening than the screeching of a thousand gulls.

"You may recall that I made a similar sketch of your sister-in-law, Isabella, of which she is said to prize. I could not help but think, with your great beauty, that a similar drawing would be any less successful. Therefore, I ask for an opportunity to compare it with the elegance of the original."

I wrote as fast as I could, my quill barking like an angry dog. "Master,"

I said, looking for any excuse to pause my writing, "might you add a sentence or two in Latin? Lucrezia is well-versed in that language."

"My dear Checco, what would you suggest?"

"You might add: 'I understand that my request may seem unduly presumptuous, and yet audentes fortuna iuvat.'"

Leonardo looked at me, his brow in furrows.

"Fortune favors the bold, Master."

"Ah. Just so. Please add the sentence and close the letter."

Part Two: Pursuit

I notice he didn't say anything about the murder. The letter seems so light and nonchalant, as if he were setting her up. Is he planning an ambush?

8VO_23

ARTIE: I'm afraid he is.

Several days later came a reply in Lucrezia's hand. She would be delighted to entertain Leonardo and myself for as long as an hour, if we would come to Ferrara on the morning of the sixth day of June. She would be certain to find his drawing as skilled and delightful as any she has seen.

On the third of June, we set off for Ferrara, having spent the night in Mestre, where our horses were stabled.

On the morning of the sixth we arrived at the castle. The sky was dark with leaden clouds, as if a storm could unleash its fury at any moment. The castle loomed ahead like a somber warning to less fortunate mortals. I had never seen such a forbidding structure. High brick walls connected four massive towers. A deep moat made access impossible except through one of three ravelins, each with a drawbridge.

We approached the western ravelin and were met by two sentries who immediately stood to each side upon hearing my master's name. We passed under the portcullis, the hooves of our horses and jennet echoing off the wooden planks. A pair of grooms helped us dismount. A servant led us through a covered passageway to a large gallery, where we were asked to wait for Lucrezia.

Here on the walls and ceiling were the paintings of Giovanni Bellini, Raphaello Sanzio, and Tiziano Vecellio. Leonardo scanned the room, unimpressed. "The young painters of today have abundant skill, but they cannot see. They have eyes only for the surfaces of things."

I knew this was a lesson meant for me. I replied, "What would you tell them, Master?"

"I would tell them to study the muscles that lie beneath the skin. I would tell them to study the rules of perspective, and of light. They should not illuminate a face from one source, and a mountain from another. There is only one sun."

I nodded, thinking of the times I had mixed my light sources for a dramatic yet dishonest effect.

Lucrezia soon appeared in the doorway, dressed in a yellow silk day-gown with black and white vines embroidered on the bodice. Leonardo and I bowed in unison. She was even more elegant than I had imagined, her hair worn in long blond ringlets, her hands and face festooned with bright jewels.

Leonardo quickly introduced me as his pupil, Count Melzi. "My dearest Duchesss, it is such a profound pleasure to renew our friendship that I scarce know what to say."

"My darling Leonardo, we have never known you to be at a loss for words. The last time we met, you played the lyre and sang us a bawdy song."

"In my much younger and more frivolous days, I fear."

"You were certainly not frivolous with my brother Cesare. The two of you were intent on conquering the world. He had the deepest regard for your talents."

"He was too kind and shall be missed. May I offer felicitations to you and the Duke regarding the birth of your son? This is very good news."

"We thank you, Leonardo. It is indeed good news. The Este family now has an heir," she said, allowing herself the faintest smile. "Tell us of this drawing you have made."

Leonardo reached into his cloak and pulled out a small portfolio bound in yellow silk. He opened it with a flourish, revealing a red-brown crayon sketch of Lucrezia's head and shoulders, as seen from the front. Her eyes were lowered as if in prayer, or perhaps contemplation. Her hair was in ringlets, as now, and her collar was buttoned up except for the top, showing a tender hollow at the base of her throat. Her eyelids were softened to contrast with the sharp line of her eyelashes, which he drew fluidly with a crayon sanded to a chisel edge. Leonardo had used his sfumato technique to enhance the saintly quality of her visage.

She accepted the drawing and studied it with interest. "You have taken liberties, my dear Leonardo."

"How so, Your Grace?"

"We are not this beautiful."

"I fear I must agree," said Leonardo, shaking his head sadly.

The muscles around Lucrezia's mouth tightened. Her eyes blinked involuntarily.

"Truly, I have done you a grave injustice. You are much more beautiful than this. I must return to the studio and remake my sketch this instant." He reached for the drawing. She pulled it back with a girlish giggle.

In that moment I experienced the unguarded charm that had made Lucrezia a figure of renown amongst the nobility. Bembo would have been powerless to resist its pull.

"You tease us, Master Leonardo. We see your more frivolous tendencies have not deserted you. Please be seated while we talk further." She waved a bejeweled hand toward a set of chairs upholstered in yellow and gold brocade. A servant arrived as if by magic and placed a tray of drinks on a small round table between us.

"Now, Master Leonardo, please tell us why you have come."

Leonardo tilted his head, as if confused. "To bask in your presence, Your Ladyship."

"My dear Leonardo, we did not ascend to the position of Duchess by imbibing flattery. We have been raised in a household of powerful men, and we have seen many attempts to manipulate our power. Again, please tell us why you have come." She laid her hands in her lap, palms up, waiting.

"Your Ladyship," said Leonardo, his voice now serious. "I have come to discuss a delicate matter."

"Proceed."

"A fortnight ago in Venice a man was found crucified on the beams of a printing press."

Lucrezia raised her hand to her mouth. If she was feigning surprise, her performance rose to the level of high theatre.

"A passage from Dante was impressed on his face," said Leonardo. "A passage that touched on the evils of scandal. Do you know it?"

"We do not, but why do you come to us with this story?"

"Because I believe the passage was a warning to your friend Pietro Bembo." Leonardo watched her eyes.

"A warning? About what, pray?"

Turning to me, he said, "My dear Count, perhaps you would wait outside while I speak frankly with the Duchess."

I left the room and closed the door quietly behind me. I am ashamed to say, Dear Reader, that I did not wander far from the door.

"Your Ladyship, I understand that you have enjoyed a platonic liaison with the poet Bembo for many years. I understand also that your liaison has at times strayed beyond the platonic."

Lucrezia started to protest.

"Wait—please let me finish."

Silence. Then, coldly: "Continue."

"I do not wish to interfere in your personal affairs, Your Ladyship, but—"

"But 'audentes fortuna iuvat'?"

"But this—shall we call it an unfortunate accident?—has had conse-quences for others, including Aldo Manuzio, the proprietor of the Aldine Press. His business has been interrupted by the Lords of the Night and cannot resume unless the perpetrator is unmasked. My aim, my hope, is to find a way to rescue Aldo's business while protecting your reputation."

"Master Leonardo, you stray too far. Our liaisons, whatever they may be, are private, and must not be the subject of idle gossip. We must ask you to leave, and never speak of this again. Do you understand?"

"Yes, Your Ladyship. The matter is closed if you wish it."

"We do wish it. And to be clear, Master Leonardo, my friendship with Messer Bembo is, and always has been, platonic."

"Yes, Your Grace. I shall take my leave now."

A bell tinkled, rather insistently it seemed to me. I hurried to the other side of the hallway and took a position at the opposite window, hands behind my back, gazing onto the streets below.

The door opened and Leonardo strode out. "Come, Francesco, it is time to go."

A servant appeared from another direction to guide us to the exit. We followed him down the corridor and descended the stairs to the ravelin. We remounted our horses and crossed the drawbridge with Violetta follow-ing obediently behind.

Leonardo had failed. Lucrezia was not fooled, and she was now more wary as a result of his failure.

"What now, Master?" I said.

"Our only hope is to meet with Lucrezia's confidant, Ercole Strozzi," said Leonardo, "and see if he is willing to tell us such things as Lucrezia will not. But we must be discreet. He is a close friend of hers, and if she finds out he has revealed anything, she may deem it a betrayal. Great power is like a stone in a river that bends the water around it. The closer the water gets to the stone, the more it bends. In the presence of power, it is difficult to know what is true."

We rode through Ferrara in silence, the first raindrops spattering the cobblestones. Our object was to find an inn where we could rest for the night. We would search for Messer Strozzi in the morning.

As we rounded the corner in front of the Church of San Francesco, we saw in the distance a group of men bending over a dark form in the middle of the road. Leonardo brought his horse to a trot and I followed suit. It soon became clear that the dark form in the street was the body of a man wrapped in a black mantle. In a single motion Leonardo swung his leg over his horse's neck and leapt to the ground. He pushed two of the men aside and knelt down to examine the body.

"What has happened?" he demanded.

"We found him here this morning," said one.

Another said he saw two ruffians with a handbarrow dump him in the street and then run off, taking the barrow with them. He pointed south along the Via Praisolo.

Leonardo pulled back his mantle. The unfortunate man had been stabbed repeatedly. His long, wavy hair lay scattered in clumps around his motionless form. Leonardo turned him over, saw that his throat had been cut, and found a crutch lying beneath him. He had been a cripple.

My master's face turned white. He rose and began pacing back and forth. He asked for help in getting the dead man over the back of his horse. We lashed him to the saddle and walked the three animals back toward the castle on foot. The rain sifted steadily from the darkening sky.

I searched Leonardo's features for answers to a hundred questions.

He finally spoke.

"My dear Checco, this man is Ercole Strozzi."

EDITOR'S EMAIL

Oh, my God. I remember Strozzi's name from the Zanetti episode—the mutual friend of Lucrezia and Bembo. What else do you have on him?

8VO_24

[HIGHWAY SOUNDS]

SCARLETT: Strozzi was a poet at the court of Alfonso. He wrote reams of paeans to Lucrezia's beauty, her intelligence, blah, blah, blah. Which pretty much guaranteed job security at the Este court. He also served as a go-between for the two lovers.

Lucrezia was lying through her pearly whites about her relationship with Bembo being platonic. More like *tectonic*—the earth moved for those two kids. They wrote torrid love letters back and forth, while Strozzi set up play dates right under Alfonso's nose.

I'll find out more when I get a chance. I'm driving now, so here's Artie with part two of the Ferrara episode.

ARTIE: Hello, Peter. Without further ado.

We arrived once again at the western ravelin. The sentries were the same ones we met earlier, but this time they refused us entry. Leonardo entreated them to raise the portcullis and announce our presence. Instead, they crossed their poleaxes to block our path.

"Let us through!" demanded Leonardo. "We have brought the body of Ercole Strozzi, a member of the court."

Our clothing was soaked to the flesh. I was starting to shiver. I could not allow Leonardo to endanger his health by waiting any longer in the cold air. He had removed his cap and his hair was dripping wet.

I said to the guards, "Can you not see that my master is too old to stand in the rain? Please let us through." My hand flew instantly to my dagger as a guard levered his poleaxe into my forehead. I fell backwards into my horse, who skittered on the wooden bridge, nearly falling into the moat.

Leonardo moved quickly. He caught the guard's pole with his right hand, pulled him forward, and with a swing of his left elbow sent his helmet flying. He struck the guard in the temple with the first knuckle of his left hand, using the merest force. The guard collapsed like a felled tree.

The second guard swung his axe at Leonardo's head, but the master ducked and spun, catching the guard in the back of one knee with the instep of his boot. The guard sunk to the ground like a penitent sinner. Leonardo jabbed his throat with the fingers of his right hand. The man dropped his axe and fell sideways, clutching his neck. Both guards lay writhing on the wooden bridge, one moaning, the other unable to speak.

"Checco, fetch Violetta and meet me in the castle."

I complied, once again astonished at the atheleticism of my aging master. The two animals and I stepped carefully over the downed men and their weapons. I joined Leonardo on the other side of the portcullis, and, as I did, an inner door flew open and two more guards emerged, followed by Lucrezia.

"Master Leonardo, we gave explicit instructions—"

She then saw Strozzi, his hair torn out and his eyes fixed in a stare, a hideous red smile under his chin. She turned away and clapped her hands to her face, shoulders hunched.

The guards stood, feet braced, cornering us with their lances.

Lucrezia inhaled deeply and regained her posture of authority. "Let them go," she said, holding Leonardo in her steady gaze. Yet it seemed to me that her features betrayed a hint of fear—and perhaps guilt—as she waited for an explanation.

"We found him on the road next to the Church of San Francesco," said Leonardo. "He has been murdered."

Her mouth opened, then closed. Finally, she said, "But why? He was a friend of the court, the gentlest person of our acquaintance."

"I can help Your Grace, but you must talk to me about Bembo."

She lowered her head and nodded slowly, as if weighing the merits of the trade. What would she get, and what would she have to give?

"Come," she said.

She led us up the stairs, holding her skirts, and down the hallway that communicated with the gallery where we had met in the morning. She dismissed a waiting servant and let us into the room herself. When Leonardo and I had taken our seats, she closed the door behind us.

"You must believe us," she said, "that we have taken no part in this deed. Ercole was a valuable member of the court, and we wished him no harm, no harm at all. Only a fortnight ago we celebrated his happy marriage to Barbara Torelli, another friend of the court. She will be shattered by the news of his death, as will his brothers. Who would do such a spiteful thing?"

"Spiteful, Duchess?"

She blushed. "I meant mean-spirited. I cannot know the motive, of course."

"Can Your Ladyship think of anyone who would wish him harm, perhaps outside the court?"

She wrinkled her brow and thought for a moment. "One does not wish to throw stones, but the manner of his death brings to mind the deeds of the assassin Masino del Forno and his accomplices."

"How so, Duchess?"

"Ercole's hair has been pulled from his head. Hair-pulling is a hallmark of Masino's killings."

"How do you know this?"

She paused. "Alfonso has had occasion to employ his services. These are treacherous times." She quickly caught herself. "Of course, we do not wish to imply that Alfonso was involved in any way. Alfonso has—or had—still has—the highest respect for Ercole. But Masino was an assassin for hire. Perhaps Ercole had other enemies, such as a rival for his wife's attentions. Barbara Torelli is a charming and talented woman with many admirers."

"Was Ercole not a trusted confidant of Your Ladyship?"

"He was, yes."

"And, from time to time, did he not arrange meetings between you and Messer Bembo?"

Her jaw tensed. She shifted her gaze from Leonardo's eyes to mine, then back again.

"Duchess," said Leonardo, "whatever you say to myself and Count Melzi shall be held in the strictest confidence for as long as you wish."

Her face relaxed, if only slightly. She said, "Let us merely observe that the heart is a whimsical master."

"In that case, is it possible that Alfonso might have desired an end to this whimsy? Perhaps by ending the means by which it was coordinated?"

Lucrezia feigned offense on behalf of her husband. "Never," she said with apparent conviction. "He can be heartless in battle, it is true, but in domestic affairs he is a lamb, a font of tenderness. Look around you," she said, taking in the room with a gesture. "This collection of paintings is an expression of his love of life, of art, and of the artists of his court, including musicians and poets like Ercole. If you knew him thus, you would never say such a thing."

"I do apologize, Your Grace. I agree that these paintings speak well of your family's tender feelings." Leonardo rose to his feet and walked over to study a small painting by Tiziano Vecelli. He reached into his tunic and withdrew his glasses. Placing them on the bridge of his nose, he said, "The young Titian shows much promise."

"Furthermore," the Duchess said, "our friendship with Bembo has not been renewed for years. He spends most of his days in Urbino and has less and less interest in visiting us in Ferrara. And my own days are devoted to caring for our young son, Ercole II."

"Of course. My sincere apologies."

"Would you agree that any connection between our family and the murders of Ercole Strozzi and the man at the print shop is unlikely? One must ask how savagery of this kind is even possible."

"There is a saying," said Leonardo, "that he who would kill a dog must work himself into a rage."

Did I see Lucrezia stiffen? If she did, Leonardo affected not to notice. He opened his notebook and removed his sketch of the crucified man.

"Duchess, may I ask you to look at a drawing?" As he bent over the table to flatten it out, his glasses fell off his nose. I moved to retrieve them, but Leonardo raised a hand. He was down on his knees, searching with his hands under the table. "Do not trouble yourself. I have them." He plucked something from the Turkish carpet.

As he rose from the floor Lucrezia gestured toward the drawing and said, "Master Leonardo, who is this man?"

"I had hoped you might recognize him. This is the victim from the print shop as he might have appeared in life. Perhaps an associate of Masino del Forno?"

"We fear we cannot help," she said. "Masino is not the sort of person one associates with."

"Of course, Your Ladyship."

The door opened. A servant brought a tray with two folded towels and two hairbrushes. "Would the gentlemen care to dry off before taking their leave?" he intoned. Leonardo and I thanked him.

Lucrezia dismissed the servant and rose to her feet. "We trust the matter is resolved as it concerns the Este family?"

Leonardo bowed. "You have been too kind, Your Grace. We shall take our leave."

"And as to the guards…"

"Your Grace's guards will recover quickly by swallowing the whites of eggs mixed with several threads of blue silk, cut small," said Leonardo. "But before I go, I have one small request."

Lucrezia waited.

"Your kind introduction to Ercole's brothers."

EDITOR'S EMAIL

Lucrezia promised to come clean, but she didn't volunteer very much. She seems to be covering something up. What's your take?

8VO_25

SCARLETT: Well, she did volunteer Masino del Forno. Then she volunteered her husband, Alfonso. Almost like she threw him under the bus. She knew *he* was having affairs, too.

But if Alfonso was responsible for the murder at the print shop, why would he need to kill Strozzi, too? Was he sending two messages, one for Bembo and one for Lucrezia? Maybe he was just using the same sort of force he favored as a military strategist, but in a domestic situation: step one, warn Bembo with the murder of a stranger; step two, warn Lucrezia with the murder of a friend. The issue need never come up again.

Did you catch the veiled threat from Lucrezia? Hands off the family rep, Leo. This might have been something new for Lucrezia—motherly instinct, Duchess-style. But would she kill her good friend Ercole to protect the Este name? She seemed genuinely shocked by his death.

ARTIE: It seems as if Alfonso would have known about her affair with Bembo. He would also have known that Ercole had been arranging secret meetings. Secrets at court didn't stay secret for long.

Bembo wrote verses and verses in praise of Lucrezia. He wrote her a poem in Tuscan in which he used the language of his hero Petrarch to describe the beauty of her blond hair. It fell to her shoulders, he wrote, and with two hands of immeasurable beauty she bound it up again, and with her hair, his heart. These poems were passed from courtier to courtier.

Two years after Strozzi was murdered, Pope Julius publicly accused Alfonso of committing the crime, based partly, one suspects, on Alfonso's failure to investigate it. Moreover, the pope may have known about Lucrezia's and Bembo's affair, which would have added weight to his allegation.

SCARLETT: Okay, but let's follow Leonardo's hunch and imagine the print shop murder was Lucrezia's idea. Given her history with Bembo, why would she warn him off in such a violent way? Why not just have a heart-to-heart like a rational person? Just say, look, my darling, I'm a mom now and I have responsibilities. Time to call it a day.

Artie, what was that saying?

ARTIE: *Fare thee well, and if for ever, still for ever, fare thee well.*

SCARLETT: See, that's why I keep her around.

ARTIE: That, and my leftover pizza.

SCARLETT: Oh, c'mon, you eat like a bird. Anyway, the whole thing doesn't make any sense. The more we find out, the further we get from nailing down the perp. Alfonso gets my vote, but Lucrezia is pretty shady in her own way. The history books say the crimes were never solved.

Peter, yesterday we drove to Ferrara to check out the castle. It's all still there—the ravelins, the drawbridges, the hallways, the gallery. The interior's been stripped of any furnishings that might have existed in 1508, but you can imagine how sumptuous and convivial it must have been. Perched on the second floor there's a pretty little garden with orange trees and a loggia. I could easily see Lucrezia trysting with Bembo on a stone bench under the fragrant trees.

A few blocks south is the street where Leonardo found Strozzi. We headed down there next. Many of the buildings on the street, including the church, are pretty much the same as they were back then. The weather didn't provide the ominous mood described by Melzi, but it's still creepy to stand at the exact spot where Strozzi's body was found five centuries ago. Everything in the story checks out.

That afternoon, Artie and I decided to grab a late lunch at a sidewalk restaurant. The aforementioned pizza. It felt nice to be outside in the sun instead of holed up in our rooms or sitting in a car. Small cars make me claustrophobic, but that's another story. We used the time to catch up on our work.

That's when I see it.

I'm just finishing Artie's pizza when a white Ford Transit crosses the intersection about twenty meters away. It's got the Shiva cartoon, the lettering that says *Il tuo Salvatore*, and the dent above the right taillight. The town of Ferrara is even farther from the townhouse than the printing museum, so this is fucking weird. What are the chances of spotting the same van in three towns that far apart?

Artie slips the manuscript into the metal box and shoves the box inside the satchel. I stuff a wad of euros under the pizza pan, and we run for the car. I don't know about you, but this kind of shit freaks me out. I can tolerate coincidences up to a point, but Jesus.

I kept an eye on the rearview as we flew out of Ferrara at a hundred and forty. Anyone following us would've had to stomp on it to catch us. No one did. We checked into a new hotel with a good view of the surrounding streets. After a while we started to breathe easier. I stood watch at the window while Artie translated the next little piece of the story.

ARTIE: Here it is, Peter.

Leonardo and I stabled the animals at a locanda near the church. My stamina had been tested severely by the events of the day, such that I begged to retire early. Leonardo kindly dressed the wound on my forehead caused by the guard's axe, applying a poultice of aloe which he had purchased from the apothecary. He had also purchased a notebook, which he now placed in my hands.

"My dear Checco," he said, "here is a small gift to commemorate your bravery."

I was touched by his thoughtfulness. It seemed to me that Leonardo was the more brave, having rescued Ercole's body and subdued a pair of armed guards with physical force.

"It is a gift that comes with an obligation," he added.

"Master?"

"You must use it to record the details of our search for the truth on behalf of Aldo. I urge you to apply your considerable skills to the telling of our adventures. Hold back nothing. Fear nothing. Order the facts as plainly as you observe them and bring all your gifts of elucidation to bear. We shall need a clear account of events if we are to prevail in our endeavors."

I must admit that Leonardo's assignment lifted my heart beyond all reason. One moment I was lying in bed feeling enervated, and the next I was scribbling furiously to capture the sequence of incidents that brought us to this stage of our inquiry. Candle after candle burned to the brass.

"Master, before I finish writing for tonight, perhaps you can explain how you managed to incapacitate the two guards at the castle. It was a wondrous demonstration. I would like to include it in my account."

Leonardo smiled. "Ah, well, someday I will give you a lesson in the Oriental art of unarmed combat. The secret lies in attacking certain points of weakness in the human body. The temple, for example, or the neck. It takes very little strength to subdue your adversary when you know the locations of his weak points." He massaged the first two fingers of his right hand.

"But where did you learn it, Master?"

"In a book, my dear Checco! One need not speak Japanese to read pictures. I simply combined the principles on its pages with my own knowledge of the human body. A guard who is weighed down by armor, or whose vision is obstructed by a helmet, is no match for a well-aimed knuckle or elbow."

"And your prescription of eggs and threads, will that really heal the wounds of the guards?"

"Of course not, Checco. I simply had silk threads on my mind. But if I had said water and rest, would Her Ladyship have believed me?"

I began to write this down when Leonardo stopped me.

"Checco, Checco. Go to bed and rest your quill for tomorrow's trials. In the morning we shall seek a meeting with Lorenzo and Guido Strozzi."

EDITOR'S EMAIL

Ah, so this is how the manuscript came into being. An assignment from the master. He must have had a great deal of faith in the boy's skills. About the martial arts episode, I'm with Melzi. How could a 56-year-old man, no matter how athletic, subdue two heavily armed guards?

8VO_26

SCARLETT: My guess? Some form of Jujutso. I took Aikido classes in school. There are like 250 pressure points in the human body you can attack with various strikes called *atemi*. What's surprising is how Leonardo could get his hands on a martial arts book in Renaissance Italy. Shows you how lively the book trade must have been.

Wait. Artie. Here, position your right hand straight up between your eyes, like this. A little higher. That's right. Now position your left hand to protect your throat. There. You got it. The woman is gangsta.

Where were we?

ARTIE: Leonardo and Checco turning in for the night.

SCARLETT: I think what Peter would like to know is, did they share a room?

ARTIE: Scarlett, dear, I'm not a tabloid historian. Remember, in those days travelers didn't expect to have their own beds, much less their own rooms. If you're asking if Leonardo and Francesco had a homosexual relationship, allow me to part the veil. After Leonardo died, Count Melzi married a noblewoman, Angiola di Landriani, and had eight children by her. Make of that what you will. But I would say no.

Shall we continue with the translation?

I was wakened in the morning by a loud knock. I quickly donned my breeches and tunic.

Leonardo was already dressed and strode to the foyer. He lifted the latch of the heavy wooden door and pulled it open, admitting a bright light to the room. We would not need to seek an audience with Ercole's brothers.

They were here.

I could tell by the disposition of their limbs and torsos that they were ready to fight. I thought I might see another demonstration of Leonardo's oriental combat techniques. But instead, he opened his arms and the two men rushed into them. They were sobbing and shaking with grief over their dear brother's death.

"Come in, come in," he said to the brothers when their anguish had begun to ebb. He introduced them, and I pulled out two chairs so they could sit.

The taller of the two, whom I believed to be the younger, placed his elbows on the table and his head in his hands. He ran his fingers through his unkempt hair and finally looked up. "We examined Ercole's body at the castle," he said with a tremulous voice. "We found 22 stab wounds. It was not enough for the assassins to cut his throat and pull out his hair. They had to defile every part of his body."

His brother draped his arms around him to quell his shuddering. Leonardo and I waited, our hearts heavy for their sorrow.

"Ercole's wife had just given birth to a daughter, and they married in joyful celebration of it. Now she will be alone." He dropped his head into his hands, his shoulders rapidly rising and falling.

His brother said, "We found his mule wandering in the marshes. Ercole had gone there to pick a spray of crocuses for Barbara and the baby. He was so happy. Why would anyone do this?"

Leonardo placed a hand on his shoulder. "There are wheels within wheels, my dear Guido. We shall endeavor to find out. Do you know if he had enemies?"

"I am sure he had. He inherited our father's title as magistrate, and with it all the enmity which is naturally entailed in that position. But what sort of deed would warrant such brutal revenge? He was physically harmless, a mere cripple."

"Tell me," said Leonardo. "What was the nature of his relationship with Alfonso?"

"Cordial, I believe. And yet he was much closer to Lucrezia. Yesterday we entreated her to persuade Alfonso to investigate his death."

"Did Alfonso agree?"

"He refused."

"Did he provide a reason?"

"He said he had more pressing military matters to attend to, but that he would do everything in his power to protect Barbara Torelli and her family against future attacks."

"And what will you do?" asked Leonardo.

"With Barbara's permission, we shall petition Gonzaga."

"Francesco Gonzaga, the Marquess of Mantua? Ferrara is not his jurisdiction."

"Barbara is a good friend of Isabella d'Este, the Marchioness. Isabella could persuade Gonzaga to investigate on our behalf."

I knew that Lucrezia and Isabella were rivals. I could not imagine a circumstance in which Isabella would happily intercede on behalf of Barbara Torelli, Ercole being a close friend of Lucrezia's.

The mystery of the Aldine Press seemed to become muddier and muddier with every revelation. The faster we ran, the further we fell behind. I was relieved, therefore, when Leonardo announced that we would begin our return to Milan in two days. There was much work to do at the studio, and we had made little progress on behalf of Aldo. It now seemed as if our venture was but a fitful dream, another stray dog that Leonardo would do well to shake from his boot. Perhaps the publication of his notebooks was not meant to be. Some things are predestined by the Will of God.

We began to organize our belongings for the journey. The weather was improving, and the roads were now favorable for the long ride home.

SCARLETT: Setbacks like these are familiar to me. At some point in every project, whether it's a piece of research or an experiment or an investigation, you hit a wall. Your best bet is to back off, let the problem simmer, and give the old brain cells a rest.

On that note, Peter, I think Artie and I will do the same. It's been another long day. We'll rest here in the hotel and hit the road in the morning. Just a sec—

[LIGHT SHUFFLING SOUNDS]

Thought I heard a truck. Nothing. Tomorrow we'll swap out our rental car, just in case, and move to another hotel. Peter, please allow an extra day for the next installment.

Say goodnight, Gracie.

ARTIE: You're mad.

EDITOR'S EMAIL

This business with the van is making me nervous. I know you can't reveal your security measures, but I hope you're taking strong precautions. These guys aren't playing around.

Things are heating up around here, too. Yesterday we got a warning from your client's attorneys. Now we know what Dickson's real name is. Needless to say, we found it unnerving. You've certainly made a powerful enemy. How could he have known about our arrangement? Did you say anything, Scarlett?

At this point we still feel we're on firm legal ground, so please continue translating and fact-checking as before. We'll try to take care of this on our end.

8VO_27

[TRAFFIC NOISE]

SCARLETT: That fucking bastard. I can't say I'm surprised, but I didn't think he'd be on top of us that fast. That's why I don't trust men. In fact, that's why I don't trust people. Everyone has an agenda.

Artie and I feel relatively safe. Yesterday we returned our rental and picked up a new one from a different dealership. Now I'm waiting in the car while she uses the ladies' at the AutoGrill. No sign of the creepy Transit van.

I'm trying to be logical about this, Peter. The laws of probability say there's a good chance our six-armed Salvatore is just an ordinary handyman with a fairly large territory. Not to get into the weeds, but the background rate for the same van popping up in different locations is probably a bigger number than I thought.

Believe it or not, this is the kind of shit I obsess about when I don't understand something.

The X-factor is that the Transit van is eye-catching—you know, with the Shiva cartoon and all. We didn't notice the other vans cruising around in multiple towns, because, well, they're ordinary. Who pays attention to plain white vans? See what I mean? We only noticed Salvatore's van because it stood out from the others.

By the same token, it's tempting to use logic as a security blanket. Our handyman could be exactly what he seems—one half of a pincer movement designed to crush us. Dickson sets his legal dogs on Harker, and at the same time sends Salvatore to collect the manuscript from me and Artie—by force if necessary. Sometimes you have to go with the obvious.

I have to say I'm starting to question my judgment. First, I drag Artie into a situation she isn't equipped to handle, then I bring a pack of wolves down on you and Harker. Thanks for shielding us from Dickson's macho posturing, but I feel like this whole enterprise could end up a smoking crater, courtesy me.

I confess I haven't been straight with you, Peter. Or myself. I believed my motives were pure. But I have to admit I saw this little caper partly as an offramp—a chance to leave my student loans in the rearview mirror. I feel ashamed about it now, and even more ashamed that I enlisted honest people like you and Artie in my scheme. This whole thing is wack. Trying to outmaneuver Dickson's surveillance is just sending cracks up the wall.

The docent at the printing museum said the graver might be worth ten thousand, but that's only because he doesn't know its provenance. What if I just returned the manuscript and sold the graver on the black market? This little item could be worth a hundred grand if I can make a case for it. With a single stroke I could cancel Salvatore, save Harker, repay our advances, and have enough money left over to shove a few pounds into Artie's lotion-fresh hands.

Not exactly kosher, I know—

Wait! Here she comes. Please don't mention any of this until I've talked to her. She's loving all this cloak-and-dagger stuff. Been translating her little paisley heart out.

[CAR DOOR OPENING AND CLOSING]

This next part is where we get to meet the genius in his lair, right, Artie?

ARTIE: Right you are, Scarlett. Leonardo and Melzi have returned to Milan. They're falling back into the familiar rhythms of work.

According to historians, the Milan studio was located in the parish of Santa Babila, an artisan quarter near the Porta Orientale, close to the various services they would need to produce their work. Here we can place Salaì, now relieved of his management duties, along with the pupil Melzi, the pupil Lorenzo, and an artist known as Giampietrino, one of Leonardo's most talented followers, plus the household servants.

Melzi takes us straight into Leonardo's ambit—his ideas, his work, his conversations with friends. We get a level of intimacy that didn't exist before we found this manuscript. I suggest you pause the recording here and make yourself a hot cuppa.

Our return journey to Lombardy was uneventful, but our arrival was tumultuous. Salaì had not received my letter telling him of our return, or perhaps chose not to read it, and had failed to put the studio back in order.

Leonardo discovered his newly written notebooks scattered across the dining table, with several lying on the floor. A number of other books had been pulled from the shelves in the library and not returned to their places. There were piles of plates on side tables and in Salaì's room, most of them with dried bits of food stuck to them. Wine bottles littered the floor, along with blankets and stray pieces of clothing.

Salaì had given the servants two days' leave, no doubt to eliminate any witnesses. He told the other assistants the studio would be closed for spring cleaning. This was a lie from the mouth of Hell, and in any case the spring cleaning should have been done before Easter.

Leonardo was furious. He cornered Salaì and lifted him from the floor by his tunic.

"I do not pay my assistants to get drunk and carouse with their derelict friends," he hissed through clenched teeth. "I know full well that you bought all this food and wine with the household money, not with your own purse." He glared at Salaì, who hung mute against the wall like a painting being mounted for an exhibition.

He dropped him to the ground and swept off to his study, shutting the door with force. The door rebounded slightly. As I walked by, I could see Leonardo standing in front of his wardrobe. He bent down and picked up a pair of shoes made from vegetable-tanned Tuscan leather. The shoes were covered with mud and had dried into strange shapes. He took out a satin cloak and saw that it was stained and torn. He slowly shook his head.

Then he began to laugh.

The next day I busied myself in tidying up the studio. Leonardo had sent Salaì to the shops to buy supplies, or perhaps to avoid further confrontation.

The mess was concentrated in three rooms: the library, the dining room, and the kitchen, all on the Via Spiga side of the house. The cook, Domenica, had already started on the kitchen. I made a plan for the other rooms.

Leonardo's notebooks, perhaps the residue of a night of boasting—Salaì no doubt taking credit for the master's inventions—lay in careless disarray in the dining room. These items I put back in the master's private study, stacked carefully according to their numbers. I moved to the library and replaced the bound books, which Leonardo had wanted organized by subject, onto their proper shelves. There were circular wine stains on some of the covers where Salaì's guests had rested their goblets. I knew from experience that Leonardo would forgive these transgressions.

As the sun rotated to the Porta Orientale side of the house, I moved with it into the main studio. I examined the large wooden panel of the Virgin Mary, which had been the cause of so much handwringing over the years. It was a figure of Mary surrounded by an angel, the infant Jesus, and the infant Saint John. It rested on small wooden blocks instead of an easel so that Leonardo and his collaborator, Ambrogio de Predis, could reach the arched top with the aid of a foot stool.

This was the second version of the painting. The first stood to the left of it, having been rejected by the patrons, the Confraternity of the Immaculate Conception, on the grounds that Leonardo had not followed their instructions. He had made alterations in an attempt to appease them, such as causing the angel to point to the infant John, who in turn gestured toward Jesus with clasped hands. But he had already lost their trust. They refused to pay for it.

"Patrons from Hell!" Leonardo had cried, throwing down his brush when told the news. "They would drain the blood from my veins!" The very next day he transferred the work to Ambrogio and refused to put his *hand to it further. The panel had been the source of too many disputes, not only between Leonardo and his patrons, but between Leonardo and Ambrogio. He was done with it.*

I saw that one of Salaì's friends—or perhaps Salaì himself—had glued a radish to the tip of John the Baptist's nose. It appeared as if the infant Jesus was blessing a wine-reddened proboscis. I carefully removed the object and cleaned off the glue. I did not want this sacrilege to create further tensions.

I looked around the room. Positioned prominently in the main studio, where the midday light could illuminate Leonardo's vibrant colors, were two Madonnas of different sizes that he had promised to King Louis XII. He would deliver these in several weeks after adding his final touches. I examined their surfaces and found no damage to either panel. I also examined a half-finished painting of the Leda, and another painting of the Virgin with Saint Anne. Their easels had been knocked sideways, but there was no damage to the paintings.

On the back wall above a worktable hung a series of studies on paper for the funeral monument of Giangiacomo Trivulzio, the marshal of Milan. This was to be a bronze equestrian statue, so there were several clay maquettes on the table. The marshal sat regally on a muscular, well-proportioned charger, which in turn stood on top of an elaborately carved marble arch. Those who knew Trivulzio would be surprised by the handsome visage given him by Leonardo. This, of course, was by instruction.

The brittle maquettes had been disturbed in our absence, and one was lying broken on its side. Yet these were early models and not important.

Hanging on the wall next to the studies were three lyres crafted by Leonardo in his earlier days. His ability to compose and perform music, often spontaneously, had been his entree to the Sforza court. With the death of his patron, he no longer had occasion to play. One of the lyres had been replaced improperly and hung at an angle from one hook. I examined it and found a scratch on the back side. I made a mental note to repair it. Leonardo would not need to know about the scratch, and Salaì would not need to fabricate one of his preposterous lies.

I looked around the studio for other signs of damage. It was at that point I realized that my portrait of Leonardo was missing.

EDITOR'S EMAIL

Was that the portrait of Leonardo from the townhouse? I'm definitely feeling the Vertigo Effect. It's exhilarating, the experience of flashing backwards 500 years.

Scarlett, don't panic about the project. We can handle whatever Dickson throws at us. Besides, we've invested way too much to turn back now. The main thing is to complete the manuscript and get the book out there. Everything else is secondary.

8VO_28

ARTIE: What do you mean, Peter, turn back? Don't panic about what?

SCARLETT: Nothing, Artie. I was having a minor freakout. I'm feeling better now. Peter's asking if Melzi found the painting.

ARTIE: He found it alright. Can you guess where?

I turned and bounded up the stairs from the reception to the first floor, remembering that we sometimes moved finished pieces to the laboratory to make room for new work.

The laboratory is a large open space with a high ceiling. It sits atop the main studio and stays locked against prying eyes. Access is allowed in three ways: from the wide utility lift in the main studio below; from Leonardo's bedroom directly above his private study; and from the door at the top of the stairs where I found myself now.

I took a key from my robe and turned the lock.

The laboratory appeared to be just as we had left it. This is the room where Leonardo works on his more elaborate experiments, in subjects such as mechanics, hydraulics, sound amplification, and architectural physics. There were models of fantastical machines, mostly made from wood, metal, and leather, including a large flying machine that was based on his observation of birds and bats in flight. On the table were bat wings in various stages of dissection, with larger models of mechanical wings lying to the side.

Whereas the main studio was tidy, clean, and organized, so as to impress visiting patrons, the laboratory was a wild, unkempt forest of strange inventions. Against the walls were tables and shelves littered with miters and saws, hammers and chisels, planes and drills, boxes of wood and metal fittings. A fine coat of sawdust covered every horizontal surface. The moment the surfaces were cleaned, the dust would begin to settle again.

At the far end of the room was the door to Leonardo's sleeping chamber. Although I have never entered it, I have glimpsed the interior from the laboratory side of the door. The center of the floor has a set of doors that hinge downward into his study, allowing him to raise and lower his worktable, with the aid of levers and winches, between his study and his private bedroom, so that he can protect his ideas from the prying eyes of assistants and patrons. I did not see the worktable in his study the day before, so it must have been in the upstairs position.

Seeing no sign of my portrait, I locked the laboratory and returned to the ground floor. Domenica had finished cleaning the kitchen, and now stood at the back door talking with Pagolino, the groom, her small hands set on her wide hips. Pago was holding up articles of clothing, saying he had found these in the stables. This led to lamentations about the younger generation and a deplorable lack of morals.

I only half-heard their complaints. I was standing in the library, scanning the shelves for the book that Leonardo had described to me in Ferrara. I was eager—truly most eager—to learn more about the Japanese art of weaponless combat. As I pulled the book from the shelf, the door to the library burst open. I jumped as if I had been caught in the execution of a crime. It was Salaì, his arms full of packages.

"What are you doing, angioletto? Stealing the master's ideas?" He

dumped his bundles on the table and plucked the book from my hands. He flicked the pages and sneered. "Stop pretending you can read this, angioletto patetico. Anyone can see it is written in Arabic."

Salaì is nearly twice my age and had been Leonardo's assistant since before I was born. As a boy, he had tended Leonardo's vineyard. Yet he behaves as if we are rivals for our master's affections. I have come to believe there is nothing I can do to alter his manner towards me, so I resign myself to being the poor dog he keeps around to kick. Having thus resigned myself, I have come to feel inexplicably powerful. I understood that his ill manner has little to do with me, and more to do with his own fears and insecurities.

"I am so tired, Checchino," he mewled, as if he now expected my sympathy. "Can you carry these materials to the laboratory? I wish to retire to my room for a rest."

I bowed, and carried the packages upstairs behind him, reflecting on the parable of the vineyard workers and the general unfairness of life. How is it that I can work all day to clean up his mess, and when he comes home after an hour of shopping, I must also carry his packages to relieve his exhaustion?

As I unlocked the door to the laboratory, I turned around and saw him enter his bedchamber.

On the wall above his bed was my portrait of Leonardo.

EDITOR'S EMAIL

Salaì really *is* a little devil. I have to say, though, I've always found the parable of the vineyard workers baffling. The owner pays every worker the same whether they worked all day or just for the last hour. How is that fair to the ones who started first thing in the morning? What lessons are we supposed to take from that?

8VO_29

SCARLETT: If you're looking to the Bible for logic, good luck. I've read it cover to cover and I can tell you it wasn't written to make sense. It was written to impose control over a weak-minded populace. If I were writing that parable, I'd have the early workers rise up and beat the shit out of the vineyard owner.

ARTIE: Don't be a helmet.

SCARLETT: Okay, so maybe I need an editor.

ARTIE: It's true that Salaì was a bit of a wide boy. An accomplished painter, yes, but he lived by his wits and caused bedlam on a daily basis. It's not surprising he would claim Francesco's first competent painting as his own property. He could steal the portrait and assert his dominance over Melzi at the same time.

To give you a sense of Salaì's character, we can go back to his first year in Leonardo's household. The boy was ten.

Leonardo writes in his notebook that, quote, I had two shirts cut for him, a pair of stockings and jerkin, and when I put aside the money to pay for these things he stole the money from my purse, unquote. The next day Leonardo brought Salaì to dinner at a friend's house, where the boy broke three table flasks and knocked over the wine.

Later, at the house of Galeazzo Sanseverino, Salaì robbed the purse of a footman as he was dressing for a pageant. After the pageant, a friend gave Leonardo a gift of Turkish leather to make a pair of boots with. The next month Salaì sold it to a shoemaker and used the money to buy sweets.

The list of Salaì's misdeeds would fill pages and pages. Leonardo wrote in his notes that he was a thief, a liar, obstinate, and greedy. The historian Charles Nicholl summed it up more simply. He called him a right little tearaway.

Why did Leonardo keep him around? Beauty? Entertainment? Love? I believe there's a strong possibility he saw something of himself in the boy.

SCARLETT: By the way, Peter, I tried to verify the location of Leonardo's studio. It turns out historians don't have a clue, so we'll have to take Melzi's word for it. At the time, the corner of Corso di Porta Orientale and Via della Spiga was just inside the ancient gate at the time. Spiga, the side road, was probably just a horse path that gave access to the kitchen and stables.

Naturally, things changed as the city grew. The gate was moved farther out and renamed the Porta Venezia. The Corso di Porta Orientale is now called the Corso Venezia, and the horse path on the right side of the studio is a la-di-da pedestrian street where shoppers can spend shitloads of money on Italian shoes made in Mexico. Your girlfriend would love it. Yes, I know who she is. Google tells all.

ARTIE: Please forgive Scarlett. She may have flunked charm school, but she makes up for it in bad manners.

SCARLETT: Ooh, sick burn.

ARTIE: Shush, dear. Let the grownups talk.

When one considers how prolific Leonardo was, it's quite interesting to note the amount of time he spent on his projects. For example, the Leda, the Virgin and Child with Saint Anne, and the two Madonnas each took five to ten years to complete. The second version of the Virgin Mary, now known as The Virgin of the Rocks, took Leonardo and Ambrogio thirteen years to complete.

One painting Melzi didn't mention is the *Mona Lisa*. It must have been in the studio at the time of his writing. Leonardo had finished it only three years earlier, and it was not a commissioned work.

Perhaps *completed* is too strong a word. He carried it from place to place until his death, adding small touches as if it were a Pekingese needing constant grooming, or an imaginary friend with whom to discuss the finer points of art. He often said the *discorso mentale,* the mental discourse, was more important than the finished work.

What the average person fails to recognize is that there were a number of *Mona Lisas*. Only one of these found its way to the Louvre. It was as if he'd set out to create the perfect woman, or perhaps the perfect mother, and carried on trying until the end of his life.

His own mother was certainly less than perfect. She gave birth to him out of wedlock. She then abandoned him—at least in his telling. His father, a notary public, was already married and refused to include him in the family. Leonardo lived with his uncle until he entered Verrocchio's studio at fourteen.

Yet one would be hard pressed to say that his seemingly Dickensian childhood had a detrimental effect on his progress. Some might argue that being left alone to experience the world without guidance or formal education was the making of him.

Did he feel a need to re-create his mother in the *Mona Lisa?* Was he trying to replace his imperfect mother with a better version? The origin, the history, and meaning of the *Mona Lisa* lay just beyond our grasp, like a mirage receding with each new discovery, each new theory.

SCARLETT: Oh no, please no. Not the woo-woo again. Can't we just stick to the facts? How can we possibly know how he felt about his childhood? Everyone has unresolved issues with their parents. Why get all Freudian about it?

ARTIE: All I'm saying is that we can't be sure of the reason for Leonardo's fascination with the *Mona Lisa.*

SCARLETT: Big D, little uh.

ARTIE: I think we're both tired after a long day of unproductive research, Peter. I'm feeling a bit punch-drunk myself. Shall we continue tomorrow?

EDITOR'S EMAIL

You two must be exhausted. There's so much to speculate about, so many leads to follow up. I really admire the insights you've managed to turn up so far. I had no idea there were multiple versions of the *Mona Lisa*.

Scarlett, I'm curious. What do you actually know about my girlfriend? For that matter, what do you know about me?

8VO_30

SCARLETT: Okay, Peter, ready? First of all, you didn't trudge two miles through the snow to pay your library fines when you were ten. You've admitted that. Now you're in your mid-thirties and you're hoping to rise to the rank of publisher by the time you're forty. You're serious, smart, and ambitious. You've been known to bend the rules to acquire a book, because—hey—it only takes one blockbuster to make your bones. You've convinced your colleagues you're just a fun guy who goes with the flow, which beats the hell out of getting a knife in the back. But you actually *would* trudge through the snow to return a library book. You grew up on the East Coast in a middle-class family and fought your way through Columbia on a partial scholarship. You're so caught up in the rat race that your whiskers twitch at the faintest whiff of a manuscript. You've had some notable successes, but nothing that matches the grandeur of your ambitions. Every year at the Frankfurt Book Fair it's the same old story: Peter, long time no see. Anything new since *A Girl Named Aptly?* When's the next blockbuster? Stephane, come over here and meet Mister Aptly! Every year it gets more stale, this experience of being defined by a handful of oldies. Your girlfriend, who you met five years ago at Art Basel, is a fashion-obsessed shopaholic who's never worn the same outfit once. The two of you bonded over Ed Ruscha's works on paper, the ones that say SCUM, SUDS, SIN, and HEART ATTACK. You've thought about proposing, but lately you're not sure you love her. You feel terrible about it. Your vacillation messes with your self-image as a Boy Scout. Something has to change but you're not sure what.

Is that about right? I'm good at online people-watching, you gotta admit.

EDITOR'S EMAIL

Scarlett, I'd appreciate it if you'd refrain from making my personal life part of your research. Right now I'm dealing with a pack of legal pit bulls, a boss who's developed a nervous twitch, and a general counsel who thinks I've lost the only two brain cells I ever had. Didn't you once say that you don't do personal? I have enough to worry about without your amateur psychoanalysis, and so do you. Agreed?

8VO_31

SCARLETT: I have a superpower. I can sense the perfect time to stick my foot in my mouth. Sorry for my behavior, Peter. You're right. I wouldn't want you to investigate *my* life, and I'm happy to accord you the same courtesy. I promise it won't happen again.

ARTIE: Peter, we've come so far on this journey, and none of us wants to lose the trust we're building. We imagine you're under enormous pressure with all the legal attacks from Dickson.

Perhaps we can look to Leonardo for lessons in perseverance. For forty years he had to overcome hundreds of obstacles to become the most original thinker of his day. I don't mean to minimize the threat from Mr. Dickson, but you see what I mean. The important thing is to have faith and keep going, don't you agree?

In this next installment Melzi reveals Leonardo's thinking habits, so methodical and relentless, as he follows the trail like a beagle with the scent of fox in his nostrils.

I sat next to Leonardo at a bench in the laboratory. The light from a round window illuminated a small wooden frame that held two pieces of glass in precise alignment. I had constructed the frame myself according to my master's specifications, while he ground pieces of glass into lenses. We mounted the lenses into two metal tubes, fitting the smaller tube into the larger. We then designed a crank that caused the smaller tube to rise and fall inside the larger one, thereby altering the distance between the lenses.

Leonardo turned the handle forward and backward until he was satisfied. "Here, Checco, see for yourself."

I peered into the smaller tube and saw a rusty stain, the mark left by a bloody finger on the broken chase from Aldo's shop. It was now enlarged many times, so that I could clearly see swirling lines, like furrows in a field or ripples in a stream. I looked at my own fingertips and noticed similar furrows.

"The patterns on our fingers remain unchanged during our lives," Leonardo said, adjusting the lenses. "They develop in the womb and stay with us until death. Notice how the loops and concentric lines of this mark differ from those on your own fingers. Place your index finger under the lens and look closely."

I was startled to see my own fingertip enlarged to the point of unrecognition. The parallel ridges of skin glowed from the light of the window, the furrows seeming deep enough to hide oneself within, like a child in a garden maze. I saw a small scar crossing five or six of the rows, the reminder of an accident I had last year with a shop tool. I could see particles of dust, and a tiny translucent insect moving along the ridges on six legs.

"Now look at the same print again," he said. I removed my hand so he could place the chase back under the lens. "Memorize the shape of the pattern. Do you have it? Now view another print."

He moved the chase slightly to the right. Another pattern came into view, this one made by black ink.

"It is the same!" I cried, pleased by my ability to recognize the features they shared.

"Correct," said Leonardo. "Because it was made by the same finger, which belonged to the same man. And who was that man?"

"Master, it must have been Griffo! He was Aldo's compositor, the one

who readied the formes for the press. Naturally, he would have ink on his fingers from proofing the type. He must have left the other print during the morning of the murder, after crushing the victim's head in the press. He nailed him to the uprights, then, with bloody hands, threw the chase on the floor, scattering the type while leaving this token of evidence."

"My dear Checco, I shall make a police inspector of you yet."

"But, Master, we already knew that Griffo was the perpetrator of the crime. What we did not know is who the instigator was, the one who poisoned the man and set the crime in motion. We have guessed Lucrezia, but we still have no evidence."

"Checco, I am pleased with your logic. Can you see the advantage of favoring facts over superstition? Necromancy and augury have little place in the pursuit of truth. Now, as to the instigator…"

He began to hum as he removed the section of chase from under the lens and pulled his notebook from his belt. He opened it to the final page, still folded from the night at the morgue. He carefully extracted the thread he had found on the victim's knee and placed it under the lens.

I could barely contain my excitement as I moved my eye toward the device.

"Wait!" he said, lightly tapping the back of my head. He extracted a slip of paper from his robe and placed it on the bench. Inside was another thread, which he set next to the first one under the lens. "Now."

I peered down through the top to see two threads, enlarged so many times that I could see all the smaller threads twisted together to make a larger one. They were different colors—one ultramarine and the other indigo—but their formation and luminosity were the same. "Where did you find this second thread?"

"I pulled it from the carpet when we met with Lucrezia the second time."

I suddenly recalled the moment when Leonardo had dropped his glasses under the table. He refused my help in finding them. I now gazed into the face of my master with newfound awe. I suddenly remembered his humorous remedy for Lucrezia's guards: egg whites mixed with threads of blue silk, cut small.

He returned my gaze with crinkled eyes. "I noticed that her carpet threads had strands of silk in them, like certain carpets from China. The same strands of silk can be seen in the thread I found on the murder victim's knee. What does this suggest, my young inspector?"

"That the victim had visited the same room and perhaps genuflected in front of the Duchess."

"Or perhaps fell to his knees after ingesting poison?"

My heart stopped. I could see the chain of events unfolding in front of my eyes. The victim was summoned by Lucrezia, whereupon she poisoned him with cantarella. Griffo came and carried him to Venice that night. Believing he was already dead, Griffo crushed his head in the printing press as a message to Bembo and revenge against Aldo.

I recited my version to Leonardo.

"Well done, Checco. Let us call this a working hypothesis, as we now have evidence to support this construction. But we do not have an answer to the larger question."

"What is that, Master?"

He looked at me in disbelief. "The question of why!"

EDITOR'S EMAIL

Did Leonardo invent the microscope, too? How about fingerprint analysis? I don't think I've ever heard that about da Vinci. He gets more and more intriguing all the time.

8VO_32

SCARLETT: Only a fraction of Leonardo's notebooks have survived, so we can't say for sure if he invented the microscope. Most historians place the invention of compound lenses somewhere around the 17th century. So Melzi's account, if true, is breaking news.

Fingerprint analysis, by contrast, goes way back to ancient China. It's hard to know if Leonardo got it from the Chinese or hit on it independently, but I suspect the latter, since the study of fingertip patterns would have been right in his wheelhouse. The rest of Europe didn't recognize the importance of fingerprints until the 1600s.

What really wigs me out is his grasp of forensic science. I mean, he was hundreds of years ahead of modern investigators. The idea of using trace evidence to place a suspect at the scene of a crime? Precocious, to say the least. Today we call it the Locard Exchange Principle. When a person comes into contact with someone or something, there's an exchange of materials that can be used as evidence. Leonardo used it centuries before Locard was even born.

ARTIE: He also invented a complete system for dating trees by counting their rings. Peter, you might recall our surprise at finding the outer edge of the tree on the back side of Melzi's portrait of Leonardo. We thought it a lucky coincidence, but perhaps he was leaving a clue for posterity, a way to date the painting using nature's abacus. In fact, Scarlett and I are convinced of it. It was too deliberate a choice to be otherwise.

In this next bit, Melzi receives several doses of the most concentrated mentoring one can imagine.

Leonardo's "why" hung on me like a hair shirt, offering discomfort but little enlightenment. What would cause Lucrezia to poison a stranger and then risk discovery by making common cause with Griffo, a man whom she hardly knew and had scant reason to trust?

I peered into the glass once more, transfixed by the vibrant color of the giant carpet threads, laid side by side like twin corpses in luminous satin shrouds. When I finally looked up again, I found Leonardo lying motionless on his pallet, eyes closed in deep meditation, or perhaps sleep.

I recalled the first time he had visited my family home in Vaprio. He and my father were discussing military engineering with a great deal of enthusiasm, when suddenly Leonardo excused himself and fell immediately into a deep sleep. My father remarked on it for years afterwards.

I gently closed the door to the laboratory and descended the stairs to resume my work in the library.

Left to his own devices, Master Leonardo would not bother to keep his library in regular order. I would often find his books lying about on worktables, on shelves meant for maquettes, or piled haphazardly on the floor, covered with wood chips or metal dust. He claimed to appreciate my attempts to organize them, but within days I would find them in new piles and in different places.

Pacioli's "Divina proportione" would have befriended Aesop's "Fables," and Visconti's "Rithmi" would have formed an attachment for da Como's "Arte coquinaria." How poetry and cookery could end up coupled, I cannot say. I would simply pick up the books and return them to their proper places.

After an hour of reorganizing his volumes by subject and author, I heard footsteps. I turned to see Leonardo standing at the door of the library, whence he thanked me once again for my efforts. Sensing his willingness to talk, I ventured a delicate question.

"Master," I said, "I cannot but wonder about the books you have chosen to read."

"What would you like to know, mio fanciullo?"

"You have collected books on cosmography and medicine by Ptolemy and Euclid, and books of strange poetry and fabulous stories by Aesop, and still others on mathematics and alchemy. All of these are written in Latin, a language you do not understand. How can you learn from these books?"

"Unlike you, my dear Checco, I cannot read Latin nor write with sophistication. I am unlettered. I was born to a peasant woman and have little schooling. But with sufficient effort I can decipher Latin, and I can understand pictures and numbers better than most men. To me, Euclid becomes a limpid mountain pool after a period of quiet contemplation. I need not understand his every word to follow his thinking."

"And if you desire to exchange ideas with educated men, then what?"

"I may not be able to quote from other authors, but I can quote from a more worthy source—Nature itself. Too many men believe the knowledge found in books is sufficient. They become trumpeters and reciters of the works of others. Their ideas are only objects reflected in a mirror, not the objects themselves."

"But, Master, do we not stand on the shoulders of giants?"

"Checco, it is one thing to stand on their shoulders. It is another to cling to their ankles. Men learn best by thinking and doing without prejudice, by interrogating experience, by asking why. One should not let one's schooling limit one's education, Checco."

I thought for a moment. I reached up and pulled down a book, "Opus majus" by Bacon, and laid it open on the table. "Surely it would not be wrong to cling to the ankles of Roger Bacon. He advocates the same process you yourself subscribe to, that of studying Nature through empiricism."

"I have the greatest of respect for Friar Bacon. His treatises on science—mathematics, perspective, and astronomy—have opened my eyes. But like many Englishmen, he was too much in the thrall of Aristotle. His was the logic of deduction, whereas true invention requires a different kind of logic, the logic of what might be, not of what already is."

"Which is better, Master, science or art?"

"It is not a question of which is better, my dear Checco, but of how well they dance. Science is powerful, but art is nourishing. Would you want one without the other? Someday I shall set down my thoughts on this."

"Will you add these to your notebooks?"

"Perhaps."

"Master, why do you write all your notes backward? Are you afraid that if others can read them they will steal your ideas?"

"Dear Checco, you must think with more precision. If that were my aim, I would most certainly fail. A simple mirror would cause my writing to give up all its secrets. No, Checco, I write that way because I am

lefthanded and fear I might smudge the ink as I write, and because I was not taught properly, as you were."

I felt shame at having asked such a foolish question, but also at having embarrassed my master once again. To a man of letters, his backward writing might betoken a backward education. His lefthandedness, his lack of Latin, and his peasant upbringing might be seen as disqualifying birthmarks in a society of intellectuals.

SCARLETT: Christ on a bike! It just hit me. His problem wasn't a lack of schooling. The man had access to the best minds and the best libraries in Italy.

His problem was *dyslexia!*

That was the reason he didn't learn Latin. *That* was the reason he couldn't write well—he couldn't *read* well. I know the symptoms. The term dyslexia didn't exist in those days, but how else can you explain the failure of a brilliant man to master the basic skills of his time? We know that left-handedness and dyslexia are strongly correlated. And that both are correlated with creativity in the arts.

ARTIE: Fine deduction, my clever girl. Roger Bacon would have been proud.

EDITOR'S EMAIL

Nice insight, Scarlett. Is there any speculation about this in the literature?

8VO_33

SCARLETT: Fuck me. I did some research and found out that *everybody* knows he was dyslexic. I'm apparently the last one to the party. What an idiot. Artie was kind enough not to laugh.

ARTIE: I never mock the afflicted. And could you please watch your mouth, young woman?

SCARLETT: Sorry, Ms. Paisley Puss.

ARTIE: She doesn't mean it, Peter. It's a game we play. She tries to curdle my cream and I try to keep it from curdling.

I'm about to read the next chapter, which gets to the heart of Leonardo's relationship with Melzi. Leonardo often referred to the boy as a *bellissimo fanciullo,* a beautiful child. I believe Leonardo did find him beautiful, but there's no evidence of a sexual relationship. Instead, I think he saw Melzi as his protegé, his amanuensis, his connection to the next generation. More son than lover. Notice his fatherly tone in this next passage.

Leonardo sat on the edge of the table and extended his arms toward me. I came closer and he grasped my shoulders warmly. "My dear Checco, you must promise me something."

"Anything, Master."

"No matter what happens to me, whether my mind is intact or befuddled, whether I am free or in prison or confined to a sickbed, you will see to it that my notebooks are published. They must be published. Can you promise me that?"

"Certainly, Master. I shall make it my life's work if you wish it."

He gazed into my face, his aging blue eyes growing moist. "You are a good boy, Checco." He squeezed my arms. "You must ensure that my notes are written properly and illustrated clearly. The printing must be precise, and the books themselves must be portable and easily read by anyone who wants to learn from them."

"How would you like the books to appear?" I asked.

"As if God Himself were the printer. I would like them to be as fresh and beautiful as your own youthful face."

"So you don't want the text printed backwards?"

"Of course not—this is Italy, not China!" He shook his head and laughed, then pulled me into a long embrace. "Checco, Checco."

"Master, why do you want so dearly to publish your notebooks?"

"Because, young Checco, whosoever receives much, owes much." He jumped off the table and pulled me by the hand. "Come, let me show you a new way of making images."

I followed him out of the library to his private studiolo. He unlocked the door and led me over to a long worktable at one end of the room. Arranged on it were four sheets of paper, each with an engraved image of an apple. One was printed in yellow, one in blue, one in red, and the other in black.

"Observe, Checco, that in front of us we have four versions of the same image, each in a different color. What happens when the four colors are printed over each other in perfect alignment?"

He opened a drawer and pulled out a fifth sheet of paper, placing it on the table under the light from the window. It showed a bright red apple with rose, orange, and yellow highlights, resting on a pale blue and purple shadow. I had never seen anything so beautiful on a printed page. It looked as if one could pick up the apple and devour it.

"This came from a printing press, Master?"

"Not this one, Checco. This is only a proof. Let me show you how the trick is done."

On one side of the table was a wooden easel with a copper plate mounted to it. On top of the plate was a sheet of drawing paper he had used as a cartoon. He peeled it back, revealing that the underside was covered with graphite, allowing him to trace the image onto the plate. The image he had drawn was the illumination of a human heart, showing the veins and arteries and various chambers.

"You see, Checco, you have to etch the same image four times onto four different plates, one for each color. Unlike painting, where colors are mixed on a palette, here the colors are mixed in the eye."

"It is witchcraft."

"It is not witchcraft. It is the science of optics."

I peered once more at the apple proof. Leonardo handed me the glass to view it more closely. I could see that what seemed like a purple shadow *was actually a combination of tiny red and blue hatchings laid at angles on top of one another. An orange highlight was a combination of red and yellow hatchings. Leonardo had added black hatchings to give depth and weight to the shadow side of the apple.*

"You must train your eyes to know how the colors combine to make particular variations. In time it will become instinctual."

"Can you teach me?"

"I can, I shall, and I must. Because you, Checco, shall redraw all the images in my notebooks so they can be printed in color. Aldo understands the theory of this process and has agreed to attempt it. That is why I cannot trust the printing to anyone else. Are you ready to learn engraving?"

"Yes, Master!"

SCARLETT: Did you see what just happened? Leonardo invented color printing—four hundred years before the first commercial application. If we can find a sample of it, we can see if the colors he picked were the same four we use today: cyan, magenta, yellow, and black. But in any case, it sounds like he got the basic idea right.

ARTIE: For some reason, Leonardo's technique was lost to future generations. One can only imagine the effect it would have had on publishing. Naturalistic color in books would have made an impact similar to the shift from black-and-white movies to Technicolor. Readers would have swooned.

8VO_34

SCARLETT: Today we're on the move, Peter. I have a strong sense that it's dangerous to stay in one place for more than a day or two. Yesterday we swapped our rental car for a new one. On the way back to the hotel, I ducked into a Carrefour and bought an electric hair trimmer. Artie now has a stylish buzz cut after thirty years of elaborately quaffed bouffants.

ARTIE: All the better to accommodate my growing collection of wigs.

SCARLETT: We're getting to be pros at this. I've changed my hair seven times already. Whoops—probably shouldn't have said that out loud. Listening, Dickson?

ARTIE: Peter, it would be difficult to verify all the items in the previous chapter, but I do feel encouraged by the fact that most of the books he mentioned are also listed in other documents, so I'd venture that this last tranche of material is as accurate as the earlier ones.

Now the story is moving in a new direction, which I feel could shed additional light on daily life in the studio, as well as Leonardo's relationships with his colleagues. Here we go:

The next day saw a whirlwind of activity in the studio. Leonardo announced his wish to host a dinner celebration, a ten-year reunion of the Academia Leonardi Vinci. Bramante and Bramantino will be in Milan, so it was only a matter of persuading some of the others to join us at our table. The date was set a fortnight from now. My immediate duty was to send invitations to all the masters.

I was a mere child when the Academia was disbanded, so I knew little of its purpose or achievements. I only knew what Leonardo and Salaì had told me—that their meetings were often raucous and their conversation lively and even subversive. When the Duke of Milan was captured in 1499, the members scattered like seeds to the far corners of Italy.

Naturally, some were too far away to make the journey back to Milan, but Leonardo insisted I invite them in spite of this. He asked me to title the invitation "The Last Supper," referring to the mural that touched so many of their lives at the Sforza court.

On passing through the library, I noticed two volumes missing: the cookbooks of Platina and Martino da Como. I knew then that Leonardo would be taking a personal interest in the menu, and perhaps even the cooking itself, as he was quite inventive in the kitchen.

Three days before the event, we had received letters from the architect Donato Bramante; Bramantino, his talented follower; Alvise da Marliano, our esteemed doctor from the Sforza court; Galeazzo Sanseverino, a condottiere and Ludovico Sforza's cousin; Zoroastro, a metal worker and alchemist; and Fra Luca Pacioli, the famed mathematician and perhaps Leonardo's dearest friend, all saying they would attend.

That morning Leonardo sent Salaì to the shops with a purse of three lire. He told him to bring back five loaves of bread, eight bottles of good red wine, a large bottle of flaxseed oil, a bottle of rosewater, an assortment of root vegetables, a pound of almonds, a half-pound of Cyprus powder, a variety of cheeses, and various spices including curcuma, aloe, saffron, cinnamon, ginger, and mustard. The remaining ingredients for the meal would come from the garden and the stores of our pantry.

Giampietrino had nearly completed a linen tablecloth on which he had embroidered the Academia emblem, an elaborate figure of curvilinear interlocking knots. Leonardo had designed the emblem himself after the patterns used by the basket weavers in his home village of Vinci. He once told me that the twists and turns of the knots reminded him of watching the rhythmic movements of his mother's hands as she wove osier branches into baskets. He smiled as he said it, but there were tears in his eyes.

Around midday Salaì came through the kitchen door with sacks of wine, spices, and other foodstuffs. Domenica lifted them off his shoulders, whereupon he slumped into a chair.

"So many trials sent by the Lord!" he exclaimed with a dramatic wave of his hand. "First, the wine merchant tried to cheat me on the price of Sangiovese. Naturally, I refused to accede to his usurious demands. Next the cheesemonger sold me a moldy Gorgonzola, which I unwrapped on the spot to prove I was not a simpleton. And lastly, the spice merchant tried to substitute curcuma from Turkey, when I plainly asked for India. I feel weary even recounting these tedious tests of patience. God preserve me from the petty schemes of shop owners."

Domenica rolled her eyes and sorted the purchases onto the shelves in the pantry.

Salaì turned to me. "Why do you stand there like a gaping gargoyle? Help Domenica with the unpacking!"

I complied, and after a few moments he slithered off to the slovenly crevice he calls his bedchamber. I despaired to think of my portrait of Leonardo hanging in that den of duplicity and lassitude.

Later that day, as I was picking fruit from the cherry tree in the court-yard, I heard loud voices coming from the kitchen. I descended the ladder and moved gingerly toward the door. I could hear Leonardo scolding someone at a raised pitch. Normally, his voice was high and reedy, but now it was an octave above that.

"I told you to get good Sangiovese, you Devil, not this swill that passes for wine! Where is the rest of my money?"

I heard Salaì's puling voice. "But Master, the wine merchant assured me—"

"Assured you! Assured you of a tidy profit for your pocket! Did you think my friends and I would be too drunk by the second course to tell the difference? You thieving magpie! I should have thrown you out of my house the day after I took you in."

Salaì mumbled something below the threshold of my hearing.

"You spend all my money, you ruin my garments, you drink my wine, and then laugh about it with your friends when my back is turned. I cannot abide scoundrels in my house!"

"Master, please do not expel me," he whined. "I will do anything to please you. Truly. Command me, and I shall do it."

There came a lengthy silence. I imagined Salaì throwing himself into Leonardo's arms, sobbing pathetically, sliding down his master's robes to the floor and embracing his legs.

"I cannot promise to forgive you until you return the money and do penance for your treachery."

"I will, O Master, I will. Please command me."

"You shall not be allowed to sit at the table of the Academia. Instead, you will assist Domenica and Lorenzo in the serving of the meal. If you perform your duties with humility and grace, I shall consider whether to welcome you back into the household. Do you understand?"

"Yes, yes, good Master, I do. You can trust me to serve your friends as if they were royalty, even better."

With that, the argument seemed to end. I went back to my task of picking cherries, that Domenica could bake a sweet torta for the end of the meal.

On the morning of the celebration, Leonardo called me to his study and bade me sit on a stool next to him. "Checco," he said, "have you been adding your thoughts to your notebook, the one I gave you in Ferrara?"

"I have, Master."

"Good. I would like you to join the table tonight and bring your book. I will introduce you as my secretary and say you will be taking notes on our conversation, and that you shall send copies to everyone afterwards. I believe the guests will be pleased, and not a little flattered by the attention. Yet you must not join the conversation unless asked, and comport yourself according to the very model of deference. Can you do that?"

"I can, Master."

"And no matter what happens, you must refrain from discussing our adventures in Venice and Ferrara. I believe we will make progress on our investigation tonight, but we must keep our cards hidden up our sleeves."

"And if they already know about the murders in Venice and Ferrara?"

"Do not be alarmed by anything that is said or done. Just nod and take notes. Adopt the face of a card player and allow me to direct the conversation."

"Yes, Master."

The rest of the morning was filled with happy chatter as Leonardo orchestrated the work of the kitchen. His favorite smooth-coated terrier, Mimi, patrolled the floor for morsels, occasionally chasing field cats who had the temerity to enter the kitchen. Domenica busied herself in boiling eggs, chopping apples, sugaring almonds, and making sauces. Giampietrino decorated the surface of the cherry torta, while Lorenzo set up the roasting spit for meat. All the time Leonardo's knife flashed, like the sword of a circus performer, as he turned a mound of simple vegetables into fantastical shapes to be roasted in the oven.

In the afternoon I retired to my bedchamber to dress for dinner. The guests would soon be arriving.

EDITOR'S EMAIL

I wonder what the maestro expects to learn at dinner. I can hardly wait to learn what a group of Renaissance subversives would choose to talk about.

Did you get a chance to fact-check the last chapter? Can we even call them chapters? And what's an osier, anyway?

8VO_35

ARTIE: Peter, an osier is a willow used in basket weaving. I believe Leonardo may have designed the basket-weave emblem as a visual verbal pun. The name Vinci derives from the old Italian word for osier, which in turn comes from the Latin word for bond, or vinculus. Osier branches, you see, were often used for binding. Leonardo loved wordplay, so you can imagine his delight at designing an emblem that not only reflected the character of his village, but characterized the close bond forged by the members of his inner circle.

SCARLETT: Good God, woman! You sound like a textbook! Complete sentences, like everything's already written and all you have to do is recite it. I could flip you to any page and you'd read yourself to me, punctuation intact, all proofed and perfect. What's up with that?

ARTIE: It's called English, my dear girl. May I continue?

SCARLETT: If you have to. But please, please, *please,* make a mistake once in a while. I need to know you're a regular human person.

ARTIE: I'll try. But keep in mind I was *not* expelled from charm school, unlike some I could name. Perhaps all those books they piled onto my head made an impression.

SCARLETT: A joke! I guess that counts for human, at least a little. Let's keep going and see what happens. Did you know, Ms. Smartypants, that Leonardo was a vegetarian foodie?

ARTIE: I did. Several historians have noted that he preferred to avoid animal flesh in the later years of his life. And yet he wouldn't think of imposing his views on those around him. Melzi mentions a spit for roasting meat, so we can assume he made allowances for other tastes.

SCARLETT: What about Salaì? Vegetarian, or equal-opportunity glutton?

ARTIE: It appears that Salaì would eat or drink anything to excess, especially if it were deemed unhealthy. He grew up in Leonardo's vineyard, so one might visualize a rascally fox with unfettered access to the henhouse. He may have developed his bad habits early.

SCARLETT: Do you *have* any bad habits?

ARTIE: Yes. I've been known to keep questionable company.

SCARLETT: That hurts.

ARTIE: Of Leonardo's guests, the only one who was not a member of the Academia was Tommaso Masini—Zoroastro to his friends. He was a metalworker, alchemist, augur, and daredevil assistant on Leonardo's riskier projects. In many ways, he was a folkloric version of Leonardo himself. Mad as a box of frogs. He might have served as a sort of court jester on occasions such as this.

SCARLETT: Mad as a box of frogs. Is that a complete sentence?

ARTIE: A sentence fragment. The words *Zoroastro was* are understood. Contemporary usage, my dear.

SCARLETT: This sentence no verb.

ARTIE: Scarlett, stop faffing about. Peter is a busy man.

SCARLETT: Yes, sir.

ARTIE: In various references, Zoroastro, or Astro, is alternately described as a clumsy giant, a fool, a half-wit, a mad genius, a charlatan, even a cyclops. He was blinded in one eye when a white-hot metallic cinder flew out from the forge. Later he had the eye sewn shut. As one can imagine, he was a bit bockety from all his misadventures.

Part Three: Heresy

SCARLETT: So let's recap. We have a Renaissance genius who's not only an artist but a boundlessly creative scientist before the term science was recognized. Now we find out he's a super-sleuth. On top of that, he's a left-handed, gay, dyslexic, illegitimate, vegetarian atheist. Tonight he'll be entertaining a monk, a doctor, a cyclops, the cousin of a duke, a teenage Boswell, and two architects with the same name.

That's what I call dinner for eight.

ARTIE: Indeed. And now the guests are starting to come.

A clatter of horse hoofs announced the arrival of Leonardo's dear friend, Luca Pacioli, as his carriage drew to a halt outside the main entrance of the studio. My duty was to welcome each of the guests as they arrived, and escort them to the library where Domenica would bring them a bowl of cool, scented water and a freshly laundered hand towel.

Fra Luca stepped from the carriage wearing the brown robe and hood of the Franciscan order, bound with a cream-colored cincture knotted in three places. He carried a woven sack, which I knew to contain proofs of a new book on which he and Leonardo had been collaborating.

I introduced myself as Leonardo's assistant, whereupon he ruffled my hair and said, "Jupiter's beard! So this is the young Latin scholar who writes like an angel and paints like the Devil. I have heard much from Leonardo."

I blushed and said, "Nemo sine vitio est," no one is without fault. He laughed heartily. "And not without wit, I see!"

Upon hearing the voice of his old friend, Leonardo hurried through the reception with his arms outstretched. "Luca, Luca, it has been too long!" He embraced his friend warmly. They then held each other at arm's distance as if they could not believe their eyes, and walked into the library where Fra Luca began spreading out the pages of their book.

"Look, Leonardo, how beautiful! The engraver has done justice to your illustrations, do you not agree?"

Leonardo nodded as he turned the pages, but I could see he was disappointed. Perhaps not disappointed but determined to improve the quality in future printings. Fra Luca, being a mathematician and not an artist, could not discriminate between journeyman work and true mastery. Leonardo refused to cast a shadow over this sparkling moment, so he merely smiled and changed the topic.

"Luca, you must tell me of your recent travels in the Veneto. Let us sit in the garden while you regale me with your stories."

I took my leave. As I did so, I saw Pagolino through the window, leading Fra Luca's horse up Via Spiga to the stables. Pago was an excellent groom, perhaps the only one in Milan that Leonardo would trust with his stable. He never pulled on the horses' mouths or let them stand in water, and always made certain they had the proper blankets on cold nights.

The next guest to arrive was Marliani, who came on foot, as he lived close by in central Milan. He was short and stout with a trimmed beard and oval glasses, which made him look more like a prominent merchant than a doctor. He blinked once and said, "My name is Alvise da Marliano. And who, pray, are you?"

"I am your servant," I said, bowing. "Count Francesco Melzi of Vaprio, a student of Leonardo da Vinci."

"Ah," he said. "Then I have come to the right address."

I assured him he had, and escorted the doctor into the library. "If you wish," I said, "you can join the master and Fra Pacioli in the garden." He thanked me and passed through the dining room into the courtyard.

A loud knocking called me back to the reception. I opened the door and found Bramante and Bramantino just outside on the street, arguing about something they saw on the exterior of the building. I invited them in, yet they ignored me as if I were a mere annoyance that would soon disappear of its own accord. I waited until they agreed to disagree, then repeated my words of welcome. They seemed surprised to see a person standing in front of them.

"My dear boy," said Bramante, finally focusing on me. "You must pardon our rudeness. We were just discussing the fenestration of your building, which in our experience is unique."

"You said 'impertinent,'" corrected Bramantino.

"I may have, my friend, but only in the heat of argument."

I smiled politely and gestured them inside. They followed me past the stairs and into the library, where they were drawn with evident interest to the proofs lying on the table.

"Messers," I interrupted.

Their heads come up in unison, two question marks with hair.

"These are the pages from a newly printed edition of 'Divina proportione.' Would you like to join the authors, along with Dr. Marliani, in the garden? They are eager to see you."

At that moment I heard a brisk tapping, so I excused myself and hurried to answer the door. Before me stood Galeazzo Sanseverino, a tall man with a crooked nose and a scar below his left temple. His hair was gray, and so were his eyes. I had never seen a sadder, more intelligent face. I introduced myself and led him straight to the garden, to the delight of the other guests. They rushed over and took turns embracing him.

"Domenica," called Leonardo. "Bring the aquarosa to the garden!" Within minutes she appeared, smiling, with a tray of goblets and a carafe of pale liquid—a mixture of rosewater, lemon juice, Cyprus powder, and alcohol. On the surface floated a blanket of rose petals.

"That cook of yours is such a sweet woman," said Bramantino. "I'll wager she was a beauty in her day."

"She once sliced the throat of a French soldier who tried to steal

an egg," said Leonardo.

The men turned toward the kitchen with newfound respect. I myself felt a shiver.

"Leonardo," said the doctor, taking a sip of aquarosa. "It is good to meet again after so long. Has it been ten years? I knew you before you could grow a beard. And now look at you. The very visage of a wise old man!"

"It's true, Marliani," said Bramante to Marliani. "And I knew you when you could still see your feet." This produced laughter from all the guests, including Marliani.

"Bramante," said Galeazzo, "what brings you to the north from Rome? I understand you have a contract with Julius to rebuild the Basilica. Does he know you are in Milan talking treason with the likes of us?"

"He does not, and I wish you would kindly keep it to yourself. As far as Julius knows, I am here only to enlist the services of my young friend Bramantino in decorating the papal apartments. If he knew I was sharing aquarosa with a cousin of Sforza, he would instantly give my position to Michelangelo."

Bramantino snorted. "They deserve each other. Julius will keep Michelangelo on a string for the rest of his life with that monumental folly called a tomb. For his part, Michelangelo will torture Julius to the end of his days with his constant demands for money. And now Julius has shut the purse to Michelangelo and diverted his funds to Bramante. They are like two fighting dogs who have roped themselves together for eternity. It is all too droll."

"I heard that Julius refused to let the people kiss his feet on Good Friday," said Marliani, "on the grounds that it would be too painful. His skin is covered with lesions from syphilis, I am told."

"Syphilis is a disease very fond of priests," said Fra Luca, shaking his head. "Especially rich priests."

"Especially rich priests with a taste for men," added Marliani. "I understand that Michelangelo likes to play that Florentine game as well."

I glanced at Leonardo, who showed no expression.

What did he mean, "Florentine game"? Was Marliani implying Michelangelo and Julius the Second were gay? That they were sexually involved? What's the connection to Florence?

8VO_37

ARTIE: Peter, the most damaging epithet one could throw at an adversary was Florentine, since Florence was widely reputed to be a hotbed of homosexuality.

SCARLETT: Hotbed!

ARTIE: You'll remember that Leonardo was jailed for sodomy in his youth, an experience that altered his behavior toward authority. Perhaps this explains why he said nothing in response to Marliani's remark. In the Renaissance, the word Florentine could be used as a synonym for homosexual, a fact that undoubtedly fed his discomfort with his own heritage.

SCARLETT: What about Julius and Michelangelo? An item?

ARTIE: Hmm. It's difficult to discount the possibility that Julius harbored repressed feelings for Michelangelo, given that the young artist had an animal intensity that many found charismatic. Yet there's no record of an explicit sexual relationship. Julius fathered several children with mistresses before becoming pope, and was considered virile, if not manly, by most in his generation. Certainly, his coarse manner and humorless conversation did not contribute to an overall impression of homosexuality. Perhaps life in the Vatican made it difficult to consort with women, so he took what was available.

SCARLETT: Sounds like a charmer.

ARTIE: He was known as *Il Terribile* to his friends, if that helps. Peter, I think you'll find this next scene intriguing.

After a brief pause, Bramantino turned to Leonardo and said, "I under-stand you do not care much for Michelangelo, but you must admit he brings a dramatic expression to his figures. His work on the tomb, and the chapel ceiling before it, is quite impressive."

"Oh, I admit he is a sincere and energetic artist," said Leonardo quick-ly. "But my wish for him is to pay more attention to what activates the muscles beneath the skin. Unless the body to which they belong is in a state of exertion, or under great strain, there is no need to exaggerate them equally. The artist is then in danger of producing a sack of walnuts instead of a human being."

"A sack of walnuts!" exclaimed Marliani.

"Do you not agree, Doctor, that a painting or sculpture should indi-cate what lies beneath the surface?"

"I was merely reflecting that a sack of walnuts would go well with this rose-flavored drink. My appetite quickened with the mere mention of food."

"My good Marliani!" said Leonardo. "Let us adjourn to the kitchen to see what may await us."

The air in the courtyard was growing cool, and the guests were pleased to follow the two men into the house. In the kitchen, Lorenzo had just lit the fire for the spit, and as the heat was building up, the gears began to turn.

"Leonardo, what magic animates this machine?" asked Bramante. "The roast appears to be turning itself." The others crowded around with curiosity, especially Marliani.

"The principle is simple, my good Donato. The heat from the fire rises upward past the meat into the funnel. As it compresses inside the funnel, it forces a set of gears to turn, which then turns the spit. The greater the heat, the greater the speed of turning. In this way the meat cooks evenly, and is less likely to burn. It makes an improvement over cranking by hand, does it not?"

"What a marvelous invention!" cried Luca. "I could easily calculate

the cooking time by counting the turns per minute, and create a table to account for various cuts and sizes of meat. Perhaps our next book should be a cookbook."

"Perhaps it should, my dear Luca. And we would undoubtedly expand the girth of our good friend the doctor." Leonardo winked at Marliani.

"I would be happy to assist with the testing," said Marliani.

I filled their glasses from the carafe, and before long they drifted into the studio where they continued their reminiscences.

"My dear Galeazzo," said Luca, "we were saddened to hear the news of your cousin, the good Duke. God rest his immortal soul. He brought us together, and together none of us could save him. Our powers were too weak. We are only glad that you yourself are free of that foul Touraine prison."

"Ah," said Galeazzo with a sigh, "perhaps they grew tired of my poor Italian wit. But our dear Ludovico. After eight years he was half-mad from captivity. He felt in his heart there was no chance of release. I believe it was the lack of hope, not the imprisonment, that killed him in the end. First his spirit died, then his mind, and finally his body."

"Such a sadness," said Bramante. "None of his works were completed, including the giant horse he had commissioned from you, Leonardo. I watched in disgust as the Gascon bowmen used it for target practice."

"Let us drink to the memory of the Duke," said Leonardo, raising his goblet. "And to the memory of our dear friend Giacomo Andrea, the first of us to die at the hands of the French."

"Beheaded and quartered in the castle courtyard, was he not?" said Marliani, his hand caressing his throat. "Such a good man, Giacomo, a magnificent architect. And no one could intercede on his behalf?"

"Oh, many of us tried," said Bramante. "But the French were persuaded he was a close conspirator of the Duke. He was not, of course, but their minds were fixed upon the matter."

The guests murmured their toasts and drained the balance of their *drinks. I collected the cups and brought them to the kitchen. When I returned, I found the group admiring the two Virgins in the fading light of the southwest-facing windows.*

"And the Confraternity was still not satisfied?" Bramantino said.

"They were not!" said Leonardo. "They refused to let me do the work as planned. Whereupon I presented a new composition with the Virgin Mary kneeling over the infant Jesus, whilst a different angel with beautifully rendered wings looked over his shoulder. They rejected this new version as well. Instead, they asked me to return to the first angel—without the pointing hand that they themselves had insisted on!"

Bramante shook his head in disbelief. "And what, pray tell, did you do then?"

"I complied, my dear Donato. And here is the result."

To my own humble eye, the second version on the right seemed richer and more assured than the left, employing the same techniques of chiaroscuro and sfumato that Leonardo had been teaching me.

Hues like jewels, made from pigments ground by Ambrogio's brother Evangelista, gave it the supernatural appearance of a church window, as if the panel had been fashioned from colored glass and not painted on wood. The interplay of light and shadow, the minute observation of plant life, the laws of anatomy, the mechanics of drapery, the spirals of female hair—which he compared to the eddies in a stream—combined to form a silent symphony to the Virgin Mother as if she were Nature herself.

With equal love and attention, he had formed the dimples in the infant's elbow, the crevices in the ancient rocks, the veins in the iris petals, and the shimmering surface of a distant spring. My heart swelled when I realized anew my good fortune at being his student.

"Leonardo," said Galleazo from a distance, "what is this panel over here?" The last rays of the sun fell upon a small half-length portrait of a woman.

"It is nothing," said Leonardo.

"In that case, would you sell it to me? It would look well on my wall next to your other works."

"I fear it is not finished, my dear Galeazzo. I can apply my brush to it only in stolen minutes, of which I have very few these days."

"Of course, my good friend. You have an eager patron whensoever you wish," said Galeazzo with a courtly bow.

Leonardo looked distinctly uncomfortable. I quickly announced that dinner would commence in the dining room.

EDITOR'S EMAIL

Am I crazy, or was that the *Mona Lisa*? The same *Mona Lisa* that ten million people pay to see every year. And Leonardo said, "It is nothing"?

8VO_38

ARTIE: Indeed, Peter, I thought we might find the *Mona Lisa* there. It seems to have been a personal project, not a commission, though it may have started out as one. Whatever Leonardo's reasons for painting it, they were not related to the output of the studio.

Salaì often referred to the painting as La Gioconda, the joking woman—a pun on the woman's smile and her husband's last name, Giocondo. Perhaps Salaì was jealous of the time Leonardo had spent with her. Some historians say the beautiful Lisa Gherardini—her actual name—sat for Leonardo once a week for a year whilst he was in Florence painting *The Battle of Anghiari*.

Based on the interchange between Galeazzo and Leonardo, we can surmise that, for some reason, the subject of the *Mona Lisa* was out of bounds for Leonardo.

SCARLETT: Leo and Mona had something going on.

ARTIE: Perhaps, but what? A friendship? A romance? A purely professional relationship? If the painting was not a commission, what was the purpose of it? Did he paint other works for the Giocondo family that didn't survive? And why did he make so many drawings and paintings of similar-looking women in similar poses over the years? I thought it was telling that Melzi changed the subject. He moved the guests into the dining room before the last one had even arrived.

The room was alive with candlelight, reflecting off the surfaces of the cutlery, the vessels, and the pewter plates that had been expertly arranged by Lorenzo and Domenica. These gleaming objects gained in elegance when set against the magnificent backdrop of Giampietrino's linen tablecloth, embroidered in metallic thread with the emblem of the Academia.

Leonardo had made the candles himself by carving wax heads of the absent members, including the Duke of Milan, architect Giacomo Andrea, theologian Fra Domenico Ponzone, painter Giovanni Boltraffio, and author Gasparé Visconti, who died shortly before the Duke was captured.

"Poor Visconte," said Leonardo. "His death marked the death of an epoch. But at least we can eat in the remembered presence of our dear old friends, whose bright light still shines within us."

The members were delighted by the preparations, especially Bramante and Bramantino, who would soon be engaged in the creation of elegant rooms for Pope Julius and were eager for inspiration. Bramante pointed to Giampietrino's tablecloth and whispered something to Bramantino, who nodded in appreciation.

Leonardo introduced me as his youngest pupil, explaining that I was joining the table as his secretary, and was eager to record their conversation if the members would be kind enough to permit it. I waved my notebook, and they readily assented.

"Ah, so the young Francesco is your Titus Livius," said Luca. "May the Holy Ghost sharpen your quill, my son, for the words will fly. Is your pen filled with honest ink?"

"Veritas odit moras," I said.

Luca leaned toward Leonardo and said quietly: "Truth hates delay. Your pupil is not without a quick mind." He raised his goblet toward me with a wink. He then stood up and led a prayer thanking the Lord for our good fortune in finding ourselves together this evening, and for the bounty which soon would grace our table.

As if by prearrangement, Lorenzo and Salaì entered with four bottles of white wine, a Malvasia di Candia from Leonardo's own vineyard, to fill our cups.

The pouring was interrupted by a knock at the door. Lorenzo set his bottles on the side table and attended to it, signaling to Pagolino through the window. Within minutes a tall figure appeared in the doorway of the dining room, wearing a long cloak made of oak galls, and a broad, flat hat with oak galls dangling from the brim.

"The Gall Nut!" cried several of the masters in unison.

He stepped into the light, grinning like a madman. "I apologize, my dear friends. It took me some time to find the proper attire." Lorenzo stepped from behind and relieved him of his odd-looking cloak and hat.

Leonardo rose to his feet and hugged this giant of a man most heartily. "Welcome, welcome, dear Astro! I was worried that you had written the wrong day!"

"It is the day of the reunion, is it not?"

Leonardo nodded.

"Then it is the right day!" he said joyfully, taking his seat at the table.

In the light of the candles I could see that his face was scarred in places, and his right eye sewn shut. His neck was bent sideways and his hair stuck out at unexpected angles. His clothing, while not as odd as his gall-nut overrobe, was the rumpled clothing of a peasant, fashioned from linen instead of fine wool and leather. It was said that he refused to wear the furs or skins of animals and would never so much as harm a flea.

"Astro, let us fill your goblet," said Leonardo, motioning to Salaì, who smiled broadly. Salaì and Zoroastro had a history of playing pranks together, which had forged a longstanding bond between them.

When the conversation grew quiet, Domenica and Lorenzo entered with the antipasto: roasted carrots with cinnamon, asparagus, braised and fried with saffron and leek, and blanched mountain mushrooms with onion and spices. To everyone's delight, Leonardo had twisted the vegetables into miniature dragons, devils, and chimeras, as if Hell itself had been unleashed onto the table.

"I am not certain who will eat and who will be eaten!" said Fra Luca.

"If they breathe fire on you," said Leonardo, filling Luca's cup, "douse your tongue with this."

Luca shook with laughter. He and the others devoured the devilish creatures with obvious pleasure, and indeed found the need to quench their thirst between bites.

Salaì circled the table, recharging all the cups except for mine. I knew he resented my privilege in dining with the masters while he was forced to serve me. Yet I only pretended to drink, on the grounds that a biographer must remain alert while working. As I dipped my pen, I recalled a wine-soaked night in Venice and my terrifying inability to keep the room from spinning upside down.

"Has anyone noticed the similarity of our friend Salaì to the woman in the painting?" said Bramantino. "It is quite remarkable."

Salaì snatched a kitchen towel from the side table and draped it over his head. He folded one wrist over the other and shaped his lips into an insipid half-smile. The room exploded with laughter. Zoroastro knocked over his goblet, so great was his mirth.

"The resemblance is uncanny," said Marliani, gasping. "One might think the model was Salaì himself!"

I glanced at Leonardo. He pretended to enjoy the joke, but his face turned a bright shade of crimson.

EDITOR'S EMAIL

The plot thickens! If there's one thread that runs through Leonardo's story, as you say, it's the mystery of the *Mona Lisa*. Who was she? Why did he hang onto her for so many years? How did she end up at the Louvre instead of the Uffizi or another Italian gallery? If we get answers to some of these questions, I can forecast an extra million copies.

One thing that confuses me, though. I don't get the inside joke about gall nuts. Do you have any information on Zoroastro's outfit?

8VO_39

SCARLETT: Ah. Now you're getting into my territory. Zoroastro was a metallurgist, but he was also the guy who ground the pigments for Leonardo's paintings, like *The Battle of Anghiari* in Florence, and the ink for his drawings. He would've been familiar with iron sulfate, or $FeSO_4$. It's the compound used to make iron-gall ink. When you combine iron sulfate with the tannic acid from oak galls, you get the permanent purple-black ink that was common all over Europe at the time.

Melzi's manuscript, for example, was written in iron-gall ink. You can see how the iron has rusted and the acids have eaten through the paper in certain places. Very typical of manuscripts from that period.

Allow me to get a little geeky on you. Oak galls are formed when a wasp lays its eggs on the branches or the leaves of an oak tree. The tree reacts by producing a small sphere, or gall nut, around each egg. Eventually, the egg hatches into a worm, and the worm eats its way out, leaving a small hole. The gall nut can then be processed for its tannins.

Astro was Leonardo's go-to guy for ink, paint, and chemical formulations, so he'd have had bushels of gall nuts to make the stuff with.

The story goes that Leonardo needed a nature-boy character for one of his theatrical events, so he cast his giant friend in the role. He stitched up a long robe of gall nuts and fashioned a matching gall-nut hat with the little balls hanging from the brim.

The play would have been staged for the Duke of Milan and members of his court, including the Academia crowd. So when Astro showed up at the dinner wearing the costume, the place cracked up.

ARTIE: Zoroastro was 48, but had the expression of a child. His skin was often covered with soot from his work in the forge. Some people thought him a simpleton, even a lunatic. And yet to Leonardo he was Maestro Tommaso.

SCARLETT: That's right. When Leonardo wanted to cast a giant bronze horse for the Duke of Milan, he called on Astro. When he wanted pigments that could resist erosion, he called on Astro. When he wanted a test pilot for one of his flying machines, he also called on Astro.

Astro was totally committed to Leonardo's quest for human flight. A couple years earlier he volunteered to fly a prototype of the ornithopter in the hills above Florence. He launched it from the top of Monte Ceceri, flapping madly, then face-planted a thousand yards down the mountain. He broke his leg, too, which may explain the bockety-bockety walk.

ARTIE: One might think this would have discouraged him from flying again, but it did not. He begged Leonardo to repair the machine and give it another go.

Now, shall we return to the party?

When the laughter subsided, Donato Bramante turned to me and said, "My good Francesco, please lend me your quill." On a blank page of my notebook, he drew from memory a simple outline of the woman on the small painted panel in the main studio. "Here is what I noticed about the painting."

He drew a vertical line starting at the top of the woman's forehead, down through her nose and her mouth, all the way to the point where her hands were crossed. He then drew three horizontal lines across the parting of her hair, her eyes, and her mouth. "See how these are equidistant."

Next, he connected these lines to make a six-pointed star that centered on the place between her eyebrows. He drew a circle that connected the points of the star, whereupon it defined the right side of her hair. "Notice, despite this symmetry, that the main vertical line is positioned to the left of the center of the panel."

Marliani and Zoroastro peered at the page.

"Do you not see the sacred symmetry?" said Bramante. "And do you not see the violation of it with the asymmetric positioning of the figure? Leonardo's painting succeeds through its architecture. Great architecture mixes symmetry with anomaly, and here we have both in perfect tension." He closed my book and slapped it down on the table as if it were a verdict.

"I do not disagree with you, Bramante," said Fra Luca. "For without mathematics there can be no art. And with nothing but mathematics there can be no art. Mathematics is the mind of God, and we are but human. Every human endeavor must contain a flaw or it cannot be beautiful. We are not perfect beings. What sayest thou, Leonardo?"

Leonardo smiled and looked toward me. He then leaned down and gave Mimi a pat on the head. She wagged her tail in appreciation. I quietly reached for the book and extracted the quill from Bramante's hand.

Marliani said, "Euclid believed that mathematical proofs should be judged on their aesthetic qualities, not merely on their practicality. Do you agree, dear Luca?"

By now I was writing furiously.

"I agree that mathematical truths have a spiritual beauty. That is why I became a Franciscan. I wanted to speak to God in his own language."

"Oh," said Bramantino, "does God keep account books?"

"You jest, dear Tino, but do not underestimate the good that proper accounts can bring to the world. Regular accounting preserves friendships."

Leonardo coughed loudly and glared at Salaì with particular meaning, raising an eyebrow for emphasis. Salaì quickly looked away as if he were listening for Domenica.

"And yet," said Galeazzo, "too many men of business confuse plus and minus with right and wrong. They believe their riches are proof of their rightness."

Bramantino said, "Perhaps, but Luca shall have no argument from me. There is certainly beauty in accounting. Who could fault the perfection of a column of figures summed up correctly, or the usefulness of *charting the inward and outward flows of funds? The master Vitruvius believed that beautiful architecture embodied the qualities of solidity, usefulness, and delight. I myself am delighted when my accounts, not only my buildings, prove solid and useful."*

Fra Luca leaned back in his chair and clasped his hands over his brown robe. "You speak truly, Bramantino. The beauty of mathematics lies in its precision. Equations," he said, "articulate relationships. They define truths that exist beyond mere opinion or interpretation. Mathematical truths, like artistic beauty, evoke timeless harmonies that transport us to the realm of enchantment. One need not die to experience the infinite."

Just then Lorenzo and Salaì brought more trays to the table: boiled eggs stuffed with cooked egg yolks, raisins, saffron, marjoram, and mint leaves, alongside a sauce of sweet-and-sour must and ginger. The members lunged at these as if a pack of wolves.

"Fra Luca," said Marliani, his mouth full of egg, "we may die anyway from this enchanted and certainly poisonous food. As a doctor, I cannot recommend that any of you eat this wicked concoction. The vilest serpent in Eden would hesitate to recommend it."

"And yet you must admit that it sorts well with the Malvasia," said Bramante.

Before the doctor could respond, Salaì refilled his goblet.

EDITOR'S EMAIL

If I didn't know better, I'd say Salaì is trying to get the doctor drunk. Every time Marliani turns around, someone is filling his glass. Same with the others, come to think of it. What's going on?

8VO_40

ARTIE: Scarlett and I had the same impression. They seem to be drinking a lot, with the exception of Leonardo and his staff. Shall we press on and see?

"*My good doctor,*" *said Leonardo.* "*I understand you have called on Her Ladyship, Lucrezia Borgia, in recent months. Is she doing well after the birth of her son, Ercole II?*"

I held my breath. I feared the others might know we had seen her more recently. Moreover, it seemed to me a breach of etiquette to ask a doctor about a patient, especially one so prominent. The others looked up from their plates expectantly. Bramantino's face wore an expression of concern, but the doctor seemed to think it a fair question.

"*She is doing well, praise God, and so is her little heir. But she has suffered heartache from the misfortune of another Ercole—Ercole Strozzi, her friend at court. He was found murdered in the streets of Ferrara.*"

The guests stopped eating and stared at Marliani. Leonardo gave me a sharp look as if to say, "*Silence.*" *I put my head down and kept writing.*

"*Indeed, my friends. Shocking. He had just married Barbara Torelli when a band of assassins caught him out alone and stole his life. He was stabbed mercilessly, I am told. It is such a shame. Ercole would not have hurt a mouse.*"

"*Was there a reason given?*" *said Bramante.*

"*No reason was found, and the assassins have not been caught.*"

"*Dear doctor,*" *said Leonardo,* "*did Her Ladyship say anything on the topic?*"

"*She was in a foul mood that day,*" *he said.* "*She had just received the scholar Pietro Bembo, and became effusive about her distaste for octavos, of all things. She believed they would undermine the Church, destroy the universities, and destabilize the powerful families of Italy.*

"*She felt it was beneath one's dignity to express lofty thoughts outside the courts. Scholars, poets, and historians may share their ideas with their patrons, but to disseminate their works to audiences who are not ready for them is unseemly, and a sin against God. She said the printers of these books should be arrested and given ten drops on the strappado.*"

The masters looked around, waiting to see who would speak.

Bramante shrugged. "*Ovid might have agreed with her.*" *He said,*

'Bene vixit qui bene latuit.'"

Luca leaned over toward Leonardo. "He lived well who hid well."

"And yet we know him only from his books," said Leonardo. "We are indeed fortunate he did not stay hidden. The same can be said about Pythagoras, Plato, Euclid, Aristotle, Pliny, Plutarch, Homer, Virgil, Bacon, and our dear Dante. And now, as with the books of Dante, anyone who reads can read them in Italian. Learning need no longer be confined to Latin scholars."

Fra Luca snorted. "I have often been asked if universities stifle theology students," he said. "In my view they don't stifle enough of them. We should be glad they can no longer claim a monopoly on learning."

Leonardo emitted a high-pitched laugh. The room soon grew animated with the topic of education in a time of easily obtainable books. Domenica came in with a frictella made from apples. Salaì poured more wine.

"I am surprised to hear Lucrezia has turned against Bembo," said Bramante. "They were very close."

"Perhaps too close," said Marliani with a wink. "More than once I had to examine her for, shall we say, female irregularities. Her Ladyship had taken enormous risks with Bembo, even if their relationship was merely courtly as she claimed. The Este, as you know, have a reputation for ruthlessness."

Marliani hesitated. He looked up and down the table and continued in a loud whisper: "Many years ago, in the Torre Marchesana, Niccolo d'Este beheaded his adulterous second wife," gesturing with his thumb across his throat, "along with her son."

Lucrezia, it seemed, was attracted to danger. She reminds me of someone else I know.

SCARLETT: Surely not! Moi?

ARTIE: She and Bembo had been exchanging torrid love letters for six years. Scarlett and I found a number of these in the Ambrosian

Library in Milan. In one of them, after Lucrezia had suffered a mis-carriage, Bembo wrote this to her:

> *If during this period you chance to find your ears ringing, it will be because I am communing with all those dark things and horrors and tears of yours, or else writing pages about you that will still be read a century after we are gone.*

Lord Byron called these the prettiest love letters in the world. And indeed, centuries later we're still reading them.

In addition to the letters, the two lovers used Ercole Strozzi to set up various trysts around Ferrara. Lucrezia must have known she was being watched. After all, she was still the Este's best hope for an heir.

SCARLETT: Yeah, but what was that rant? Ten drops on the *strappado* for printing a book? Peter, the strappado was a punishment for breaking censorship laws. You got a stiff fine, several years in prison, and tor-ture by strappado. They bound your hands behind your back with a long rope and dropped you from a tall contraption to dislocate your shoulders. It's still de rigeur in S&M circles—without the dislocation, one would hope.

ARTIE: In those days it wasn't about kinky sex. It was about using the force of the law to preserve the status quo. The power structure then—same as today, if we're honest—was driven by three questions: Who gets to learn? Who gets to choose who gets to learn? And who gets to choose who gets to choose? The printing press was a threat to the elites of the day. It had to be controlled. The censorship laws en-sured that any author who offended an aristocrat was branded a traitor.

SCARLETT: Right, so authors and publishers like Bembo and Aldo came up with a slick workaround. They affected a snobby disdain for the printing process. They were *Educated Gentlemen* who brought beauty and enlightenment to respected readers, right? The dirty, sweaty, noisy work of making books was left to less sensitive souls. Like Griffo.

And yet, that same dirty-sweaty-noisy process was the bridge from the Dark Ages to the Enlightenment. Once you had printing, you could spread science. Once you had science, you could invent any number of things, some of which were bound to shake the halls of power right down to their foundations.

Theologians viewed mass-produced books and scientific experiments as subversive—attacks on the Church. Widespread reading would sow chaos, they said. And it did. The safest place for a publisher to stand was as far away from a printing press as possible. Me, a publisher? No, no, no. A scholar!

EDITOR'S EMAIL

Point taken. Modern education, publishing, religion—all invented during the Renaissance. These same institutions are now under attack from new technologies like online learning, digital self-publishing, and DIY video. It's as if a 500-year cycle were repeating itself. Our own company is suffering from this same disruption. Traditional bookstores are disappearing and authors are taking their books straight to readers. Amazon is the new Aldine Press, only much, much bigger. We complain about it every day, but the truth is, the revolution caught us flat-footed. You'd think, as book people, we would have seen it coming.

Which begs the question: Why didn't you two simply publish the book yourselves instead of coming to us with it?

8VO_41

SCARLETT: Knock, knock. We're on the lam, remember? We can't just sign up with Amazon. We'd need to open a bank account. Even a numbered bank account can be frozen by Interpol.

ARTIE: Peter, please excuse my colleague. We've been under considerable pressure—moving from place to place, exchanging rental cars, altering our appearance every day.

The true reason we chose Harker is that we needed the distribution and marketing muscle of an established firm with a strong legal team. But we also chose Harker to get you. We saw you as a fellow traveler.

SCARLETT: Well, there's that. Sorry to snap at you, Peter. Despite being suspicious, judgy, and vengeful, I can also be reactive.

ARTIE: On the subject of publishing, we think you'll find this next chapter rather stimulating.

SCARLETT: Artie always knows when to change the subject.

ARTIE: Yes, well.

"Indeed, Marliani," said Bramante, "we have heard these stories about the Este. And about the Borgia, too. Some have called Lady Lucrezia the Whore of Babylon, but I must say that she runs her state with capable wisdom in her husband's absence."

"Competence and ruthlessness are not incompatible," said Leonardo. "The many hours I have spent with her brother Cesare persuaded me that the most sublime intelligence can coexist with the most violent impulses."

"I myself feel safer with his bones in a grave," said Fra Luca. "He was much too bloodthirsty for my taste. He took far too much and gave far too little. In the eyes of the Church, his accounts did not add up."

The other guests murmured agreement. The fragrance of the roasting meat had begun to act on their senses. The sound of knives heralded its imminant arrival. Dr. Marliani moved his cutlery from side to side, anticipating the sweet and savory flesh that his nose assured him was coming.

"Leonardo, I understood from Sforza that you prefer to eat plants," he said. "Did I understand wrongly?"

"My good doctor, you are correct. In my philosophy, there is more beauty in a single broccoli, more dignity in a carrot, than in a dozen golden

pots filled with flesh and bones."

"But surely one should not have to choose. Why, pray, have you given up meat as if Lent were eternal?"

Leonardo paused. "My dear Marliani, I do not wish to impose my views on my good friends. I can only say that my experiments with Nature have shown me that animals are sensitive to pain in the same way humans are. My conscience will not allow me to inflict harm on them, nor pay others to do so on my behalf."

"But Leonardo," said Bramantino with a wink, "are you so sure that plants cannot feel pain?"

"You jest, but I have seen them recoil when wounded, and I have seen them send messages from leaf to leaf and branch to branch that they may protect or repair themselves. Still, I do not believe they are designed for pain. Creatures that feel pain are given wings or legs with which to escape it."

"And yet you have prepared a hearty leg of meat for us."

"My dear Bramantino, I would not deprive my guests of a proper second course, although I myself will eat vegetables. The wild boar that shall soon grace our table was speared by Salaì's father, Pietro, who runs my vineyard. The beast had been tearing up the very vines that brought you this heavenly Malvasía."

"Then we shall feel no remorse!" cried Bramantino, raising his goblet. "To the beast who brought us dinner. We salute you!" The guests clinked their cups, and when they were drained, Salaì recharged them with Sangiovese.

Lorenzo and Domenica entered the room with two glittering trays, one with slices of spit-roasted boar in a pomegranate wine sauce and the other with boiled and sliced turnips, alternated with layers of soft cheese. Marliani's eyes flickered, bright as candles. He raised his eyes heavenward and crossed himself in gratitude for the good Lord's abundance. All conversation ceased except for groans and grunts, and the clatter of knives on plates.

When they had eaten well, all the masters leaned back in their chairs, all except Zoroastro, who had done nothing but eat since he arrived. His tunic was stained with splashes of wine and vinegar, and his hands were oily, as if he had used them in place of utensils.

"Tell me, Leonardo," said Bramante, "what was the process you used to make the illuminations for 'Divina proportione'?"

"They are woodcuts designed from my drawings, dear Donato. But I am now experimenting with a newer, more refined method. Would you like to see it?"

Bramante said he would. Leonardo motioned for Lorenzo to bring the materials into the dining room. He returned with a small easel that held a copper plate and placed it on the sideboard. He then laid five proofs upside down beside it. All the masters except Zoroastro crowded around to look. Lorenzo brought over a candelabra for extra light. Bramante leaned forward with ferocious interest.

"As you see," said Leonardo, "there are four engravings of the same object, a human heart. Each is printed in a different color." He turned them over one by one. "These engravings are far more delicate and refined than the ordinary woodcuts in 'Divina proportione,' because they are etched into copper plates, like the one you see here, using a ruby-tipped stylus.

"And now, my good friends, when the four images are printed one atop another, they appear thus." He turned over the fifth proof and the guests drew a sharp breath. The heart was so lifelike that it seemed to be pumping blood. His calligraphic precision of line and the fine shading of his cross hatches made the image more real than reality itself.

Bramante appeared to have no words. "But—but—how is it done?" he said. "If there are only four colors, how can it glow with every hue from Nature's own spectrum?"

"It is like a painting, is it not?" said Leonardo. "And yet it is not a painting. In a painting, the colors are mixed on a palette before being applied to a surface. In color engraving, the mixing occurs afterward, in the mind of the viewer."

Bramante and the others seemed puzzled.

Leonardo explained further. "When in the distance you see a garden of red and yellow roses, the effect is not one of red and yellow, but of orange. And when you see a field of yellow and blue crocuses, the effect is not of yellow and blue, but of green. The flowers are too far away to be seen in their individual colors. Instead, they blend together in one's eye to make a third color. It is the same with color engraving." He handed Bramante a magnifying glass.

"It is remarkable," he said, peering closely at the delicate cross hatches. "Not like a painting at all."

"A painting cannot be reproduced indefinitely like a printed page," said Leonardo. "It cannot be copied like a book, where every copy has the same value as the original. In that way its utility is limited."

Bramante nodded slowly.

"The first task of the painter is to make a flat image appear as a lifelike object in relief, standing out from the surface. This is the soul of painting. But now it can be the soul of printing as well."

I stared at Leonardo's bulino lying on the easel, a silver snake with a coiled tail, awaiting the return of the artist's hand, longing to be brought back to life, impatient to once again sink its ruby fang into copper flesh.

I would soon become its keeper.

EDITOR'S EMAIL

A silver snake with a coiled tail? That's your graver! The one you have in your hair! I can't believe it was just lying around the townhouse like a piece of junk. You should hold onto that thing.

8VO_42

SCARLETT: Yeah, I'll bet my auntie's undies it's the same graver. And I was ready to sell it for pizza money.

Artie, I have to come clean. Peter's rattling my cage. I told him I was having second thoughts about our mission. I was thinking about scrapping the whole thing and selling the graver for cash. Don't worry. When we finish the translation and validation, I'll hand it over with the manuscript. I may be a thief, but I do have standards.

ARTIE: That's my girl. Don't let down the side. We all know there's a soul in there somewhere trying to get out.

SCARLETT: Artie, the hopeless romantic.

ARTIE: Speaking of souls, Peter, this next chapter reveals some of Leonardo's views on the religious beliefs of the time. It's remarkable that men holding such different views could remain friends for so long. It's a tribute to their shared spirit of inquiry that they could discuss their differences with equanimity instead of throwing food at each other.

"This is indeed a feast!" cried Marliani as Lorenzo and Salaì brought in trays of cheese and fruit, and bowls of sugared almonds. The guests hastily resumed their seats. Marliani rubbed his hands whilst Salaì poured more wine to accompany the cheese.

Galeazzi spooned a mound of almonds onto his plate next to a slice of aged cheese dripping with honey. He said to Leonardo, "I understand you have recently returned from Venice. How are things on the Rialto?"

"I am afraid Venice trembles on the precipice of war, my good friend. The League of Cambrai threatens to enter Venetian territory, and the Council of Ten is at a loss about how to stop them."

"And that was the cause of your visit?"

I looked at Leonardo, who glanced back at me. Our eyes locked for the briefest of moments.

"Not at all, my dear Galeazzi. I had an opportunity to continue my studies in human dissection. I made some drawings. Would you like to see them?"

"No, Maestro, no! Let us end our dinner with happier thoughts. I care not for nightmares on top of indigestion."

Marliani spoke through a mouthful of almonds: "I for one would take a great interest in your drawings. Perhaps you could show them to me another time." The doctor was beginning to slur his words. "I have always applauded your utter disregard for convention. Let the petty priests and bishops be damned!" he said, grinning like a fool at Fra Luca.

Luca shrugged. "The Church takes no official stand against it, except to express a concern that dissection may encourage grave-robbing. I trust your cadavers come from a reputable source, Leonardo?"

"They have not been buried, if that is what you mean."

"Then it is not desecration. As long as the soul has left the body, there is no difficulty. We must never interfere with a soul returning to God."

"Or to a lizard," said Zoroastro, rocking from side to side.

"My dear Astro," said Luca, "you are talking about reincarnation. The Church does not hold with such beliefs."

Leonardo tapped his cup. "Have you not heard about the man who tried to prove on the authority of Pythagoras that he had lived before?"

"I have not," said Luca, tilting his head.

"The second man would not accept his argument, so he said, 'As proof that I am right, I remember that you were a miller.' Whereupon the second man said, 'Ah, yes. Now I remember! You were the ass that carried my flour!'"

Bramante laughed so hard he knocked his goblet to the floor, splashing wine against the wall. Lorenzo rushed in to clean it before it could leave a stain.

"Maestro Ruinante is at it again," said Marliani, raising his hands and bringing them down to the table with a crash. "First the old Basilica, and now the house of Leonardo!"

Bramante caught Marliani's chair as he tipped back. "And who shall rebuild you, dear Doctor, when you collapse in a heap?"

"I shall," said Zoroastro, grinning. "Taxidermy is a particular talent of mine. I have a large collection of lizards and frogs."

Leonardo said, "I do not know if a lizard has a soul, but I can tell you this. By logic, the soul desires to stay with its body. The soul gives the body life, and the body gives the soul form. When the body dies, the soul therefore dies with it. A soul cannot be transferred to another body, like the title to a property, nor can it ascend to heaven as if a bird."

"But the Church believes the soul is immortal," said Galeazzo.

"One has to beware of beliefs," said Leonardo. "We cannot let our beliefs keep us from learning what we might find out."

"So you do not believe the body and soul are separate entities?" said Galeazzo.

"It is like these sculpted candles," said Leonardo, indicating the waxen heads on the table. "Just as the wax has a certain shape—here the likenesses of our absent friends—a living organism has the property of life, its soul. The wax is mere matter without its shape, and the shape cannot exist without the wax. They are inseparable. If you should melt down the wax, it would still be wax. But it would have no meaning or connection with its previous existence."

Luca frowned. "In your conception, physical life is the mansion of the soul, and death its eviction. There is no transmigration. Very well, Leonardo, but your theory attacks a core tenet of Church doctrine, the belief in life after death. Without the promise of immortality, the Church would lose many followers."

"I do not suggest immortality is impossible," said Leonardo. "On the contrary, one can receive a measure of immortality through one's deeds on Earth. The things we contribute to the world live on without us, do they not? If we behave badly, our children will suffer for many years. If we behave well, our children and our children's children will perpetuate our good deeds. Is that not a kind of immortality?"

"It is heresy! But I cannot refute it with logic. In your philosophy, a book such as 'Divina proportione' would lead to immortality more surely than dying in a state of grace. Perhaps publishing should become a sacrament!" said Luca. "Or perhaps I should have more wine." He pushed his glass toward Leonardo with a broad smile. Salaì appeared as if a ghost to fill it.

"To heresy!" cried Zoroastro, and the masters raised their glasses.

EDITOR'S EMAIL

Atheist or not, Leonardo doesn't seem like he's on board with the Church of Rome. And yet his best friend was a Franciscan friar. His other friend, Astro, believed in reincarnation—and who knows what else. You've said you don't believe in God, Scarlett, so I'm guessing eternal life is not on the agenda. What about you, Artie? Does religion hold any significance?

8VO_43

ARTIE: I'm not one to wear my religion on my sleeve, Peter. But I must say it doesn't seem irrational to imagine a second life based on the mysteries we encounter in this one. None of us knows exactly what's going on in this bedlam we call reality. That's why art is so important. It's the best tool we have for contending with the ineffable—that which defies logic. It's how we try to understand the parts of ourselves that science can't reach.

SCARLETT: Hooey. The way to contend with the ineffable is with effing science. Why believe something when you can find out about it?

Look, we're all gonna die. Leonardo was right. If you want to live forever, discover something. Contribute something. Teach something. Write a book. After most people die, we talk about them in the past tense. But if they've written a book, we talk about them in the present tense. To us they're still alive.

There's no empirical evidence proving life after death, except for the residue of our actions. Sorry, but I got too much of this metaphysical crap from my parents. There's no daddy in the sky waiting to give us a big hug. Time for the human race to grow up.

ARTIE: Finished?

SCARLETT: I feel much better.

ARTIE: And now, Peter, we can sit back and watch as Leonardo's little plan unfolds. The tongues of the guests have been loosened and soon the trap will spring shut.

Leonardo's smooth-coated terrier, Mimi, was sniffing under the table for errant scraps of meat. He picked her up and placed her on his lap, gently stroking her ears.

"Good Marliani," said Leonardo, "did you happen to see Pietro Bembo while visiting Ferrara?"

"He left before I arrived. However, on the subject of the soul, here is a coincidence. Her Ladyship Lucrezia showed me a beautiful medallion she wore over her bodice. A gold coin with an image of fire, engraved with the words, 'Est animum.'"

Said Bramante, "It is the spirit?"

"It is the soul," corrected the doctor.

"Hah!" said Bramante. "Of all people to claim one! Lucrezia knows less about the soul than I know of Latin. And yet some people describe her as pious. It is quite remarkable, I think, how easily we mistake beauty for goodness."

Marliani lowered his voice. "She confided to me that the inscription was recommended by Bembo, and that she wore it for his visit. I must say, despite her displeasure with their conversation, she seemed as giddy as a girl about the medallion. She could not wait to show it to Isabella."

"Isabella d'Este?" said Leonardo.

"You must know that the two have been locked in jealous combat ever since Lucrezia married Isabella's brother Alfonso. Who is the prettier? Who is the more elegant? Who has the better taste? Who owns the finest treasures? Did you know that Lucrezia commandeered Isabella's old bedchamber when she first arrived? She had it altered so that nothing remained of Isabella's childhood. Isabella retaliates by acquiring works from the greatest artists of Italy—Mantegna, Costa, Perugino—and making sure Lucrezia hears about it. She sends messages through her chamber maids."

"Is she still pestering you for a portrait, Leonardo?" said Galeazzo.

My master sighed. "She treats an artist like a monkey on a leash. I keep refusing her in the gentlest possible way, but she persists, using various acquaintances to intercede for her. I once made the mistake of drawing a sketch of Her Ladyship on a visit to Mantua, and now it hangs over me like the sword of Damocles. I find her shallow, vain, and given to tantrums when vexed. I shall never be rid of her."

Galeazzo's brow grew knotted. He appeared to be deciding whether to speak or stay silent.

"Leonardo," he finally said, "a fortnight ago, on my last visit to Mantua, Isabella approached me to write you a letter. I said you could no longer stand the sight of a brush, and that your days were entirely devoted to working on your notes. Naturally, she found this answer unsatisfactory. But as we spoke, I noticed she wore the same gold medallion that Marliani has described, an engraving of fire with the words, 'Est animum.' Is it not a remarkable coincidence?"

"Galeazzo," said Marliani, "the explanation is simple. Isabella found out that Bembo had given her a pretty medallion, so she had one made for herself. She cannot abide Lucrezia having anything she does not."

Leonardo turned to Bramante. "Donato, of all of us, you are the most versed in the works of Dante. What does 'The inferno' say about such petty behaviors?"

"Ah, yes, the Fourth Circle of Hell is reserved for avaricious people:

> *For all the gold that is beneath the moon,*
> *Or ever has been, of these weary souls*
> *Could never make a single one repose.'*

"Their punishment," said Bramante, "is to strive ceaselessly for meaningless trinkets, never satisfied and never getting a moment's rest."

"I see," said Leonardo. "And what do you make of this passage:

> *'See how mutilated I am;*

Before me, another weeps as well,
His face split from forehead to chin.'

"That is from the Ninth Circle. It warns that people who damage the rep-
utations of others will create harmful divisions in society. As their punish-
ment, they must weep for eternity with their faces split in two."

EDITOR'S EMAIL

Leonardo netted some rare fish in *that* chapter. A new character in the person of Isabella, the medallion that appears in two places at once, the poor slanderers who spend eternity in the ninth circle of hell. I have a feeling the master is making progress.

On another subject, ladies, I have a question related to our legal matter with Dickson. (I'll continue to use your name for him.) Did either of you sign an NDA?

8VO_44

SCARLETT: Of course we did. He's too cagey to hire anyone without a non-disclosure. Why should it matter? We haven't discussed him with anyone except you.

EDITOR'S EMAIL

If you check your agreement, it probably states that you can't discuss Dickson—or the assignment—with anyone, *including* me. The problem is, you already have. I'll let you know if it becomes an issue. Please tell me in your own words what the NDA says. No names.

8VO_45

[PAPER RATTLING]

SCARLETT: Okay, it says we're not allowed to blab about you know who. Or the objects. Or the location of the objects. Or the current owners of the objects. Or the nature and details of our arrangement. All output from the authentication process belongs to him. It's pretty draconian. I'm surprised it doesn't say we have to kill ourselves on completion of the work.

Can't your legal team work around this shit? You have some leverage. If he wants to acquire the painting, he won't make a big stink about the manuscript. Otherwise, we'll tell the world he's been looting the patrimony of the Italian people. There goes half his collection, along with a chunk of his company's brand.

Peter, now is probably a good time to tell you how much we appreciate your support. I know I can be difficult. And Artie tends to get nervous—

ARTIE: Alas, my first time in the international heist business.

SCARLETT: But we're learning on the job. Have you heard the definition of an entrepreneur? It's someone who dives into an empty swimming pool and invents water on the way down. That's us. A larceny startup.

ARTIE: Peter, this next chapter illuminates changing views about the nature of God in the Renaissance.

SCARLETT: There is no God.

ARTIE: Don't be cheeky. You're too young to have a closed mind, much less on a subject like religion. Shall we listen in?

"Leonardo," said Marliani, his eyelids drooping from drink, "I have always thought you a man who does not believe in Hell. You have no fear of dissecting the dead, nor of contradicting the Church, nor of…nor of…" he hiccoughed, "nor of many things."

"My good doctor," Leonardo said kindly, "I believe that men are capable of inventing whatever they wish, and if they wish to invent Hell, then they are more than capable of believing in it. I sometimes think that men

invented Hell as a weapon with which to bludgeon their enemies and control their wives."

Galeazzo laughed. "Oh, come now, Leonardo, surely you believe in a higher intelligence than that of men. There is a deep reverence in your paintings—the Virgins, the Madonnas, the Magi, The Last Supper. These works shine with an inner light, a light that must originate in your soul."

"All light comes from the sun, dear Galeazzo, or from the combustion of earthly materials. If there is light in my soul, I have not seen it."

"Light can also come from understanding, which comes from God. Your paintings have the radiance of the divine, which should prove to you that He exists."

"Surely God exists whether I believe in Him or not," said Leonardo. "He does not need help from me, nor does He need my devotion. I shall endeavor to express my reverence by studying Nature's creations. The universe is suffused with the power of life, and in studying life I have learnt to create. Perhaps the imitation of God's creativity is the highest form of worship."

"But man can never create as God creates," said Galeazzo. "Man cannot perform miracles, for example. He cannot change water into wine or raise the dead."

"We shall see." He winked at me, then turned to Astro. "Shall we prove our friend wrong with a man-made miracle?"

Astro rose and limped to the kitchen.

Bramantino leaned forward and whispered to the others, "Astro does not eat animals either. I once saw him cry when a fly died. A fly!"

He returned with his gall-nut hat and a tall glass with white wine, or perhaps it was vinegar.

Leonardo spoke as if to a theatre audience. "Our abilities are poor compared with those of God," he said majestically, "so we will attempt only a minor miracle. Astro, please demonstrate the raising of a copper coin."

Astro dropped a quattrino into the wine, whereupon it sank to the bottom. He touched the outside of the glass near the coin and slowly raised his finger upward. As if by magic, the coin followed his finger to the top of the glass. The guests were transfixed.

"Bravo!" said Luca. "A miracle indeed! What form of trickery is this?"

"It is not trickery," said Astro, gall nuts dancing on his hat, "but alchemy. I merely rubbed a small amount of magnetic powder on the coin, and another small amount on my finger. The coin had no choice but to rise upward."

"I must include this magic in my next book," said Luca. "Do you have more of that powder?"

"Of course. An alchemist keeps many such powders. I have another powder, made from certain mushrooms, that, when swallowed, gives one the visions of a saint. You would not need your Franciscan robes to visit the realm of the divine, Fra Luca! I can also take auspices from the positions of the stars, from decks of cards, from piles of dung, or from the livers of bats."

"Leonardo," said Galeazzo, gesturing toward Zoroastro, "do you hold with the beliefs of your gall-nut friend?"

"I hold all beliefs lightly, my dear Galeazzo. Although I do know the mushroom powder to be effective in parting the gates of Heaven. The priests would do well to ban such potions, or the faithful may no longer be willing to pay their tolls."

"I am not a priest," said Fra Luca. "I am a follower of St. Francis, a saint who had familiarity with mushrooms. Do you have any of that powder in your bag, dear Astro? I would fain sample it."

Astro stared at Luca as if he were mad. His face grew so rigid that the gall nuts on his hat stopped dancing. His one eye grew wide. With the speed of a conjurer he slammed a small wooden box onto the table.

"I do."

Fra Luca laughed and reached for the box. Within minutes all the guests, with the exception of myself, had taken a pinch of the powder in their wine.

"You must remember that the effect is not immediate," said Zoroastro.

Domenica entered with a large torta made from the cherries I had picked three days earlier. It was now decorated with a graceful spiral of rose petals. The guests admired it greatly, which pleased Domenica.

Salaì poured small cups of Moscato Passito and handed one to each guest. "From Valcalepio," he said. This was one of the wines Salaì had tried to cheat with. Leonardo narrowed his eyes at Salaì with remembered annoyance.

"Statistically, more Italians believe in God than do not," offered Bramante, his mouth full of torta. "I was told this by a census-taker in Rome."

"Statistically," said Luca, "Italians have one breast and one testicle. We must by wary of statistics, Donato. We must also be wary of superstitions such as augury, astrology, necromancy, and palm reading. They neither come from God, nor from science."

Zoroastro looked hurt, as if he suddenly realized his genius would not be appreciated in his lifetime.

"Superstitious beliefs are what killed the Duke," said Marliani, taking a bite. "Oh, yes, did you not know? Ludovico began to substitute augury for military strategy, and astrology for medical advice. After that, it was only a matter of time."

"Both he and his astrologer were imprisoned by the French," said Galeazzo. "Those were dark days."

Leonardo turned to me. I stopped writing. "Checco, what was that Latin saying about darkness?"

"In absentia luci, Tenebrae vincunt?" I offered.

"That is the one," said Leonardo. "In the absence of light, darkness prevails."

"Well remembered, young lad," said Fra Luca.

Salaì studied me with the eyes of a lynx. After a moment he walked up with a bottle of moscato, and seeing my cup still full, knocked it onto my notebook.

"Young lad," he said mockingly, "I am so sorry! Allow me to clean this up." He took his apron and smeared the ink all over the pages.

I glanced at the others sitting around the table. The doctor had closed his eyes with his head on his chest.

Bramante held a cherry between his finger and thumb, admiring it in the light.

Bramantino had arranged his own cherries into perfect rows on his serviette.

Galeazzo reached over to move one of Bramantino's cherries as if it were a chess piece.

Fra Luca and Leonardo conversed with great animation about the theories of Pythagoras, comparing his genius with that of Euclid.

Zoroastro stared straight ahead with his one eye wide, swaying slightly in his chair with a grin painted across his boyish, scarred face.

EDITOR'S EMAIL

Is this well known about Leonardo's circle? It sounds more like San Francisco than Milan. Personally, I'm too young to remember, but my mother was there. She doesn't remember, either. Leonardo doesn't come right out and say God doesn't exist, but he definitely has his own views on the subject. What's more interesting is that Luca Pacioli, a Franciscan friar, is so open to experimentation.

8VO_46

SCARLETT: We've been searching for evidence of psychoactive experiences in Leonardo's past, but so far, nada. If this account is correct, we can add drug-using to the growing list of descriptors—right after left-handed, gay, dyslexic, illegitimate, vegetarian, and atheist.

ARTIE: The ritualistic use of sacred mushrooms was long established in primitive societies. Indigenous people in Mesoamerica used psychoactive plants as a shortcut to the divine, very much as Leonardo implied. We know, because around this time Columbus's sailors brought back devotional stone carvings in the shapes of mushrooms.

SCARLETT: And if they brought back any actual mushroom spores,

Astro could have cultivated them. Right, Artie?

ARTIE: It's possible. A few years later, when the Spanish arrived in Mexico, they put an end to these mushroom cults. They complained that the Aztecs were communicating with the devil. The real reason was that hallucinogens undermined the hegemony of the Catholic priests. So they tried to substitute the Eucharist for mushrooms.

SCARLETT: Hah. Unleavened bread for psychedelic mushrooms? I don't care how many times you bless a slice of bread, it's a lousy substitute for psilocybin.

ARTIE: Peter, you must understand that we're only speculating. We can't verify Leonardo's use of hallucinogens, merely that the timing makes it possible. Most of the sailors from Columbus's fourth voyage returned five years earlier, and one of their stops had been Costa Rica.

As to the prevalence of superstitious beliefs amongst Italian nobles, we have ample evidence. Astrology, augury, necromancy, readings from tea leaves—these were all rampant in the Italian courts, despite the scorn of intellectuals like Leonardo.

Ludovico Sforza's doctor, Giovanni da Rosate, doubled as his astrologer. One would think that a competent astrologer would be clever at avoiding imprisonment, but the French caught them unawares and threw them both in jail without so much as a by-your-leave.

SCARLETT: Mercury was in retrograde.

ARTIE: Yes, well, we mustn't look down on the Renaissance Italians. We're all just tapping our canes on the cobblestone streets, straining our ears for a future we can't see.

SCARLETT: After three centuries of scientific debunking, 29 percent of U.S. adults still believe in astrology and 77 percent still believe in angels. Can we stop tapping now? All this mystical shit is getting to me.

ARTIE: Scarlett, please. We need to be careful to separate superstition from mysticism. People use the word mystical to describe the indescribable—experiences beyond ordinary understanding. If science can't prove the existence of what we feel, does that mean we should reject it out of hand? Or should we try to express the inexpressible in the spirit of art? I, for one, think we mustn't throw out what we don't yet understand.

Peter, I apologize for injecting my own opinion on this subject. Shall we return to the story? There are more depths to plumb while the gates of divinity are still open.

Leonardo held Fra Luca's forearm firmly and shook it. "My dear Luca, we are so adept at explaining the universe with mathematical models that we forget they are just models. Nature is much less predictable than a model!"

"On the contrary, my friend, mathematics is absolute and immutable. A correct model is truer than anything the senses can perceive in Nature. Experience is suspect. Only numbers are truth!"

"Luca, any brain that is clever enough to imagine models is clever enough to delude itself. No, no, to find the truth you must begin with experience. You must observe how something works, theorize from observation, and create experiments to prove or disprove your theory. Only then can you make a model, keeping in mind that all models are simulations, not Nature itself."

I looked up from my writing to find Bramantino building a pyramid of cherries.

Bramante looked on intently.

I feared that Dr. Marliani had lost consciousness, but then his eyes shot open as if he had received an epiphany from the Holy Spirit.

Galeazzo had left the room.

Zoroastro sat swaying, as if in a trance, both arms wrapped around his chest.

It felt strange to be recording these behaviors in my notebook, but I remembered that the master had said, "Hold nothing back."

"*Furthermore, Luca, my sweetest Luca, if you wish to invent something new, old models will not be useful. You must work without models until the invention at last appears, fully formed. Only then can you fit a model to it. Inventions are wild birds that must be captured on the wing.*"

"*Leonardo, you know I am a Franciscan. The work of our order is the preservation of knowledge, not the invention of it. Knowledge is a divine thing, created by God. It was perfect and complete before we were born, and shall be perfect and complete after we die. There are no ideas that are not God's ideas. At best there are clever recapitulations of timeless truths.*"

Leonardo shook his head in disbelief. "*Do you not agree with Roger Bacon that the study of Nature can reveal new truths through the application of empiricism?*"

"*Reveal, yes, but not create. I have read his 'Opus majus,' and I find him detestable. He was an Englishman without a heart. A head, I admit, but no heart.*"

"*But his head was remarkable, don't you think?*"

"*I do, and no doubt it led him to Hades.*"

"*In that case, I shall call on him when I get there, and we shall argue the merits of religion.*"

Luca laughed in spite of himself. He turned to me and said, "*Be wary of your master, Francesco, or he will lead you down the path to perdition.*"

"*Dulce periculum,*" *I said.*

"*Danger is sweet!*" *said Zoroastro, surprising everyone.*

"*Fra Luca,*" *said Bramante,* "*there is more God in these cherries than in all of your theories.*"

"*I have tasted them, and I praise the Lord for His bounty.*"

Galeazzo had returned with Leonardo's painting of Lisa Gherardini and placed it on the sideboard against the wall. "*I love this woman,*" *he said, straddling a chair with his head resting on his forearms.* "*She is perfection itself. A goddess, a true Italian beauty. Look at those lips, those eyes. She knows the secrets of the world, and yet she doesn't share them. She is a tease, an earthbound siren.*"

Lorenzo began removing unnecessary items from the table, and as he did, Bramante took a deep interest in Giampietrino's tablecloth. He traced his finger over the embroidered lines of the Academia emblem, feeling its golden threads as he followed the loops and knots.

"It is remarkable," he said. "When I close my eyes I see the most beautiful geometric patterns, gold and silver and brown, forming and reforming in my inner field of vision, like the patterns on this cloth. Do you see it?"

"I do see it," said Zoroastro, his good eye closed. "It never stops moving. It writhes and coils and weaves like a thousand eels, writing and rewriting the secrets of alchemy. Everything is connected. Everything is beautiful."

"It is beautiful indeed," said Galeazzo. "Vines growing from an enormous head, the head of a woman, curling and branching and sprouting with leaves as luminous as dew. Is this not God? This must be God."

I glanced at Fra Luca, expecting a curt objection to this line of conversation. Instead, he sat quiet with his eyes closed. A look of concentrated awe passed over his features. He opened his mouth to speak and closed it again. Finally, he said: "It is the Theotokos. The Mother of God. So beautiful. So beautiful. Unlike anything I have seen."

EDITOR'S EMAIL

They were tripping! Is it possible that the design of the emblem wasn't the *cause* of hallucinations, but the *result*? Could the intricate patterning of the emblem have appeared to Leonardo on some previous occasion? Maybe all he did was draw it from memory.

8VO_47

SCARLETT: Now there's a hypothesis. We know Zoroastro was into fringe pursuits. Weird animals. Taxidermy. Alchemy. Augury. Necromancy. He was convinced he could fly like a bird if Leonardo could perfect his machine. Is it a stretch to imagine him cultivating plants and supplying various powders and potions to Leonardo?

As a scientist, I steer clear of mind-altering drugs. I like to stay focused on reality, so I won't comment on the visions of the guests.

ARTIE: Scarlett is taking the view that hallucinations aren't real. But I assure you, to the person hallucinating, his or her visions are very real indeed.

SCARLETT: Artie, are you telling me you're an acidhead?

ARTIE: I was young once, too, my dear. And I can tell you that the visions described in Melzi's account align closely with those of my own experience. Not just *my* experience, but the experience of artists, scientists, and saints throughout history.

Naturally, everyone's hallucinations will be colored by their personal experience. An artist may see profound new dimensions of art, a scientist may see natural connections never before glimpsed, a clergyman may see the power and the glory of God. But one thing they will agree on is the realness of their visions.

SCARLETT: But *are* they real? Or did their brains just serve up a theatrical version of what they already believed, using whatever ingredients were there? I'd be much more impressed if Fra Luca had a visit from Chinese goddess Wangmu Niangniang instead of the Western Mother of God. He only saw what he already believed.

ARTIE: Don't rush your fences, Scarlett. Reality is not black and white. Why not entertain a broad range of perspectives before deciding what's true? I find that's where art can be helpful.

SCARLETT: What rattles my molars are people who default to subjectivity and call it truth. Leonardo said he's all about evidence, and yet here he is indulging in hallucinations.

ARTIE: Scarlett, there's no need to take up Peter's time with our personal views. Shall we continue with the story?

I wrote as fast as my hand allowed, but I could not keep pace with the flood of ideas, opinions, and visions I heard that night. The hour was late, and yet the conversation showed no signs of abating.

Fra Luca reached into his bag and pulled out a bottle of grappa he had obtained on his recent trip to the Veneto. He offered it to the others as a digestivo. Domenica had already gone to bed after cleaning the kitchen, so Lorenzo came out with clean cups and poured small drinks for everyone save me. My eyes were heavy with the desire for sleep, but I noticed the guests were still full of energy and had returned to their normal senses. Even Marliani was alert and talkative.

"Surely you don't think the Bible false, Leonardo. The word of God should never be questioned."

"So it is said, Marliani. But answers that we cannot question are more dangerous than questions we cannot answer. How can I believe the Bible to be the word of God? Has God written it, or have men written it? Perhaps it is better to read the Bible as a book of fables, written on behalf of God, and not by God Himself, to instruct us in our earthly affairs. To do otherwise is to place the word of God in opposition to the facts."

"What facts do you mean?" said Fra Luca, setting down his grappa and peering at Leonardo.

"There are many stories in the Bible that do not accord with the evidence, my dear Luca. The Deluge, for example. The Bible says that all the waters prevailed exceedingly upon the earth and the high hills were covered by fifteen cubits of water. As proof of this, the scholars point to fossils of sea creatures on the tops of mountains. For their theory to be correct, the fossils would have to include other animals in the layers of the rocks, not just sea creatures. The Bible says all flesh on earth had drowned.

"But when you examine the fossils," he continued, "the only ones you shall find are those you would expect at the bottom of the sea. You shall not discover any birds, cows, horses, lions, dogs, lizards, or men in the layers of stone. The only explanation is that these fossils began in the seabed, and over many thousands of years, the seabed was lifted to the height of moun-

tains. *Therefore, the story must be a fable, not a fact.*"

"*Your logic may be correct as far as it goes, Leonardo. But God can do as He pleases. He can place fossils wheresoever He chooses.*"

"*Yes, and He can lift mountains, too. And if He did lift the mountains, why would He write a story that contradicted it? The answer, my dear Luca, is that He did not write it. Why do you doubt the evidence of your senses? Your fellow Franciscan, William of Occam, says that the simplest explanation for any phenomenon is most often the correct one.*"

"*Another Englishman I detest.*"

"*Please, Luca, charity. He spoke the truth as he knew it.*"

"*Perhaps, but I prefer the truth of St. Francis.*"

"*The truth does not change according to one's language. How can we know if the mystery we call God is not actually the mystery of Life? What if Life is a sublime and mysterious force against the deadness of the universe, and in our ignorance we created God?*"

"*We created God? Leonardo, you blaspheme!*"

"*Calm yourself, Luca,*" said Leonardo, gesturing with his palms. "*What I am saying is that fables can simplify understanding. Our minds are constructed of stories, are they not? One does not have to believe that Noah was five hundred years old to understand the lesson from the Bible—that God punishes the wicked and rewards the faithful.* *Donato,*" he said, turning to Master Bramante, "*Shall I tell you a fable? Then you can tell me the lesson you have drawn from it.*"

"*As far as my addled brain will allow.*"

Bramantino snorted, and the two clinked their cups.

"*The fable concerns the queen of a beautiful realm that was ruled by a powerful king.*"

The others leaned forward, eager for the tale.

"*The king wanted an heir, but the queen was secretly in love with another man. She kept this secret locked in her heart, and soon she gave birth to a boy.*

"*One day a messenger arrived to tell her that her lover was about to betray their secret. She was furious. The king, without further need for an heir, might well decide to lock her in the tower. So she poisoned the messenger and paid a tradesman to deliver his body to her lover as a warning to hold his tongue.*

"Yet the tradesman had a secret, too. The queen's lover had caused him to lose his position with his master. So he added his revenge to the warning by signing his name to the messenger's body. The result was a scandal that led to widespread misery, but no satisfaction. Can you tell me the lesson, Donato?"

Bramante looked at Bramantino and back at Leonardo. He shrugged and said, "The lessons are many: do not betray your husband; do not kill the messenger; do not cause scandals; do not send confusing messages. It is a tangled knot."

"True," said Galeazzo. "A tangled knot. But something is missing." Our eyes shifted toward Galeazzo. "Who sent the messenger in the first place?"

The table fell silent while they pondered this question. Leonardo shot a meaningful glance in my direction.

"It is obvious," said Dr. Marliani. "The lover, of course. He wanted the queen to himself." The doctor had just finished the last piece of torta. "What a meal!" he said, dropping his fork on the plate and slapping his ample stomach. "I cannot in good conscience eat another bite."

Galleazo had returned his gaze to the portrait of Lisa Gherardini. "A beautiful painting," he said, "so simple on its surface, yet giving one a sensation of depth beneath depth, of falling through its levels in light-headed ecstasy."

I glanced up from my notebook and saw a faint light from the east. The sculptured candles of the absent friends had burned down to formless lumps of wax, leaving only a few candles to light the room. Salaì had gone to bed after drinking the remaining wine, and Lorenzo lay asleep on the kitchen floor.

Leonardo looked at me and smiled. "Dear Checco," he said. "You are a good soldier. Now it is time for us both to rest. I shall be extremely displeased if you rise before dinner tonight."

"Quite correct," said Luca, pushing back his chair with a scrape. "Young people need more sleep than old people. The old have slept too much already and shall soon be sleeping for eternity."

Lorenzo roused himself to help Pagolino with the horses, while I showed the masters to the door.

EDITOR'S EMAIL

That Leonardo is a wily one. Did you notice how at the end of the evening he slipped in his little fable about the queen? A perfectly baited hook. And yet no takers. We can probably assume his friends had little more to offer. But what a conversation! "Life is a sublime and mysterious force fighting against the deadness of the universe." It's thrilling to be in the same room with the brilliant minds of the day. It also shows they were just people, figuring it out like the rest of us.

8VO_48

SCARLETT: Leonardo might not have gotten new information, but Galeazzi's observation about his fable was right on point: Who sent the messenger?

I happen to agree about the way our minds are constructed. Most people are believers. And what they believe most are stories, not facts. With the right story, they'll swallow just about anything.

Me, I'm not a believer. I'm a finder-outer. Leo seems like a finder-outer too, big-time, but he's also a storyteller. And he seems to be training Melzi in the same tradition. Makes me wish I could write.

ARTIE: Peter, those who read the book will be reminded that human beings are boundlessly creative, insatiably curious, and ravenous for meaning. Leonardo was arguing for learning as a multi-dimensional pursuit. It's not only what we can measure, mimic, and memorize, but what we can invent, imagine, and interpret.

SCARLETT: Double alliteration. I see what you did there.

ARTIE: You daft article.

SCARLETT: There are so many phony scientists trying to turn technology into a religion these days. It shows how easily some people revert to monkeyhood. You can have the biggest brain in the world, but when someone offers you a magic daddy you're right back in the Paleolithic. Only now the magic daddy is a machine. Anyone who buys into that shit can't call himself an atheist. He's a full-on cultist. Sorry, Artie.

ARTIE: All religions start as cults. They simply need to satisfy a few basic requirements to become religions.

SCARLETT: Such as?

ARTIE: They need to encourage mystery, and then get followers to see the mystery in everything around them. They need to build a mutually supportive community. They need to teach followers to live a moral lifetime, no matter what befalls them. The rest is ritual and tradition.

SCARLETT: Yeah, and that ritual and tradition can wall you off from reality. There's a statue of a guy named Giordano Bruno on the very spot in Rome where the Church burned him to death in 1600. His crime? Claiming the sun couldn't possibly be orbiting the earth. Heresy! they said. He wouldn't retract his claim, so they torched him.

Galileo was smarter. He also claimed the sun didn't orbit the earth. But he was careful not to insist on it, so they let him off the hook. It took the Vatican 400 years to apologize for their minor astronomical error. I looked it up. Every year the Italian Association for

Freethinking celebrates Bruno by inviting the mayor of Rome to say a few words in front of the statue. If you listen to these speeches, you might think Bruno died of a car accident instead of a Church decree. Heresy and hypocrisy are two sides of the same quattrino.

ARTIE: No one ever accused the Catholic Church of being scientific.

SCARLETT: What I'm saying is that science-based religions are even worse. Peter, sometime let me tell you more about my encounter with Dickson in the museum. It'll show you what kind of cray-cray you're dealing with.

EDITOR'S EMAIL

Now might be a good time, Scarlett. I'll continue to shelter you from the gory details of the lawsuit, but Dickson's legal team is putting a full-court press on us. They're threatening to take us down unless we agree not to publish.

Dickson also wants all the items you have in your possession, including the silver graver you took from the townhouse. How could he know about that? He thinks you have something else, too—a letter, in addition to the one you found with the manuscript. Do you? Anything you can tell us about the letter, or Dickson's character, or his background, would be helpful at this stage.

8VO_49

SCARLETT: Holy shit. This is serious. But another letter? There's no other letter. The only letter we have is Melzi's cover letter to Manuzio. He's making that up.

The graver is much more concerning. There's only two ways he could know about it. First, the owners of the townhouse noticed it missing and said something. That's unlikely, since they didn't itemize the graver on the list of artifacts. Second, he's been intercepting our emails. That's possible, because he has access to some pretty sophisticated technology. Because, duh, his business is security software.

Remember back in the art museum? All that bullshit about keeping people safe and stewarding their lives? What if instead of stewarding, he's surveilling? What if instead of stopping the bad guys, he *is* the bad guy? Who would know? Who would know how to stop him?

I've made some changes on our end to throw him off, but there's a real chance he's already got our communications, including the ones between you and your legal team. We should both take a fresh look at our counter-surveillance tactics.

Okay, Peter, I told you about Dickson's theory about Transhumanism, right? The concept of reversing the forces of entropy and living forever. He and his buddies will leap the natural boundaries of human biology. They'll plug their brains into an AI and live forever in non-corporeal space, the modern equivalent of sending your soul to heaven without doing the work. No good deeds required.

So there we were, standing in the warm light of the museum. The color is set precisely at 2700 degrees Kelvin, the ideal temperature for viewing art. I'm studying the tiny craters on his pockmarked face and wondering: What was his childhood like? Was he a pimply nerd? Was he victimized by bullies? Did girls laugh at him behind his back?

He tells me that extended life should only go to those who've earned it. It needs to be distributed on the basis of merit. After all, he's built a business that keeps people safe from security risks. Hasn't he earned the right to steward their lives?

Stewardship is cool, I say, working hard at coy. But how can you steward *soooo* many people?

Let me tell you something, he says, dialing his voice to late-night deejay and getting all mansplainy. It's no secret that privacy will become a luxury. It already is. We live in the world's most advanced surveillance system. If you're online, you're being tracked. Your location is being recorded in real time. Your attention is being sold by the terabyte. It may not seem like a problem right now, because it's still fairly painless.

He puts his arm around my shoulders and walks me over to a deserted section of the gallery, as if there might be spies behind the sculptures. His skin smells like fresh cement.

What you don't realize, he says, is that the surveillance industry is getting the best part of the deal. They're harvesting your data free. Before you know it, you'll look around and find they've not only stolen your data, but your liberty, too. And not just yours, but everybody else's. At that point your life will be manipulated six ways from Sunday. These companies are amassing power in such a thorough and disturbing way that they're threatening the survival of civilization.

Then he says: I happen to think someone should protect us from that. Someone with the track record of a steward and a lifespan long enough to see it through.

Suddenly Dickson's the Most Interesting Man in the World, a bundle of buddy-buddy and social responsibility.

Peter, my father is an evangelical preacher. I grew up a PK, a preacher's kid. I know a cult when I see one. This whole extropian thing is nine parts cult and ten parts bullshit.

I move within perfume range of Dickson and twiddle the sleeve of his two-hundred-dollar tee. So what is it, I say, with you and the Renaissance?

His eyes start to dance and shift into the distance, as if he can see the 15th century from here.

It was the birth of Humanism, he says. It was a time of the Universal Man, the beginning of technological innovation. What most people don't understand about technology is that it's a very human activity. It's not just machines. It's hope. It's the desire for a better life.

I never thought about it like that, I say, his own personal acolyte.

Take evolution. What is evolution but a constant tug toward greater complexity, greater elegance, greater beauty, greater *love*? These are the same qualities that the world's religions look to God for. Evolution brings us closer and closer to that ideal, but at a painfully glacial pace. Technology speeds things up. It wants to be more than useful. More than human. It wants to be God.

I'm thinking I don't know what planet Dickson is orbiting, but they should sell tickets. His eyes finally come in for a landing, resting on the alluvial plain of my blouse.

Did you know, he says, that Leonardo da Vinci's father lived to be seventy? He fathered eleven children, the last one born just before he died. Now, five centuries later, Humanism is evolving into Transhumanism. Technology is letting us extend our lives far beyond our allotted three score and ten.

He stands back and gives me a mic-drop look, like I'm supposed to break into wild applause. Well, why not? People flick their Bic at anything these days.

Peter, I can see the appeal of extending your life, even for healthy people. Every ten years of extra life could probably double your wealth. Plus, you might actually use it to do some good.

But as a PK, I can easily see it going the other way, like the sex pervert in the news who wants to use cryonics to freeze his penis. He wants to stick his dick in as many holes as possible, and if babies come out, so much the better. All part of his plan to colonize the gene pool.

What do I really think? I think Dickson is part of something insidious. A kind of patriarchal capitalism that lets you pass down not only your financial wealth, but your genetic wealth, too. The strong get stronger while the rest of us pay the bills.

Me, I've had no choice but to work for douchebags. I've got ninety-five thousand dollars in student debt. I'm too far in debt to hang with my YouTube-celebrity-wannabe friends, chasing social clout and shopping for the latest drip to fuel their viral dreams. At some point, being young is no longer an excuse for stupidity.

Be careful with Dickson, Peter. He's much smarter than you think. And he's not about to let people like you or me get in his way. He wants the manuscript, and he'll kill for it.

Part Four: Epiphany

You don't have to convince me, Scarlett. We're in the process of adding more security right now. But you're the ones whose lives are at stake. You've got the manuscript. For Dickson, you're the line of least resistance. I know you can't tell me what security measures you've taken, but I hope they're clever. The main thing is that you stay safe. In the meantime, let's keep our eye on the ball. Have you made any progress on the next chapter?

8VO_50

[TRAFFIC SOUNDS]

ARTIE: It's all tickety-boo on our end. We've seen neither hide nor hair of the handyman, and we've made a new plan for eluding Dickson's surveillance. We're on the move again. Scarlett will tell you more when she feels it's safe. In the meantime, I'll read whilst she drives.

I slept until late in the day, so fatigued was I from writing all night. My notebook overflowed with the most astonishing thoughts, opinions, and reactions from the lips of the masters. I was eager to ask Leonardo about these, that I might clarify a few points from the discussion. He was still in his studiolo with the door locked.

Three days passed with no sign of the master, except for the empty plates that left his chamber with Domenica. I had seen this behavior many times before. He would spend weeks in gregarious conversation with friends or patrons or assistants, and then suddenly barricade himself in his chamber for up to a month. He might be thinking or working or sleeping—no one knew.

On the fourth day, he emerged from his chamber, his mood surprisingly light. He squeezed my shoulder and thanked me for comporting myself according to his wishes at dinner. He then asked my impressions of the conversation.

"Master, I thought it was the most remarkable conversation I have ever heard. Naturally, I am too young to understand all of what was said. But I have many questions."

"Shall we meet in the courtyard after dinner, my dear Checco? I shall answer them as I am able."

That night I brought my notebook and a candle to the bench under the cherry tree. The cicadas chirped loudly and the fireflies flew lazy arcs through the warm air. The horses made rustling sounds as they moved around on the fresh straw Pagolino had laid down for them.

Leonardo came through the dining room doors with a bottle of sweet wine. He sat down next to me and poured the liquid into two small cups. He smiled and handed one to me.

"Now, Checco, what are your questions?"

"Master," I said, with some hesitation, "can you tell me about the powder you took with your wine after dinner?"

"Checco, you are too young for such knowledge. Ask me something else."

I quickly understood that certain doors would be locked. I tried a different door. "You said to Bramantino that you refuse meat because you do not want to inflict pain on animals."

"That is true, Checco."

"Master, I am confused. If you do not wish to inflict pain on animals, which are of a lower order, why do you design weapons of war to inflict pain on men, as you have for the Duke and Cesare Borgia?" I peered at his face, fearing I had transgressed.

A shadow crossed his features. He said nothing.

Then finally, "Your arrow has found its tender heel, my dear boy. Why must I—why must any man—harm others' lives in order to live? I have no simple answer. All I will say is that we do what we must to survive. Virtue asks a price that only the powerful can afford, and even the powerful are loathe to pay it. Many would rather corrupt the less fortunate and increase their power than use it for virtuous ends."

"Does this mean we are destined to live in sin?"

"Perhaps. I myself have no more stomach for war. I regret that I sought the patronage of men like Cesare. I was eager to apply my skills to the machinery of war, and take the money and learning it offered. I was weak. I lied to myself, saying that fewer people would die with more fearsome weaponry."

"Master, then how can we be virtuous?"

"You shall learn in time that virtue is a right that must be earned through wisdom and strength. When we are young, we must take the work we are offered. When we are middle-aged, we must be strong enough to refuse it. And when we are old, we must repay the world for the damage we have caused in our youth."

The snares of the Devil are indeed infinite. I thought carefully about my role in this. "Am I causing damage?"

"Checco, I fear you shall. You are still a boy, but soon you will make your way amongst adults. The burden will be greater." Mimi sidled up to his legs, wagging her bony tail. He raised her to his lap and began scratching the scruffy hair on her chest. "Are you worried about your soul?"

"No. It is said that God will forgive our sins if we have faith and worship Him. But I fear you do not worship Him. You are old now, and I worry that you shall die and not be admitted to the Kingdom of Heaven."

In saying this I felt a pressure forming behind my eyes.

"Checco, dear Checco," he said. "I have more faith in the need of men to believe than I do of God's need to be worshipped. Why must we worship a God that we have mostly created ourselves? Why are we content with imagined realities when we could, with diligence and courage, confront

the truths of Nature? The universe is more intricate and beautiful than most men can conceive. We do not need faith when we can open our eyes and see it for ourselves."

"Master, please do not speak thus. It shall count hard against you. We must have faith to receive His blessings. Amor est magis cognitivus quam cognitio."

Leonardo blinked, uncomprehending.

"We know things better through love than knowledge," I said.

He encircled me with his arms and pulled my head into his shoulder. "O, sweet boy," he said softly.

EDITOR'S EMAIL

Obviously, Melzi was upset. I imagine Leonardo's unorthodox views on religion rocked his world. It's so touching that he was worried about his master's afterlife. Was he raised with traditional Roman Catholic values?

8VO_51

SCARLETT: I'm pretty sure they didn't call them values. The Church was simply the air the Melzis breathed. When you're raised in a religion, you don't question its teachings. You defend them. That's what Checco was doing with Leonardo. The Jesuits used to say, give me a child for the first seven years and I'll give you the man. It would take an event of titanic proportions to dislodge Melzi's beliefs.

Leonardo escaped all that religious programming because his uncle left him alone most of the time. He wasn't in school much, and he didn't go to church except on rare occasions. He was free to explore the world on his own.

People always accuse materialists of reducing everything to boring matter—stripping all the mystery and majesty from life. For Leonardo it was the opposite. He accused the Church of reducing everything to comfort food, an elaborate fairy tale that shielded people from the fearsome and awe-inspiring truths of the universe. He was your basic heretic. My kind of guy.

What do you think, Artie?

ARTIE: It's hard to know what he believed. I would say his conception of God was more akin to nature with a capital N than it was to an authoritative supernatural being. In that sense he had more in common with primitive people, like those who might use mind-altering plants to gain direct access to the divine. I'm not saying he was a bog-standard hippie. I'm just saying he distrusted the Church to mediate his experience of the universe.

SCARLETT: Peter, I think I know how Dickson intercepted our emails. We all carry the perfect tracking device in our pocket, or purse. It's called a phone. Right from the start, I worried that his encryption software might be doubling as an eavesdropping program, so I deleted it.

The real culprit was something called Spyjinks. It activates your phone's mic from a remote location, then reads your emails, texts, and photos. So I deleted that, too. You shouldn't get any more nasty surprises from Dickson. Unfortunately, he probably knows everything up to this point.

ARTIE: We're both very sorry, Peter. I suppose all we can do now is correct course and carry on.

On the bright side, I believe this next chapter will be mother's milk for creative people. Melzi reveals the essence of what made Leonardo Leonardo, including what he called his *discorso mentale*, the internal dialogue that informed his work. The new chapter opens in his private study.

In the morning I entered my master's studiolo to find him sitting amid a large number of drawings and notes that were scattered about the tables and pinned to the wall. There were studies of water, birds, architecture, astronomy, optics, and more. Perhaps this was the explanation for his absence over the last few days. He had been working on his notebooks.

"Sit, Checco," he said, rising to close the door behind me. "As you see, I have made more drawings with which to tax your talents. You will be sick of making engravings before I am finished with you."

"I will endeavor to be worthy of them, Master. These are quite beautiful to behold."

"I have every faith you will succeed." He picked up the drawings one by one and stacked them in the corner. "But now we have more urgent work. We must clear Aldo's good name so the Aldine Press can revive its business and begin printing my notebooks. Let us make an inventory of what we learnt from the masters at dinner. Do you have your little book?" I took it from my belt and opened to the first page. "I made many entries, but I found three of these especially curious in light of our mystery.

"First, Marliani said Lucrezia was in a foul mood after visiting with Bembo. She said those who printed books should get ten drops on the strappado. Bembo does not print books, but he does write them.

"Second, Lucrezia was wearing a beautiful medallion with an inscription suggested by Bembo. Marliani said she was 'as giddy as a girl' despite her displeasure with Bembo, and could hardly wait to show it to Isabella.

"Third, Galeazzo said Isabella had asked him to intercede with you about finishing the portrait you had started. He said she was wearing a medallion that looked like the one Lucrezia had."

"Well done, Checco. And what do you make of these oddities?"

"I cannot say, Master. These are questions without answers. How can we possibly know what they mean?"

"We cannot know before we know. We must find out through logic. There are two main types of logic, dear Checco: deduction and induction. Do you know between these which is which?"

"I believe so," I said. "Deduction starts with a general principle and leads to a specific conclusion. Induction starts with a set of observations

and leads to a general principle.”

“Checco, I am pleased to find such erudition in one so young. Yet neither of these types of reasoning can solve our mystery. Do you know why?”

“Because our mystery has no discernible shape. It is a shifting fog in a floating mist. We cannot see what the missing pieces are, much less where they might fit.”

“This is so. A mystery is a mystery because it has no simple pattern, and thus eludes simple logic. Therefore, we must use a more subtle form of reasoning, called abduction.”

“I have not heard of it.”

“Abduction is the logic of hypothesis. It requires that we start by imagining the pieces that might be missing in order to make sense out of the few pieces we have. We must ask, ‘What if? What if? What if?’ until, like staring through a glass, some semblance of cohesion appears. When a model finally comes into view, a model with a credible internal logic, we can measure the imagined pieces against the truth. Do you see what I mean?”

“I think so.”

“And what pieces have we thus far?”

I opened my notebook to a page entitled “List of Knowns.”

“In order of occurrence,” I said, “we can name the following seven facts, or what we believe to be facts.

“One, the victim had gone to see Lucrezia. We have the carpet thread to prove this.

“Two, Lucrezia poisoned him and sent for Griffo. We know the messenger was poisoned because of his discolored skin.

“Three, Griffo carried the messenger to the Aldine Press, where Aldo had been printing Bembo’s book. We have Griffo’s bloody fingerprints on the chase to prove he was there.

“Four, Griffo impressed a passage from Dante into the messenger’s skin and nailed him to the press. Only Griffo would have had the necessary skill and strength to do both.

“Five, the passage warns of God’s punishment for those who create

scandals. The chase with the passage came from Bembo's translation of Dante.

"Six, Aldo, Bembo, and Lucrezia said they knew nothing of the motive or the victim. They did not recognize his face from the drawing.

"Seven, the victim was only seeming dead from Lucrezia's poison. Perhaps without knowing, Griffo became the actual murderer."

"Excellent, Checco. These are the facts as we understand them. And what do we suspect but cannot prove?"

I turned to another page entitled "List of Motives."

"We suspect the relationship between Lucrezia and Bembo was more than platonic. We have this from gossip since we could not interrogate Strozzi.

"We also suspect that Lucrezia was angry with Bembo, and yet still harbored strong feelings for him. We have Marliani's story about the medallion.

"We suspect that Griffo sought revenge against Aldo for damaging his reputation in the trade. His actions have all but signed his name to the crime."

"Anything else?" said Leonardo.

"Master, I think anything further would be speculation."

"Very good. Checco, we have driven the horse cart up the mountain to the end of the paved road. From here we must proceed on foot. And now I have work to do. Let us both think about this puzzle and meet again in three days' time."

As I closed the door to the studiolo, I saw a small box next to a cup on a high shelf. I thought about the dinner with the masters and wondered if the box contained Zoroastro's mushroom powder.

EDITOR'S EMAIL

Oh, my God. Melzi is about to take the psilocybin. I can feel it. His very first question on the night after the dinner party was about the mushroom powder, and Leonardo shut him down. Melzi was too young to know.

8VO_52

SCARLETT: See, that's why you're the editor and I'm the scientist. You grok the story before I can even glimpse a theory. People are opaque to me. I'm all about logic, and most people are the opposite of logic. I can hardly talk to Artie. I try to follow her reasoning, and afterwards all I can think is, I want those brain cells back.

The type of logic Leonardo was explaining to Melzi is the centerpiece of something we now call design thinking. It's a modern problem-solving approach based on applied imagination. News flash: Leonardo was using it 500 years ago!

ARTIE: If I gave my logic a fancy-sounding name, would it be easier to follow?

SCARLETT: No.

ARTIE: Well, dear, you didn't have to answer so quickly. Peter, brace yourself for the story of Melzi and the mushrooms.

I confess, Dear Reader, that my curiosity got the better of me. After Leonardo went down to dinner, I tried the door of his studiolo. Unlocked. I slipped inside and found the wooden box on the shelf where last I had seen it. I took it down, opened the lid, and found it half full of a soft, gray powder. I bent my head to sniff it, and as I did a large amount flew into my nostrils. The pungent scent of mushrooms exploded in my head. I thought I might cry out, so sharp was the pain. I shut the box quickly and returned it to the shelf.

Closing the door behind me, I ran to my chamber and locked myself inside. My ears were ringing ominously like leaden church bells. I fell onto my pallet and pulled a pillow over my head, and yet the dull pounding in my brain continued. I pulled the pillow tighter.

Then, as quickly as it came, the pain ebbed away. All that remained was a peaceful sense of alertness, a supreme calm, as if nothing at all had happened. I waited. Calmness and quietude, nothing else.

I went to my table and began to work on the mystery.

As I sat there contemplating the inexplicable chain of events I had recorded in my notebook, the candle danced in my peripheral vision, throwing shadows across the pages of my book. Soon the flame began to move more rhythmically, more intently, as if in thrall to the music of some distant African chant. I watched with strange fascination as it drew me into its flickering rhythms. So compelling did I find this flame, this rhythm, that I felt I must tear my eyes away or risk being consumed by its white hot center.

I forced my gaze downward and saw Leonardo's silver bulino lying on the table before me. Had it been there all along? I noticed keenly, perhaps for the first time, the delicately inscribed circles, interlocking like the looping lines in the Academia emblem, covering the silver surface of the handle. The circles were moving, growing like vines, knotting and unknotting like reeds in a magical basket.

Before long the handle began to bend. The bulino straightened and then curled itself into a circle, its ruby point separating into jaws, straining to reach the end of the handle to complete the circle.

It was the ouroboros, the snake that devours its tail, the symbol of rebirth.

A feeling of supernatural grace swept over me. No. Not supernatural grace. Deeply natural grace, as if I were on a journey through an ever denser, ever more beautiful jungle, a journey toward the womb of the earth.

I reached my arm through encroaching vines for the bulino. It felt alive in my hand. Just as its jaws were about to meet its tail, it twisted into a three-dimensional figure, a flower-shaped knot. The snake-like form moved within this figure, never changing the shape of the figure but moving along its course, its jaws straining to reach its tail, but never closing the distance. The bulino grew hotter as I held it—so hot that I dropped it on the table. It hit the surface and broke into three smaller figures, each a replica of the first. The three snakes moved along the same pattern, each set of jaws straining, but never reaching, the tail it sought.

I knew that the secret of the universe had been revealed to me, and yet I could not hold it. It hovered beyond my grasp like the tails of the snakes.

More visions followed, each more fantastical than the last, opening like flowers within flowers. No sooner did one blossom open, when a bud hidden within it followed suit. This continued for what seemed like an eternity, yet it was probably only hours.

I saw that the candle had nearly burned to the brass. I rose from the table and lay down on my bed. As I closed my eyes, my own face appeared before me, crawling with the most intricate patterns—veins twisting like vines, leaves unfurling, wheels turning slowly, wheels within wheels, pulsing with the red rivers of life. Beneath these I saw the bones of my face, the hollows of my skull, all the way to my very thoughts, my mind a roiling sea of words and images, tides running first in one direction, and then the other. The sea was pounding against my skull, pounding, pounding.

A voice called my name. Was it God?

"Checco!" it called.

I sat up in the semi-darkness, listening intently. "Yes, God, is that You?"

At that moment, the vision I had of my own face became that of God's face, His long white beard cascading onto a rose-colored robe. He sat down next to me, holding a lighted taper in His sinewy hand. He placed the other hand on my forehead. He lowered me gently back down to the pillow.

Then, rising to His feet, He went to the door. "Domenica!" He called out. "Bring me a bowl of water and a clean serviette!" Does God know Domenica? Of course He does! He knows the merest creature in his infinite Kingdom. He knows all and sees all.

Before long Domenica brought the water into the room, her dark hair glowing with a heavenly radiance. Never before had I seen such a beautiful woman.

God received from her the serviette, dipped it in the bowl, and laid it on my forehead. It was the most wonderful sacrament one could imagine.

Cool water ran down my temples in long, blue-green rivulets. My mind floated with them to the sea. My eyes slowly closed.

God said, "Sleep, Checco, sleep."

And so I did.

When I woke the next morning I was alone in my chamber. The bowl of water stood on the side table and the serviette lay on the floor, dry. My eyes ached from the many things I had seen during the night. I rose stiffly from my bed and went to the table. The bulino had returned to its original shape, and everything in the room was back to the way it was.

But something had changed. It was I.

And suddenly I knew what the missing pieces were.

EDITOR'S EMAIL

Christ, the kid could have died from that experience. He was only fifteen! What if God or the snake or some crazy creature had told him the path to everlasting life was through the window? Leonardo was right to discourage that sort of experimentation.

8VO_53

SCARLETT: Experimentation is one thing. Experiments take place in a controlled environment. This was pure juvenile insanity.

Me, I'm still reeling from the news that my paisley-garbed partner is an acidhead from the sixties. This is a woman who doesn't complete a sentence before checking with the Oxford Manual of Style. Her clothes are always pressed, and her nylons—nylons!—never have nicks. She keeps all her wigs on little stands in separate boxes. Even on the lam, she won't go out until her makeup is flight-attendant perfect.

Don't worry, she can't hear me. She's in the other room translating. We splurged on a suite so we could get a break from each other.

I have to tell you, Peter, Artie's brilliant and all, but her work habits are driving me nuts. She talks to herself! She sits there and gives lectures to—I don't know—somebody—her less-professional alter ego?

No, no, no, she'll mutter. You can't say that. Compound words are not the sum of their components. Or, you fool! That's the local idiom for lynx, not caracal. There are no caracals in Italy. Look it up! On and on.

Last night was the first decent night's sleep I've had in weeks. And forget trying to do research while she's working. Two days ago I was on the—wait, she's coming out.

There she is, at last! Artie, you ready now?

ARTIE: Ready steady. Sorry I'm late, Peter. I had to check on a few words that weren't in the normal vocabulary.

Scarlett dear, don't give me that look.

I cannot tell you how excited I am about this next chapter.

Before I could finish dressing there came a knock at my door. I threw my tunic over my head and brushed my hair into place with my hands. It was Master Leonardo.

"Good morning, my young adventurer," he said. "How are you feeling today?"

"Master, I have a confession to make."

He raised one eyebrow and brought his hand from around his back. "Is it in the shape of a small wooden box?" he said, holding it up.

I was humiliated. I had betrayed my master's trust and now I must pay for it. I searched his face for signs of mercy. "How did you know, Master?"

"Well, it might have been the layer of fine powder on my worktable with a box-sized silhouette in the center, yes? Or it might have been your dilated pupils when I came to visit last night. Would you care to tell me what demons have slipped in through those eyes of yours?"

"I am truly sorry, Master. I feel ashamed and unworthy of your gener-ous trust. I deserve whatever punishment you deem fit—I will clean your

brushes, groom your horses—"

"Yes, and change the chamber pots for a month. I know. Checco, please tell me what you saw, and we shall speak of it no more. I want to be certain that your mind has been returned to us undamaged."

At that moment Domenica entered with a tray containing a pitcher of water, two cups, and an almond cake with a dusting of powdered sugar. In the middle of the powder was a rectangular silhouette. I could feel my face reddening.

"I said we would no longer speak of it. I did not say we would no longer joke about it."

We both burst out laughing. I knew this was to be the extent of my punishment.

"Master," I said, unable to contain my excitement. "I had the most beatific visions last night. Not of God, as I had imagined when you came into the room. No, these visions were of Nature. Of the connectedness of all things under God's Heaven. I saw jungles and oceans and flowers and animals. Your bulino, your silver bulino, turned into a snake trying to eat its tail."

"I know this symbol," he said. "It is the ouroboros, the symbol of eternal renewal. The snake bites its tail, completing the circle. And having done this, is reborn as something new."

"Yes, but it could not reach its tail. It tried and tried, and then broke into three smaller snakes, and none of them could reach their tails. They bent themselves into the shape of knots as they tried."

Leonardo looked into my eyes, uncomprehending.

"But do you not see? The snakes are questions seeking answers. They keep moving and cannot rest until they find the truth that will complete them."

"And what are the questions, Checco?"

"The questions are three: Why was Strozzi murdered? How did Griffo know Lucrezia? And most important, who sent the messenger to Lucrezia in the first place?"

"Ah," said Leonardo, "that is the question Galeazzo had posed. I won-

dered how long it would take you to come back to it. Excellent, Checco. And how do we go about answering these questions?"

"We have no choice. We must use abductive logic. We must imagine what's missing, and then build a model. When we find a model that yields a believable story, the ouroboros will be complete. We must test our story against reality."

"You are a good student, my boy. Do you have a hypothesis for any of the missing parts?"

"Perhaps, Master. We know that Lucrezia was seeing Messer Bembo, and at the same time hoping for an heir. We also know that Ercole Strozzi was the person who arranged their secret meetings. What if—what if—Lucrezia's husband Alfonso suspected Strozzi of interfering in his marriage—at the very moment when the honor of the family was most vulnerable? Would he not have a motive to murder Strozzi? If the public found out that Alfonso had been cuckolded by Bembo, the legitimacy of his heir would be in question and his reputation forever damaged."

"Checco, you are wise beyond your years. I fear you may be right. Let us accept your hypothesis. Go on."

"What if—what if, Master—Lucrezia feared that Bembo might injure the family's reputation by publishing something intimate, perhaps their love letters? Remember what Lucrezia said? 'All publishers should be given ten drops on the strappado.' Perhaps she was thinking of Bembo, whom she had just seen, when she spoke about this to Dr. Marliani."

"Very good, Checcho, but who sent the messenger to Lucrezia?"

"Why, Bembo, of course! When he threatened to publish their letters, she did the only thing she could think to stop him. She sent him a violent warning in the form of a murdered messenger. She could not know that Griffo would distort her message for his own purposes."

"Perhaps, Checco. But how was she acquainted with Griffo in the first place?"

I admitted I did not know.

Leonardo gazed out the window. "There is no mystery so tangled," he *finally said, "that when viewed in a stronger light, it does not become more tangled."*

Leonardo had a good point. How could Lucrezia, a high-born duchess, be acquainted with a tradesman like Griffo? They moved in very different circles. She might have known Griffo through Bembo, of course, but why would she trust him enough to handle such a delicate errand?

8VO_54

SCARLETT: My money's still on Alfonso. It's just like a man to pull something like that. Talk about ego. He might have accepted Lucrezia's infidelity, but the idea of being exposed as a cuckold?

No fucking way.

Of course, that doesn't explain why he'd choose Griffo to do the deed. He could have hired one of Masino del Forno's assassins much more easily. And then there was Alfonso's brother, Cardinal Ippolito, the fixer in the family. But I checked the records and Ippolito was in Bologna, while Griffo happened to be right there in Ferrara.

ARTIE: Ladies and gentlemen, all will be revealed in the next chapter. Once again, we shall see one of history's greatest minds at work.

I have related to you, Dear Reader, that my master had a habit of secluding himself in his studiolo for long periods of time. I believe he used these periods to concentrate his mind on the problems he found most vexing. Two full weeks passed before I saw him again, except for brief comings and goings in which he spoke to no one.

One morning, he burst into my studiolo. I had been practicing his engraving techniques and was eager to show him my progress.

"Never mind, Checco. Today we have more urgent work!"

He paced the floor in front of me.

"We are such magnificent fools!" he cried, pounding his fists against his head. "It is human nature to be blind to the truth, Checco, but we have been more blind than Zoroastro, more blind than the blindest of bats! If our eyes had been plucked out by eagles, we could not have been more blind. What does it profit a man to probe the deepest secrets of Nature if he cannot see what is right in front of his nose?"

"But, Master, I..."

"Checco, one does not need an education in Latin or Greek to know that punchcutters are former goldsmiths, and that goldsmiths are people who inscribe medallions. The two of us will have a bright future in the circus when we grow tired of solving mysteries. We can use our talents to paint frowns on each other's faces!"

"Master, I..."

"Do you not see? Bembo gave the medallion to Griffo to engrave the inscription. Griffo delivered it to Lucrezia in Ferrara. We cannot be certain what they spoke of, but they made common cause in their distrust of Aldo. Lucrezia found her accomplice."

"But, Master, that does not explain who sent the messenger to Lucrezia in the first place."

"Checco, we have been the fools of fools. What did Galeazzo tell us? That Isabella was wearing the same medallion Lucrezia wore. O, we are such clowns that we sully the reputation of clowns."

"But, Master..."

"The medallion is the key that unlocks the mystery! This was not a copy of Lucrezia's medallion. This was the original. Isabella wore it as a prize. We do not know how she obtained it, and yet we must entertain this interpretation of the facts. Occam's rule states that the simplest explanation is most often the correct one. Think—which explanation is simpler, that Isabella somehow obtained Lucrezia's medallion, or that Isabella commissioned an exact copy of Lucrezia's medallion?"

"I see, Master. To make a copy, one must first have the original. And yet there could be other explanations."

"Indeed, Checco, but it does not profit us to imagine more complicated possibilities when beginning to assemble a model. We must start with the simplest interpretation and see how the pieces fit. Then we can alter the model as needed. For example, we know that Isabella and Lucrezia are bitter rivals. We also know that someone sent a messenger to Lucrezia to start this murderous chain of events. What if…what if…?"

"What if the messenger were sent by Isabella and not by Bembo?"

"Yes, YES!"

My heart jumped at this bold thought. But that is all it was, a thought. "Master, we have no evidence."

"True, but we can see, as a consequence of our imagining, that Isabella might be connected to the mystery. She possessed a medallion that belonged to Lucrezia and that also passed through the hands of Bembo and Griffo. What was the Latin proverb spoken by Bembo at the print shop?"

"Quien quiere matar perro ravia le levante."

"He who would kill a dog must work himself into a rage. What did you make of that?"

"I could not be certain what it meant. But I remember his face had the expression of a hunted animal when you questioned him about it. Later, in Ferrara, you repeated the proverb to Lucrezia and her face changed to a similar expression."

"Well observed, Checco. Now we must risk a larger leap of imagination. We know that Lucrezia and Isabella are bitter rivals. We also know that Lucrezia has known other men besides Bembo. What if Lucrezia had begun a secret relationship with Isabella's husband?"

"Gonzaga, the Marquess of Mantua?"

"Think of it, Checco. Could there be a better way of getting strong on a rival than by sleeping with her husband? And if Isabella had discovered their relationship, what then?"

"She would be furious. She might even hire a messenger to threaten Lucrezia. But, Master," I said, "why would Lucrezia threaten Bembo instead of retaliating against Isabella?"

"My dear Checco, you are not following. Using Occam's rule, there can be only one answer: She believed the message came from Bembo."

My head was spinning. I felt that I was the fool, not Leonardo, as none of this made sense to my young mind. His thinking seemed more magical than logical. There were so many causes and so many effects that I could not tell which was which. I shut my eyes, the better to concentrate my thoughts.

"Master," I began slowly, "in the morgue you said that murder begins with a cause and ends with evidence—but that, as investigators, we must follow the opposite path. We must begin with the evidence, and by means of it, discover the cause. And now that we have a story—a provisional one at best—should we not arrange the elements in chronological order to see if they hold together?"

"Excellent, Checco, most excellent. Please proceed."

"I shall try. To start, Isabella learns that her husband Gonzaga is secretly meeting with her rival Lucrezia. Is that correct?"

Leonardo widened his eyes, nodding.

"She decides to send Lucrezia a message, but disguises it as coming from Bembo. The message says that he, Bembo, will publish certain letters unless she halts her relationship with Gonzaga, Isabella's husband. Lucrezia reacts with fury—a public scandal would place her reputation and the reputation of the Este family in jeopardy. She acts quickly. She poisons the messenger with cantarella and hires Griffo to deliver his body to the Aldine Press as a visceral warning to Bembo.

"Griffo, however, has his own plans. He embellishes Lucrezia's message by leaving a passage from Dante on the man's cheek as he crushes his head in the press. To achieve the fullest measure of horror, he nails his body to the uprights using type punches. In this way Aldo will understand that he, Griffo, is the author of Aldo's demise. Griffo then goes into hiding."

I glanced at Leonardo for reassurance. He bade me continue.

"Later, in Ferrara, Lucrezia's husband Alfonso sends his own gruesome message. He hires Masino to assassinate Ercole Strozzi and leave

him in the streets outside the Church of San Francesco. Without Strozzi, Lucrezia can no longer arrange trysts with Bembo. Her wings, once so dazzling and bright, have been clipped."

"Well told, Checco! You have a gift for words. And now you must use that gift to write a letter."

EDITOR'S EMAIL

Astonishing—isn't that the word Melzi used to describe his master's talents? I'm starting to see the beauty of Leonardo's methods. If he'd waited for proof of these assumptions, he couldn't have constructed a working hypothesis. There wouldn't be enough data points. So instead he taps his imagination to supply what's missing and goes from there. In a way, it's like making a sketch of something to learn how to draw it. What was the term he uses? Abductive thinking?

8VO_55

SCARLETT: Also known as design thinking, like I said. You imagine possibilities that don't yet exist, then you create testable models. No need to prove anything in advance. Just take an educated guess and learn from your mistakes. Imagine, prototype, test, learn. Rinse and repeat.

ARTIE: I did some research on the medallion. It turns up in various accounts, but always as a sidebar item, an historical orphan. I found nothing in the record that suggests the medallion had fallen into Isabella's hands. This was pure conjecture on Leonardo's part. Provisional, as Melzi said. But I have to admit that it makes a compelling linchpin for their hypothesis.

Peter, this is probably as good a time as any to tell you about our plans. We're very sorry to surprise you with this, but we felt silence was necessary. We feared you might not approve.

SCARLETT: Promise not to bust a blood vessel, okay? We know you're ass-deep in legal crap from Dickson, but that's why we did it.

Ready?

We decided to go public with the portrait of Leonardo.

I know, I know. Dickson will freak out. It'll fuck with his efforts to buy the painting on the sly. Sorry, Artie. It'll *mess* with his efforts to buy the painting. The object of his obsession will go straight to auction, and that's only if Italy doesn't claim it first. Even if he's got the painting, Italy may claw it back.

The downside is that we'll no longer have any leverage against him. Nothing to stop him from coming at us with everything he's got. He who kills a dog must work himself into a rage, right? Don't think we haven't considered this. I've started my aikido workouts again, and I'm upping my anti-surveillance game.

In fairness to Artie, she argued against the idea. She says I sail too close to the wind. Which I can't deny. But we're both in agreement that we have to keep the portrait out of Dickson's vault, along with the manuscript.

Here's what we did.

First, we leaked a hi-res image of the portrait to AFAR, the American Foundation for Art Research. It's a nonprofit that keeps track of major international artworks, including stolen pieces. Our ask was to publish the image in their journal without any provenance or claims of authenticity. Just get it out there. Let the world's art researchers get a good look at it. After that, it doesn't matter. The genie's out of the bottle.

They refused.

They wanted our names, our CVs, our research notes—everything we can't give them. That was two weeks ago. There's still a chance they'll publish it later, but later is too late.

Plan B was to go straight to the public. So we sent it to *BuzzFeed News*. We're expecting a big story tomorrow, complete with lurid speculation about the painting's value, its possible whereabouts, and its massive importance to the art world. They'll probably have a few second-rate historians weigh in on it. Don't worry, Peter, they can't trace the painting to you or Harker. They won't know that Dickson's involved, either. His name won't appear.

I'm sure I don't have to convince you of the upside. The reaction will drive demand for the book into the stratosphere. People will say, *wait*—the greatest art discovery of the 21st century has a backstory? Yeah, baby! If you slap Melzi's portrait of Leonardo on the jacket you could ride Leomania right into publishing history.

Peter, I don't mean to make light of the spot we've put you in. But after all our investment in this project, we just can't let that slimeball get away with it. I hope you agree.

EDITOR'S EMAIL

Agree? Are you two out of your minds? We heard from Dickson as soon as the news ripped through the internet. His legal team is accusing us of planting the article to damage his negotiations for the painting. Have you read this? Do you realize what kind of jeopardy you've put us in?

Lost Portrait May Be Worth $200 Million

by Madeleine B. Sagmeister

Yesterday the editors of *BuzzFeed* News received a photo of a painting that may be an authentic portrait of Leonardo da Vinci, made in the later years of his life. The providers of the photo say the painter was Francesco Melzi, a pupil of da Vinci who worked for the Renaisance master from 1507 until his death in 1519.

The portrait, painted in oil tempera on wood, was discovered under the floorboards of a 15th-century

workshop in Northern Italy. The experts who authenticated the painting wish to remain anonymous,
promising to share more information with the Italian
government as soon as they complete their work.

Sir John Clockwright, a spokesman for Sotheby's, said,
"If the painting is what it says on the tin, this piece will
fetch in the neighborhood of 150 million pounds. Not
because of the painter, but the subject. This would be
the first full portrait of Leonardo da Vinci."

The editors of *BuzzFeed* News cannot verify or falsify
the authenticity of the painting, therefore we welcome
the observations of qualified professionals as we
develop this story.

Please send bio and comments to "Leonardo" via Buzz-
Feed's SecureDrop page.

Scarlett, I can't believe you did this without consulting me. We're supposed
to be partners. "Trust us," you said! What kind of partners make existential
decisions on their own? I don't know what to say. I am so disappointed in
both of you. My only hope is that we'll still have a company when it's over.

8VO_56

SCARLETT: Shit, Peter. I didn't mean to upset you. I should have lis-
tened to Artie. *Of course* we should have consulted you. Please tell us
how we can make it right.

ARTIE: Honestly, Scarlett is gutted about this. We both are. She says I
tried to talk her out of it, but she's covering up for me. I encouraged
her to do it.

SCARLETT: It's not really so bad, is it? I mean, look on the bright side.
AFAR is now begging for a second chance. I got six emails from various publications with questions for Anonymous. A *BuzzFeed* tweet

got, like, 700 thousand hearts and 11 hundred comments in the first three hours. Facebook went bonkers with conspiracy theories. *Fox News* called it a hoax. *The New York Times* wants an interview. The demand for the book will go through the roof the minute you announce.

Don't worry, don't worry. I deleted the emails and closed my account.

Peter, let's think this through. You said Dickson's attorneys accused you of trying to damage his negotiations. That proves he had access to our emails, right? Could your legal team build on that?

Better yet, why not keep the illegal surveillance card up your sleeve? There's no way Dickson should know anything besides what's in our report—unless—cue scary chords—he had us hacked. I mean, how would it look if the head of a large security company was caught surveilling a couple of women?

ARTIE: A sexy one and a younger one.

SCARLETT: That's right, a sexy one with a vast collection of wigs and a younger one with shit for brains.

EDITOR'S EMAIL

Scarlett, I'm furious. I'm in no mood for cute apologies. You two have no idea what you've done. You've put the whole company at risk with your boneheaded move. Dickson could crush us with legal fees alone.

Let's talk about trust, Scarlett. Remember what you said at the start? "Please understand that we want to trust you. But also understand if you betray that trust, even a little, the deal's off."

Trust goes both ways. It extends outward in chains of mutual responsibility— from me to Katherine; from Katherine to the board of directors; from me to my staff; from my staff to the other employees; from the employees to their families. Trust is a web. It's not just about you and your personal crusade. Doing what you did was a slap in the face to all these people.

I don't like speaking to you like this, Scarlett, but someone has to do it. I have such high regard for your ethics and your sense of fairplay that I hate to see you betray your own principles.

If you still want to get this book out, you'd better pray we still have the resources to do it. In the meantime, please get back to work and stop pretending you're a marketing genius.

8VO_57

[DRIVING SOUNDS]

SCARLETT: Peter, I'm appalled by my carelessness. I didn't look at it that way. I asked for your trust, then paid you back by withholding my own. There's only one word for this mess—fuck, fuck, fuck.

ARTIE: That's three words.

SCARLETT: You get my drift. Dickson will probably double down on the manuscript now that the painting is out there. Shit. Well, at least our evasive maneuvers are working—we haven't spotted the white van since Ferrara. We know that could change in a Milano minute, so we'll have to keep moving.

ARTIE: Peter, we're so sorry about everything. Can we start over? We promise to be perfect little girls going forward.

On the manuscript front, Melzi's story seems to be entering an exciting new phase. I'll read whilst Scarlett drives.

Leonardo had raised his worktable up to his private chamber on the first floor. He sat behind it with his back to the tall, west-facing windows. The low afternoon light illumined the rim of his long white hair and yellow tunic.

As he bade me enter, I noticed his room was tidier than usual. The master always put his work away when preparing to leave the studio for any period of time. The box of mushroom powder was nowhere to be seen.

I felt a twinge of guilt as I recalled my earlier episode.

"Do you have the letter?" he asked with eagerness.

I opened the small portfolio in which I keep my stationery and correspondence. I read from my draft:

To Lady d'Este, Marchioness of Mantua

Is it possible that eight years have passed since Your Ladyship had so graciously entertained my household at the Ducal Palace? Whilst I regret that my busy schedule has not allowed me to return as soon as I had wished, not a day goes by that I fail to recall with delight Your Ladyship's hospitality. I do hope the chalk portrait I sketched of Your Grace has counted as some small repayment for the kindness I received in Mantua.

Several years ago, you wrote to ask for something else from my hand. At the time I was preoccupied with less exalted commissions, but I would now like to balance the accounts of our friendship. You had recommended a youthful Christ of about 12 years old, the age at which he disputed with the doctors in the temple.

I believe this is far too modest. I would like to suggest instead a marvelous spectacle to entertain your esteemed guests at the festival of Carnivale in February. I would like to propose a major undertaking, requiring twelve weeks' use of a workshop for myself and three assistants. My intention is to create a spectacle so wonderful and elegant that all of Italy will remark on it for decades to come.

If this proposal meets with your approval, please send your acceptance so that my assistants and I may begin making arrangements for our journey to Mantua.

Also, please accept my felicitations on the birth of Your Ladyship's daughter Livia. I will bring with me a special present, a newly painted miniature of the infant Christ, to mark her joyous arrival.

Your most obedient and grateful servant,
Master Leonardo da Vinci
Milan
27 August 1508

"Very good, Checco. Please copy it fair and send it to Isabella."

I never question the instructions of my master. But I must admit on this occasion my curiosity got the better of me. "Master," I said, "I believe you have resisted Her Ladyship's overtures many times in the past. You called her 'a spoilt little girl who keeps artists in cages as if they were pet goldfinches.' Are you not now walking straight into one of her cages?"

He leaned forward and gazed at me with cold blue eyes. "Checco, how many years have you?"

"Fifteen, Master."

"Do you think fifteen years qualifies you to doubt the judgment of your master?"

I looked down. "No, Master."

"Then listen to me. We now have a working hypothesis for the chain of events leading up to the murder. I am satisfied that the logic holds. But we are lacking proof. Furthermore, if we should obtain proof, we cannot be certain that the Venice authorities will open Aldo's shop on the strength of it. The investigation will not be concluded until our object has been achieved. We must find a way to save the Aldine Press. If our path runs through Mantua, perforce, to Mantua we must go. Do you understand?"

"I understand, Master. We are not merely investigators. We are saviors. I pray the saints are with us."

In a fortnight's time a letter arrived from Mantua, written in Isabella's hand. It said the festival is planned for the first week of February, and the spectacle set for February 21, on Carnival Day, in the grand piazza of the palace. Her Ladyship will be pleased to welcome us in late October, and urges us to begin our work on November the first. A workshop shall be made ready on the castle grounds.

Leonardo scheduled our journey to begin on October the fifteenth. His three assistants would be Zoroastro, Salaì, and myself. Salaì and I had the task of preparing the studio for our departure, which in practice meant I would do it. Salaì was likely to spend most of his time buying clothes for his social activities in Mantua.

No sooner had Leonardo received Isabella's letter than he forgot about it. He threw himself into sketching his thoughts on the properties of water. The door to his studiolo remained closed for several weeks, whilst Salaì tended to the studio's commissions and I to the master's correspondence.

Zoroastro, for his part, had made a list of materials to purchase and pack for Mantua. These included:

4 skins of tanned goat leather
1 skin of top-grain horse leather
Various metalworking tools
Various sizes and types of springs
Rolls of wire in various weights
Lightweight wooden struts to build a framework
A spool of strong raw-silk cord
Flexible copper tubing
6 sheets of thin metal
A full set of paints and brushes
Chemicals with which to create smoke
A large bellows

What these items would be used for I could only imagine.

EDITOR'S EMAIL

At least Leonardo had a plan, which is more than I can say for us. Our attorneys are gathering oppo on Dickson's business to see if they're up to anything illegal. Meanwhile, Dickson is cranking up the threat level. His attorneys promised to "inflict pain" on the company if we don't agree to their demands. It's a total nightmare. There's not much I can do to help, so I'm trying to stay focused on the book.

Is there any way you can check and see if this journey to Mantua ever happened? You'd think a spectacle designed by Leonardo da Vinci would be listed in the records of the Ducal Palace.

8VO_58

[STREET SOUNDS]

SCARLETT: Can you hear me? Wait a second. We're walking through a covered market. Lotta racket here.

That's better. Artie couldn't find anything online about a visit to Mantua. On the other hand, it doesn't contradict the record. The stuff about Leonardo's earlier visit and the chalk portrait—that's known fact. It drove Isabella crazy that he never completed her portrait in oil.

But we did find something suggestive. The previous year, after King Louis XII had put down a rebellion in Genoa, he hired Leonardo to choreograph several days of festivals and pageants to celebrate his triumph. Isabella d'Este, her desire still burning bright for a small Leonardo masterpiece, had attended the masked ball. She must have been impressed with the wizardry of his theatrics.

Later, when he wrote her to say he'd give her the same treatment that he gave to the king of France, she probably fainted with joy. What's a little oil painting compared with a full-blown Leonardo spectacle for five hundred of your closest friends? I'll bet my last green M&M she was already scheming on some way to get Lucrezia into the front row.

We'll drive to Mantua and see what else we can find, but first we've got an errand to do. Sorry, but we have to keep the specifics to ourselves. I know I'm on thin ice when I say this, but trust me.

ARTIE: In this next chapter, Peter, Leonardo and his crew arrive at the Ducal Palace. Allow me to set the scene. In those days the palace and the town of Mantua were surrounded by marshes—treacherous if you're trying to invade, strategic if you need to defend. The palace was further guarded by a natural moat, an L-shaped lake that hugged the town on the north and east.

Leonardo's party would have ridden in from the west, with the moon still high and pale in the morning sky and the meadows trembling with dew. The roads into town would have had wooden planks to improve the footing, and wooden bridges to allow passage over the canals. Mantua was atmospheric in 1508. This would be late October, when the days were getting shorter and the nights more brisk.

Zoroastro turned the key in the lock and lifted the metal bar that secured the two massive doors. Each door had a window fitted with a wrought-iron grille in the upper half. These had no glazing. We would need to find a remedy before the weather turned cold. Set in the archway above the lintel was another window, this one slightly smaller and glazed. It was protected by an outer grille fashioned into a diamond pattern.

Astro pushed open the doors, and daylight flew across the stone floor. My eyes followed it along the pietra serena tiles, up the plastered walls, and across a high ceiling supported by heavy wooden beams. The room had a large fireplace suitable for use as a forge. Tables had been stationed about the room. Shelves containing tools clung to the walls.

"A fine space for working," I said.

"It would be," said Astro, his one eye casting about. Sometimes I wondered if his experience with chemicals and powders had damaged his ability to reason. He appeared to be unaware of our purpose in coming.

The workshop lacked illumination, as it was served only by the three windows in the main doors and the small round windows above. A stairway to the upper level ascended the wall at the far end of the room and let onto a balcony that gave access to the upstairs chambers.

Astro and I began unloading the cart and storing our materials in the workshop.

In the meantime, Leonardo and Salaì were in the village arranging credit with the local shopkeepers, no doubt brandishing the letter from Isabella, which guaranteed payment.

When the cart was unloaded, we carried the bags upstairs to their respective chambers. Salaì had the greatest number of bags, Leonardo the second, and myself the third. Astro had only one bag.

My own chamber was small but ample for my needs. A good-sized window opened onto the courtyard, its light falling softly onto a rustic oak desk that sat beneath it. I placed my garments in a musty wardrobe that stood by the door, save the ones I would need for our audience with the Duchess. These I hung on the back of a chair. I pulled out my notebook, sat down at the desk, and began making notes on our journey.

In the evening I went downstairs to the workroom and joined the others for dinner, a simple meal of roasted vegetables, bread, oil, and white wine, prepared by Leonardo and Zoroastro.

The next morning a grey mist hung like a veil over the palace grounds. I followed Leonardo across the Piazza Castello, the square in which the festival was to be held, to the massive archway that opened to the older part of the palace. A servant met us at the entrance and showed us down a long corridor, up a spiral staircase, and to the vestibule of an ancient tower. He opened the door and stepped aside.

Suddenly my head felt light. I had never seen such color. Ceruleans, mauves, cobalts, turquoises, crimsons, lavenders, and yellows of every kind, all applied with magnificent confidence to scenes of surpassing splendor. It seemed as if the chamber had no walls, only vistas with figures of important men in the foreground. With the simple opening of a door, a rather plain palace was transformed into a paradise of illusion. Every surface was covered with both real and frescoed architectural elements, so that their intermingling sowed confusion as to which was which.

"This is the work of Andrea Mantegna," Leonardo said, looking around. "A master of perspective."

There were triple vaults on each wall, a fireplace on the north wall, a doorway on the west wall, and another doorway on the south wall through which we had entered. Two large windows offered actual views over the Lago di Mezzo, in contrast to the views displayed in the frescoes. A curtain rod was painted on each wall so that scenes appeared to be revealed by the drawing back of gold brocaded drapes, which had also been painted.

As my eyes traveled up the pilasters that separated the vaults, they slid up painted ceiling ribs that met at a central oculus, through which putti and courtiers peered down with curiosity at the viewer. The effect was altogether dizzying, making it difficult to maintain one's balance whilst looking up.

Just then, the other door opened and the Duchess Isabella entered in a cloud of perfumed air, her pale hand extended palm downward toward Leonardo. She was dressed in a flowing gown made of alternating ribbons of gold fabric. Her hair was held in place with a crespine of fine black silk. A simple circlet of gold adorned her head and a necklace of knotted gold cords rested against her throat. Attached to the necklace was the medallion that Galeazzo had described. The inscription: "Est animum."

In the years before her brother Alfonso married Lucrezia, Isabella had been hailed as the most beautiful noblewoman in Northern Italy. It came as a shock when her peers turned their attention to Lucrezia, a woman seven years her junior. And now, after giving birth to several children, Isabella's figure had grown slightly plump, though still attractive in a charming way. And yet I saw little of the furtiveness and guile that I perceived in Lucrezia.

Leonardo took her hand, bending from the waist to kiss her ring. "Your Grace, how can it be that in the intervening years I have become a grizzled old man whilst you have continued to grow younger?"

"Master Leonardo, you are too kind. I fear that time marches forward, and soon enough we find it has left its tiny footprints on our face."

Leonardo pulled his eyeglasses from his pocket and placed them on the end of his nose, pretending to study her as an artist would a vase of flowers. "I see no footprints, Your Grace. And I am renowned for my powers of observation."

Isabella turned pink. Her green eyes danced as she looked into his face. "I understand you can no longer bear the sight of a paintbrush, Master

Leonardo." Her brow then wrinkled and her lips turned downward. "And yet my spies tell me you have already used my hands and bust for another painting."

It was true. La Gioconda. But how could she have known? Perhaps Galeazzo had written to her. Leonardo pretended not to hear what she said. He turned to me and introduced me as Count Francesco de Melzi, his protegé and personal secretary. Isabella acknowledged my presence, but nothing more.

"I cannot be angry with you," she said coquettishly, "for I am ever beguiled by your air of sweetness and gentleness. Now please sit and tell me about the wondrous delights you are planning for me."

We rested ourselves on silk-embroidered chairs arranged around a low table with ivory inlays. Leonardo leaned forward, his fingertips forming a pyramid.

"Your Ladyship, I can only say that your festival will be an event not easily forgotten. Italy will be altered when news of the Mantua Carnivale spreads through the courts and the high streets. Your elegance will be spoken of widely, so I hope you do not mind your ears crackling like forest fires."

"Oh, I shall try not to mind," she said, suppressing a giggle. "Can you not be more specific? My ears have not yet turned to ashes."

Leonardo leaned farther forward and spoke in a confidential manner. "Part of the success of the spectacle, Your Ladyship, depends on the element of surprise. You must—MUST!—refrain from asking to see the work or trying to discover its intent. When it is done and the festival is over, you will understand why secrecy was in the best interests of all. These are my terms and my humble request. May I have your word?"

Her smile spread as if saying yes, but her lips tightened so that the word could never escape. "I assure you," she said, "that all the keys to the workshop shall remain with you."

"Then it is settled. But there is one more thing."

She tilted her head, prepared to rebuff any further demands.

I handed Leonardo the parcel I had secreted in my robe. He untied the blue velvet bag and pulled out a small painting—a portrait of the infant Christ playing with an infant girl, set against the background of the Ducal Palace.

"For the baby Livia," he said.

Isabella took the painting and held it at arm's length, then clasped it to her breast. Tears filled her eyes as she gazed at Leonardo. No words came, so great was her joy.

EDITOR'S EMAIL

What just happened there? That whole performance seemed to be aimed at getting Isabella to butt out. What was he up to? Have you found if any of this is true?

8VO_59

SCARLETT: Leo played her like Nero's fiddle. He was taking control of the spectacle—the whole spectacle, including Isabella's part. She'd been trying to wrangle a piece of art from him for umpteen years with total non-success. She used every go-between she could think of, including Fra Pietro Novellara, the vicar-general of the Carmelites.

Once she even traveled down to Florence to meet our boy in person, but when she got there she found out he was off in the countryside studying birds. In her portraits she looks petulant, like a little girl who got the wrong gelato. He knew exactly how to pluck her strings.

And no, we haven't had time to locate any records of his visit. We'll circle back on that when we get to Mantua.

Right now, while Artie's translating, I have something more important to talk about. I couldn't tell you about our special errand before. Now I can.

This afternoon we had lunch with a former student of Artie's. She's a mucky-muck at one of the history departments of a major

Italian university—I can't reveal the name. Our goal in meeting was to set up a channel for handing off the manuscript.

We drive to the university and park the car in a faculty lot. Artie has a courtesy pass. We navigate our way down colonnaded streets to a piazzetta near the history department. The place is crawling with students. The city and the university are so mixed up that they're like Isabella's tower room—you can't tell one thing from another. We're a little nervous about being seen in public, but Artie's wearing one of her more concealing wigs, and it's cold enough that I can pull my hoodie over my head without looking like a gangbanger.

We grab some menus from the food kiosk and sit down at a four-top on the edge of the piazzetta. There's a pedestrian lane running along the side and one-way street in front of us. No way Mr. Handyman can sneak up in the Ford Transit. I put on my sunglasses and look at my watch.

Where is she? I say.

Artie says, it's Italy, she'll be late. As soon as the words are out of her mouth, I see a woman walking our way in a tailored gray jacket over a black T-shirt. The shirt has a white silkscreened logo for a rock band. She breaks into a broad smile when she recognizes Artie under her wig.

Ciao bella! she cries and flings her arms wide. Artie jumps up and gives her a big hug. They spin around and laugh.

Scarlett, says Artie, this is my star student from before the flood. Look at her now: a full professor with a whole department!

She's about my height, olive complexion, close-cropped hair, gold earrings with dangling hearts. She turns to greet me and does a double take, her dark eyes fixing on my face. I wonder, does she know who I am? But no, it's something else. She thinks I'm a lesbian. I get that sometimes, and now that I'm incognito I look more tomboyish than ever.

I flip back my hood and extend my hand. Hi, how are you?

She says very well, and sits down at the table with us. Then, turning to Artie: I did not recognize you at once. Your hair is new.

Fresh out of the box, says Artie.

The professor—let's call her Paola—says: Oh. *Mi dispiace.* Do you have an illness?

Artie smiles and says, no, no, Paola. I'm fine. It's an experiment.

I love experiments! she says. Are you traveling together? She wonders if we're an item. Like maybe I'm just a crazy fling for her old prof.

We *are* traveling together, Paola. You might say we're on a mission. I thought you might be able to help us.

What kind of mission? she asks. A secret mission?

Actually, says Artie, raising her eyebrows and nodding.

Oh my God! I was joking! She leans forward and clasps Artie's hands, her face full of concern. She whispers, tell me.

Paola, what would you say if I told you we have in our possession an historical find of great interest to Italy, and to your department in particular? And that we would like to hand it over to you. Anonymously.

Is it a painting?

It's connected with a painting, yes.

Her eyes go blank. Then grow huge. Two fried eggs with black yolks.

You! You have the *portrait*—she lowers her voice—of Leonardo! The one on the internet. No!

Artie looks around to make sure they weren't overheard. Not the portrait, she says, just a photograph of the portrait. What we have is something more important. A manuscript, written by the person who did the portrait—Leonardo's last pupil. A manuscript that reveals intimate details of Leonardo's life, his thought processes, and a stunning piece of history that somehow escaped the official record. Much better than a portrait.

His last pupil? Francesco Melzi?

The same.

You stealed it?

Well, yes and no. We borrowed it from Italy, and now we want to give it back.

You stealed it! You cannot do that, you know. I am not a—how do you say in English?

A fence.

You will be arrested. I will be arrested. The ROS will come and take us away. You must give it to the police.

Paola, we can't do that. We need to hold onto it a little longer, and then we want to give it to you.

No, no, e no! she says. I will not help you!

Artie glances at me with apprehension. I wait a few seconds, then put my hand on Paola's wrist. Paola, it's okay. Let's have lunch and you can tell me all about your work at the university. It sounds so fascinating.

She calms down. We look at our menus and Artie walks our order to the kiosk.

Paola, I say, taking off my sunglasses, tell me about your department. What's your role at the university? I scan her face as if she's *La Gioconda* and I'm a tourist at the Louvre. She blushes and begins to relax.

Allora, she says. I am sorry for react so crazy. I am Italian.

I smile. Where did you get that cool shirt?

Oh, is a band from the Veneto, Jennifer Gentle. They make *musica psichedelica*. I like very much. She opens her jacket so I can see the lettering. Haight-Ashbury Bold.

Listen, Paola, we don't want you to do anything you're not comfortable with. We sometimes forget we're hardened criminals and other people are normal.

She smiles back. Artie is not a hardened criminal, she says. But you are. I can see it. You have the eyes of a thief.

You have the eyes of a victim, I say. I might have to rob you.

She touches her left earring and pretends to be shocked. International art thieves can be so sexy.

Artie comes back with a tray of sandwiches and drinks. *Buon appetito*, she says in a sing-song voice, setting the food on the table. We dig in and talk about everything except the manuscript. Music, movies, restaurants, travel, cars. She loves the new Alfa Romeo Giulia.

Just as we're finishing, I notice two boys, maybe 17 or 18, in the pedestrian street near our table. They've got a younger girl backed up against the wall. They're taunting her about her small breasts. I don't speak Italian, but I can see what's going on. I get up from the table and walk straight toward them. I grab one by the ear and pull him away. The other takes a swing at me but misses by a mile. I grab his wrist with my other hand and yank it behind his back.

Paola is right behind me, shouting in their faces. *Basta, bastardi! Che problema avete, il pene piccolo?*

Hah! *Pene piccolo.* Tiny penis.

Andatevene da qui, bastardi! she yells, gesturing toward the street.

I let go and they tear off, looking back with abject fear in their eyes, thinking we'll tell their parents. The girl slides down the wall, sobbing, hands hiding her face. I pull her up and wrap my arms around her. *Bastardi*, I say quietly. My first Italian swear word.

Paola crouches, turns the girl around, and wipes the tears from her cheeks with her thumbs. *Stai bene?* she says.

Sì, signora. Grazie. She manages a weak smile.

Paola tells her not to play with the older boys. She nods obediently and runs in the opposite direction. We go back to our table arm in arm, where Artie is waiting.

Everything OK? she asks.

Paola says something in Italian and Artie says she's proud of her. *Sono fiera di te.* Paola turns her gaze to me and seems to exhale all the air from her lungs.

I will help, she says.

On the way back to the car, Artie won't talk to me. She's never been what you'd call chatty, but I haven't seen her like this before.

Artie, what's the matter, I say.

She shakes her head.

Artie, tell me. Whatever it is, I can take it.

She stops cold and turns to face me. Are you a lesbian? she says.

Surprised, I say, well, more like a tomboy.

Not a lesbian, she says.

Tombo ain't lesbo.

Right. Someday you'll go too far. You're attractive and full of confidence. Too *much* confidence, in my opinion. If you keep leading people on this way—men *or* women—eventually you'll find yourself in real trouble. Beyond that, it's not very kind.

Yeah, I say, but we got her cooperation, didn't we? Who are you, anyway, my mother?

I have no idea where that came from. My mother never gave me any advice. She just prayed all day and did whatever my father told her to do.

EDITOR'S EMAIL

Artie's right, Scarlett. Someday you'll find yourself in real trouble. Although I can't imagine how much more trouble you could find yourself in beyond the trouble you're already in.

I'm happy to hear you have a receiver for the manuscript. I'm even happier you didn't give away her name or location. Dickson has resources we can't even imagine. Judging by the legal moves he's making, he knows everything we're doing.

Please watch out for yourselves, and above all keep moving. That's the one thing that seems to be working for you. If it weren't, let's face it, he'd already have the MS. Keep your eyes peeled.

8VO_60

SCARLETT: Don't worry, moonpie, we'll look both ways.

ARTIE: Peter, in this chapter, Melzi's description of life in Mantua doesn't need much corroboration. Most of Europe still bore many of the attributes of the Middle Ages, despite the stirrings of modernity brought on by printing and science.

The November air had turned cold. The heat from the forge could not countervail the icy wind that came through the open windows at the entrance to the workshop. Leonardo instructed me to purchase two panes of glass with which to arm the doors against the elements.

"Take care that the glass is of a type that admits light but impedes curious eyes," he said. He was mindful that Isabella had not explicitly agreed to restrain her spies from reporting on our progress.

"Yes, Master."

I pulled on my boots and threw my cloak over my shoulders, turning up the collar. On my way out, I quickly measured the workshop doors, then followed the passageway down to the arched gate and out into the village. The simple act of passing through the gate seemed to shatter the quiet into a thousand fragments. Sellers of eels shouted their wares over the singsong pitches of tallow men, barkers, and auctioneers. The streets stank of manure and urine, and the clatter of hooves ricocheted off the cobblestones and walls, assaulting my ears and fracturing my concentration.

I looked back at the archway to mark my bearings. The contrast between the relative calm of the palace grounds and the cacophony of the village streets could not be more pronounced. Nor could the contrast of rich and poor, learned and ignorant, clean and filthy. People brushed by roughly as they bustled through the town, stinking of unbathed bodies and unwashed clothes. From their mouths came the vapors of decayed teeth and sour milk, from their skin the stench of rancid cheese and rotting tumors.

On the corner, a charlatan stood on a box, surrounded by a large and willing audience that was stretching and bobbing to glimpse the stranger. Coiling around the man's wrist was a deadly viper with silver and black scales, copper eyes, and a horn jutting forward from the top of its head. Its menacing black tongue flicked from side to side as if testing the air for opportunity.

"People of Mantua, heed my words!" his voice rang out. His tattered black cloak swirled around him like dank river water. "Satan has sent a plague of snakes to visit the marshes of Mantua. You have seen them! They threaten your innocent children as they play in the streets! They murder your beloved elders as they lie in their beds!"

Heads nodded and eyes met eyes in shared alarm.

"And yet," he bellowed, holding the serpent high in one hand, "You need not fear this unholy Demon!" He brought the snake down and let it slither around his neck like a glistening noose.

The crowd gasped, recoiling from the frightful sight.

"I need not fear this serpent, dear people of Mantua, because I have swallowed a potion which renders its deadly poison harmless." He pulled back his sleeves to reveal a series of red-tinged holes in his wrists and forearms.

"It is a miracle!" someone cried from the crowd.

"A miracle, indeed! And I have come to Mantua to share this miracle with you. Every vial contains Earth of Malta, an element discovered centuries ago by Saint Paul, from whom I am descended. This powerful concoction will protect you without fail against venom, poison, and diseases of all types. Who will buy the first vial and be safe from sickness and dread?"

An elderly man, his face covered in boils, rushed forward with a fistful of coins. A boy about my age, the charlatan's assistant, stepped in front of the man, arms wide, to guard him from the snake. He accepted his coins and handed him a vial. Several others rushed forward, and soon most of the crowd had spent their money on bottles of what was likely no more than bitter grappa. I feared these poor townspeople would find themselves poorer still, and yet no safer from the snakes that prowl the marsh grass.

It was early afternoon, and the housewives and the daughters of the townsmen had thrown wide their windows and doors. As I passed each house, I inhaled the redolent atmosphere of individual lives. Parlors smelling of stale dust, bedrooms reeking of greasy beds and chamber pots. Stairwells rank with rat droppings and mildewed wood, kitchens promising meager dinners with the aromas of onions and mutton fat.

Farther from the palace, the streets grew more ramshackle. Streams of pungent sulphur-gas poured from chimneys and clawed at my eyes. From the tanneries came the bite of caustic lyes, from the abattoirs the stomach-churning stench of congealed blood. The wind shifted and brought the familiar fetor of the palace stables, where the Marquis kept 650 horses for the use of courtiers and laborers.

In this part of town, prostitutes mingled with merchants, and courtiers glanced furtively as they came and went from their assignations. A woman beckoned me from a doorway. Her dress was pulled past her stockings; her face was a mass of scars. She must have been a courtesan, slashed by a jealous courtier. Such is the fate of women of the night, whose beauty is bound up with their livelihood.

SCARLETT: Peter, I did some digging and confirmed that the lives of courtesans in the Renaissance were, to say the least, precarious. They continuously exposed themselves to the risk of *sfregio*, or face-slashing, at the hands of vindictive lovers. I use the term *lovers* ironically. Alternately, their revenge might take the form of the *trentuno*, a ritualized rape by 31 righteous assholes. Or even the *trentuno reale*, by a total of 79. Can you believe that? Men can be so kind.

ARTIE: Men can be monsters, but I think you'll agree that Leonardo and his circle were not of that ilk.

SCARLETT: He was gay.

ARTIE: And you're a nutter. Shall I continue?

I quickened my pace and found the door to the glazier's shop. After a half-hour's work in scoring, breaking, and polishing the glass, an apprentice of my own age wrapped the panes in paper and handed them over. I paid the invoice and retraced my steps to the workshop, carrying the package past the throngs of townspeople, careful not to drop it or let it be bumped.

"Perfection," said Leonardo, holding one of the panes up to the doorway. "Prying eyes cannot penetrate it, yet the daylight passes through it undiminished."

I set out to install the windows immediately. The temperature had dropped since the afternoon, and the four us could already see our breath. By evening we would be shivering in our cloaks. I put on a pair of fingerless gloves and finished the work by dusk.

That night at dinner, Leonardo revealed his plans for the spectacle. It would be an angel, he said. A mechanical angel descending from heaven to symbolize Isabella's heavenly love for the people of Mantua.

"Heavenly love?" I blurted. "The people of Mantua are sick and starving! Isabella spends the profits from their desperate labors on lavish artworks and meaningless trinkets to flatter her station!"

Astro shifted his gaze nervously between Leonardo and myself. Salaì smirked in anticipation of the vengeful satisfaction he knew would be his. Leonardo thrust his cold-blue eyes into mine as if driving two steel blades into my soul. He waited until my cheeks flushed red with embarrassment.

"Young Count Melzi of Vaprio," he said sternly. "Her Ladyship is a saint. A saint! There is no other word for it." He paused to let his disapproval sink in. "Except for one or two words we cannot say in public."

Salaì and Astro exploded with laughter. I had been tricked. My sense of justice withered in the face of Leonardo's impish humor.

He raised his cup and offered a conciliatory tribute. "To our most excellent Checco, without whom we must surely suffer death by freezing."

EDITOR'S EMAIL

I have to say, life in Mantua does sound difficult for those outside the palace walls. Talk about inequality! I'm starting to despise Isabella and her cronies. It's as if they're keeping their subjects in a constant state of helplessness so they have no option other than total dependency.

8VO_61

SCARLETT: Straight out of the authoritarian handbook. Let them eat cake, but don't give them any cake. And be sure to demonstrate fearsome power at regular intervals. Sometimes I despair of humans.

ARTIE: Peter, it took me a little longer to finish the translation—the vocabulary is specific to the time, place, and craft skills involved. What's the English word for a Renaissance tool with a wooden handle and a forked scraping blade? I've no idea. I called it a forked scraping tool. But I won't bore you with nits. Shall we get on with the next chapter?

As November became December, the days grew shorter and the nights colder. And yet the workshop maintained a comfortable temperature with the aid of Astro's forge. His first task was to create the body of the angel using sheets of copper, molded to form the necessary shapes and then soldered together.

The soldering work could only be done outside the shop on bright days. It required a special device to concentrate the rays of the sun to a fine point. To accomplish this, Leonardo calculated the precise curvature needed to make the concave mirror. He then sent out for a large block of glass, which was delivered in a cart by the glazier's assistant. Using abrasion tools and a slurry of grit, he demonstrated the art of grinding glass, a craft he had learned while apprenticing at Verrocchio's studio.

This he taught to me.

It took two days to grind the glass to the proper depth, which I was able to gauge against his drawings with a straightedge and measuring stick.

Astro then mounted the heavy mirror on a wheeled frame so we could move it inside from the courtyard the moment Isabella's spies appeared. Several times we had already seen a man standing under the colonnade, gazing in our direction. Whenever we returned his gaze, he vanished.

When the frame was finished, Astro fell to his knees in prayer. "Mithras, Lord of the Light," he intoned, looking upward. "Please help us, Father of our Fathers. Send your fire to our mirror so we may build a weapon to banish the darkness. In the light we are invincible, for Mithras is our crown." He made the sign of the cross and wobbled to his feet, confident now that the work would go well.

Whilst Astro and Salaì built the body of the angel, Leonardo designed its wings. These would be articulated in such a way as to simulate the flight of a bird. But in fact his wings were not based on those of a bird at all.

"We must imitate none other than the bat," Leonardo asserted. "For the wings of bats have one advantage that the wings of birds do not. They have membranes that connect and protect the underlying framework, and which are not penetrated by the air. For this, we may use deer leather."

"But Master, leather and wood and copper are heavy materials. How will the angel fly?"

"Poor Checco, the angel does not have to fly. It must only appear to fly. Remember, we are not creating an angel, but a spectacle. It is the illusion that must be real."

"A real illusion?"

Leonardo tilted his head and stroked his beard as he thought about how to answer. "Checco, do you recall the night you spent in thrall to the mushroom powder?"

My face must have reddened, because I saw Leonardo stifle a smile. I lowered my head in shame. "Yes, Master."

"And were your hallucinations real?"

I recalled the bulino twisting into an ouroboros in front of my eyes. "I know not, Master, but they seemed real."

"They seemed real because the human mind bends reality like a prism bends light. We do not experience the world directly, but through the mechanism of our senses. This does not make our experience less real. On the contrary, we are so eager to believe the evidence of our senses that we fail to question what we are seeing. Seeing is believing, so we say."

"Should we doubt the faithfulness of our senses, Master?"

"We must observe every phenomenon from many angles, Checco. We must question, question, and question again. Seeing is believing, but we forget its opposite: Believing is also seeing. Our senses are willing to betray us whensoever our minds desire it."

Leonardo bade me follow him to his worktable. He unrolled a sheet of foolscap, on which was a drawing of an angel with flowing white robes and glorious feathered wings.

"Imagine, Checco. When our angel flies down from its perch, its great wings will move volumes of air and its robes will billow like the white clouds of Heaven. Its head will turn to face the members of the crowd, penetrating the eyes of each in turn. Its voice will shake the piazza as thunder shakes a city. People will gaze upward in awe. They will not see the cords and pulleys that guide its descent, nor the gears and springs that animate its movement. They will see what they wish to see, and nothing else. They will see an angel."

I nodded. "Because we are creatures of self-delusion?"

"Because we are creatures of stories."

I was not certain of his meaning.

"My dear Checco, everything we perceive is part of a theatrical play," he said, his gesture taking in the workshop, "a spectacle staged by our senses for the entertainment of our minds. There is but a small step between believing the stories of our senses and believing the stories of astrology, or necromancy, or evil spirits, or God. Do you see? This is the reason we fall prey, like children, to the mountebanks and charlatans selling miracle prayers and potions in the street. We would rather believe than know."

"If that is so, Master, where should we look for the truth?"

He turned to the drawing of the angel, lifted it, and slapped his hand on the table. "Here, Checco, beneath the surface of our fears and desires," he said, returning the drawing to the table. His eyes peered sharply at mine, waiting for a response.

"I think I understand, Master. If Zoroastro causes a quattrino to rise to the top of a glass whilst pointing his finger at it, many would call this a miracle. They will find it more enchanting—or perhaps less effortful—to believe it thus than to find out how the trick was done. But an artist must look beneath the miracle if he is to master the trick."

"My brilliant boy!" he said, eyes sparkling. "You have hit upon the secret of all the arts. Any work which lies sufficiently beyond the grasp of its audience is perceived as magic. Therefore, it is in the artist's power to wield that magic as a soldier wields a lance. We pierce the armor of our audience's beliefs and disembowel its expectations." He made a corkscrew motion with his finger.

"Then, Master," I said, "are we not exploiting a weakness of the human mind?"

Leonardo smiled. "Checco, you are right to question this. You are right to question everything you hear and see around you. Curiosity, not obedience, is that which leads to truth. I would answer you thus: The artist has an obligation to use his unfair advantage for the good of mankind. To do otherwise is to be unworthy of the gift."

I have thought of this many times in the intervening years. It seems to me that Leonardo was not always faithful to his obligation. Was it for the good of mankind to design cannons and armored chariots for Ludovico Sforza? Was it for the good of mankind to make military maps for the political advantage of the cruel Cesare Borgia? Was it for the good of mankind to divert the Arno, thus depriving Pisa of its waters and its trade routes?

Or was it merely good for Leonardo and his patrons, to the detriment of mankind? My heart ached whenever I thought of this, for one wishes to believe the best of one's master.

As Christmastide approached, the angel took shape. Astro had finished crafting the body and was now working on the wings. He and Salaì sculpted thin bones from pieces of poplar to resemble those of a bat's wings. With the aid of a forked scraping tool, they cut twin dovetail joints into the wood, allowing the pieces to slide back and forth, shortening and lengthening with the movements of the wings. They connected the bones to the framework with horse leather and covered the framework with goatskin.

Whilst Astro and Salaì worked on the wings, Leonardo designed the head, which at this stage was a clay model with holes for eyes and a hinged jaw. From this he would make a mold, and from the mold a metal head, which I myself would paint to resemble the face of an angel.

Upon completion of these tasks, Leonardo gathered us near the entrance of the workshop where the light was strongest. On a large table, he unrolled a drawing that showed the mechanical instructions for how the angel would operate. There were levers and springs, cables and gears, axles and balance cocks. A winding stem at the back of the machine would drive its movements, much as the mainspring of a clock.

"A flying machine needs great resistance and strong rigging," he said. "Like a bird, it will weigh more when it draws its wings together, and less when it spreads them out. As you can see," he said, tapping the drawing, "the forces transmitted by the levers and pulleys are designed to simulate muscles and joints."

Barely visible wires would guide its descent and counterbalance its weight. As it neared the ground, its wings would make shorter strokes, beating with great power against the air, to land the machine on the surface as lightly as a bird. Leonardo demonstrated the motion of the wings with his arms, and Astro mimicked him with comic fidelity. "Just so, Maestro Tommaso," said Leonardo with a smile.

After eight days of soldering, stitching, and calibrating, the angel was ready to test. It was far from complete, merely a skeleton with wings, but the test would serve to prove or disprove the theory of its design. Astro had wound the mainspring tight and hoisted the machine high up onto the railing of the balcony, like a huge hawk crouching on a branch.

On a signal from Leonardo, Astro released it. Gears whirred and wings began to extend. Legs pushed off the railing, and the whole mag-nificent assemblage leapt out into space above the workshop floor. The rush of air from its leather wings felt like a battering ram to my chest, so great was the force they generated. As the creature approached the ground, its descent slowed and its legs stretched downward to soften the landing. Its wings folded neatly and its head came up, proud and victorious.

A raucous cheer rose from the floor. Astro and Salaì fell into each other's arms, laughing ecstatically, and Leonardo gripped my shoulder as he gazed at the creature in astonishment.

We had a working model of our angel.

EDITOR'S EMAIL

This is the Leonardo that fires people's imaginations. Flying machines! Mechanical angels! Any work which lies sufficiently beyond the grasp of its audience is magic! Great stuff. Are you excited?

8VO_62

SCARLETT: Excited doesn't cover it. When he said that everything we perceive is part of a theatrical play, my hair stood on end. This goes straight to the heart of what scientists call the hard question of con-sciousness. Where does the redness of red come from? Is it in the skin of the apple, or the wiring of our brains? Scientists are obsessed with truth, but how do we account for the limitations of the human mind to perceive it?

ARTIE: Leonardo said we're creatures of stories. I take this to mean that, for artists, finding objective truth is not the top priority. Find-ing personal meaning is. Enlarging on what it means to be alive. The redness of red is not as pressing as the *is*-ness of *is*. Who are we? What is existence? How can we live a rich and authentic life?

Meanwhile, in Mantua, the direction of the story is about to shift again. Leonardo was holding something back. His plan all along was much darker than his comrades could have imagined.

Dawn broke amidst noisy preparations for Saturnalia. The weather had turned warm, and the sky would soon be a cheerful blue. Workers moved tables into courtyards, trunks of trees onto hearths, large casks of wine under arcades. Soon the palace would erupt in a blur of feasts, revelries, and continuous merrymaking, all leading up to Twelfth Night.

In the main piazza, carpenters began to assemble a nativity scene with a lifesize stable and a creche for the baby Jesus. In the halls of the palace, servants decorated fireplace mantles and covered nearly every surface with festive branches and boughs of greenery.

In the workshop, however, the mood was darkening.

"We have created the structure for a magical angel," said Leonardo, pausing for dramatic effect. "And yet there are two forms of magic—that of angels and that of more sinister forces."

Salai smiled crookedly, his face betraying a wild anticipation. Astro leaned forward, his one eye gleaming like a faraway planet. I myself was not prepared for what Leonardo was about to propose. He unfolded a large drawing and placed it on the table.

We gasped in unison.

"This is what we shall build," he said, staring at each of us in turn. "We have until Epiphany Eve to complete the work. At that time, we shall stage our first spectacle. Afterwards, we shall return to the angel and finish it by the start of Carnevale. Do you understand?"

We nodded dumbly, our voices deserting us like cowards at the start of battle. My throat felt as if steel hands had squeezed it shut. The image before us was more horrible than the crucifixion at the Aldine Press, more sickening than the mutilated cadaver at the churchyard morgue. Unearthly. Unnatural. Abnormal and depraved. What was Leonardo's thinking? Had he lost control of his reason?

Outside, beyond the walls of the workshop, the joyous celebrations of Saturnalia raged on. Courtiers and servants danced and drank and ate with abandon. The only person not taking part was Isabella's spy, who stood motionless under the arcade across from the workshop.

Inside the workshop, we toiled without ceasing to complete our new machine before Twelfth Night. The days blended one into the next as we transformed Leonardo's drawing into a terrifying reality.

Astro had fashioned the scales of a reptile from thin sheets of lead, scoring each with a comb-like scraper. Salaì had collected clumps of hair from the refuse piles at the abattoir, sewing them into a mane. Leonardo had designed a fearsome head with glowing eyes like a depraved lion. I fabricated talons from the forked branches of olive trees and covered them with dark, wrinkled leather.

In the days to come, Leonardo would design a mechanism to make a booming voice, and Astro would experiment with ways to conjure smoke, fire, and lightning.

"Boil ten pounds of brandy until it fills the room with fumes," advised Leonardo. "Then throw some powdered varnish into the air. Enter with a lighted torch and—boom!—the chamber will be ablaze."

Whilst Astro worked on these theatrics, Salaì and I began to assemble the new machine on the same plan as the angel. Salaì insisted we make a hinged double door in the chest of the machine, for reasons I did not comprehend. I have learned not to cross him, for he can be vengeful, and Leonardo often forgave his behavior.

On the morning of the tenth day of Christmas, Salaì called me over to his worktable. Whilst Astro was shopping for chemicals in the village and Leonardo was meeting with Isabella, Salaì had heated a pot of brandy in the forge. The air smelled strongly of alcohol. On the table lay a dish of powdered crystals.

"Checchino, I need your assistance in testing Leonardo's formula. When I clap my hands, will you throw these crystals into the air?"

I nodded and positioned myself at the table. Salaì slipped around the corner just outside the main workroom and gave the signal.

I threw the crystals upward as a fiery torch landed on the floor beside me. There came a sudden roar and the room flashed a blinding white. When I finally opened my eyes, I was looking up at Zoroastro, who was pressing a cold cloth onto my face. His lips were moving, but there was something wrong with his voice.

I pulled myself onto my elbows and saw Leonardo in the far corner of the workshop with Salaì. He appeared to be shouting at him, but no sound emerged from his lips.

I saw that I was lying on a worktable, and all about me were scorched papers and overturned objects. Then the room went black.

Later that day I regained my senses well enough to hear. A quick glance at my reflection showed only minor wounds. My hair had been singed, I had lost an eyebrow, and my face was a bright carmine on one side. The only serious damage was to my pride. I had let the trickster Salaì make a fool of me again. He had been so helpful and productive these last few weeks that I had forgotten who he was.

Just before dusk, the master called us all to his private chamber. I ascended the staircase with Astro, and when we arrived we found Salaì already there, slouched in a chair with a chastened expression. And yet when he looked in my direction his eyes were daggers.

Leonardo sat hunched in a heavy robe behind a wooden desk covered with drawings and tiny models of fanciful beasts. They appeared to be made from parts of lizards, crickets, locusts, beetles, bats, and other such creatures. As he regarded these, he rubbed his temples with hands that were wrinkled and splotched. His long white hair hung limp at the sides of his face. When we had all arrived, he raised his aging head to speak.

"I have just come from an audience with Isabella," he said. "She has not paid us in a month. She was cordial but firm in her refusal to make any more payments until we reveal our progress."

Salaì groaned, and Astro opened his eye wide.

"But, Master," I said, wincing in pain. "Master, you have been clear in your terms. You told Her Ladyship that she must refrain from asking to see the work or trying to discover its intent before the festival. She promised that all the keys to the workshop would remain with you."

"Yes, Checco. I reminded her of that. She replied thus: 'If you do not show us your work until you are finished, then you shall not mind waiting to be paid until you are finished. Not a scudo more until we see the work.' In the circumstances, I felt it necessary to reveal part of our plan. I told her about the angel."

I closed my eyes and ceased to breathe.

Yet Salaì brightened. "But surely Her Ladyship was glad to hear it!"

"Oh, yes, she was," said Leonardo. "Her mood changed from night to day. She was giddy with delight. Now she desires more than ever to see the angel. She begged me show it to her, and when I said I could not, her face shut tight as a clam. Her eyes narrowed to slits and she said, 'In that case, you shall see no money.'"

"And then?" said Salaì.

"And then I left."

"The woman is the Whore of Babylon," spat Salaì. "We do not need her cursed money. In two short days she shall be begging our forgiveness."

Astro nodded vigorously. The galls on his oak-gall hat bounced in time with his head.

"Perhaps, dear Salaì. But there is a problem. My purse is now reduced to 17 scudi. I have not yet been paid by the Confraternity for the large panel of the Virgin, and we have spent all of Isabella's money on two spectacles instead of one. I had hoped to surprise her with the first spectacle on Epiphany Eve, but now we have no money to finish it. We have yet to purchase a mainspring for the new machine, and it will not operate without one."

The four of us grew silent as we thought about the hours and days we had toiled to reach this point. So many trials sent by the Lord!

I said, "Master, is there nothing we can do?"

Leonardo shook his head slowly. "Delaying our plans will not aid us, *dear Checco. Soon we shall not be able to feed ourselves, much less finish the machine. Perhaps the money from the Confraternity will arrive in time, but that would require a miracle. You know my mind on miracles. Therefore, let us complete the work of which we are able, and tomorrow I shall make a decision."*

I trudged downstairs to the workshop, my heart heavy with regret. That afternoon I found working difficult. I had forgotten my burnt face, so painful was the thought of not completing our machine.

During the night I could not sleep as my mind went round and round, trying to solve the problem of money.

EDITOR'S EMAIL

Speaking of money, I have some bad news. I know I promised to shield you from the issues surrounding Dickson, but the situation is deteriorating. It looks like his legal team is executing a scorched-earth attack against us. Their lawsuit has little merit, but it does have a huge war chest.

Like a number of other publishers, Harker has been trying to stay independent in the face of falling revenues. Dickson's strategy is to drive our company so far into the red that we'll never recover. At that point we'll be forced to sell. A member of the Big Five will buy us for our backlist and fire the editing staff. The book will almost certainly be abandoned due to "unacceptable risk."

Scarlett, Artie, I want you to know we still believe in you. In fact, at this point, the book now looks like our only hope of saving the company. The stakes couldn't be higher.

I have a big favor to ask. Would you consider a delay to your advances until we get through the lawsuit? We're asking our other authors to do the same. When the book hits, we'll make good on everyone's royalties, plus a generous amount of interest. I'm sorry to have to ask you this, but we're running out of options.

8VO_63

SCARLETT: Shit, shit, shit. This is our fault. We brought a time bomb into your camp, and now it's about to blow. Dammit! I feel terrible about this. You've been so upbeat and encouraging, and all we've done is make it harder for you.

Dickson! The man is fucking evil.

ARTIE: Fucking *evil*.

SCARLETT: Artie!

ARTIE: Sorry, but it's true.

SCARLETT: Peter, there's no question of accepting a hold on our payments. We have enough money to get by, so please do what you need to do. Right, Artie? It'll be our turn to shield you from problems. I'm just worried about the impact on all the other authors.

ARTIE: We're your partners on this journey. In for a penny, in for a pound. Don't worry about us. Focus on the legal issues, and we'll finish up the manuscript. The book will turn the situation around, you'll see.

This next chapter should give you hope. It's a real corker.

When the sun came up in the morning, Salaì was gone. His clothes were missing, and so were his personal effects. As the accounts were my responsibility, I hurried downstairs to check the cash box.

Empty.

I searched the shelves, the tables, the drawers. No sign of Leonardo's 17 scudi.

I leapt up the stairs two steps at a time and burst into his private chamber. "Master," I said, breathing hard, "Salaì is gone, and so is the money."

Leonardo looked up from his desk, uncomprehending. His eyes grew large. He banged his palm on the desk, knocking over a herd of miniature dragons. "That thieving rooster!" he cried. "I shall wring his scrawny neck!"

He strode down the hallway to Salaì's quarters and kicked the door open. There was nothing in the room but a tidy bed. He flew down the stairs to check the cash box. He opened the lid and slammed it down on the table.

"By Jupiter's beard! I should never have let that Devil into my house," he shouted.

He slumped onto a stool and put his head in his hands, rocking back and forth. Astro put an arm around his shoulder. Leonardo looked up and said, "My dear Tommaso, I fear we are sunk."

I felt his dejection deeply. Not only were his plans undone, but he was betrayed by the one person in whom he had invested so much of his love.

After a long silence, he stood up and pulled back his shoulders. He inhaled slowly. In a voice as clear and strong as a Roman orator's, he said, "Astro, Checco, we must march forward as three. Tomorrow is Epiphany Eve. We must spring our trap during the night's festivities, when Isabella least expects it. Astro, continue your work on our theatrical effects. Checco, complete the exterior of the machine. Meanwhile, I shall design an alternate means of propulsion to replace the mainspring."

Whilst Astro mixed chemicals at his workbench, I peered through the window. Across the courtyard, Isabella's spy stood in the shadows of the arcade, searching for clues as to the nature of our spectacle.

By the afternoon, Leonardo was no closer to solving the problem caused by the lack of a mainspring. His only solution was to place the machine on the ground and forgo the drama of its descent from the balcony. I feared this might compromise its purpose, but as Leonardo had not fully revealed its purpose, I kept my thoughts to myself.

The air turned colder as the sun began to set. Leonardo called us to his worktable. "My darlings," he said, clasping our hands in each of his, "we have only one day left to prepare our spectacle. I wanted you to know this before tomorrow night: No matter what happens, no matter whether we *succeed or fail, you have made me very proud. I could not wish for a better pair of assistants, nor a better pair of friends." He gave our hands a squeeze.*

I felt I might cry and so turned away. Astro's face broke into a comical grin.

Before I could recover, there came the scraping sound of a key in a lock. The door burst open. Our heads swiveled in unison. In came Salaì with two large bags and a rush of cold air. He placed the bags on the ground and slammed the door against the wind.

Leonardo stood up, dumbfounded.

"I am back!" cried Salaì. "I believe I have what we need." He carried the bags to where we were standing and dropped them at our feet. He pulled back his cloak and produced a mainspring.

Astro took it, his eye gliding over its polished surfaces.

Salaì then reached down into one of his bags and pulled out a cage of live snakes. "For the guts!" he squealed, delighted with his contribution.

He reached into the other bag and pulled out an empty glass jar, handing it to Astro. "I borrowed this from your shelf."

Finally, he reached into the bag again and produced a cured ham, a loaf of bread, and two bottles of wine. These he placed on the table. "For tonight!"

Leonardo embraced him like a father welcoming a prodigal son.

Salaì disintangled himself and reached into his cloak. "One more thing." He pulled out a purse and plopped it on the table. "Your 17 scudi."

Leonardo tried to talk but words would not come. Finally, he said, "Salaì, Salaì, what have you done? How is this possible?"

Salaì smiled so broadly I thought his face would break in half. "Open the wine and I shall tell you."

Astro placed four cups on the table and poured the wine while I cut the ham into slices. When everything was ready, we sat down to eat.

"First of all," said Salaì, stuffing his mouth with bread, "I was sorry to disappear without telling you. I had to leave early, before Isabella's spies had moved into position. I went down to the marketplace, where I got a

good price for my clothing, my ivory comb, my dagger, and a small baby Jesus I had painted for Christmas.

"Then I searched out the charlatan who sells snake-bite potions to gullible townspeople. He was setting up his table for a day of trickery. I made him a wager that I could draw a larger crowd with one jar of water than he could draw with all of his potions put together.

"My wager was this: If I should win, he would give me all his serpents, plus 20 scudi from his own purse. If he should win, I would give him all the money I had made selling my goods, plus my purse of 17 scudi—for a total of 55 scudi."

Leonardo was aghast. "You risked all the money we had for a bag of snakes?"

"Ah, but there was little risk, Master. Do you remember Astro's magic of raising a quattrino in a jar of white vinegar?"

Leonardo smiled, and then began to laugh. Soon Astro began to laugh as well, and then myself. We were laughing so hard that we could barely eat, and soon could barely breathe. Wine bubbled from Astro's nostrils. His oak galls bounced wildly as he howled with delight.

"I told the Mantuans that potions may well guard against snake bites, but my secret prayer can raise the dead as surely as it can raise this quattrino. My crowd grew to nearly twice the size of the charlatan's crowd. At the end of my demonstration, people were shoving money into my hands to buy my life-giving remedy.

"The charlatan was so excited that he gave me all his serpents, plus the 20 scudi, and another 35 scudi to reveal my secret prayer. When I left him he was still trying to make the quattrino rise, and wondering if there might be something amiss with his finger!"

Astro fell to the floor with a thump, so filled with mirth was he. Leonardo simply shook his head in wonder. It was then that I understood he was right. People would rather believe than know.

"Let us finish the wine tonight," said Leonardo, "and tomorrow we shall finish the machine. Perhaps, Salaì, you can compose a prayer to draw

Isabella into our trap!"

"Master," he said, "what exactly are we trying to do with our spectacle?"

"To make Isabella confess!"

EDITOR'S EMAIL

I have to say, that really cheered me up. Also your willingness to bear with us on the payments. I was worried we might have to call it quits—not just the three of us but the whole company. But something you said gave me pause. You said it's your turn to shield me from problems. What problems? Is anything wrong?

8VO_64

SCARLETT: No, no, we're fine. It's just that we had another van sighting. A few days ago. We can't shake the feeling that sooner or later we'll be meeting Signore Six Arms in a dark alley. We made a decision to stay out of dark alleys.

In any case, we're getting close to the end. Soon we'll be able to wrap up the translation and fact-check the remaining details. We're satisfied that Melzi told the truth from beginning to end. But. We're professionals. I-dotting and T-crossing are part of the service.

ARTIE: You won't believe what happens next, Peter. I must say I had some difficulty with this chapter. You know my aversion to horrific scenes. And yet, in spite of my squeamishness, the show must go on.

The festivities began at dusk on Epiphany Eve with a lavish dinner in the main dining hall. Courtiers passed to and fro outside the workshop, and distant music wove its enchantment into the cool streams of evening air. Christmas carols, derived from the drab plainsong chants of long ago, took on new life when rendered by the drunken harmonies of revelers.

Leonardo wore an Arab-hooded cloak of silver satin with green velvet trim, a pink cap, and purple stockings. Salaì had sold his good clothes for a mainspring, so Leonardo lent him a long purple cape with a wide collar and velvet hood to cover his work breeches and tunic. Astro dressed in the gall-nut robe that matched his hat, and I wore a crimson cloak with a bonnet of black velvet, golden tassels at the corners.

We left the workshop together, talking loudly of our plans for the evening. Upon locking the doors, Astro stretched to his full height and placed the key on the ledge above. I watched as Isabella's spy slipped behind a column.

We turned right at the corner and walked through the passageway that led into town, gossiping like a gaggle of old geese. As soon as we disappeared from sight, Leonardo gave a signal. Salaì pulled up his hood and walked back through the passageway, around the corner, and into the courtyard.

Reappearing at the corner, he sounded a low whistle.

We hurried back to the workshop, whereupon Astro reached up to the ledge for the key.

"It's gone," he said. I nodded and handed him another one.

Back inside, we made our final preparations.

All was dark and silent before midnight. We heard a key rattling its iron bones in the lock. The door gasped open, then slammed shut with the wind. A soft light moved into the room, along with a flutter of silk and taffeta.

Isabella.

She was alone, with only a lantern to guide her way. She took a step forward and stopped as a rat skittered across the stone tiles. She opened the doors of the lantern wider and saw in the corner of the workshop a large object covered in white linen. She ventured toward it, glancing nervously from side to side. Before she could reach it, she heard a stirring high in the rafters.

She froze where she stood.

In the high blackness of the balcony, two eyes began to glow like bellowed coals. They blinked slowly and then narrowed. A faint tide of wind flowed down from the balcony and moved along the floor, rustling her skirts. From behind my screen I could see the two coal-eyes reflecting in Isabella's enlarged pupils. I could feel her senses standing on edge.

Suddenly, a deep voice that rumbled like funeral bells issued from the blackness of the balcony.

"Isss…a…BELL…a," the voice tolled.

She dropped her lantern to the stone floor, extinguishing the light.

"You…have…sssssssinnnned," rasped the tolling bells, like the hissing of a thousand snakes. A violent rush of wind, caused by the flapping of huge leather wings, tore at her clothing. The odor of burning sulphur filled her nostrils.

"I…have…WAIT…ed," rang the rusted bells, more insistent now.

Great wings began to beat the air and a flash of lightning illuminated the whole frightful scene. As if frozen on a painted panel, the beast was revealed in all its hideous horror.

It had the head of a mastiff, red glaucous eyes, and three rows of sharp yellow teeth. It had the wild mane of a lion and the cracked neck of a prehistoric terrapin. Its body was that of dragon, with a double row of spikes lining its spine. Its wings were scaly and bat-like, its feet the talons of a giant raptor. Between its legs was a red penis, erect and bristling with dark gray thorns. Curving forward above its back was the tail of a scorpion, twitching and ready to strike.

If Isabella was afraid, she hid it well. Her spine seemed to stiffen in defiance.

The beast kicked off the balustrade into the air, and as it descended to the ground, smoke and fire erupted around it. It landed two arm-lengths from Isabella, its breath stinking like sulfur and its hide reeking of dung. The light from the fires illuminated its fearsome face.

Another fire sprung up in a dark corner of the room under the balcony, casting light on the cloaked figure of Salaì. He wore a death mask of Il Serpente, which I had made from Leonardo's drawing. In a voice that seemed to come from beyond the grave, he recited the passage from Dante:

"See how mutilated I am;
Before me, another weeps as well,
His face split from forehead to chin;"

With this he peeled back the skin of Il Serpente's face, revealing the muscles and tendons and frightening teeth beneath.

"And all the others you see here
Were those who spread scandal
And divided people up."

Isabella cracked open. Her defiance turned to recognition. She began to understand the horror of what she had done. Wordless noises tumbled incoherently in the back of her throat.

"You have sinned against the Lord," cried the beast, its voice clanging off the walls. "You have stolen the soul of another. You are mine!" The wails of eternity echoed in that voice, the pitiful howls of the damned, the protests of a billion dead sinners wishing they had never been born.

Isabella plucked the medallion from her neck and threw it to the floor. "I repent! I repent!" she bleated. "I did not mean to hurt anyone!"

"WHYYYYYYYYYY?" boomed the beast, its eyes flashing red.

Tears streamed down Isabella's face. Her breathing came faster. Finally, she blurted out: "Because Lucrezia stole my husband!"

With that, the mystery unfurled like the petals of a deadly morning glory. Now we saw the root of all of this treachery.

The beast boomed again: "You have KILLED!" it tolled. "You will join us tonight!" Its scaly chest opened to reveal a writhing nest of vipers, coiling around the twisted branch of a tree.

I watched in anguish as Isabella's soul submerged. She fell to her knees, hands covering her face. "No, no, PLEASE! Do not take me. I meant no harm to Il Serpente. It was an accident! An accident! I promise, promise, promise. I will never sin again!"

Her eyes rolled up and she slumped to the floor. Leonardo ran from *behind the folding screen to raise her head, whilst Salaì brought a cup of water to her lips.*

EDITOR'S EMAIL

Whoa, whoa! What a scene! Incredible! The lightning, the fire, the booming voice like a bell. Can you imagine being alone and having a hideous monster come down at you like that? Isabella must have been petrified. Petrified! I mean, that was spectacular!

8VO_65

[HIGHWAY SOUNDS]

SCARLETT: They don't call it a spectacle for nothing. I hope your movie guy is on this. We weren't expecting anything this cinematic, but Melzi's story is a natural for the screen. Leonardo really did a number on Isabella, don't you think? Getting her to walk into that trap? And the big reveal: *Lucrezia stole my husband!*

Gonzaga certainly didn't have the refinement of someone like Bembo, but he had an animal magnetism Lucrezia would have found irresistable. He was much more like the men she'd loved as a child— her father Rodrigo and brother Cesare.

And then, of course, Gonzaga was married to her rival. How can you put a pricetag on revenge?

Artie and I checked into this whole spectacle business. It turns out that when you look at all of Leonardo's celebrated inventions— the ornithopter, the diving suit, the machine gun, the self-propelled cart, the clever painting techniques—what he was really getting paid for were his spectacles. He was doing tons of these.

Unfortunately, none of the sketches for these events have survived. He probably tossed them as soon as he finished. He considered spectacles his bread-and-butter projects—not part of his serious work. But as you can tell, he was the Cecil B. DeMille of Renaissance Italy.

ARTIE: I'd say more like a Ridley Scott—*Alien, Blade Runner, Gladiator, The Martian.*

SCARLETT: You *would* say that. The man is all eye and no head. And a Brit, too.

ARTIE: Are you saying I can't be objective?

SCARLETT: I'm saying Leonardo was more than an artist. Fuck sake.

ARTIE: Don't be gobby.

SCARLETT: Yes, Mother.

ARTIE: Sorry, Peter. I think we've been cooped up in the car too long. I'm sure you'd rather hear what happens next than listen to our bickering, so allow me to read on.

Leonardo returned from his visit with Isabella. This time his mood was quite jovial. He gathered us round in front of the forge, where Astro had prepared a fire.

"Her Ladyship sends her warm greetings. She is resting quietly in her chamber after suffering a blow to the head. Happily, her speech is normal and her thoughts are coherent. She is much chastened after a frightening ordeal with a certain beast," said Leonardo, a sly smile crinkling his eyes. "I assured her we had seen no evidence of supernatural activity in the workshop."

Astro grinned crazily at this. Salaì slapped the table with his palms and gave a sharp laugh.

"She believes what she saw was not merely a vivid dream but a visitation from Satan, and perhaps a final chance to atone for her sins. Her Ladyship was most interested in my advice on the matter. I asked her to lay out the chain of events from the beginning, and I assured her I would

do my best to give her fair counsel.

"She told me that one day in March she received a trove of letters from one of Lucrezia's maids. The young woman had hoped to leave Lucrezia's employ for a better position with Isabella. For Isabella, any opportunity to annoy her rival was a victory, so she hired the maid and accepted the letters. Some were bundled in red ribbons, others in blue. And what letters they were! The bundles tied in red came from Bembo—beautiful letters and poems that made Isabella blush. She grew even more jealous of her rival, if that were possible. In one of these letters Isabella found a medallion, a gold disc engraved with the inscription, 'Est animum.' The accompanying letter was so touching that her jealousy turned to irritation.

"'How dare she treat Bembo with such disregard,' she asked me, 'as to use the medallion as a test of affection without intending to wear it?'

"Isabella herself had taken no lovers since her marriage to Gonzaga. Of course, Gonzaga was not a poet. He cared only for the military and other manly pursuits. She decided then and there to wear the medallion herself so news of it would get back to Lucrezia.

"And yet it was the letters tied up with blue that sent her into a cold fury. As soon as she opened the first one she recognized her husband's handwriting. She could barely read it, so ardent were Gonzaga's words to Lucrezia. He had never directed such passion towards Isabella, and now her rival—her rival!—was the recipient of all the affection she had been denied."

I could feel a welling of tears behind my eyes. I had never heard a more heartbreaking story in my life. "Master, what did she do?"

"She grew clever. She plotted revenge against the villains in her treacherous circle. She hired the assassin Il Serpente to deliver a message to Lucrezia. He was told to say that Bembo had sent him, and if Lucrezia did not end her affair with Gonzaga, Bembo would publish their love letters."

Astro's eye grew as large as a dinner plate. Salaì leaned forward on his elbows.

"But we know the plan went awry. Lucrezia is not one to be trifled

with. It took her six years to produce an heir for the Este, and she was not about to relinquish her new status to appease Bembo's jealousy.

"We can imagine that when Il Serpente arrived at the castle bearing the message, Lucrezia took the news calmly and asked him to wait while she composed a return message. She re-entered the waiting room with two cups of wine, one for her and one for the messenger, the latter infused with cantarella. Il Serpente drank from the poisoned cup and fell to his knees on the carpet."

"The silk thread!" I cried, recalling the ultramarine filament he had found on Il Serpente's breeches.

"Well remembered, Checco. Lucrezia then sent for Griffo, whom she knew had the skills, access, and desire to carry out her treachery. Griffo brought Il Serpente to the Aldine Press in a donkey cart, and there impressed a passage from Dante onto his face as a warning to Bembo—and revenge against Aldo."

"And this was the act that killed the messenger?"

"It was. Il Serpente was only seeming dead. He might have recovered had his skull not been crushed by the press."

"Ah, yes, Master. This you had surmised from the start." I opened my book to my earliest notes. "Here, on the page from the morgue, I wrote that we seemed to have two murderers: one who intended to murder and failed, and another who did not intend it and succeeded. And now we have a third murderer: Isabella, who meant only to protect her marriage, but unknowingly set a dozen dark planets in motion."

Leonardo smiled, his pale eyes shining. "Checco, you could be a poet."

I was unaccustomed to such praise in the company of my elders. I felt embarrassed, and pretended not to hear it. "Does Her Ladyship realize the mischief she has wrought?"

"I think not. And yet she knew something was amiss. She had learned about the assassination of Strozzi from one of her spies. She then wrote about it to Pope Julius. It was he who reinforced her belief that Lucrezia's husband had given the order.

"Meanwhile, Gonzaga would not talk to her and Lucrezia would not torture her. She became isolated. When the beast penetrated the secrets of her heart, she fell to pieces."

Astro glanced at Salaì, and Salaì turned to Leonardo, saying, "Does she know everything now?"

"Almost everything, my dear Salaì. I completed the chain of events for Her Ladyship, except for the making of the mechanical beast and a few other details that would only vex her. These she can learn when she reads the excellent octavo by Count Francesco da Melzi."

Salaì and Astro turned to look at me. "Count Checco?" said Salaì, twisting his visage into that of a clown.

EDITOR'S EMAIL

I'm stunned. This is one tragic tale.

8VO_66

[CAR RADIO PLAYING]

ARTIE: A tragic tale, indeed. What a tangled web we weave when first we practice to deceive.

SCARLETT: Shakespeare.

ARTIE: Sir Walter Scott, Marmion. You Americans think everything came from Shakespeare. Scarlett—put your tongue back in your mouth. It's unbecoming.

SCARLETT: Holy shit—we're fucked!

ARTIE: Scarlett, what did I—

SCARLETT: No, Artie, look! We're being followed. Check your side mirror. That same pair of headlights has been stuck to our rear end through the last three interchanges. I sped up and slowed down a couple of times, but the headlights are keeping pace.

Here—take the phone.

[SOUND BREAKING UP]

I'm getting off…autostrada…see what he…

Shit…right behind…Peter, we're on a side…off the E45, heading…Mantua. I guess it can't hurt…tell where we are…already been spotted…lonely road, no streetlights, just the lights from the oil refineries that seem to be, like, everywhere.

Artie, hold on!

[SILENCE]

Well, that was exciting. A bit of a nightmare, honestly, but we managed to get ourselves to a safe hotel. We were so shook up that we downed two bottles of Prosecco, one from each minibar. Artie's asleep in her room.

Let's see, where did we leave off? Oh, yeah, with headlights following us onto a side road. At that point I tossed the phone to Artie and clamped both hands on the wheel. Artie shut the recording off.

I know you want to hear what happened, so I'll do my best. Excuse my thick tongue. Prosecco sneaks up on you.

Okay, so we're in this, I don't know, random part of Italy when we get a bogie on our tail. I drive deeper into the darkness, and all I can see is black trees sliding by against rolling marshland. I have an aversion to darkness, Peter. It always feels like the walls are closing in, even in a wide-open landscape. I started to panic. I wondered how I got here, how I ended up trapped in a car with a partner I barely know on a mission I can't control.

Artie senses my anxiety. She grips my shoulder and says, be brave, love.

I stomp on the gas and take it up to 160. Now Artie's clutching the dashboard like we're plunging downhill on the Coney Island Cyclone.

This puts enough distance between us and our follower to give me some options. I take a sharp curve to the right and the tires squeal like steel-belted pigs. I cut the lights and swerve onto a deserted refinery road. Taillights shoot past in the rearview and I think, *whew*, lost him. But then he slows down and makes a three-point turn.

I roll the car further into the refinery, looking for a shadow we can pull over ourselves like a blanket. But the thing about refineries is this: they're covered in lights. Our only shot is to drive so far into the lights that we disappear like a black hole in a star-filled sky. Luckily, our rental is a deep blue, so we have a fighting chance.

I find a small space between some shoulder-high shrubs and pull the car straight in, taillights facing out. Don't want the reflective metal inside the headlights to give us away.

Our follower creeps along the road and slips past us as if we weren't there. But I can see *him* in the mirror. Sitting in the white van with a stupid cartoon on the side. Salvatore.

Artie grabs my hand.

I lower my window halfway to listen, but all I can hear is the hissing of marsh grass. The stink of sulfur smacks me in the nose like a handful of cowshit. I quickly close the window. I back the car out and leave the way we came.

And that's it. Adventure over.

We manage to locate a two-room suite with secure parking on the outskirts of Mantua. Artie's a wreck, and I'm not doing great, apart from the buzz. At least now I know what Salvatore looks like. Tomorrow we'll swap our car and do some recon in Mantua.

EDITOR'S EMAIL

Jesus, you two are going to give me a heart attack. I won't sleep until you've wrapped all this up and made your escape. How much more do you have? Can't we just agree that the manuscript is authentic? Nothing you've found so far has proven it false.

8VO_67

SCARLETT: Peter, I'm a scientist. I can't just take a leap of faith. Artie's a stone-cold professional. We only have a few more pages to go. We want to make sure the project is all tied up with a nice big bow. A *pink* bow, if Artie has anything to say about it.

Today we located what we think is the workshop. Mantua looks just the way Melzi described it—the palace, the piazza, the courtyard, the whole nine yards. The only difference is a huge church opposite the shop, the Basilica di Santa Barbara, which hadn't been built at the time.

The workshop itself is truly atmospheric. Looks like it still has the original dust. Three double doors across the front, each set within a stone arch. In the middle two are the windows Melzi had glazed against the cold. No glass anymore, just ancient wrought-iron grilles with wire screens to keep out the mice. To the left of the doors is the passageway into town.

This evening the streets are lined with office workers honking their way home in tired resignation. Boys on skeleton bikes blasting radios from discount backpacks. Girls wondering who they'll marry and knowing they'll end up alone anyway. Evening shadows running up cooly to overtake the elderly. Let's face it, no one here is going anywhere.

Can you tell I'm feeling discouraged?

ARTIE: It's bloody hard to miss, young lady.

Peter, you'll be pleased to know there's light at the end of the tale. Here we go.

The first day of Carnivale felt like the beginning of spring. The air was warm and clear. The piazza was filled with flowers, placed there by the workers to welcome guests who had traveled long distances to join the festivities. The scents of lilies, irises, and columbines mixed with those of primroses, heartsease, and pinks. Olive and ivy branches lay across ledges, wound around columns, cascaded from windows.

Inside the workshop, Leonardo adjusted his green velvet cap. He tied his beard in two places to create diminishing volumes of silky, white hair that flowed softly over his favorite rose tunic. This led one's eye down to green wool stockings and finely tooled boots, much as in my portrait of him. Leonardo had remained dedicated to the principle of La Bella Figura, the studied illusion of beauty and wealth, even when his purse was down to 17 scudi.

Salaì had purchased new clothes from the proceeds of his wager, and now equaled Leonardo in his display of finery. He wore a doublet of pale blue silk with white brocade in the French style, along with white buskins and a four-cornered hat of blue velvet, adorned with a tall white plume.

Even Zoroastro had made an effort at elegance. He abandoned his oak-gall costume in favor of a gown made of golden taffeta and a silver cap.

I myself wore my best brocade doublet, silk-ribboned breeches, and a new pair of boots that Salaì had bought from his winnings. He seemed a different person after our adventure, and I now felt a great deal of affection for him.

By the time we reached the Piazza Castello, the servants had set up rows of chairs and benches from which to view the opening spectacle. Nestled in the crescent-shaped entrance to the Castello di San Giorgio was a broad stage festooned with flowers and a low fence of olive branches. High above the stage, perched on the ridge of the old tile roof, was the mechanical angel. It stood quiet, covered in a pale blue sheet to match the sky, making it nearly invisible.

We seated ourselves at the corner of the entrance under the arcade, our chairs hidden from view by a set of folding screens. From here we could operate the angel and observe the audience at the same time. Zoroastro and Salaì set about climbing the interior stairs to the roof, leaving me alone with Leonardo.

"Master," I said, unsure of how to ask my question.

"Yes, Checco."

"We began our long journey nearly a year ago. It led us from Milan to Venice, Venice to Ferrara, then back to Milan, and now to Mantua. Slowly and with great effort, we have managed to unravel the knot. We know who the messenger was, how he was murdered, and who the perpetrators were. We understand the motives of the parties involved, and we have a confession from the instigator, Isabella."

"That is correct."

"We have solved the mystery, have we not?"

"Yes, Checco."

"But I fear we have not resolved the problem. How will we save Aldo's business? How will we get your notebooks published?"

"Dear boy," he said, removing a piece of lint from the collar of my cloak. "You have learned much as my pupil. I am very proud of you." He turned to gaze across the piazza as the guests began to arrive. He seemed pleased by what he saw.

He lowered his voice and said: "I have not forgotten the purpose of our efforts. Today we will know if victory is ours or if our considerable efforts have been in vain. Isabella has agreed to undo the damage she has caused. She pledged to apologize to Lucrezia and ask her forgiveness. If she can do this with sincerity, I believe Lucrezia will reciprocate by ending her affair with Gonzaga.

"Together, dear Checcco, they must intercede on behalf of Aldo. I agreed that if their efforts to reopen the Aldine Press are successful, it would not be necessary to supply my evidence to the Venice authorities. And in fact, I should be the soul of discretion for at least five years. After that, I shall make a judgment as to whether to continue my silence.

"As for Il Serpente, I fear nothing can be done. He was a known assassin, and since Griffo believed he was already dead when he killed him, I prefer to leave the scales of justice as we found them."

I was about to respond when the blast of trumpets echoed off the build-

ings enclosing the piazza. A cheer rose from the crowd. As the trumpets faded, the orchestra followed with the martial anthem of Mantua, ending in a rousing crescendo of horns and drums.

The piazza then grew quiet. A servant whispered something to Leonardo, who in turn gave a signal to the rooftop. Salaì, hidden behind the ridge, pulled the sheet from the angel with a dramatic flourish.

The crowd gasped.

The mechanical angel stood motionless on the roof, its white robe fluttering in the afternoon light. Church bells began to ring, first quietly, and then with more insistence. More bells joined these, and then more, as if all the bells in the world were ringing in unison. When the ringing ceased and the echoes died down, the angel's wings began to move.

Would it fly? A thousand insects raced up my spine. My palms began to sweat.

The angel leaned forward, crouched, and with the strength and grace of a massive bird, pushed off the roof. It soared out over the stage, its white feathered wings pounding the air, its white robes flowing out behind. It slowed as it descended, its wings beating faster, and settled softly on the stage. It took two steps toward the crowd, fell to one knee, and opened wide its robes. Inside was the most extravagant bouquet of flowers I had ever seen. Roses, the symbol of friendship. The crowd gasped again and jumped to its feet in wild applause.

Leonardo grabbed my forearm. "Look," he said, indicating the front row.

Isabella and Lucrezia sat side by side in the seats of honor. Lucrezia found Isabella's hand and squeezed it. Isabella leaned over and kissed her cheek.

"There it is," said Leonardo.

The angel reached into the cavity of its chest and began to strew roses, one by one, into the crowd. In a voice that shook the palace walls, our magnificent machine roared:

"Welcome, dearest friends of Mantua, to CARNIVALE!"

The orchestra struck up a bracing tune, and the guests began to dance.

Isabella and Lucrezia stood to face the dancers and clapped their hands in time with the music, their faces glowing with happiness.

EDITOR'S EMAIL

You can't see me right now, but tears are streaming down my face. Amazing. I actually think someone like Ridley Scott would be perfect for this. Our film-rights guy is on it. Is there more?

8VO_68

ARTIE: One chapter to go. An epilogue, if you will. Melzi recounts what happens to the two women, and Leonardo leaves his pupil with some encouragement and a few final thoughts.

In the months to come, Dear Reader, the happiness of Isabella and Lucrezia would give way to a sense of duty.

Alfonso and Gonzaga went to war on opposite sides, leaving Isabella and Lucrezia to run their states by themselves. The two women exchanged war news almost daily, sharing hard-won lessons about the management of their domains.

Lucrezia's heir, the infant Ercole, would grow ill and recover during the summer, and soon Her Ladyship would find herself pregnant again. She took respite from her concerns by indulging in the redecoration of rooms that had once been occupied by Isabella. This time she would honor her former rival by returning the rooms to their original style.

In August, the Venetians would capture Gonzaga, leaving Isabella to manage Mantua by herself. Far from finding the task burdensome, she blossomed into a capable leader, free of the cold restraining presence of Gonzaga.

And Aldo? Aldo had secretly moved the Aldine Press into the house of his partner, Andrea Torresani. There he continued to work while awaiting permission to reopen the business. Lucrezia and Isabella soon prevailed with the Venice authorities, clearing the way for Leonardo's notebooks and the introduction of color engraving. The printing of his octavos could proceed.

Upon our return to Milan in March, the Master called me to his studiolo. He bade me sit, positioning his own chair opposite mine. His face was more lined than I had seen it before. The strain of our adventures had taken a toll on his aging body, and yet he seemed as optimistic and brimming with life as ever.

"My dear Checco," he said, "you have been a good pupil. It is time to assume the full responsibilities of a master-in-training. This means you must produce your work at an increasingly rapid pace, for there is no rest in the pursuit of art, writing, and philosophy. You must also strive to be original. The world has little need for those who simply repeat the achievements of others."

"I understand, Master. But tell me, how is it that you, above all others, have conquered so many subjects and produced so many inventions? Have you been blessed by God with divine grace, as people say?"

"Perhaps," said Leonardo. "I feel my good fortune and accept it with gratitude. But I will tell you the secret of creativity, and it does not depend on special gifts from God. The secret is this: One can accomplish little in one day, but much in a year. Take care to work carefully and steadily with the energy that comes from joy. If you do this, you will soon look behind you and see a trail of accomplishments. Do not fear of using up your ideas. The more you use, the more you will get. Over time, your momentum will release its creativity as a flywheel releases energy."

I exhaled, nodding.

"And now, my dear Checco, you have two challenges before you. The first is to prepare my notes, the fruits of my life's work, for publication. I have every faith you will accomplish this feat.

"The second is to publish your own octavo. You will have five years to finish it, and at the end of five years, if the houses of Este and Gonzaga have not yet acknowledged their roles in this tragedy, you must print your

account. In absentia luci, Tenebrae vincunt."

"In the absence of light, darkness prevails. Master, you remembered!"

A smile creased his kindly face. "I am learning, Checco."

He leaned forward and shook my right wrist. "Take care, as you move this hand across the page, Checco, to write with dramatic urgency. History will fail to heed the ordinary diaries of men, but the world will always embrace eloquence and spectacle. Inspired words are the means by which past deeds gain meaning and future deeds gain purpose."

"Yes, Master."

"If the artist wishes to invent beauties that make one fall in love, he is the lord who can create them. And if he wants to make monsters that frighten, or things that cause people to laugh, or even things that rouse them to action, he is their lord and god. I pray you, young Checco, do not shrink from this duty."

Leonardo had always taught me to be observant rather than obedient; to refrain from imposing my wishes on a situation or event; and to record true facts, no matter how much discomfort they may cause. And so it is, Dear Reader, that I have resolved to write only what I have observed and what I believe to be true.

Three fingers hold the pen, yet the whole body aches, so say the monks who taught me to write. I rest my weary hand this day, November 28, the year of our Christian salvation 1514.

Count Francesco Melzi
Rome

SCARLETT: *Mic drop!* Leonardo, where have you been all my life? Be observant rather than obedient. Don't impose your wishes on a situation. Record true facts. Can you imagine having this man as your mentor in 1508? I can hardly wait to see what the science community makes of this. He was doing science before we even knew what to call it.

So there we are, Mr. Chenoweth. The astonishing story of how the greatest genius of all time used abductive logic to solve a riddle that deduction couldn't reach. Step aside, Sherlock Holmes, there's a new sheriff in town.

ARTIE: Indeed.

SCARLETT: What do you think, Mr. Editor? Good story, or best story ever?

EDITOR'S EMAIL

This will certainly rock the foundations of the publishing world. It's rare to get a non-fiction book that's not only a page-turner but a historical blockbuster to boot. We just need to keep our business alive until we can get this thing out there. Then it's a whole new ballgame, and Dickson can shove it up his ass. Sorry if that sounds unprofessional.

8VO_69

ARTIE: Perfectly understandable in the circumstances, Peter.

Scarlett and I still have a few loose ends to tie up. We've scheduled a meeting tomorrow with the palace historian to see if she has any records of Leonardo's visit. I must say, I'm not hopeful.

However, we did clear up one little mystery. It's about the date that was added in the margin of Melzi's letter to Aldo: *m. 6 feb 15.* I checked with Paola, who knew instantly what it was. In Italian, *m.* stands for *morto.* Dead. Melzi discovered that Aldo had died two weeks earlier, and never sent the letter. This explains why the manuscript never got published, and why it was still in Melzi's leather portfolio. As to how the portfolio came to be hidden under the floorboards of a converted workshop, that's a riddle we may never solve.

Meanwhile, Paola had a brainwave. She thought the archives of the Biblioteca Nazionale Marciana in Venice might be worth a look, since they have a collection of Aldo's correspondence. Perhaps he and Melzi had exchanged some letters before he wrote the one we found.

She'd be happy to connect us directly with the archivist if we'd like.

SCARLETT: You forgot to tell me that. Jesus, what is it with you? Are we on the same team or not?

ARTIE: You didn't seem interested in my conversations with Paola. I thought we might discuss it later.

SCARLETT: Pro tip—when you're being chased by bad guys, tell your partner everything. *Everything.* In real time. Not later. Not when it's convenient. Not when the woo-woo is in the seventh house and Jupiter aligns with Mars. What if there *are* letters, and they give context for Melzi's story? Shouldn't we know?

Artie, sometimes I'm not sure if you're working with the same level of urgency as Peter and I. You seem to be more concerned about your clothes and your wigs and your makeup than you are about the mission. You spend an hour in the bathroom every day before going out. You need to bear down. It's time to show some grit.

Peter, help me out here.

EDITOR'S EMAIL

Scarlett, please don't share this email with Artie. I have a few more things I need to say to you. Believe me when I tell you I don't enjoy being put in this position, but I have to speak up.

Do you understand what Artie has done for you? She's turned her life inside out to become your sidekick. This is a woman of dignity, of erudition, of surpassing grace and civility. How can you be so rude as to question her loyalty? How can you treat this refined woman as if she were a senseless buffoon, or a useless appendage? Leonardo showed more respect for the nutty Astro than you've shown for Artie. He called Astro "Maestro Tommaso."

You, on the other hand, have called Artie a priss, a textbook, and an acidhead. You've made her feel superficial, priggish, and utterly disposable. And what has she called you? Confident. Brilliant. A truth-seeking missile.

If you two were contemporaries, I could write your insults off as youthful banter. But she's twice your age. She's had to combat racism most of her life. Her husband's dead, she's never had kids, and her university has no further use for her. What does she have to look forward to? Only this adventure and the privilege of your company.

All this should arouse your compassion, Scarlett, not your contempt. You couldn't have done any of this without her. In fact, you wouldn't even know about Salvatore without Artie's sharp eye for details.

This isn't right, Scarlett. And don't give me any stupid jokes about charm school. You're a bully.

SCARLETT'S REPLY

Message received.

EDITOR'S EMAIL

Scarlett, where are you? Don't leave me like this. If you're angry, just tell me. You can feel free to rant.

EDITOR'S EMAIL

Scarlett, what happened? I haven't heard from you in two days. Should I call in the cavalry? Let me know what's going on.

8VO_70

[TRAIN SOUNDS]

SCARLETT: Sorry to disappear on you, Peter. I'm not angry. I'm more in the scared-shitless camp. We met Salvatore yesterday, close up and personal.

Can you wait a sec? I have to move to another part of the train—sorry about the noise.

[INTERIOR DOOR OPENS AND CLOSES]

Okay, that's better. I'm sitting by myself in the back of the dining car where I can keep an eye on everyone. Artie's resting in the sleeping car.

Here's what happened.

Yesterday we were heading to the office of the palace historian to ask about the visitors' log. I started to apologize for my recent behavior, but it blew up in my face. We started bickering again. I was *that* close to calling it quits—sick of the criticism, the unsolicited advice, the understated British sarcasm. I figured our work was 99 percent complete, so what the hell. She and Paola could finish up in Venice if they wanted to. I'd be on a plane to Fiji or wherever.

As we're crossing the courtyard toward the main piazza, a worker is fussing with a water faucet near the archway. He suddenly stands up. He's big. He shoves a pipe wrench into his toolbelt and walks straight at us.

The roots of my hair quill up over my scalp. I grab Artie's hand and pull her through the side door of the church—the basilica I told you about, across from the workshop. I shut the door and try to lock it from the inside. A sexton comes out of nowhere and wants to know what we're doing.

Non potete entrare da questa porta, he says. You can't come in this way. *Posso aiutarvi?*

I yank Artie right past him, through the vestibule and into the nave, where we take refuge behind a pew.

Daylight floods the vestibule as the handyman kicks the door open. Without a second thought—*BANG!*—he shoots the sexton in the forehead with a Ramset. That's a powder-activated nail gun designed to penetrate steel and concrete. The poor man drops like a sack of spuds.

I quickly shove Artie into a confessional and pull the curtain. I walk slowly over to the altar and kneel in front of it with Artie's paisley scarf over my head. I'm not wearing my usual ratty jeans, so I look like a devout cat lady. Salvatore rushes right past me, and, one by one, starts ripping back all the curtains on the confessionals. He gets to Artie's and then…and then nothing.

She's gone.

A priest comes out from behind the wooden door of the last confessional and starts yelling at Salvatore in Italian. Sal reaches for his nail gun but thinks better of it. Probably a double mortal sin to kill a priest—even Italian goons have their limits.

I spot a room just to the left of the altar, labeled *Sacrestia*, and disappear into it. On the right side of the room is a wooden bench with a hinged lid. I lift it open.

Artie.

She's breathing hard and seems to be in a state of tharn, a terrified rabbit cowering in its hole. I put my finger to my lips and close the lid.

Salvatore sees me and sprints full speed toward the sacristy. I light out through the back, slamming the door behind me. There's another door at the end of a hallway that leads to a triangular walled garden. I open it, then turn back and shut myself in a small restroom off the hall. When he races past me into the garden, I tiptoe out of the restroom and lock the door behind him.

Artie's a shivering wreck. I grab a dish of holy water from outside the confessional and splash it on her face.

What are on earth are you doing? she hisses.

What am I doing? I'm saving your life, that's what I'm doing. You're not a Catholic. It's just water.

It's *blessed!*

Well, that should help, shouldn't it?

It's simply not the done thing, she says, and her body starts to sag. Scarlett, she says, I'm mafted. Her eyes flutter and close.

I pull her slowly to her feet and put my arm around her waist. We have to go, I say. *Now.*

Salvatore is still in the garden, but it sounds like he's removing the hinges of the door with a power driver.

I hurry her past the priest, who's kneeling over the sexton. He's loosening the man's collar with one hand and holding a phone to his ear with the other. There's a nail sticking out of the man's forehead and blood streaming onto the marble floor. We hobble out through the passageway by the workshop and down to the car. I help her in from the passenger side and crank the seatback flat. Then I drive us to the rental car dropoff at the train station.

[WAIL OF TRAIN HORN]

My phone shudders and I press the button. It's a text from Dickson: Turn over the MS, he says. There is no alternative and no way out.

Shit, I think. How did he find us?

You'll have to leave your wigs, I say to Artie. All we can take are the two bags and the satchel. Hold onto your purse.

I open the trunk and place my latest phone in the fuse compartment above the wheel well. Whoever rents the car next may get a six-armed visitor. I pull Artie's bag over her shoulder and hand her the metal box.

Can you make it? I say.

She nods.

We walk slowly to the *tabacchi* at the train station, where I buy some tickets and a burner phone, just in case.

Peter, I'm not sure when I can get back to you. Our plan is to keep switching trains and check for followers at each station. Right now I have to stop. I'm exhausted.

Talk later.

I feel so helpless. You're clearly in serious danger, Scarlett. I googled the Mantua news and saw that the sexton was pronounced DOA at the Ospedale Carlo Poma. They said he died instantly. That could have been you.

Dickson is getting desperate. His legal team is losing ground, so he's stepping up the pressure in creative ways. I really don't know how he's tracking you. It's spooky.

Is Artie okay? Does she need medical attention?

8VO_71

SCARLETT: Artie's feeling better, but she's terribly fatigued. This whole adventure has taken a toll, poor thing. I feel like such an jerk, the way I've treated her.

Peter, I need to get a few things off my chest. Please don't put any of this in the book. It's just for you…I was going to say it's just for your benefit, but let's be honest. It's for mine. The episode in the church brought me face to face with my own mortality. You know how I am about balancing the scales. If I don't make it through this nightmare, I want the record to show that I gave props to the people that mattered to me.

When I look back, Artie's probably the only one who ever gave a shit about me. My parents never did. My boyfriend moved on years ago. I never really bonded with my classmates. Seems like all they thought about was As, Bs, Cs, Ds, and Fs—Allowances, Bingeing, Cocktails, Drugs, and Fortnite. I got so tired of hearing about video games and whose tats are the dopest that I finally tuned out. Not that I'm against any of that stuff, but there's a whole world out there. Social inequality will never autocorrect. The planet is not going to heal itself. Business won't save the future without a bunch of new rules. Education won't make us smarter until everyone has it.

Peter, I think we should gather up all of our shallowness, our selfishness, our unfairness, our greed, toss it onto a big pile and burn it. Bonfire of the stupidities. Get rid of it for good. I promise to throw my own stuff on top—my meanness, my bitterness, my lack of empathy.

Last night I was standing at the rear window of the last car, watching the silver snail-gleam of the tracks feed out endlessly, receding into the darkness. I was thinking, is this my new life? A sleepless passenger on a train to nowhere? I turned to head back through the cars, past the slumbering, dreaming cabins I can never enter, looking for another place to stand and wait.

What got under my skin about Artie was the whole mothering thing. My own mother was absent. She was there, but she wasn't. She never stood up for me, encouraged me, had any expectations of me. It was like she gave up before I was born. Whenever Artie gives me that look, whenever she gets real with me, it just reminds me of how much I missed. It surfaces a ton of bitter feelings. I realize now I'd been taking it out on Artie.

What kind of penance do I have to pay for that? Now I have my own confessional prayer: *O wah, tah jer, kye yam. O wah, tah jer, kye yam.* I say it ten times fast, every night at bedtime.

Peter, are we still friends? After the episode in the church, I feel like I have to unload on somebody. You asked me to be more forthcoming, right? If it's too much, just hit stop.

[TRAIN NOISE, THEN A SIGH]

I can't really blame my mother for her lack of actual mothering. She was trapped by the twin beliefs that women should be oh-so-biddable and oh-so-devout. And my father was right there, ready to take advantage of both, an alcoholic misogynist and religious bully. He'd deliver his sermons in the morning and come home at night stinking of Jack. My mother would tell him I hadn't read my Bible, because, well, I hadn't. He'd drag me down to the cellar and lock me in the utility closet. In the morning he'd let me out and beat me until I recited to perfection some obscure piece of scripture. He said I had to be punished for my pride. When I was fifteen, he not only beat me, but raped me.

You probably don't need to hear about my second-hand sob stories. I don't know why I'm sharing this shit with you. Really, hit the stop button before I embarrass myself.

[TRAIN HORN]

My older brother was gay. My father badgered him to death. Called him an abomination in the eyes of God. Said he should never have been born. My mother kept quiet the whole time, didn't say a word. When he killed himself on his 18th birthday, I ran away from home. I put myself through school and never spoke to either of my parents again.

You called me a bully, and yet I can't stand bullies. I can't stand the Bible. And I can't stand small spaces. That's why I haven't slept in so long. I'd have a five-alarm freakout if I locked myself in a sleeping compartment. I pace the train and hang out in the restaurant car or stand in the gangway between carriages and stare out the window. Windows keep my claustro down to a dull roar.

So here I am, watching the landscape go by, and I'm seeing my reflection superimposed over it. I'm thinking, who are you? You've got no friends, no identity, no future. You've been washed with fear, rinsed with hate, dried with blood. You really *are* lost in translation. You're no longer who you were, and you have no idea who you should be.

They say language is more than language. It's a way of thinking about life.

What's the language of me?

As a little girl I used to lie on the floor and write stories for hours on end. But when my father's drinking got worse, I lost the ability to put words to paper. They say it can happen like that with dysgraphia. Maybe the trauma of mental and physical abuse rewires your brain. My workaround in college was recording my thoughts electronically, then transcribing the words with speech-to-text software. Bockety, as Artie would say, but better than nothing.

I truly admire Artie's ability to manipulate language. She would say, well, dear, I *am* English, in that supercilious way that always sets me off. The fact is, she wasn't born in England at all. English was her second language, and she learned a bunch of others after that.

Artie, you never swear, I tell her. Why is that?

When I was a schoolgirl, she says, six or seven, I became over-excited and peed on a school bench. The girl sitting next to me screamed and ran, and soon I found myself in the office of the head-mistress. She was quite stern.

What the devil got into you? she demanded. I felt angry at myself and started to swear.

I fucked up pink murder, I blurted.

What?

My English wasn't very good, so I just strung together every bad word I could think of.

Pink?

I learned to swear from my father, and he hated pink. Said it was for sissies.

Then what happened?

The headmistress called my mother to tell her what I'd said. I was so ashamed. From that day on I resolved to stop cursing and learn proper English. I became an obedient little girl, and never peed in public again.

And now look at you, I say. A partner in a larceny startup with half the world chasing you. You've come a long way, baby.

Yes, says Artie, I suppose I have.

Peter, I seriously misjudged the old girl. In the beginning I found her so boring I wanted to grab her piping hot tea and throw it in my face just to break the monotony. Now I see there's a vibrant life behind that staid British façade.

I've been calling Artie Artie so long that I've almost forgotten her real name. Our transition to non-entity, to nameless nobody, to worm in the woodwork is almost complete. Sometimes I'm overcome by the enormity of what we've done. The price we'll have to pay. Erasing ourselves. Disappearing without a trace. As if our DNA, our dreams, our names, have been wiped away with a damp sponge. Our memories, our footprints. Like we'd never been born. So something else could be born. Something better.

I feel so guilty about dragging Artie down the road to oblivion. I never understood why she said yes. Last night I get up the nerve to ask her, and you know what she says?

I thought you needed a mission, dear.

I needed a mission. *Me.* And this whole time I thought *she* was the one who needed a mission.

I tell her so, and she says, no dear. I discovered what *I* needed was a daughter. Now I have one. I'm so proud of you. Then she puts her hand on my cheek. I totally lose it. Explode in tears. And you know I never explode in tears.

Several days from now, if we're lucky, we'll go our separate ways. No more Scarlett and Artie. But neither of us will ever forget this adventure. The time we planted a tiny seed that set an example for generations to come. A seed for connecting science and art—truth and beauty—just the way Leonardo wanted it. Maybe it's not much in the scheme of things, but it's not nothing.

I'm a scientist. I don't need no stinkin' mythology. But someone inside me does. Somebody in here needs the soul-stirring voodoo of human stories to make me a real person. A whole person.

Peter, are you there?

Here comes the big thank-you. I know I've been a pain in the ass. Whereas you, you've been a gentleman from start to finish. I hope this book does everything you hoped it would, and that once in a while you think of me. I'll be forever grateful for this chance to make a difference.

I'm so sorry we'll never meet. A girl never knows when she might need a good editor.

EDITOR'S EMAIL

Scarlett, wait. It sounds like you're signing off. You haven't gone to Venice yet. There might be something to Paola's theory about the letters between Aldo and Melzi.

8VO_72

SCARLETT: I think it's best if we pause our correspondence for now, Peter. I just got another text from Dickson, and then one from Salvatore. They're hacking my phone and issuing ultimatums.

ARTIE: Peter, halloo!

SCARLETT: As you can tell, Artie's back. Give us a few days and we'll get back in touch. Don't try to contact us. Assume Dickson knows everything we're saying and doing.

EDITOR'S EMAIL

Got it. If I don't hear from you in a week, I'm sending in the cavalry. I have a bad feeling about this. Stay alert, Scarlett. Artie, glad you're back.

EDITOR'S EMAIL

What's going on? It's been more than a week. Are you alright?

Scarlett?

8VO_73

[SOUND OF MOTORBOATS OUTSIDE]

SCARLETT: It's been a long ten days. I have tons to tell you. For the first time since we've been corresponding, I think it's safe to talk. You'll be hearing mostly from me, for reasons that will become apparent.

Jesus, where do I start?

In my last recording, we were still on the train. Man, that was ages ago. Artie and I spent three days riding around Northern Italy, trying to lose Salvatore. After a long stretch of zero bad-guy sightings, we finally felt it was okay to get off the train. We changed one last time and headed for Venice.

Our three days on the train gave us time to think. We realized Dickson would never stop hounding us until we gave him the manuscript.

Unless.

Unless he believed we didn't have it. At this point we started strategizing like Leonardo. How many ways were there to make it look like the manuscript was no longer an option?

Well, we could hand it over to Paola in a flood of news coverage. What could Dickson do? He might try to make a quick deal with the owners of the townhouse and back it up with legal muscle, but the university would still prevail in the long term. Problem is, in the short term he'd make Paola's life a living hell. All we'd be doing is shifting the problem from our shoulders to hers.

Or we could turn it over to the ROS, the Italian equivalent of the FBI. There's no way Dickson would mess with those guys—he'd be risking an international scandal if something went wrong. Still, the ros gambit could blow up, too. What if Dickson managed to bribe them, say, with free security software framed as a beta test? Or what if the Italian courts decided the manuscript belongs to the owners of the townhouse after all? We'd be cooked.

That's when Artie gets a third idea. Straight from Leonardo's playbook. What if there *were* no manuscript? What if the physical document had been totaled? Wouldn't Dickson simply give up? He's not the sort of guy to waste energy on revenge—he's too practical. He only wants the manuscript, and if he thought it was destroyed, he'd simply call off the dogs and move on to other quarry.

Okay, I know—if we actually destroyed it, we'd be robbing the world of a great treasure. Stay with me, Peter.

Let's say the manuscript were only *seeming* destroyed, as Leonardo would put it. What if we created a spectacle—an event so convincing that Dickson believed the manuscript was a goner? We could get Salvatore off our backs and quietly slip the real manuscript to Paola for safekeeping.

At last, our train pulls into the Santa Lucia station after passing through Mestre, the spot where Leonardo and Melzi had stabled their horses before taking the boat to the Rialto. The station in Venice is a Brutalist monster built by Mussolini. Looks like a massive concrete slab balanced on tall glass windows, fronting the Grand Canal.

The shock of walking from the modern lobby straight into the ancient city is jarring, like an endorfin cream pie in the face. Gondolas, vaporettos, and speedboats gliding gaily back and forth over pale green water. The greenish light reflecting into the buildings across the canal. The air alive with accordions, so corny and so right that it takes your breath away.

We exit through glass doors and descend the wide concrete steps toward the canal, me lugging our two bags and Artie toting the satchel with the manuscript. She feels strong enough to walk, so we turn right and head south along the canal. Best not to engage a water taxi on the principle that, you know, we're on a secret mission. How strange it is to feel like spies in the midst of all these carefree tourists.

As we near the section of Venice that contains the University Ca' Foscari, the buildings grow plainer. Our Airbnb is in a stand-alone structure facing a canal in an ex-industrial section, a no-man's land between a minimum-security prison and a cluster of rundown student apartments.

The owner is waiting out front. He's a paunchy, unshaven slumlord whose *modus operandi* is luring students and their parents out of their comfort zones with low rent. The paint is peeling, the façade has a deficit of visual interest, and the whole area is bland and half-deserted. All this splendor can be yours for 86 dollars a night, American.

Don't worry about noise, he tells us. There's nobody else in the building.

Gee, what a surprise.

He hands over the keys. We haul our meager belongings, bump, bump, bump, up to our flat, a forlorn set of rooms at the top of the stairs. Can't really complain about the amount of space, though. We have our own bedrooms, plus a shared bathroom, a sitting room, and a spacious kitchen. But the linoleum tiles are curling, the surfaces are sticky, and the furniture looks like it might collapse under the weight of an actual human. No place like home.

We stow our stuff and walk down to the supermarket for groceries. After that we head over to a cartoleria near the university, where Artie buys an X-acto knife, a package of number-eleven blades, some gum arabic, a drawing pad, and a sack of goose feathers. Next, we locate a used bookstore and pick up a couple of ancient, ratty-looking books. And finally, we stop at a ferramenta for two sheets of sandpaper, a bag of sand, a roll of duct tape, and a box of steel wool.

After dinner we get to work.

The lighting in the kitchen is a bare bulb trying to look like a fashion statement. Harsh, but at least bright. Artie gets comfortable at the kitchen table and pulls one of the feathers from the paper sack. I sit down next to her, ready to learn.

First you have to scrape off the downy barbs and the after-feather, she says. She takes the X-acto knife to the lower part of the quill. Then you sand off this wispy outer membrane, here, like this. You cut the end of the quill at an angle, and then cure it.

I go to the stove and stick the shaft of the feather into a pan of hot sand.

That should do it, she says, after a few minutes.

I pull it out and hand it back to her. I'm utterly fascinated by the whole process. I ask, where did you learn this?

She lowers her glasses and looks at me like I'm fresh off the saucer from Clythereon 4.

Calligraphy class?

Oh.

She takes her blade and makes a lengthwise cut at the tip of the feather. You have to thin it down at the point, she says, so it's flexible. She cuts away the sides in graceful arcs and sands the underside of the tip. Then she chops a tiny bit off the end to give it a chisel edge.

The tip should separate at the slightest pressure, she says. Don't cut off too much—Melzi used a fine point, which is how he got those delicate thicks and thins.

There. Now you try it.

I press down on the tip and it separates. I take the knife and get to work on the next quill.

Meanwhile, Artie starts cooking the ink. Ink in the Renaissance was made from oak galls and iron sulfate, but the process makes an ink so dark that it wouldn't suit our purposes.

So I give her my own recipe.

First we burn a few of the blank sheets to get a sooty black that'll carbon-date to the 15th century. We mix that with linseed oil, bees-wax, and some tannic acid, which we get from boiling the bindings of our old used books. Then we add a little peroxide so the ink dries a nice rusty brown, like it's been there for centuries. It may not test perfectly, but perfect isn't on the menu.

And, honestly, who's going to bother testing when half the manu-script is burned to a crisp?

Part Five: Inferno

PUBLISHER'S EMAIL

Scarlett, I'm Katherine Cavel, the executive publisher. Peter Chenoweth's superior. He tried to contact you, but when he got no response, he left on sabbatical and handed the project over to me. I've been following your adventures since the beginning, so rest assured that I'm up to speed and ready to assist you. I'll try to be every bit as attentive as Peter was. Please continue sending your recordings. We're very interested in your safety, as well as the possibility of getting additional material for the book. We'll of course be willing to renegotiate if something interesting turns up.

8VO_74

SCARLETT: What the fuck! He leaves? Just like that? Sorry for my language, Ms. Cavel, but I'm really pissed about this. After everything we've been through I'd expect a little more courtesy. I know the project is almost complete, but this makes me feel, I don't know, used. Betrayed. *Violated.* Was this just a game for him?

PUBLISHER'S EMAIL

I understand how you feel, Scarlett. I feel a little used myself. Frankly, we're not sure why he chose this particular moment to take time off. It may have been the pressure of the lawsuit, or maybe the strain of working so long on a difficult project. I'm sure you're aware that *Octavo*—that's what we're calling it—is a make-or-break book for us. Peter had postponed a long-planned vacation with his girlfriend, so I believe they're traveling together. Let us know if there's any way we can help you going forward.

8VO_75

SCARLETT: Apologies, Ms. Cavel, I lost it this morning. I'm back from the edge. This is all my fault. I do hope Mr. Chenoweth is okay, and I wish him the best, wherever he is and whatever he's doing.

And yes, we'd be happy to work directly with you. You're the boss, right? The one who approved the project? The only important thing is that the book gets published so the world can see the real Leonardo.

[LONG SIGH]

Okay, where was I? The spectacle. You may have guessed it was me who made the fake passports. But Artie is on a whole different level. Honestly, I had no idea I was working with a master forger until this week. She has an incredible eye—I mean *incredible*—and the hand of a true craftsman.

She showed me how she holds the quill at a horizontal angle to get the best ink flow. To make this easier, I went into McGyver mode and rigged up a writing desk on the kitchen table, using a cutting board and what's left of our bag of sand. I settled the board onto the bag at a 55-degree slant and secured it to the table with duct tape.

Artie opens the metal box and takes out the leather portfolio. Unties it. Removes the blank sheets from the top of the stack and sets them on the table. It's the same paper Melzi used for the manuscript, complete with fox marks and easily identifiable fibers. She'll have just enough sheets to copy the entire manuscript if she doesn't make any mistakes. She dips her quill into an espresso cup with our home-made ink.

She starts writing.

3 December 1512

*The events I wish to relate, Dear Reader, might be taken as the
ravings of a lunatic were it not for the details I have recorded
in my notes…*

Her handwriting is a dead match for Melzi's. It took a few pages on
the drawing pad to establish a rhythm, but now she's got it.

*Even so, I myself have difficulty believing that such events did
ever take place, so gruesome and fantastical they seem to me
now…*

I ask her how she can write with such fluidity, such small, graceful
letters, like a silk line spinning out from a fishing reel.

Well, dear, it starts with how you hold the pen. You rest the shaft
on your second finger and use your thumb and first finger for control.
This allows you to see the pen tip as you write, so your hand and
eye can work together. If you can't see what you're writing, there's
no feedback loop, so your penmanship is a *fait accompli* and you can't
correct as you go.

*Yet I shall strive to serve the truth as I have served my master,
with diligence and humility.*

Yeah, I say, but I don't know anybody who writes like that.

Sadly, no, she says. It's a lost art. Educators stopped teaching penmanship in the Sixties. They thought it might restrict the personal
expression of students. Unfortunately, they didn't realize that art—
which this is—thrives on craft, discipline, and rules.

Yes, I say, but don't the best artists break rules? Leonardo told
Melzi to be original. He said the world doesn't need people who just
repeat the achievements of others.

You misunderstood, dear. The best artists don't break rules, they
make rules. They set the bar higher for future artists by revealing

new truths, demonstrating new skills. Discipline and craft are the keys to expressing one's imagination. I've always felt that so-called creative freedom is an excuse for people who don't want to do the work.

> *My aim is not to shock or titillate. It is merely to shine a light*
> *on the prodigious creative powers of my master, Leonardo da*
> *Vinci.*

She writes calmly and steadily. The lines appear magically, like waves on the ocean, rising out of nothing and washing onto the shore the color of dark wet sand. Line after line, page after page, her quick brown eyes and rust-splotched hand are locked in a graceful dance, waltzing across water, across time, across the hills and valleys of the ancient paper.

I never realized artists cared so much about discipline. Discipline is one of the reasons I went into science. I like the rigor, the proofs, the tangible outcomes of physics and math. The uncertainties of art give me motion sickness. It's like there's no left or right or up or down. No features on the horizon to help you steer a course. Now I can see that, to be an artist, you need rules and rigor every bit as much as a scientist does. The difference is you have to create them yourself.

I only have one question, Artie, I say. Why didn't you tell me all this before?

She peers at me over her glasses. She says, well, you didn't seem very keen. You were so defensive and fearful about what you were doing that you wouldn't listen to anyone. I have to say, though, I loved the way you laid down the law for Peter: If I don't hear back from you in the time it takes to pee, you said, we're moving on to another publisher. Of course, he saw through you, but he liked you all the more for it. As did I.

I throw my arms around her shoulders and bury my face in her last wig. I love you, Artie, I say, blurting it out like a child.

The ink! What the devil are you doing?

Sorry, sorry, I said. Sorry about everything.

What are you going on about, silly girl?

Nothing, Artie. It's just that it's been so long since I said I love you to anybody.

The next morning my phone nearly leaps off the table with excitement. It's an all-caps text from the Biblioteca Marciana saying they've found something. No letters between Francesco Melzi and Aldo Manuzio, but one letter from Melzi to Aldo's friend, Pietro Bembo. If I would like to come in and pay a small fee, they'd be happy to furnish me with a photocopy.

Venice is a tangle of canals and bridges, but it's suprisingly easy to cross if you know your way. Since I don't, I take my new phone and follow the map from Santa Marta to St. Mark's Square.

The Marciana's a magnificent library that occupies the place of honor across from the Doge's Palace in the shadow of the lion column. The structure was built specifically to house the output of Venice's printing revolution.

I locate the office, sign the form, and pay the fee. *Grazie molto*, I say, slipping the packet into my bag.

No sooner do I start back than I feel an ominous shiver coming from the bag. I grab my phone from the side pocket and check the screen. Another text. This time from Dickson. My heart stops like a smashed clock.

Where R U? it says.

I check to make sure I'd disabled the GPS when I left the Marciana. Off.

You have it and I want it, continues the text. Hand it over to Salvatore at Oke Pizza in Dorsoduro with whatever you got from the library. Tonight 21:00. You know what he looks like. Last chance, bitch.

I have no idea how he's doing this. I drop my phone into the canal, knowing I have a spare back at the flat. I hurry across the bridge to the *ferramenta* where we bought our supplies. I pick out a length of wooden post, the equivalent of a two-by-four in the States, and a small block of poplar. I toss a claw hammer into the basket along with a handful of hundred-millimeter nails.

When I let myself in, Artie's still working away. She's got a stack of sheets piled up to the right of her writing board, filled with perfect cursive.

What on earth is that for, she says, aiming her quill at the wooden post.

Dickson's onto us, I say. He doesn't know where we are, but I'm not taking any chances. Salvatore could shoulder that door right off its hinges.

I reach into the kitchen drawer where I stashed my spare phone and uninstall the SIM card. That's the easy part, I think. How do you uninstall anxiety?

I paint my face all brave and tell Artie not to worry. Salvatore can't bring his van into Venice. Keep working.

I nail the block of poplar to the floor inside the door, then wedge the wooden post between the block and the doorknob. I tack both ends down, just in case.

PUBLISHER'S EMAIL

Scarlett, this is getting way too risky. We recommend you drop what you're doing and get out of Venice now. Activate your escape plan. You can send us Melzi's letter some other time when it's safe.

8VO_76

SCARLETT: Safe? Hardly, Ms. Cavel. If we leave now, there *is* no safe. Safe is getting Dickson to believe there's nothing left to take from us. He won't quit until he tracks us down, at which point we'll be alone and unprotected. There's only one way out of this.

Last night I stood Salvatore up. There's no chance I'd get within a hundred yards of that goon, much less hand over the prize. He'll have to rip it out of my hands.

Meanwhile, Artie's exhausted. She's been writing for nearly thirty hours with only the merest break for a nap. Her face is pale and lined. Her eyes are bloodshot. She looks a thousand years old. I tell her to stop and get some rest, but she refuses. The ink supply looks like it'll hold out, but the quills are almost gone. I cut a few more and line them up on the table.

On the afternoon of the third day, she finishes. All the sheets but two are used up, and the ink is almost gone. She's delirious with fatigue. I finally persuade her to take a nap. She drops off the second her head hits the pillow.

While she's sleeping, I use the time to make dinner. We still have some ciabatta for garlic bread, so I cook up some pasta to go with it. Primavera, in Leonardo's honor. We don't have any wine left, but I'm not leaving the flat unless it's absolutely necessary. Water will have to do.

At four in the afternoon, I can hear her moving around in her room. The door opens and she comes out, looking slightly dazed.

I had the strangest dream, she says, rubbing one eye with the palm of her hand.

Oh, really?

I was just standing, looking over the rooftops, when a hummingbird came right up to me, hovering just outside the window. It's feathers were a beautiful iridescent blue. You know that kind of blue that shifts from ultramarine to cerulean as the light changes? We stared at each other for what seemed like minutes. I couldn't tell what kind it was, since I didn't have my glasses on. I found it a rather spiritual experience.

A hummingbird?

Yes.

I run into Artie's room and look out the window. Nothing. I close the blinds. I go around the rest of the flat and close all the other blinds.

Artie, I say, that was no hummingbird. There *are* no hummingbirds in Italy. That was a micro-drone.

She goes blank.

I turn off the stove and gather up the finished sheets. I stick them in the metal box with the original manuscript and shut the lid. Then I take apart the writing desk, dump the ink down the drain, and stick the used quills into my bag.

C'mon, Artie. We gotta go.

She doesn't move.

Artie, *come on!* I lead her into her room and point to her bag. She starts to pack, mechanically at first, then more quickly.

Good, she's waking up.

Leave the clothes in the closet, I say. Just take your tools and purse and bathroom stuff.

I pack my own bag and do one last check. Looks like we got everything. I pull the nails out of the wooden post and stick them in the pocket of my bag, along with the hammer.

I open the door of the flat and peer out. All clear. No sounds coming from the stairwell. I lean the post against the wall in the outer hallway and lead Artie down the steps to the street. I've got both our bags, so all she has to carry is her purse.

We get to the bottom. I look out the door. I see a couple of students crossing the bridge, chattering away in German. There's an old woman across the canal, small and bent, pushing a flowered baby stroller with groceries in it. No sign of drones.

I lead Artie by the hand onto the *fondamenta*, where we extend the handles of our rollaboards and pull our bags behind us like ordinary tourists. We cross the bridge to the other side and turn left. I put on my sunglasses. Artie follows suit. We disappear through the door of an upscale boutique hotel.

The receptionist looks up and smiles. I smile back and pretend to be relaxed.

Got any rooms? *Camere?*

Sì, sì, abbiamo due camere, una singola e un appartamento.

I look at Artie.

Take the apartment, she says.

L'appartamento.

The receptionist takes my fake passport and hands me the key. I lean forward and whisper. Do you speak English?

A little, she says.

I lower my sunglasses just enough to let her see the seriousness in my eyes. We don't want to be disturbed, I say.

I understand, she replies. *Capisco.*

If any strangers ask about us, tell them you haven't seen anyone of that name or description, will you? Fans can be so tiring, as I'm sure you know. Artie looks away, a bored Vivian Leigh in her declining years. Me, her personal assistant.

Sì, sì, signora. Ho capito tutto, she says with a conspiratorial wink. Will that be all?

PUBLISHER'S EMAIL

I'm caught between two emotions. I'm awash in admiration for your resourcefulness, but I'm scared to death you won't survive the night. I must say the second emotion is winning. Will you promise to be cautious?

8VO_77

SCARLETT: No, but I can promise to be courageous. Ms. Cavel, the future of—I don't know, humanity—is at stake. This is no time to be cautious. We're on a life-or-death mission here. If we all end up as blips on a computer screen in some Transhumanist future, whose fault will that be? You know what I mean? The world needs Leonardo's thinking, ASAP. Is it worth dying for? I don't know. Maybe.

The hotel appartment has a clear view of our flat directly across the canal. Since we moved in, I've seen no sign of drones or Salvatore. As for Dickson, I'm crossing my fingers that he isn't reading this, but who knows what kind of tricks he has up his sleeve.

The new place feels calm. An oasis. Sleek Italian furniture contrasting with rustic beamed ceilings and undulating white walls. No kitchen, but the bathroom is outfitted with plush towels, heated floors, and soaps from Santa Maria Novella. Quite a change from the dumps we've been used to.

At noon I check on Artie. Still sleeping. I tiptoe over to her bed and place my hand on her forehead. A bit too warm?

My capacity for recall is off the charts, Katherine, but the memories I have of the next few days will be vivid for the rest of my life.

I gently rock Artie's shoulder and say, ready to wake up?

Oh, hello, she says brightly, like she hasn't seen me in weeks.

Artie, you okay?

I'm fine.

Really? Because you don't look so fine. No offense.

Scarlett, really, I'm fine. But there is something I have to tell you. Something rather awful.

I nod.

She struggles up on one elbow. Sorry I haven't been of more help to you in the last few weeks.

That's what you have to tell me?

No, I'm afraid it's not. The truth is, I'm dying.

Artie, don't be absurd. You're strong as an ox. You worked three days straight without sleep is all. You're tired.

Listen to me, she says. I've been diagnosed with leukemia. It's the real reason I left my teaching job. I knew I was losing the fight, but I couldn't decide what to do about it. Then you came along, and I knew I wanted quality, not quantity—one last chance at life.

I reach for her hand and close my eyes. Shit, shit, shit. I take a deep breath and ask, how much time do you have?

Let's just say I won't be getting a telegram from the Queen. I'm in the red zone, dear. The light is blinking.

Jesus, Artie, why didn't you tell me? I could have done something about it.

Like what, love?

For starters, I wouldn't have dragged you along on this stupid adventure.

Nonsense. I wouldn't have missed it for all the tea in Bengal. How many people does one meet who would willingly pledge their lives for the sake of an ideal? You, young woman, are a beacon. I feel privileged, if you want to know the truth.

I squeeze her hand and give her a kiss on the forehead. I can honestly say I've never felt so good and so bad at the same time. I ask, what can I do for you?

You can carry on. Don't stop now. I don't give a flying flock what happens to me, as long as you complete the mission.

Artie! Such language!

Just like that, she closes her eyes and drifts off. I check her pulse. Weak but perceptible.

As the shadows grow longer and the light turns a golden yellow on the buildings, I come away from the window. Time to get ready. I force Artie's situation into a dark compartment in the back of my mind. She's counting on me.

I open the metal box and take out the two manuscripts. I untie the strings of the portfolio and remove the original pages, replacing them with Artie's forgery. I feel bad about sacrificing a 16th century folder, but it's a small price to pay for a convincing spectacle.

Outside on the *fondamenta*, I scan the area for anything out of place. I see children playing on the stone pavement down from the hotel, squeezing the last drop of happiness from the day. Nobody else in sight.

I look across the canal at the Airbnb building. The windows are dark. No drones. No handymen. No assassins in trenchcoats lurking in the crevices.

The dying light reveals a particular kind of doom in this part of Venice, the fate of a neighborhood written in the sad calligraphy of ancient cracks and peeling plaster, of electrical cables layered one over the other because no one thought it was worth hiding them. Buildings too nondescript to invest in, with the sole exception of our new hotel. Who knows? Maybe gentrification is just around the corner as the rotting foundations sink and derelict walls are razed. I'm happy to push that process forward.

I glance down and see a plastic bag floating in the canal. In the dim light I can make out the fur, the legs, the tail of a cat in rigor mortis, its mouth pressed against the bag, teeth bared in a frozen wail. A shimmy of fear ripples down my spine. I hurry across the bridge and let myself into the building.

Upstairs the blinds are still drawn. I flip the switch in the sitting area.

The fireplace is fitted with an iron stove, its belly pre-stocked with newspaper and kindling. I take the matches from the top of the stove and start the fire. Within minutes the paper flares and the kindling catches. I take the portfolio from the box and place it up-side down in the stove. Close the door. Yellow flames dance around like cannibals, licking the edges and biting into the leather. First the strings go, and then the leather starts to buckle. I let it run for a few seconds, then open the door.

With a flick of my hand, I snatch the portfolio and let it drop to the floor. I dampen the flames with a piece of crumpled newspaper. I turn it over and carefully pry open the cover, or at least what's left of it. The top pages are mostly burnt, but intact. I can still see the writing, black ink on black paper, if I hold it to the light in just the right way. The sheets underneath are less damaged, but still charred and ugly. No one in their right mind would want a manuscript in this condition.

I lay the remains back in the box, set it aside, and go into the kitchen for a candlestick. I place the candle on a side table in the sitting room, then move the table up to the drapes. I crumple a few sheets of newspaper and form them tightly around the base of the candle, then stretch a large rubber band around to hold them in place.

I light the candle, take the metal box, and lock the door on my way out.

PUBLISHER'S EMAIL

Scarlett, that's arson! What about the neighbors? The nearby buildings? People could die! Couldn't you just burn the manuscript and call it a day? Why the whole building? My God. Please get back to me right away.

I'm serious.

8VO_78

SCARLETT: Not to worry, Ms. Cavel. Way ahead of you. First of all, we knew the building was empty. Second, it's a freestanding structure at the intersection of two canals, so the fire was unlikely to spread given the absence of wind. Third, the landlord could use the insurance money to renovate the place. You can't go halfway with a spectacle. It's all or nothing.

It takes the candle about 45 minutes to burn down. Soon we see a wisp of black smoke rising from the chimney. Artie and I pull our chairs up to the window and watch the scene unfold.

Let me tell you, Ms. Cavel, it was a thing of beauty.

After the first appearance of smoke, we see light flickering behind the blinds on the top floor. The drapes go up in flames, then the shutters, and within minutes the glass explodes outward. Yellow flames shoot from the windows of the sitting room facing the canal.

Within minutes we hear the sirens of fireboats. They come roaring up the canal, sloshing water over the walkways and up against the buildings. Boats moored on the sides of the canal bob wildly, straining against their ties. A few boats that happen to be putt-putting down the canal, innocently going about their business, swerve to the side at the sight of flashing blue lights.

Now the firemen in their black jackets and yellow hoods are aiming their spotlights at the top floor, streaming canal water in lazy arcs through the lidless eyes of the flat.

An inverted image of a building in flames flickers in every ripple on the surface of the canal. A ribbon of black smoke drifts upward, curls west, slices the three-quarter moon in two. Sour scents of burning wood and boat exhaust slip in through the cracks and mingle like sweat-stained sailors.

A crowd gathers on the hotel side of the canal. Our room is on the first floor, so we open the window and listen to what they're saying.

Che liberazione, snorts an old woman just off to the right.

I look at Artie.

She translates: Good riddance.

The owner of the Airbnb is standing just to the left of the window. For a crazy second, I almost feel something like sorry for setting his building on fire. A middle-aged American man stands next to him, shaking his head in disbelief.

What a shame, says the man, all that history, gone up in smoke. The slumlord turns to him, his face positively gleeful.

I have been dreaming for this, he says. As if to add an exclamation mark, he does a little happy dance on the *fondamenta*.

I'm glad we could be of service, I say under my breath.

Artie huffs. He doesn't care whether we're in there or not.

I quickly shut the window so the owner doesn't hear us laughing, then I call down to reception for a bottle of Prosecco. We drink a toast to The Great Spectacle of Santa Marta.

Artie raises her glass and says, well, dear, I'm dying of leukemia, I'm down to my last wig, and we just set fire to our clothes. And somehow, I've never been happier in my life. Cheers!

And then, almost as soon as it started, the fire was out. The firemen are satisfied that the building's empty, and now they're stringing caution tape across the front, criss-crossing the gaping entrance several times. The splintered door is off its hinges, leaning up against the wall inside the doorway. The crowd disperses except for a few students sharing a beer from a paper bag.

I wait by the window. Hours drift by.

It's three in the morning and Artie's sound asleep. The electricity is out on the far side of the canal, so I grab the flashlight from the closet and go downstairs with the metal box. Reception is closed and the door is locked. I check to make sure I have the key.

Outside the hotel there's very little activity. I see a figure, perhaps a female student, wearing a parka and a pair of Nikes. She's leaning on the railing of the bridge, looking the other way. I wait in the shadows until I see her leave in the direction of the train station. The night is so hushed that I can hear the wind teasing the tiny hairs on my cheeks. I put up my hood and cross the bridge. I duck under the caution tape and wedge myself through the plywood barrier.

PUBLISHER'S EMAIL

We never should have let you go to Venice. Are you okay, Scarlett? What happened inside the building?

8VO_79

SCARLETT: Sorry, I had to check on Artie. She's tossing around and talking in her sleep.

Our plan seemed to be working perfectly, Ms. Cavel, but holy fucking Jesus, wait till I tell you.

I'm in the building, and it's quiet except for the sounds of dripping water. The stairs are slippery and strewn with debris, so I pick my way up the four flights. There's hardly any damage to the lower floors except for the minor effects of smoke. At the top of the stairs, the door to the flat is gone. The sitting area is completely blackened. A few charred remains of furniture lie in a puddle of dank water, but everything else has burned away to ash.

The kitchen is in better shape. Most of the damage is above counter level. The pot of primavera sauce is still on the stove. The ceiling is nothing but blackened lath and exposed rafters, and the hanging bulb is nowhere in sight. The pine table, where Artie forged the manuscript, is a thick layer of ashes on the linoleum floor.

I play the light over the cabinets and find one above the counter that looks suitable. The wooden door is partially burned. I can see straight through to the shelves, blackened but still intact.

I carefully place the charred portfolio on the lower shelf. I scoop a handful of ash from the floor and sprinkle it over the top. When the inspectors arrive in the morning, they'll find the portfolio and put two and two together. It won't be long before the news of the ruined manuscript hits the papers.

Suddenly, noises from below.

Kids? Police? Salvatore?

I douse my light. Heavy footsteps. I peer out the doorway and all I can see is a flashlight beam bouncing around the stairwell. Where to hide? Not the closets or the bathroom—too obvious. I look around. The lower cabinets.

Jesus, the one place I never want to be.

I open the one farthest from the kitchen door and move the middle shelf down to the bottom as quietly as I can. I climb in with the flashlight and close the door behind me.

Now I'm curled in a fetal position with my back against the wall. Literally against the wall. My claustro is screaming like the sirens on those fireboats. I can hear footsteps getting louder. Last flight of stairs. Almost here. Shoes crunching on debris in the sitting room. A pause. The clatter of a toolbelt hitting the floor. Now moving into the kitchen. Then silence.

After several long seconds, I hear the *zzzt-zzzt* of a power screwdriver.

My heart pounds out of my chest. I can't breathe. Alarm bells are battering my brain. He's sealing up the cabinets, one by one.

Zzzt!

He's hoping I'll give up, cry out.

Zzzt!

Closer, closer.

Zzzt! Jesus, right next door!

I can't think straight. My head's filled with the wail of sirens, shiny black threads from the looms of terror, endless nights trapped in a basement closet. Will I end up praying for my life? Is this the fate of the girl who flunked charm school? The girl who flunked life? Dead in a cabinet in a scummy burned-out flat?

The drilling stops. A voice. What's he saying? I can't hear it through the sirens, the pounding in my chest, too loud, too loud. Wait—an American accent. That can't be Salvatore.

Dickson!

I know you're in here, he says.

At this point I can't speak. I wonder what his next move is—set fire to the rest of the kitchen with me in it? The claustrophobia rears up inside me. I slap it back down. I'm starting to hallucinate. My nostrils are siphoning pure fear from the pain and throb of childhood. I'm 15 years old in the basement and my father is pinning me to the floor, his breath reeking of whiskey.

Give me the manuscript, says Dickson. The original manuscript, not the clever fake. Give it to me now and you live. *Come* with me and you live forever.

He's offering me the gift of immortality. I happen to know he wouldn't give me the stink off his shit if I were starving.

He drives a screw through the door, but it doesn't sound right. I force myself to pick up the flashlight and turn it on. Drywall fastener. Missed the frame. Still time. What are my options?

If you don't give me the manuscript, he says, I'll take it from your partner. How's she doing? It shouldn't be too hard to find her, Scarlett. Isn't that what you're calling yourself these days? My, my, how crafty. You really thought you could fool us, didn't you?

Us?

My brain is starting to kick in. My fear is spent. I've got nothing to lose. If I stay in here, I die. If I don't stay in here, I die. I feel as if I've been sealed in a dark cabinet my whole life. Shouldn't I do something, anything, and at least leave this world with a spark of dignity?

Zzzt! The second screw glances off the frame, missing again. He thinks he's got me trapped.

Scarlett! Come out, come out, wherever you are. Say the word and I'll take out the screws.

I'm desperate to get back to Artie. I need to get her to safety. But my muscles are frozen, locked up. I'm stuck in one of those treacly dreams where the atmosphere is so thick you can barely move. I'm sinking in quicksand. My back is against the wall.

Then I think, my back is against the wall.

Aikido floats into my conscious mind and I remember I have double the force when pushing off a hard surface. I'm a coiled spring. I'm a rattlesnake poised to strike. I'm a bomb ready to detonate. Dickson is no Salvatore. I can take him. I scrunch up into a ball.

Oh, *Scar*-lett, he singsongs, olly olly oxen fr—

I blast open the door with both feet and Dickson goes flying. His power driver skips across the kitchen into the sitting room. He's down in the ashes, holding his head, moaning like a motherless calf.

This is my chance.

I scramble to my feet. The door's a dozen feet away. A long arm grabs my ankle and down I go. Cinders burn my eyes. Between the power outage and the ashes, I'm totally blind.

He's on me in an instant. Nailing me down with his knees. Ripping at my blouse. How can he be this strong? Is he shooting testosterone? Taking PEDs?

Then I see the outlines of his face. Fuck. It *is* Salvatore. Salvatore is American, not Italian. He's spouting a bunch of Transhumanist gibberish and telling me I should join him in the far forever. His hands are on my breasts. Snot hitting my face.

Ms. Cavel, ever hear of deliberate calm? It's a frame of mind that pilots click into when their planes are going down. A state of total concentration. Time slows and you see the whole landscape of choices laid out in front of you.

I start to calculate my situation.

On the negative side, I'd made some questionable decisions. I thought I could outfox Dickson, but I couldn't. My hubris cost me big time. One by one, I've thrown away all the strategic advantages I could have had. By becoming a thief, I gave up any hope of any police protection. By being a jerk with Peter, I drove away my best ally. By overestimating my skills, I blew my best chance to get out of Italy alive. By being selfish, I'm about to lose my best friend, my mentor, the closest thing I'll ever have to a mother. I'm unarmed, alone, and overmatched.

On the positive side, what? I'm determined. I'm resourceful. I'm on a mission. Mainly, I would do anything to save Artie. I'm all she's got in the time she has left.

Salvatore is spewing some BS about eternal life. He wants me to join Dickson's army of child-bearers. Together we'll stride the earth as giants, or some such crap.

His knees are off my arms now, but he's pinning my wrists to the floor with vice-like hands. I can feel his root-hard erection through my jeans. He's grinding his hips into mine.

I'm starting to feel something, but it's not what he thinks. It's a flood of adrenaline racing toward my heart, my brain, my muscles, every cell in my body. He suddenly feels light on top of me, like air, like a dry leaf.

I twist to the right to throw him off-balance, then come back with everything I've got. My thigh goes straight to his groin and lifts him a foot in the air. He bellows. There's no way he'll be servicing that army of child-bearers now. He grabs his gonads, gasping for breath, leaving my right hand free.

I reach back into my hair and and it—the graver. My fingers curl around its spiral handle. It feels alive in my hand. I shut my eyes and plunge its hungry tip into the side of his neck, driving it deep with the palm of my hand. He should have screamed like a batallion of banshees, but instead he lets out the tiniest of yelps. He rolls onto the ash-strewn floor, writhing in confusion more than pain.

I crawl to the cupboard and feel around for my flashlight. Switch it on. Salvatore's scrunched up on the floor, eyelids clenched, hands clutching his jewels. His nostrils are caked with black ash, like tobacco-crusted pipe bowls. Blood is pumping rhythmically from his neck, mixing with the ashes on the floor to make a tar-like goo. I struggle to my feet and brace myself, ready for another round, but there's no fight left.

The blood has stopped spurting. Now it's just oozing into a puddle of blackness. His muscular grip on life is relaxing, relaxing, finger by finger. He looks small. He looks frail. I get down to feel for a pulse, and, I don't know, apologize?

Too late. Gone.

Ms. Cavel, this is not how I wanted things to go. But there I am, crouching down in front of him. I wonder, how did Salvatore get involved with Dickson? Are they both into this Transhumanist thing together? Listen, Ms. Cavel, I can't tell you the range of emotions that coursed through me in that second. Shock. Remorse. Anger. Disgust.

Just then I hear footsteps in the stairwell and switch off the light. I retreat to the furthest corner of the kitchen. I need a sturdier weapon. I trade the flashlight for the pot on the stove, dumping the primavera sludge into the sink.

A disembodied voice issues from the kitchen door.

Making something for dinner, are we? How thoughtful of you. I see you've met Salvatore. Don't worry. The death of his body is only a temporary inconvenience. The question is, what will happen to *your* body? Such a nice body, too. It's your mouth that needs some work.

He plays the laser across my torn blouse. I can see a little red dot tracing nipple shapes on my breasts.

The electrical power in the neighborhood flutters back on, sending the barest amount of light into the room, just enough to illuminate the lunar pockmarks on his cheeks. It's Dickson. He's wearing night goggles and waving around an Ed Brown with a Crimson Trace. How do I know this? My father has one. Fucking men.

I allow myself a conciliatory grin. Okay, I tell him, you've got a gun, but I've got a pasta pot. Try making pasta primavera with a gun.

No laughs. Tough audience.

I'm going to make this simple, he says, purring the air through his teeth like a demented tomcat. Give me the manuscript now and I won't kill your partner.

It's on the shelf, I say, gesturing with the pot toward the upper cabinet. If I could see his eyes, I'm sure they'd be full of pity for my schoolgirl naïveté.

Smartass, he says, we know everything you're doing. We've got your emails, your recordings, your texts, your phone calls. All we needed was your location, and guess what? Now we don't. Tell me where the real manuscript is.

Aha, I think. There are some things he doesn't know. I would die before telling him where it is.

Fuck off, I say.

Really? I would think after killing my associate, you might acknowledge a small debt. Why not pay up? You don't want me to hire a collection agency, do you? Such an ugly business.

Double fuck off, I say.

He says, why do you think Melzi's manuscript is so important, anyway? All that stuff about creativity is bullshit. Real power comes from concentrated control. A handful of visionaries can drive enormous change. So-called creative people are pathetic. They slow progress down. They let their idealism get in the way of true greatness.

Unlike you, I say.

Little Miss Scarlett sat on a harlot. Of course, unlike me. Is that your weapon? A pot?

You're a man of industry, I say, a man of God, a man's man, a man who gets what he wants. Right?

Well, who has the gun?

Then it dawns on me. Dickson isn't obsessed with the manuscript because he loves it, but because he hates it. He hates the whole idea that a certain creative, homosexual, freethinking atheist from the 15th century might influence the world that he, Mr. Big Shot, has under his thumb. How could Dickson possibly win in a world of Leonardos? He doesn't want *more* creative people, he wants *fewer*. Creative people just get in the way. They come up with competing ideas. They don't play ball. What he wants is obedient people. People who want him to steward their lives.

And you know what? I'm not one of them.

I rear back and wing the pot straight at his head. He dodges it easily. Fucking night goggles. The wall takes the hit with a hollow clang, sifting a cloud of black dust back into the room.

Now I'm angry enough to cut off my nose.

I say to Dickson: Yes, you have the gun. Such a big man with your gun and your designer camo and your goggles and laser pointer. You do impress a girl. I'll bet the women just love your sense of humor. Why do men wear camo in the city, anyway? It stands out like a flower arrangement at the DMV. You look like a 12-year-old playing army.

Last chance, he says. Where's the manuscript? The red beam angles up through the black dust until it's jabbing my right eye.

Fuck off.

We know you're sending it to the University of Bologna. You had lunch with that dyke. Does she have it?

No.

Really? Wait a minute. Was that a diversionary tactic? You gave it to the Marciana! We tracked you there!

No.

I'd just gotten two chances to lie my way out. Gift-wrapped and presented on a silver platter. But I'm a lousy liar, and anyway, I can't put innocent people at risk.

He slides the beam down my front and makes tiny circles on my pubis. Lascivious bastard. I'm still figuring out how to play this, but my overwhelming instinct is to antagonize the shit out of him. I can't tell you how many times this strategy has failed me.

Listen, Dickson. You know why we call you Dickson?

Yeah, because my father's a bigger dick than I am. I heard. You and I are not that different, you know. We were both raised by dickhead fathers who warped our lives.

That's right. You warped one way and I warped the other. But that's not the reason we call you Dickson.

Oh, really?

It's because your dick will always be a junior dick. It's an eenie weenie peenie that can't compare with your daddy's. A *pene piccolo*.

Look at Salvatore lying there. Even dead he's more virile than you'll ever be. You're a pimply-faced, mealy-mouthed, daddy-sucking-up loser.

He's quaking now. You fucking bitch, he says. He raises the gun to my face and starts to squeeze the trigger.

In the dim light I see a shadow moving behind him. Suddenly there's a flash and a crack. Dickson pitches forward. His laser slashes the soot-filled air and the gun skitters across the floor. He lands in front of me with a thud, goggles sideways, eyes frozen wide.

A silhouette stands in the doorway with a charred wooden post. I grab the flashlight and switch it on. A man in his mid-thirties, black parka, blue jeans, pair of Nikes. Leaning on my homemade security bar as if it were a golf club.

Sorry for the dramatic entrance, he says. I heard you needed an editor.

PUBLISHER'S EMAIL

Are you kidding me? Peter? I knew he was leaving the country, but I thought he was on a shopping mission with his fiancé. I don't believe this. My head is spinning. I'm utterly flabbergasted.

8VO_80

SCARLETT: Lucky me. No shopping mission. Rescue mission. Peter was the person on the bridge. He was watching out for me the whole time. But I'm not finished, Ms. Cavel.

Before I can even say thank you, Dickson is up on one knee. He draws a second gun from the holster in his vest and fires at Peter, hitting him in the shoulder.

Now I'm furious. Never make me mad. Never. Every cell of my body is screaming for justice.

I kick the gun out of his hand with such force that it flies into the rafters before clattering to the floor. I pick up the pot and spin around, catching him full in the face. He arcs backward and lands on his back. Particles of soot rain down on his unmoving body.

I let out a growl that seems to rise from the depths of the Inferno. A growl so full of frustration, of recrimination, of primordial anger, that Peter steps back in alarm, his hand clutching his shoulder. I fling the pot through the kitchen window, shattering the glass and breaking tiles on the roof below.

I scream at Peter. What the hell are you doing here? You could have been killed!

Scarlett…

I raise my hand. I take a deep breath and let it out slowly. My shoulders slump as the adrenaline drains away to a manageable level. I bend down and brace my hands on my knees.

Sorry, Peter. Sorry.

He and I are standing together in the silence of the kitchen. Salvatore is dead. Not sort-of-dead. Not temporarily inconvenienced. Dead dead. Dickson looks like a goner, too, so I check him. A pulse, thank God. It feels like a prayer.

Suddenly we see lights bobbing around in the stairwell. Boots clatter up the stairs, and three armed men charge into the flat. Their black jackets say Carabinieri ROS in white reflective letters. Two of them check the bodies on the floor, and another takes us into the sitting room. This is going to be awkward.

I realize I'm not exactly presentable. My face is smeared with soot and splattered with blood and black-ash pasta sauce. I try to pull my blouse closed, but it's like playing whack-a-mole. Too many rips and missing buttons. But somehow modesty doesn't seem like a top-ten concern. Peter struggles out of his parka and throws it over my shoulders. There's a dark red bloom spreading across his shirt.

The agent who's taking our information shuts his book and leads us slowly downstairs. At the bottom there's a crowd forming on the *fondamenta*. Patrol boats shiver against the edge of the canal, blue lights flashing like crazy. I rifle-fire a gaze across the water and see Artie in the window of our room. She tosses a small wave.

The crowd parts and an older man in a dark suit approaches me. You must be Scarlett, he says. He hands me a business card. I study it. Artie's been schooling me on typography. She says the smaller the type, the more serious the firm. This card has very small type.

My name is Bernardo Lucchini. Katherine Cavel asked me to assist you.

How did you find me?

He lifts his chin toward Peter. Your young man gave me the address, he says. I believe he is working with you?

My young man.

Here is the situation, he says. The ROS is collaborating with the FBI to investigate your client. Your client was colluding with other partners to surveil a number of governments, including the government of Italy. Do you understand?

I think so.

This man has been quietly moving his business from cyber-security to cyber-surveillance. He may be selling information and software services to anyone who can pay for it, and this would include our adversaries. *Capisci?* In addition, it is known that he posesses a number of artifacts that rightfully belong to Italy. I believe the two agencies now have proof.

Signor Lucchini, are we in trouble with the police?

The attorney takes a deep breath, looks toward the hotel, and turns back to me. Yes, he says, you are in trouble. This cannot be denied. You stole an artifact of considerable value to Italy, and perhaps it belongs to private citizens who will press charges.

But of course, the authorities are conflicted. On the left hand you stole something that does not belong to you, and on the right hand you saved an important piece of Italian history. Beyond that, there is the delicate matter of murder.

However, he says, I know the ROS. They are good people. Reasonable. Will they arrest us?

I think perhaps too much paperwork. You are, what they say in America, small fish. If you promise to leave the shores of Italy and not return, I believe they would be happy to ignore your involvement. I can talk with them.

The gears in my brain start to engage. Why would they ignore us? The real reason would not be the paperwork. Not even the risk of embarassing the FBI by implicating an American. The real reason would be the near certainty of complicating a clean collar. If they can sweep the details under the rug, they can claim victory immediately. Their story would be something like, *of course* these criminals had enemies. Let's focus on the real culprits and tie up the loose ends later. By then I'll be gone and impossible to find.

I flash the attorney a look of soulful gratitude. *Va bene. Grazie, Signor Lucchini.*

And, *signorina…*

Yes, Mr. Lucchini?

Please do not burn any buildings as you leave Italy.

I'm starting to appreciate the Italian way of life. When the rules get in the way, ignore the rules. Shrug your shoulders and do the reasonable thing. Live and let live.

I don't know how to thank Peter. There's a water ambulance waiting at the side of the canal, but he walks me to the door of the hotel and says goodnight. The hotel receptionist comes out from the back room and recoils at the sight of me. No surprise there. I can see her making a mental note about the untidy lives of movie people.

Me, I'm looking forward to the longest bath in recorded history. I won't be able to sleep. The adrenaline is jacking my system like a thousand-foot string of firecrackers.

Artie opens the door and her face goes white. She pulls me into my bedroom and plops me onto the bed. She runs to the bathroom to soak a fluffy hand towel, comes back, starts wiping my face.

I was so worried, she says. I thought you might have died! Look at you. You're a mess. Your face is bleeding.

It feels hot, I say. I think a bullet creased my cheek.

Oh, Scarlett, come here. She enfolds me in her arms and starts stroking my hair. Scarlett, Scarlett, you poor girl. It's enough to knock your soul sideways. What you've been through, my darling girl, my brave girl.

I have to say, Ms. Cavel, I've never been treated like a real daughter before. I found it overwhelming. I collapsed in a flood of shuddering sobs, unable to keep the dam from breaking. I've never heard such moans, such pitiful cries, such godawful howls—and they were coming from me. The tough girl who thinks emotions are stupid.

I let her fuss for a few more minutes, and then, when all the water has drained into the sea, I pass out in her arms, emptied, exhausted, and feeling as if I were home for the first time in my life.

PUBLISHER'S EMAIL

Scarlett, I am so relieved. And incredibly grateful. That's the most heroic thing I've ever heard of. I think you may have saved our book, the company, and Western civilization all at once. I exaggerate only slightly.

And what got into Peter? He's a good man, but an action hero? Did he really bean Dickson with a post?

I guess we don't have to call Dickson Dickson from now on, but for me, he'll always be Dickson, and you'll always be Scarlett.

I hope Artie is holding up under the strain of her situation. Our hopes and prayers are with her. I'll be sending a medical team to Venice as soon as we get your location from Peter. I understand you've already spoken with Bernardo Lucchini. Don't say anything to the police.

8VO_81

SCARLETT: The medics came about an hour after I got your email. Thanks, Katherine. Peter was able to go out and buy me a blouse before they showed up. He's a great shopper, that Peter, even with his arm in a sling.

Artie refused to be examined, but then she agreed on the condition that they examine me first. I'm fine, just a few bruises and some stitches on my cheek.

Artie's in bad shape, Katherine. The prognosis is dire—an accelerating decline, lasting anywhere from a few days to a week. She's already lost weight and sleeps most of the time. When I think about how she worked for three days with hardly a break, I'm so ashamed— and so amazed. The woman is a dynamo in spite of everything.

The medics wanted to arrange for hospice, but it turns out palliative care isn't a thing in Italy. In any case, Artie refused to allow it. She says letting strangers into our room is bad tradecraft. I never realized how funny she is. I asked if I could get her something to read, you know, to take her mind off the inevitable, and she says, yes.

Death in Venice.

She asked me to stay with her. Me and nobody else. The head of the medical team gave me a number to call when she's getting close, or if she suddenly passes.

Last night, while I was battling Dickson, do you think Artie sat around wringing her hands? Of course not. She went right to work on Melzi's letter to Bembo.

Ms. Cavel, this is a remarkable document. I think you'll want it for the book. I'll be back in touch when she feels up to reading it. Right now she's sleeping again.

Thanks, Scarlett. Please call me Katherine.

We just saw the news that Dickson has been arrested in the hospital. Apparently, he's expected to live. The same article said he just won a humanitarian award for his work on privacy. The irony is delicious. The article also said the Italian authorities are sending Salvatore's remains back to the States. His real name is Vincent Delbosco.

Here's the article from the *Times*.

Billionaire Arrested in Deadly Scandal

Stephen Creed found unconscious, accomplice dead

by Donathan Haig and Suze Arganbright

Stephen Creed, Jr., founder of Cybex International, has been implicated in a scheme to sell highly sensitive data to multiple national governments. He and his accomplice, Vincent Delbosco, were discovered last night in Venice, Italy.

The two men were tracked by ROS agents—the Italian equivalent of the FBI—to an Airbnb flat in the Santa Marta area of Venice, which had been the site of a fire earlier in the evening.

Mr. Delbosco was discovered dead of a neck wound on the kitchen floor. Mr. Creed was lying next to him, unconscious from blows to the head and face. A spokeswoman from the fire department said the two men were not in the building at the time of the fire.

The FBI and the ROS had been collaborating for several months to gather evidence for an arrest. Four days ago, the ROS received information from a faculty member at the University of Bologna, alleging that Mr. Creed had appropriated a valuable painting from the Lombardy town of Bergamo. Acting on a tip, a team from the FBI raided his home in Silicon Valley. There they uncovered a substantial cache of illegally purchased Italian artifacts. Hours later in Venice, the ROS closed in on the two men in the Airbnb flat.

It is still unclear why Mr. Delbosco was killed, and Mr. Creed rendered unconscious. Agents found a possible murder weapon, an antique engraving tool, and a burnt piece of timber that may have been used as a bludgeon. They also found two handguns, each with a missing round. Mr. Creed was dressed in military-style gear.

A special item of interest, a half-burned manuscript, was discovered by the ROS in a kitchen cabinet. A forensics team is analyzing the manuscript to determine its relevance to the case.

Separately, it was announced on the day of the incident that Stephen Creed Jr. had won the European International Humanitarian Award for Protection of Privacy. The honor was established in 1992 to recognize contributions to the field of cyber-security.

The assailant or assailants are still at large. Currently there are no leads. This is a developing story.

Talk soon.

8VO_82

SCARLETT: Katherine, Artie's awake. She has short periods of lucidity before she gets tired again and needs to rest. She'd like to read as much of Melzi's letter as she can. I'll go get her.

[SOUND OF FOOTSTEPS]

ARTIE: Hello, Ms. Cavel. I hope you're well. We've had quite a series of adventures after scarpering off to Venice with the manuscript. Thanks to Peter, the document is now in the hands of my former student, one of the deans at Unibo. I believe it will be safe with her.

Shall I read the letter?

To the distinguished gentleman Pietro Bembo,

Many thanks for your solicitous letter concerning the death of my master, Leonardo da Vinci. I have taken a great deal of consolation from your kind words. May I also send my own condolences regarding the death of Her Ladyship, Lucrezia Borgia, only three weeks later. I understand that you and Her Ladyship were close. You must be deeply saddened by this event.

You have asked me whether it might be more respectful to the memory of Her Ladyship to postpone the publication of my octavo, perhaps indefinitely. You need not worry on this account, Messer Bembo. I wrote my narrative on the request of my master, partially to keep pressure on the guilty parties, and also to allow Messer Manuzio to profit from its publication.

Sadly, he died before he could begin the project. His partner and successor, Andrea Torresani, showed little interest in printing the book, believing, as do you, that the truth might cause more harm than good. The manuscript has since disappeared, the result of a theft of Leonardo's studio in Amboise.

You also asked me about my master's death—whether he took the Last Rites, whether he died in a state of grace, and whether he spoke any final words on his deathbed. I am pleased to report that he did die in grace, and I have filled my notebook with his final thoughts.

Messer Bembo, many people considered Leonardo a non-believer, a heretic, because of his views on the Church. I myself was fearful that he might be denied entry to the Kingdom of Heaven. And yet he possessed almost every virtue encouraged by the Church, including those of respect, kindness, honesty, charity, humility, patience, compassion, diligence, commitment, and generosity.

His conception of God was expansive, perhaps akin to the vastness and power of Nature itself, the tremendous force of life which animates our universe. His manner of worship, in my view, was both original and deeply felt. He preferred to test the laws of Nature directly, not to accept a reality mediated by priests and philosophers.

If this is a sin, I wish fervently to be a sinner.

You may judge for yourself whether Leonardo was a man of great devotion. He once told me, "Nature has a thousand times more imagination than do men. When you live within the laws of Nature, your wants and desires fall away and what is left is love—the love of everything and everyone—love as the meaning and purpose of life. In the end," he said, "all our questions may be unanswerable except by this single word. Love obeys no laws. It sees no barriers. It flies over forests, burrows through soil, and breaks down walls to bask in the heavenly light of its object."

Messer Bembo, do these sound like the thoughts of a heretic?

He then said, "Humans will never discover an invention more beautiful, more economical, nor more elegant than that of Nature. In her creations nothing is wanting and nothing is wasted."

The recurring patterns of Nature had inspired in him a sense of wholeness, of motion, of transformation. He believed everything must continually change.

"But Master," I asked, "will you not miss the beauty of life when you have left this earth?"

"Miss it how?" he answered. "Our lives are like rivers, Checco. They

begin as rushing streams, confined within narrow banks, crashing against rocks, hurtling over cliffs. As we grow older, the banks widen and the river slows. We feel its weight, its might, its purpose. Finally, before we are fully aware of the change that is happening, the river flows into the majestic sea, where there are no banks, no rocks, no cliffs, nothing but a vast unconscious oneness with Nature and Time."

"Do you speak of the afterlife?" I asked.

He sighed as he thought about what to say.

[COUGHING]

SCARLETT: Artie, would you like a glass of water? Do you need a short break? She does. I'll hit the stop button.

ARTIE: Thank you for your patience, Ms. Cavel. Don't fuss, Scarlett. I'm ready to continue.

"Checco, it is not unreasonable to find in the mystery of human experience some hope of an afterlife. None of us can fully comprehend the workings of the universe. If we should glimpse a vein of grace, or sense an unfolding of goodness, then perhaps our conscious experience indicates that further mysteries lie beyond our grasp.

"But I must say, dear Checco, that in my philosophy, the afterlife is nothing more and nothing less than one's own contribution to posterity. Posterity is to the artist as Heaven is to the priest."

SCARLETT: Oh my God! That's what you said, Artie! It doesn't seem irrational to imagine a second life from the mysteries we encounter in this one, right? None of us knows exactly what's going on in this thing we call reality?

ARTIE: Yes. I said that art is the best tool we have for contending with the ineffable—that which defies logic. And you said the best way to contend with the ineffable was with effing science.

May I resume?

"I do not understand, Master. Without consciousness, there would be no afterlife. You would have no ability to enjoy your reward. It is unbearable to think that our conscious life should end upon our death. But if we die in Christ, we can have immortality in the mansions of Heaven."

"My dear boy, do not desire immortality. If a man needs more than a lifetime to feel as if he has lived, then he has simply failed to live. The lack is not in his years, but the quality of his living.

"The artist, like the humble caterpillar, weaves a cocoon of great beauty and usefulness, then leaves it behind for others, rising on painted wings to an infinite sky. Is this not enough?

I have brought no children into the world. My children are my pupils and my works and little else. Of these, my greatest hope is for my pupils, and of my pupils, young Checco, you have been the closest to my heart."

Messer Bembo, at this juncture I failed to hide the tears that had welled up from inside me.

"Look at me when I say this," he said. "The world is but a canvas for your invention, Checco. Write, write, and do not stop. Be a Columbus to new worlds hidden within you. Create works that after your death will make you seem alive, instead of sleeping now as if your spirit were already dead. The way to eternal life is this: Take care of Nature, love yourself and those you meet, and leave wisdom to your children."

My master's face then grew bright. "Checco, listen. You have inspired me to learn Latin!" He reached for his notebook on the table next to his bed. "Can you correct my translation of Dante?"

This is what he read to me:

> *"Lying in a feather bed will not bring you fame,*
> *Nor staying beneath the quilt,*
> *And he who uses up his life without achieving fame*
> *Leaves no more vestige of himself on earth*
> *Than smoke in the air or foam on the water."*

His pale eyes glistened as he placed the notebook in my hands.

I could not focus on the text. My heart overflowed with a love beyond all words. I threw myself upon my master and tried to keep him from dying. He laughed and patted my head. He gently pushed me up to a sitting position, his hands weak on my shoulders.

He looked me in the eyes and smiled. "Francesco de Melzi, most excellent Count of Vaprio d'Adda, your apprenticeship has come to an end. You must seek your destiny as an independent man. As my parting gift, I release you from your commitment to complete my notebooks."

He made me understand, Messer Bembo, that each of our lives has its own pattern of affordances, as unique and indelible as the whorls and loops of our fingerprints. We must not waste our individual talents on dreams that are not our own.

Over many hours of conversation, I was able to persuade my master to take the Last Rites. The ceremony was somber, yet beautiful, with a dozen courtiers and His Royal Highness, Francis I, in attendance. Upon reflection, however, I now think Leonardo acquiesced to my demands as a token of his love for me, not because he feared eternal damnation. It was, I believe, his final gesture, his last spectacle.

And now, my esteemed and illustrious Messer Bembo, I must bid you good fortune in all your endeavors. I sincerely hope our paths will cross in the fullness of time.

Your servant,
Count Francesco Melzi
Amboise, France
2 August 1519

SCARLETT: Oh, man. Leonardo sacrificed the one thing he valued most in the world—his hard-won truth—to give Melzi some closure. And Melzi, to his credit, understood why he did it. Can you imagine being loved that much?

What struck me most about Leonardo's mentoring is that he recognized Melzi's true calling. The boy thought he wanted to be an artist like his master, but Leonardo saw what he really was—a writer. He put him on the proper path by giving him a notebook, a mission, and a shitload of encouragement. Sorry, Artie.

ARTIE: You're forgiven.

Ms. Cavel—may I call you Katherine as well? Katherine, we now have three important pieces of information about the manuscript. First, Aldo died before Melzi could submit it for publication. Second, Aldo's partner Torresani reneged on Aldo's agreement, most likely fearing a backlash from the families of the Este and Gonzaga. And third, the manuscript was stolen from Leonardo's studio while he and Melzi were in France. Taken together, these explain why it was never published.

SCARLETT: We're pretty sure the artifacts in the townhouse—the manuscript, the portrait of Leonardo, the tools, and Melzi's other paintings—were the stolen items in Melzi's letter. How they ended up in Bergamo is anyone's fucking guess. Artie, don't look at me. I'm doing my best.

ARTIE: On the last page of the letter, Katherine, Melzi had glued a cut-out image of Leonardo. It's a scaled-down version of the portrait, done up as an engraving. I examined the colors under a glass. They're the same four we use in modern printing—cyan, magenta, yellow, and black.

A line of handwriting at the bottom says: *Sto imparando a fare incisioni a colori*, I'm learning to make color engravings. It appears that Melzi was planning to go forward with the notebooks despite being released from the task. Rather touching, don't you think?

SCARLETT: It's time for Artie to get some rest, Katherine.

PUBLISHER'S EMAIL

The letter is clearly a major addition to the story. We'll get permission from the Marciana and add a bonus to your advance. Has Artie prepared a will? Where does she want her share of the money to go? Let us know and we'll make the arrangements.

You'll be happy to hear that Dickson's legal team has dropped their claims. They've realized everything they were doing would only make things worse for their client. We're now clear to proceed with the book.

8VO_83

SCARLETT: That's fantastic, Katherine.

I got up this morning and found Artie's respiration labored. Long pauses between breaths. I checked my phone to make sure I had the medical team's number.

Just then Peter texts me to say the *Guardian* has more news on the investigation. They've identified the prints on the guns and the blood on the wooden post as both belonging to Dickson. They have partial prints on the graver, which seem to match the prints from the handle of the pot. Nothing about the manuscript. They must be going nuts trying to picture the scene of the crime.

Despite the signals I got from the attorney, Peter thinks I'm still in danger. He's working on airline reservations for me. I told him I'm staying put for now.

Around noon, Artie wakes up. She's been asleep for 17 hours. Now she's hungry, even chipper. Full of energy. I call downstairs for some take-out, and soon they deliver a pizza to the room.

This is delicious, she says, her mouth full of Margherita. I love Italy! I just had the most beautiful dream.

Oh, really? Tell me, I say.

I saw my husband in the passenger lounge at the airport. He

looked wonderful. Handsome, vital, as if he had never died. He seemed concerned but not agitated. Calm, in fact. Wise. I was flooded with a sense of well-being.

Then what?

Nothing—we simply sat in chairs opposite each other. He leaned forward, looked into my eyes, and held my hands. That was all.

Well, that sounds mysterious and beautiful.

It was, my dear, I don't mind telling you. She pauses, then she says, Scarlett, I'm a little worried about you.

Me?

Yes, dear. I'm worried that, after I leave, you won't find what you want.

What I want? What I want is to publish our book and escape to a desert island.

No dear, it isn't. What you want is a life. With real friends and real lovers. With a purpose you can believe in. Don't do what Dickson did. Don't put off the important things until it's too late, then wish you had another life to make up for it. Remember what Leonardo said? If you need more than a lifetime to feel you've lived, then you haven't lived. Live, Scarlett. Open up to the world. Open up to people.

She made me feel terrible.

I'm not like you, I say, I don't have a grand purpose. I don't believe in religion. I don't believe in God.

She looks down, gazing at the backs of her hands. What if, she says, Leonardo was right? What if God is something we create? Like a slice of pizza.

What?

May I have another slice of pizza?

No, the other thing. I mean, yes, you can have a slice of pizza. What did you say before that?

Scarlett, what if God is something we make up? What if human beings are not made in the image and likeness of God, but the other way round? Would that be so bad?

Yes, because we'd be living in Pretend World and not on Planet Earth.

But, Scarlett, she says, swallowing, we *are* living in Pretend World. Everything we see and hear and feel and taste is an illusion. The hard problem of consciousness, remember? What is the redness of red? Is it the pigment on the apple or the chemistry in our brains?

Come on, Artie, the skin is red. Apples are real things, after all. Not illusions.

Perhaps, dear, but our perceptions are illusions. There's no red if there's no visual system to perceive it and no mind to name it. We're creatures of illusion. In the end, our illusions are what make our lives worth living. Our illusions, our perceptions, our emotions, our poetry, our sense of beauty, our *art*. Remember what Leonardo told Melzi? Science is powerful, but art is nourishing. Someone I know once said: you can't make pasta primavera with a gun.

I did say that, didn't I? What an idiot.

I thought it was bloody brill.

Artie, you once told me the redness of red is not as important as the is-ness of is. That's bonkers. Stuff like that really sets off my woo-woo alarms.

Sorry, love. I just meant that the most important thing about life is, well, life. The experience of living. It's not as easy as it sounds. You said I'd spent my whole life in classrooms and museums and libraries. You were right. Remember what you said next?

Jeez, I hate to think.

You said, why settle for a tiny plink on the grand piano when you can play the final chord from *A Day in the Life?* Well, now I've played it. I've played it. I played the fucking chord!

I start to laugh. I look at Artie and she starts to laugh. Soon her eyes turn to slits. There's no sound coming out of her mouth. Neither of us can breathe, we're laughing so hard. She's right. We did it. We played the fucking chord.

When we finally catch our breath, she says, my God, I'm so thirsty. I could die for glass of water.

I look at her. Another round of silent howls. I'm starting to wonder if its possible to die laughing.

Stop, stop, she finally says.

I go to the bathroom and fill a glass with water. I love this woman. I decide to risk being sincere, maybe for the first time in my life.

Artie, I say, handing her the glass, I'm going to miss you. I am so sorry you have this terrible disease. It's extremely unfair.

Don't be sad, she says, we all have to die of something. What counts is what we do before that. May I give you some motherly advice?

I nod. She's getting tired again. I'm not sure how far she can go. Her hands and feet are turning a dusky color.

Scarlett, you're a fetching young woman. Smart as a whippet. For you it's rather a doddle to seduce an unsuspecting man—or a woman—as long as you're willing to make a slight sacrifice of your ethics. Don't do it. Don't manipulate people. You don't need to.

I once said Artie eats like a bird, and now I know why, poor thing. I place her half-eaten slice of pizza on the side table, fluff up her pillows, lift her feet onto the bed, and pull up the quilt. Her skin feels cool to the touch.

Scarlett, I want you to promise me something.

Of course.

Promise me you'll let one or two people through the door. Not everyone is out to get you.

I promise, Artie.

I'm trying with all my might not to cry. I ask, is there anything I can do for you?

She's fighting back the next wave of sleep. She closes her eyes and forces a small, mischievous smile. *Plaudite*, she says. *Acta est fabula.*

What?

With that she's out, breathing noisily. She seems to be having trouble clearing the fluids from her throat. She's restless. Her limbs are moving involuntarily, repetitively.

I notice an envelope on her nightstand. I pick it up. In perfect tiny cursive it says: *Per l'8vo.*

Inside are instructions for the distribution of her property and financial assets. She says she's a Catholic, and she wants to be buried alongside her husband at St. Michael's in Sheffield. How a person of color from India ends up a Catholic in Sheffield is beyond comprehension, but it's in the nature of the woman to be baffling.

On page two, she says she's leaving her share of the book proceeds to me, on the condition that I use them for the education of disadvantaged girls. At the end there's a personal note:

My dearest Scarlett,

Our adventure has been the highlight of my life. Together we smashed the last chord. Go. Go now. Go write the book of you. Make sure it's full of surprises and plot twists and love. Lots of love.

Your partner in crime,
Artie

[SCARLETT SOBS, RECOVERS]

Her breathing is more erratic now. Her lips are slightly open and dry. I dab a little water on them. She doesn't respond. I slump in my chair. *Plaudite, acta est fabula.* I search the scattered remains of my freshman Latin and somehow come up with a translation.

Applaud, the play is over.

Brava, I say softly. I hold her hand. I lean down and kiss her cool forehead. I dial the number.

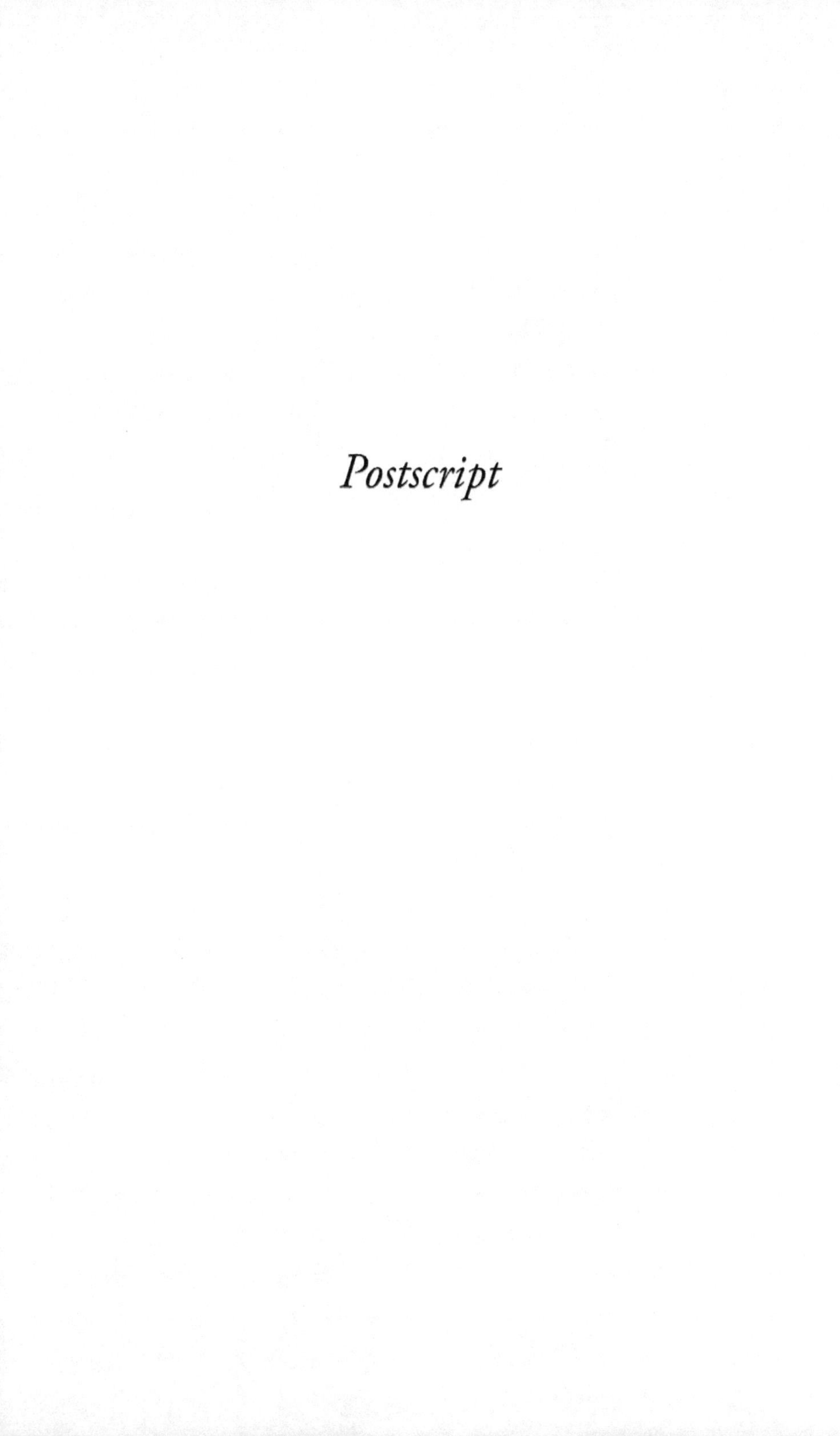

Postscript

[AIRPLANE PA ANNOUNCEMENTS]

SCARLETT: Katherine, I hope the editing of *Octavo* is going well.

This is my final recording. I've included a summary of the research I completed since leaving Italy. If my theories are right, Wikipedia will have to change a lot of its pages. There's probably a whole cottage industry waiting to spring up around da Vinci artifacts like the *Mona Lisa*. The Louvre may have to build a whole new wing to tell the full story.

Ready?

On April 23, 1519, Leonardo's last will and testament bequeathed all of his books and, quote, the instruments and portraits appertaining to his calling as a painter, to Francesco da Melzo, nobleman of Milan.

Included in Leonardo's instruments and portraits would have been Melzi's painting of him, the manuscript, and Leonardo's silver bulino—the graver—except that they'd already been stolen from his studio in Amboise. More about that in a second.

The same document willed half of Leonardo's vineyard in Milan to his former pupil and erstwhile lover, Salaì. Salaì was just a brat working the vineyard with his father when Leonardo took him in. Salaì came full circle. He returned to the same vineyard in 1513 to oversee the production of Leonardo's wine.

Here's where it gets a bit speculative, but the facts add up.

Before Leonardo's final days, Salaì sees the writing on the wall. Melzi has long ago replaced him as the master's go-to assistant. Unlike Salaì, Melzi had education, honesty, and loyalty going for him. He'd become indispensible.

Leonardo is now getting on in years. His business is drying up, and he's spending most of his time in France in a house given to him by King Francis I. All he does is work on his notes.

Salaì needs to plan for the future. So what does he do?

He travels up to Amboise in a horsecart. Doesn't write Leonardo to say he's coming. He breaks into the studio and steals the *Mona Lisa* and a trove of other paintings, including Melzi's. He's been jealous of the kid since he first arrived, and now's his chance to get even. He takes the manuscript—not to publish it, but to hide it. Why should Melzi get the spotlight instead of him? No fucking way.

He goes back to Milan and sells the *Mona Lisa* for a shit-ton of money. Within days he rides northeast to a town outside the city and buys some property, a *bottega dell'artista*, on the top of the hill.

He's now set up. He hangs his shingle outside the shop and starts taking clients. He uses Leonardo's paintings and drawings as his own portfolio, telling customers he was the master's best and most trusted assistant, and, anyway, he did most of the work on these himself. Meanwhile, he's so afraid Melzi will come back and find his stuff that he hides it under the floorboards.

That's right, Katherine. The townhouse in Bergamo was Salaì's bottega.

I kept wondering why Leonardo didn't make a big stink about the robbery of the studio. I mean, he lost his prize possession, La Gioconda, the *Mona Lisa*—the painting he'd been lugging from place to place for years, adding little affectionate touches as he went.

My guess is, he knew who the perpetrator was: Salaì, the thieving magpie. Salaì, the boy who shopped for supplies and substituted cheaper goods so he could spend the leftover money on candy. Salaì, the undependable pupil who stole his clothes and trashed his studio. Leonardo couldn't stay angry with him for more than five minutes. He found him adorable, his little Hermes plucked from a vineyard.

What does that have to do with the *Mona Lisa*? The *Mona Lisa* is not Lisa del Giocando, as everyone thinks. That was a cover story. No. The *Mona Lisa* is Salaì. Leonardo used him as the model for the universal woman—not a woman per se but the very nature of femaleness. The seductiveness, the mothering, the caring, the love he never seemed to receive.

Remember the Academia dinner? Galeazzo said she was perfection itself, a true Italian goddess. She knows the secrets of the world but she won't share them. She's a tease, an earthbound siren.

Later that evening, Bramantino asked whether anyone had noticed the similarity between Salaì and the woman in the painting. He said the resemblance was remarkable. Then Salaì did his impression of La Gioconda, and the whole room broke up. He was a dead ringer.

Think about it. If the model had actually been Lisa del Giocando and not Salaì in drag, why didn't Lisa have the painting? Why did Leonardo have it, and why did he keep working on it?

The reason was bouncing around right in front of me the whole time. He kept working on the painting because Salaì was there to pose for it. It was a ritual between them, a way to be intimate, like friends who play cards to pass the time. They start out with smalltalk, but end up going deeper, getting their hands in each other's clay.

There's one more thing, a sly clue from Leonardo. The name Mona Lisa is an anagram of Mon Salaì, French for My Salaì. Leonardo delighted in word games. It was completely in character to hide his illicit affections behind a playful riddle. And guess what—it worked for 500 years.

Now that you've read the manuscript, Katherine, could you ever visit the Louvre without seeing the real story behind the smile?

With Salaì gone from the studio and Leonardo nearing the end of his life, the maestro wanted Salaì to have the painting. I can imagine the enormous appeal of letting him steal it. Salaì not only got the painting, but got away with larceny, too, one of his favorite pastimes.

The saddest part is, Salaì never bothered to visit Leonardo in his final days. Maybe he'd already moved on, or maybe he was too jealous of Melzi. Whatever the reason, it hurt Leonardo deeply. After Leonardo died, Salaì slithered up to Amboise to collect his inheritance like the snake he'd always been.

Compare Salaì's behavior with Melzi's. Here's what the kid wrote to Leonardo's half-brothers in Florence:

> *I understand that you have been informed of the death of Master Leonardo, your brother, who was like an excellent father to me. It is impossible to express the grief I feel at his death, and as long as my limbs sustain me I will feel perpetual unhappiness, which is justified by the consuming and passionate love he bore daily towards me. Everyone is grieved by the loss of a man of whose qualities Nature no longer has it in her power to produce.*

Katherine, I freely admit I'm not an honorable person. In fact, I'm a thief and a murderer. And I swear a lot. But I do have compensating virtues. I almost always tell the truth. I'm a scientist with a degree in physics and a master's in biophysics. Suffice it to say, I have zero patience for self-delusion or magical thinking. I don't believe in all that afterlife stuff. But I do hope, as Leonardo did, that I can weave a cocoon of great beauty and usefulness before disappearing into the infinite sky on painted wings.

Now, you may be wondering where your editor is, Katherine. I have something to confess.

This morning I caught a water taxi to the Venice airport. Peter promised to meet me in departures with my ticket and a carry-on full of clothes.

When I get there he's nowhere in sight. I start to panic. I'm seeing spies behind every column and cameras inside every potted plant. Then I feel a tap on my shoulder. I turn around. It's Bernardo Lucchini, the attorney. Did he tell you?

Come with me, he says. He pulls me through security flashing an ID card, and rushes me straight to the gate where he hands me my boarding pass. Peter is waiting there, his arm in a sling. He's got my suitcase, plus one for himself.

That's right, Katherine, I stole your editor.

Peter, would you like to say a few words?

PETER: Hello, Katherine. I'm so thrilled to see the advance publicity getting so much traction. The press is going absolutely bananas trying to guess who Scarlett is. Despite the risks to her anonymity, she would like us to use her entire commentary, even the parts she originally asked me to keep private. Of course, the decision is yours. I'm so proud of all the work we did together, not to mention the courage everyone showed in the face of Dickson's threats. That's number one.

Number two, I won't be coming back.

Scarlett is planning a school for girls in a remote part of the world and I've decided to help. We're calling it the Artie Institute. My little joke.

SCARLETT: A *very* little joke.

PETER: We'll be teaching art and science to girls who've been denied access to modern education. The greatest threat to entrenched power is not an armed rebellion. It's a girl with a book.

Life is strange, isn't it? There we were in Venice. Artie was dying. Scarlett was preparing to leave everyone and everything she'd ever known. I thought, after all the editing I've done, all the books I've launched, all the effort I've poured into my career, this is my destination?

What the fuck, said Scarlett. Maybe you have to ditch the life you planned to get the one you need.

Katherine, I'm sorry to spring this on you. Your friendship means a lot to me, and I hope we'll see each other again. For now, Scarlett and I have to stay below the radar. You won't be hearing from us. You won't be able to find us on the internet. In fact, you won't be able to find us.

PUBLISHER'S EMAIL

Scarlett, we think we can mount a successful legal defense and bring you back to the US. You don't have to stay hidden. Please let us know if you'd like our help.

PUBLISHER'S EMAIL

Scarlett?

ACKNOWLEDGMENTS

I was lucky to have talented team of experts to help me with some of the key details of the story. Historian Eleanora Penzo gave my Venetian scenes an extra dash of color; translator Agnese Mandetta corrected my poor high-school Italian; and forensics expert D.P. Lyle gave me the lowdown on how blood settles, flesh discolors, and bodies decay after death.

My research included dozens books on Leonardo and his times. One of my favorites was a scholarly work on the studios of Florence, drawn from fifteenth-century tax records. I learned that the workshops of the Renaissance were remarkably similar to my own design studio, where I spent the bulk of my working life. One of the books I found indispensable in writing *Octavo* was Charles Nicholl's excellent *Leonardo da Vinci: Flights of the Mind*. Another was Walter Isaacson's biography, *Leonardo da Vinci*. Perhaps the most important, however, was Fritjof Capra's *The Science of Leonardo*, which led me to a key insight: Leonardo's failure to get his notebooks published was a tragedy of historic proportions.

I owe the quality of the print book to Jameson Spence's graphic design, Maybelyn Glanzen's map illustration, Stacy Mathewson's editing, and ORO Edition's printing and binding.

Many thanks to my early readers for plowing through the manuscript and submitting to my interrogations so joyfully: Timothy Adekunle, Samantha Alvarez, Gül Antuntaç, Christine Bruce, Colin Byrne, Alex Chikovani, Matt Davies, Kevin Doyle, Julianna Driskel, Patty Driskel, Harry Elonen, Dorothy Fulop, Mimi Heft, Michael Holliday, Renee Hunt, Gillian Hunter, Nick Jackson, Lauren Jones, Leyla Kazimova, Chris Latterell, Robert Leinders-Krog, Josh Levine, Deborah Massa, Tom McCrorie, Mitzi Overland, Stephanie Owens, Lee Ann Palmer, Stephen Pedroff, Steven Raft, Prince Rumi, Haz M. Said, Guido Scheffers, Franzi Scheithauer, Sarah Sears, Jordan

Strang, Luke Trybula, Jenifer Vogt, Chaz Wilcoxen, and Downing Wilson.

Thanks also to my sibs—Peter Neumeier, Francie Neumeier, Ellyn Lennon, Joe Lennon, Carla Girolamo, and Peter Girolamo—for their enthusiastic support.

Finally, a massive thanks to my amazing wife Eileen and daughter Sara for critiquing my progress so insightfully, and for tolerating my frequent absences as I reveled in the company of my fascinating characters.

In a book about books, it's only fair to credit the designers whose typography brought its voices to life.

For the audio communications of Scarlett and Artie, we used Bembo, based on the typeface originally cut by Francesco Griffo for Pietro Bembo in 1495.

For the email replies of Peter Chenoweth and Katherine Cavel, we chose Helvetica Neue, designed by Max Miedinger in 1957.

And to represent the handwritten manuscript of Francesco Melzi, we specified a beautiful version of Garamond Italic, first cut by Claude Garamond circa 1550 in the style of Griffo's work, and updated by Robert Slimbach for Adobe.

9 798987 158425